TROUBLE BREWING

TROUBLE BREWING

A Jack Haldean Mystery

Dolores Gordon-Smith

This first world edition published 2012
in Great Britain and in the USA by
SEVERN HOUSE PUBLISHERS LTD of
9–15 High Street, Sutton, Surrey, England, SM1 1DF.
Trade paperback edition first published
in Great Britain and the USA 2012 by
SEVERN HOUSE PUBLISHERS LTD.

British Library Cataloguing in Publication Data

Gordon-Smith, Dolores.
  Trouble brewing.
  1. Haldean, Jack (Fictitious character) – Fiction.
  2. Detective and mystery stories.
  I. Title
  823.9'2-dc23

ISBN-13: 978-0-7278-8169-4 (cased)
ISBN-13: 978-1-84751-428-8 (trade paper)

All Severn House titles are printed on acid-free paper.

Severn House Publishers support The Forest Stewardship Council [FSC],
the leading international forest certification organisation. All our titles that
are printed on Greenpeace-approved FSC-certified paper carry the FSC logo.

Typeset by Palimpsest Book Production Ltd.,
Falkirk, Stirlingshire, Scotland.
Printed and bound in Great Britain by
MPG Books Ltd., Bodmin, Cornwall.

Dedicated to Angela Churm,
old friend and fellow writer.
With love.

ONE

What on earth could the man want? Jack Haldean checked the number of the house, stuffed the letter back into his pocket, mounted the marble steps between their pillars of Portland stone, and rang the bell of 14, Neville Square. He'd never heard of a Harold Rushton Hunt and yet, out of the blue, Mr Hunt had written to him, asking him to call.

The door was opened by a magnificently portly butler with a high-domed bald head and exuberant eyebrows. 'Good morning, sir,' he said repressively.

'Good morning,' replied Jack, bracing himself under the butler's gaze. 'I've got an appointment to see Mr Hunt. My name's Haldean, Major Haldean.'

'Ah yes, sir. Mr Hunt is waiting for you in the drawing room.' He stood aside to allow him to enter. 'Allow me to take your coat, sir.'

He led the way down a gloomy green-panelled hall, pausing outside a door, before turning to Jack with an anxiety at odds with the imperturbable mask of the well-trained servant. 'You will be careful, won't you, sir? Mr Hunt is not as young as he was and the strain of the last few months has taken its toll. Any sudden excitement or upset may prove too much for him.'

'Of course,' said Jack. 'Don't worry. Wheel me in.' He received a glance of mingled disapproval and gratitude, before the butler opened the door.

'Major Haldean, sir.'

A man with blue-tinged lips and the thinness of old age sat in a leather armchair, next to the comfortable fire. A tray of medicines stood on a small table beside him. He put a bony hand on the chair arm in an attempt to get up. Jack took one look at the proud face with its pale, keen blue eyes and checked his initial impulse to help. He had a feeling Mr Hunt resented his frailty being brought home to him.

'Allow me, sir,' said the butler.

'Leave me alone, Fields,' said Mr Hunt with more than a touch of irritation. Jack was glad he had kept quiet. 'Damn it, when I can't manage to stand up, it'll be time to measure me for my box.' He slowly got to his feet. 'Major Haldean, it's good of you to call.'

'Not at all, sir,' said Jack, taking the outstretched hand.

The old man slowly re-seated himself, indicating that Jack should do the same. 'Can I offer you a cocktail? I always drink sherry at this time but my son, Frederick, keeps me up to date.'

'Sherry for me, please,' said Jack. There was something about Mr Hunt that made cocktails seem wildly inappropriate.

Fields served them with sherry then, with a doubtful glance at Jack, left the room.

Mr Hunt picked up his glass and settled back in the chair. 'I suppose you're wondering what this is all about? Smoke if you want to, by the way. The box is beside you. I gather, Major Haldean, that you have a reputation for solving problems.' The searching look Mr Hunt directed at Jack told him this was not the moment for false modesty.

'I've been successful a couple of times, yes.'

'It was George Lassiter at the club who suggested I get in touch with you. I gather you helped him with an odd business he was troubled with. Sir Douglas Lynton of Scotland Yard spoke well of you when I mentioned your name.'

'That was very good of him.' Jack was frankly puzzled. Crime in these surroundings seemed not only incongruous but in bad taste, and yet it must be a crime or why should Sir Douglas be involved? 'Is there any matter I can help you with, sir?'

For an answer Mr Hunt got painfully to his feet once more and walked stiffly to the table under the window. Picking up a silver-framed photograph, he stood and looked at it. Jack joined him at the window. 'This is my great-nephew, Mark Helston.'

Mark Helston was a dark-haired, clean-shaven man in, at a guess, his mid-twenties with an air of cheery good humour. His face rang a faint bell and Jack wondered where he had seen Mark Helston before.

'Do you recognize him?'

'I'm trying to place him, sir. I'm sure I've seen that picture before.'

'I'm sure you have. In January this picture was in all the

newspapers.' Mr Hunt turned a slightly wistful glance to Jack. 'Perhaps you remember what happened?'

The honest truth was that he didn't. 'Not really, sir.'

Mr Hunt put the photograph back on the table, letting his hand linger on it for a few seconds more than strictly necessary, before walking back to his chair. 'I'm correct in thinking, aren't I, that my name means nothing to you?' A gleam of humour in his eyes cut off Jack's apology. 'Don't apologize, young man. Have you ever heard of Hunt Coffee?'

'Well, of course I have. I say, do you own Hunt Coffee?'

'Indeed I do. My son, Frederick, is in charge of the actual business nowadays, but the firm is mine. Frederick is a widower with no children but my sister, Enid, was fortunate enough to have two grandchildren, Patricia and Mark.'

He sighed. 'My sister and I did not always see eye to eye, but she was devoted to her grandchildren. Enid took care of them both after their parents died more than twenty years ago. Patricia is married and has no interest in the firm, but Mark, under my son's tutelage, developed a keen sense of business. Mark had plenty of money and nothing to worry him. His private affairs – let me stress this, Major – were completely without fault. Completely,' he added with a fierce glare, as if Jack was going to argue the point.

'I'm sure of it, sir,' said Jack, mentally reserving judgement.

Mr Hunt subsided. 'That is more than the indulgent opinion of an old man. The police investigated Mark's life thoroughly and found nothing amiss.' He looked into the fire for a long moment. 'I told 'em they wouldn't,' he added in an undertone. Jack waited patiently for him to continue.

Mr Hunt gave a little shake of his head. 'And yet at half past seven on the evening of the ninth of January, Mark walked out of his Albemarle Street flat and from that day to this, no one has cast eyes on him.'

'What? No one, sir?'

'Not a soul. We contacted the police as soon as it became apparent that Mark was missing. We assumed he was either injured or taken ill. The police checked all the hospitals, but found nothing. The police then made a suggestion which I considered to be disgraceful and confessed themselves baffled. There the matter rested and, as far as they are concerned, will continue to rest. Meanwhile, my nephew is either dead, injured, or being held against his will.' He looked Jack straight in the eyes. 'I appeal to you, sir. Help me find Mark. The police have proved useless and until George Lassiter mentioned your name, I was completely without hope.'

Jack finished his sherry in silence. 'I'm sorry, sir,' he began, then stopped as he saw the light die out of the old man's face. He simply couldn't refuse, any more than he could have kicked a puppy. He put down his glass and linked his hands together, trying to find the right words. 'If the police have failed, Mr Hunt, then, although I'll try, I can't see how I can possibly succeed.' His voice was very gentle. 'You see, they have resources which I can't hope to match.' He glanced at Mr Hunt, seeing anxiety twist new lines around his mouth.

'But you will try, won't you?' he asked urgently.

Jack nodded. 'Oh yes, sir, I'll try.' He couldn't, in common humanity, say anything else.

'Thank you for that, Major.' A spark came into his eyes. 'Lassiter told me you wouldn't let me down. Any information you think might prove useful, I will gladly give you. Any expenses you incur, I will meet. If you can only find Mark or . . . or –' he swallowed – 'tell me what has become of him, I will be forever in your debt. Is there anything you wish to ask me?'

'I think I'll find out what the police have done first. That'll probably give me an idea of where to start. Then, if I may, I might have some questions for you.'

Mr Hunt got to his feet and stretched out his hand. 'As you wish.' He rang the bell. 'And thank you again, sir. Even if you fail, you have given me back some hope.'

'I went to see a Mr Harold Rushton Hunt today, Bill.'

Inspector William Rackham stirred a spoonful of sugar into his coffee and relaxed into his green leather armchair in the Young Services Club smoking room.

'You poor beggar, Jack,' he said, pushing his ginger hair out of his eyes. 'I thought you might get lumbered. Mr Hunt visited the Yard yesterday. From what I could gather, old Mr Lassiter has been singing your praises and Mr Hunt wanted Sir Douglas's opinion of your talents. Were your ears burning?'

'No,' said Jack, offering his friend a cigar. 'Should they have been?'

'Need you ask?' said Bill with a grin. 'Mind you, the Chief was probably so relieved at the prospect of palming Harold Hunt off onto someone else, I think he'd have given the thumbs up to anyone. I'm up to my eyes with the Leigh Abbey lot at the moment, so the last thing I want to do is get involved with ancient history. You're as good as anyone.'

Jack laughed. 'Don't go overboard, Bill.'

'I didn't. Sir Douglas might have praised you to the skies, but I was trying to get you out of it. Mr Hunt won't hear of the only explanation for Mark Helston's disappearance that makes any sense.'

'Which is?'

'Helston hooked it for reasons of his own, obviously.'

'That, I take it, is what Mr Hunt meant when he said that the police had made a disgraceful suggestion?'

'I suppose so.' Rackham frowned thoughtfully at the end of his cigar. 'It was one of Wilfred Murray's cases. He was a bit lacking in tact, old Murray, but I can't disagree with him. It must have been about the last case he took on before he retired. I don't think you ever came across Murray, did you? When he finally got his gold watch I took over some of his cases, including the Mark Helston business. As it was officially mine, I was at the meeting with Mr Hunt yesterday. I went through the file beforehand, but I couldn't tell him anything he didn't already know.' He took an absent-minded sip of coffee. 'Of course, a case is never officially closed until it's resolved, but I honestly don't think there's anything I could do that old Murray hasn't done.'

Jack sent up a thoughtful cloud of aromatic smoke. 'So that's the official explanation, is it? That Mark Helston, for reasons best known to himself, upped and left off his own bat?'

'What other explanation can there be? You know as well as I do that when someone vanishes, there's only two solutions that hold water. It's either foul play or the man's taken himself off. Even if it's an accident or loss of memory, someone, somewhere, will spot him. God knows, there were enough pictures of Helston around the place. I can't rule out foul play altogether, but I would've expected the body to have come to light by now.'

'M'yes,' agreed Jack. 'Corpses have an inconvenient habit of popping up. They make themselves unmissable after a time. He's not pretending to be someone's left luggage, is he? No, that would've been noticed. The river? That's not on, either. Even if you weighted the body down, the clothes would have rotted and the actual doings surfaced. You *could* do it by wrapping the body in chains attached to something heavy like an anchor, but it seems pretty elaborate. Is there a nice, handy, disused mine shaft or old railway ventilation chimney somewhere?'

'There might be,' said Bill doubtfully. 'But that begs the question of who wanted to put him in there in the first place. You see, even if you can do a vanishing trick with a body, there's a trail of motive and suspicion. I can't see it would be to anyone's advantage to murder Helston.'

'*Someone* must have benefited from Mark Helston turning into an empty space. I mean, if he could run to a flat on Albemarle Street he must have had a bob or two. Who collared the readies?'

'No one. No one directly, that is. Helston didn't have any capital. He had his salary from Hunt Coffee and a generous allowance from his grandmother. He was her blue-eyed boy, all right. As far as I can make out, his sister, Patricia, wasn't nearly so lavishly treated.'

'Did his sister resent it?'

Bill shrugged. 'She might have done, but if she did, it was her grandmother who got the blame. Patricia, or Pat, as she's always called, was devoted to her brother.'

'Sez you.'

'Sez me. Besides that, she married money. Gregory Jaggard, the car bloke.'

To his surprise, Jack's eyebrows shot up and he seemed to develop a nervous twitch in his neck. Bill was about to speak when an imperious glance stopped him. His friend nodded across the room. A well-built, fair-headed man was sitting at an angle to them, cigar in hand, talking to a man whose thatch of red hair was just visible above the top of his chair.

'It's him,' Jack said in an undertone.

Although it seemed unlikely that Jaggard could overhear them, neither man wanted to carry on the conversation with Jaggard in the room. Jack was about to suggest taking their drinks into the billiard room when Gregory Jaggard stood up, and, with a goodbye to his companion, threw his cigar into the fire and left.

Jack relaxed. 'How come you didn't spot him when we came in?'

'I've never cast eyes on the man,' said Bill. 'This wasn't my case, remember. All I know is what I've read in the file.'

'Of course you do. Sorry. But look here.' Jack hunched forward, keeping his voice low. 'Gregory Jaggard may seem well off, but I've heard that car concern of his is pretty wobbly. Hardly any of the quality car firms, bar one or two, are a sound bet. They all look glamorous enough, but that's usually because of the amounts going in, not coming out. It's damn good fun, but a lousy way to make money.' He frowned. 'Are you sure Helston's sister married Jaggard? I thought he married a girl called Tyler or Tyrell or something. I've seen her a few times at Brooklands.'

'She was a war widow,' said Bill. 'Are you sure about Jaggard's firm? Because if you are, that could cast quite a different complexion on things.'

'How so?'

'It's all tied up with the will Helston's grandmother left.'

Jack sighed in exasperation. '*What* will, for heaven's sake? Don't you know that where there's a will, there's a motive? Tell me, damn you, and stop being so tight-fisted with the details.'

Bill laughed. 'All right. The gist of it is that Helston's grand-mother was a very rich woman. There was some complicated tale about who she'd married, but whoever it was, they were pretty well off and left it all to her. She made Helston a generous allowance, as I said, and Patricia a far more modest one. Mark and Patricia's parents died years ago and their grandmother brought up the two children. When Mark disappeared she took it very badly and, to cut a long story short, she had a minor heart attack followed by a major one and died. Now by the terms of her first will, Patricia got five thousand, there were the usual bequests to servants and charities, but the whole of the remainder went to Mark.'

'And to come down to vulgar figures, that was . . .?'

'The best part of two hundred thousand pounds.'

'Good God!' Jack gazed at Bill with gratifying astonishment. 'I thought you said nobody gained. Hell's bells, with that sort of money kicking about you could have a line of murderers queuing round the block. Did Mark have any idea of how rich the old lady was?'

Bill shook his head. 'That's the point. No one did. Her allowance to Mark was her one extravagance. She lived at the rate of six hundred a year, paid her bills promptly and gave everyone the impression her income had declined over the years. All the time her capital was building up at compound interest.'

'Wow! And again, wow! But now Mark's out of the picture, who gets it?'

Bill frowned. 'That's just it, you see. After Mark vanished his grandmother made another will. That was after her first heart attack. She probably knew she didn't have long left. When – she firmly believed it was when and not if, apparently – Mark turned up again, the terms of the original will would stand, but in the meantime, the whole amount was to be put into a trust for him. Patricia and her husband could draw upon the income, but they couldn't touch the capital until it was proved that Mark was dead.'

'Hang on. If that's invested nice and safely at three per cent, say, that's about . . .' Jack closed his eyes and did some mental gymnastics. 'I'd say that was six thousand a year.'

'Not bad. There's actually a bit more than that, because of a block of shares she had that pay about nine per cent. The total income amounts to around eight thousand a year.'

'You told me no one benefited,' said Jack reprovingly. 'You may think those sort of dibs aren't worth having, but I bet Patricia – as was Helston – Jaggard thinks it's well worth knowing about. I bet Gregory Jaggard does too.'

'But she didn't know it existed,' said Bill plaintively. 'Nobody did. It was split up into so many different holdings even the lawyer didn't have a clue how rich she was.'

Jack drew in a long mouthful of smoke. 'That does alter things, I agree. Damn! There's another thing, too. If that was the reason, it'd make more sense to first see off grandma, then bump off Mark. It's a bit obvious, but it'd work. Doing it this way leaves an awful lot to chance. There'd be no guarantee that the will would be altered. If Mark were a properly attested corpse then his grandmother would presumably alter her will in favour of Patricia. Having him vanish like this leaves everything open. It's no end of a powerful argument against your idea that he's slung his hook, though. He'd hardly stay vanished knowing there's two hundred thousand for the taking.'

'It depends why he went,' said Bill, dryly. 'You're assuming, along with Mr Hunt, that Mark had no reason to disappear. What if he's committed a crime?'

'What sort of crime?'

'Theft, perhaps? He might have murdered someone for all I know.'

A slow smile twitched Jack's mouth. '*That's* something I wouldn't suggest to Mr Hunt. Have you got many murderees in want of a murderer? No? Because you see, don't you, that idea implies that not only has Mark Helston managed to successfully conceal himself since January, he also contrived a murder of such brilliance that nobody knows it's occurred.'

Bill grinned in return. 'Okay, strike that one from the record. I'd love to know what the devil's happened to him, though.'

'Me too. This case is growing on me, Bill.'

He stopped as the red-headed man who had been talking to Gregory Jaggard stood up and, seeing Jack, started in pleased surprise and came across the room.

'It's Meredith Smith,' said Jack in a low voice. 'He's an old pal.'

Meredith Smith greeted Jack warmly. 'I haven't seen you in absolutely ages, Jack. The funny thing is, I was going to look you up.'

Jack bowed to the inevitable. 'Take a pew, Merry. This is William Rackham of Scotland Yard and this, Bill, is Captain Meredith Smith.'

'Pleased to meet you,' said Smith, tidying his gangly limbs into a chair. 'Excuse me butting in, won't you? I'm at a bit of a loose end. Scotland Yard, eh? My guv'nor was in the police over in Hong Kong.' He looked at Jack, steepling his fingers together. 'I can do the Sherlock Holmes stunt as well, you know. And I deduce, my dear Watson, that you had a letter today inviting you to a certain house in Belgravia to investigate the disappearance of one Mark Helston.'

Jack and Bill stared at Meredith Smith in astonishment.

'How on earth d'you know that?' asked Jack.

'You know my methods,' said Smith with a laugh. 'To come clean, I wrote the letter. How d'you get on in your audience with H.R.H.?'

'With the King?'

'Idiot! Harold Rushton Hunt, commonly referred to as H.R.H., also known to minions, such as myself, as The Boss. Nice old boy, isn't he?'

'Very. But look here, Merry, old fruit, I thought you worked for the Chicago and Mid-Western Bank.'

'You're behind the times. They wanted me to move to Detroit or somewhere equally foul, and I wasn't having it at any price. Things were said on both sides and we came to a parting of the ways. After a couple of months of wondering where the next three squares were coming from, I was beginning to think Detroit might not be such a bad notion after all, when, like an angel from heaven, I received an invitation from H.R.H. to pop round and see him. I duly popped, with such satisfactory results that you are now, I'm glad to say, looking at the chief financial wizard and general factotum of Hunt Coffee Limited.'

'Well done. Er . . . what on earth made him pick you?'

Meredith Smith's eyebrows rose. 'You could find a more flattering way to phrase that.' He laughed. 'Actually, I wondered as much myself when I got the letter. Believe it or not, I'm related to him.'

'Good grief! Are you?'

Smith nodded. 'Yes. There was always a sort of cloud over it at home, so I never knew the ins and outs of it, but my grandmother was H.R.H.'s sister, Enid. She married my grandfather, who was also called Meredith Smith, but she abandoned the family and ran off with Jonathan Burbage, the actor-manager chap. Having seen a photo of Grandfather Smith, I don't know if I blame her. He seems to be all beard and whiskers. Jonathan Burbage owned a string of theatres and was quite disgustingly rich. It was their daughter who was Mark's mother. I didn't have a clue about any of this. I thought my grandmother had died long before I was born.'

He laughed. 'The funny thing is, that as far as H.R.H. is concerned, it could have happened yesterday. He pumped my hand, and asked me to overlook the grave injury his family had caused mine and all that. Well, what with not knowing the first thing about it, and having to go and fight the Great War and being rather more concerned with finding some way of keeping body and soul together, I hadn't done a frightful amount of brooding on the flighty goings-on of my grandmother in 1880 or thereabouts. After I worked out what he was talking about, I said not to worry, it was all water under the bridge and all that. H.R.H. brightened up and told me he was glad to see I'd taken it in such a sporting manner, or words to that effect. Poor old Enid had come in for some heavy Victorian disapproval and been barred for years, as far as I can make out. It was only when her daughter died that she got accepted back into the family fold once more, bringing with her Mark and Patricia.'

'When did all this happen, Merry? Mr Hunt offering you the job, I mean.'

'Just over a month ago. Mark's sliding off left an enormous gap in the firm, and H.R.H. wanted someone in the family to fill it. Fortunately I've always had a head for figures and although I'm only accidentally in the family, it was close enough to count. Between the three of us, I rather think H.R.H. had been upset by his sister's will. You know she only died a few weeks ago? She left everything to Mark, and nothing to me. As I'd never heard of the woman before H.R.H. told me about her, I can't say it bothered me much, but H.R.H. obviously thought she should have done something for Grandpa Smith's family. Anyway, he offered me a job at a corking salary, so here we are.'

Jack sat back and looked at Meredith reflectively. 'You say Mr Hunt was keen to have someone in the family. Why? Is it just sentiment or is there another reason?'

Smith gave an impatient little wriggle. 'You do ask some damn searching questions, Jack. I don't want to say too much, but I must say it had occurred to me, too.' He paused. 'Although we're doing fine at the moment, it's not where I would put my money, if you see what I mean.'

Bill sat up sharply. 'Why's that?'

Smith looked acutely uncomfortable. 'I can't tell you. I don't mean I don't want to, I mean I don't know. However, I can't help feeling *something's* been going on that's not right. There's nothing I can put my finger on, but I do wonder if Mark was quite the shining light his family thought him.'

'And if you find out, with you being part of the family . . .' said Jack.

'I'll keep quiet. Yes. I have wondered if that's the size of it. If there is anything dodgy, though, I'm sure H.R.H. isn't in on it. He's unhappy about the firm. He's asked me a couple of times if everything's as it should be and given me a sort of between-the-lines warning to keep my eyes peeled. The trouble is, if I do find anything amiss, I can't keep quiet, family or no family. Even accountants have a rudimentary sense of ethics. I don't want anything to go wrong because it's such a nailing good job, but . . .'

'But if there's dirty work at the crossroads you'll have to come clean.'

'Unfortunately, yes.' He sighed. 'I wish I'd known Mark. It's much easier to know if a man's pukka if you've actually met him. That's one of the reasons why I've taken up with Jaggard, his brother-in-law. Did you see him? I was talking to him earlier. I like the man for his own sake, but he knew Mark well. I haven't spoken about this to anyone, as they all take the line that Mark is totally innocent of anything shady. I'm not so sure. Leaving aside the idea he's wafting around in the fourth dimension some-where, he's either croaked or, seeing trouble looming, got out while the going was good.'

Jack shook his head in a dissatisfied manner. 'Perhaps. But you haven't managed to find anything, have you? If there is something dodgy it must be damn well hidden and if it's that well hidden, there'd be no reason for Helston to scoot.' He rested his chin on his hands, staring sightlessly into the fire.

'Penny for them?' prompted Bill.

Jack shook himself. 'Nothing,' he said with a grin. 'I need to look at that blessed file of yours before I start leaping to conclu-sions. D'you fancy seeing if the billiard room's free? How about you, Merry? I'm sure we could rope in a fourth if you'd like a game.'

Meredith Smith crushed out his cigarette and, standing up, delicately stifled a yawn. 'Not for me, thanks. We workers of the world have to get our eight hours. If you are going to act for H.R.H., Jack, you'll probably need to come down to the factory in Southwark. Ask for me. I'll show you around and introduce you to everyone.'

'Thanks. I'll take you up on that.'

'He might prove a useful way in to Hunt Coffee,' said Bill, watching Meredith Smith's retreating back. 'How d'you know him?'

'Merry? He was in my squadron for a time. He's a sound bloke with an absolute genius for figures. If he thinks there's something not quite as mother makes about the firm, then he's probably right. I wish I *knew* more. If I think about it much longer without getting my hands on some cold, hard facts I'll go cuckoo.'

'Come and look at the file tomorrow,' said Bill. 'You can't take it out of the building, of course, but I'm there all morning if you want to camp in my office.'

Never, thought Bill, had Inspector Wilfred Murray's compositions been subjected to such intense scrutiny. Twice he had asked Jack if he wanted a cup of tea; the third time had elicited a grunt of, 'Oh, thanks.' The cup sat, completely disregarded, at Jack's elbow.

Jack sat up, ran a hand through his hair, then smiled as he saw Bill's eyes on him. 'Sorry. I haven't been much in the way of company, have I?'

'That's not what you're here for. Did you find anything?'

Jack tapped his notepad. 'I've jotted down the main points. Helston had three hundred and twenty-seven pounds plus a few bob in his bank account. That's not been touched. The very last person to see him was Carlton, his valet, who said Helston mentioned he was dining at Oddenino's on Regent Street, but not who with, worse luck. He didn't get a taxi as it's only ten minutes' walk or so, but no one from Oddenino's remembered him being there that evening.'

'So the inference is he disappeared on the way to the restaurant?'

'Yes. No one enquired for him at Oddenino's, so it sounds as if he met whoever it was he was going to have dinner with on the way there and they went off together. Who that is, I don't know.'

Jack frowned at his notepad. 'I could do with getting to know the people involved. Frederick Hunt, for example, old Mr Hunt's son, is just a name and age in here, but he was one of the last to see Helston. What does he think happened? There's no indica-tion of that.' Jack picked up the cup of orange-coloured fluid and, with an expressive face, took a cautious sip.

'Poor old Murray wasn't writing a novel, you know. Look, there's no obligation to drink that. It must be stone cold. Let me get you a fresh cup.'

'No thanks,' said Jack hastily. 'Even scorching hot this must have been a bit above the odds.' He put the cup to one side. 'At ten o' clock on the morning he disappeared, Helston had a meeting in Frederick Hunt's office in Southwark with Frederick Hunt and the manager of Hunt's Brazilian plantation, Ariel Valdez. Inspector Murray doesn't seem to have made any attempt to get in touch with this Brazilian bloke, Valdez. Don't you think he should have done?'

Bill put down his pen and came to stand behind Jack's shoulder. 'Not really. Helston didn't disappear until half past seven that evening. Why are you interested in Valdez?'

Jack clicked his tongue. 'He's a loose end. Everyone else is accounted for. Murray doesn't say what the meeting was about.'

Bill shrugged. 'I don't suppose it matters, do you? Helston saw no end of people after the meeting broke up.' He leaned forward and ran his finger down the page. 'Martin Crowther from United Stores for lunch at Simpson's and the waiter who served them, his sister, Patricia, that afternoon, all the office people in Southwark and finally the porter and valet at his flat in Albemarle Street that evening. Besides that, Valdez is accounted for. He's gone back to Brazil. Look, it says he sailed for Rio on the tenth of January.'

'The day after Helston vanished.'

'So what? No one knew at that stage that Helston had gone. It wasn't until the eleventh that anyone sounded the alarm.' He glanced at the clock on the wall above his desk. 'I've got to see Sir Douglas at twelve o'clock. I should be finished in an hour or so. D'you fancy a spot of lunch afterwards?'

'Absolutely,' said Jack, picking up the pencil once more.

When Bill came back into his office, Jack was perched on the corner of his desk, holding the telephone.

'Are you sure?' he said into the phone, nodding a greeting to Bill. 'Yes, of course it's important . . . Thanks, Merry. Yes, I will. Before very long, I should think. Goodbye.' He put the earpiece back on its rest and folded his arms across his chest. 'That was Meredith Smith. I hope you don't mind me using your telephone.'

'Not at all. Did you get anywhere?'

'Perhaps. Hunts seem to be having an unlucky time with their managers in Brazil. They've appointed a new bloke, a De Oliveria. Their previous chap, an Australian, resigned without giving notice.'

'Hold on. I thought that other character, Valdez, was the manager. Or is there more than one plantation?'

Jack shook his head. 'No, there's only one. But Valdez arrived in London on the twenty-eighth of December, took a brief holiday, had his meeting on the ninth, and that, Bill, is the last that anyone from Hunt Coffee has seen or heard of him. He should have gone back to Brazil. I don't think he did.'

Bill looked at him in disbelief. "What? But why did no one from Hunt Coffee tell us, for heaven's sake?'

'Inspector Murray had completed his investigations by the time the S.S. *Montevideo*, the ship Valdez *should* have been on, docked in Rio. I've been on to the shipping office and, although his passage was booked, he didn't sail. I then tried various other shipping offices and he isn't listed on any of the boats that were a possible. So, unless we find out anything to the contrary, it rather looks as if Valdez never sailed at all.'

Jack shrugged. 'It takes fifteen days to sail to Rio. Murray had everything done and dusted by then. As for afterwards – well, Hunts didn't tell anyone about Valdez because no one asked. There's also the point that their anxiety about Helston took first place over anyone else's disappearance. I owe you an apology. I remember laughing last night at your idea that Mark Helston might have faded into the woodwork rather than face a murder charge. But now we know that both Helston and Valdez have gone missing . . .'

'I don't like it,' said Bill slowly. 'I don't like to jump to conclusions, but the fact that no one's seen this Valdez chap since the ninth of January has an ugly suggestiveness about it.'

'It does, doesn't it? Mark Helston could've murdered Valdez or Valdez could've murdered Helston. But if either of them *did* commit murder, what the dickens did they do with the body?'

TWO

'**M**r Hunt's in his office,' said Meredith Smith. 'He's put off a meeting to see you.'

Jack raised an eyebrow. 'Has he? I hope his temper's okay.'

'So-so,' said Smith, making a face. He knocked on the door and entered. 'Major Haldean is here, Mr Hunt.'

Frederick Hunt, a short, bespectacled man in his fifties with a thinning aureole of fluffy blond hair, rose to his feet and came out from behind his desk. 'Ah, Major. My father said he had consulted you. That will be all, Captain Smith, thank you. It's about time for afternoon tea. Can I offer you a cup, Major? Please, do take a seat.'

'Thank you,' said Jack, drawing a chair up to the desk. He glanced out of the window where the factory chimney loomed like an emaciated and gloomy Titan over a huddle of buildings. A rich, concentrated and oddly unpleasant smell of roasted coffee funnelled in through the open window. He smiled. 'I wouldn't have expected you to drink tea, sir.'

Frederick Hunt looked mildly surprised, then smiled in return. 'What? Ah yes. The factory. Much as I esteem our product, Major, my enthusiasm does not stretch to consuming it at three in the afternoon.'

He smiled at his own pleasantry, then fussily adjusted his glasses, hesitating before he spoke. 'Major Haldean, I have agreed to see you chiefly to fall in with my father's wishes. He is an old man and I feel obliged to humour him where possible. However, it is only fair to tell you that I do not see eye to eye with him about the wisdom of consulting an amateur in the matter of my nephew's disappearance. I feel it could have been safely left in the hands of the police. Inspector Murray struck me as a very able officer.'

'I agree with you, Mr Hunt,' said Jack mendaciously. His reading of Murray's file had led him to characterize that worthy as a conscientious plodder. 'However, I do have the full support of Sir Douglas Lynton.'

'That makes a difference, of course,' said Mr Hunt without much enthusiasm. 'What precisely do you wish to ascertain?'

Jack stretched out his long legs. 'I'd like to know the sort of person your nephew was, Mr Hunt. Was he, for instance, careful with money?'

Frederick Hunt was obviously surprised at the question. 'He certainly wasn't in debt, if that's what you mean.'

'Did he enjoy his work?'

'Certainly, Major. He always had the interests of the firm very much at heart.' He picked up a pencil from the desk and twirled it in his fingers. 'Mark took a very great interest in the business, Major, to the point of actually going to Brazil last year to inspect our plantation in person. There he made a number of suggestions which, if we could afford to finance them, would, I am sure, prove valuable. He was, for instance, concerned about our coffee processing methods. We currently use the tried and tested Dry method. Mark wanted to instigate the newer Wet method. The capital outlay is not, in my considered opinion, justified. I applaud the youthful enthusiasm that informed his preference, but I was able to bring to bear my many years of experience to the proposal and argue against it.'

'I'm sorry, Mr Hunt, you're going to have to give me a couple of footnotes,' said Jack. 'I haven't a clue what you're talking about.'

Frederick Hunt gave a superior and benign smile at this expression of ignorance. 'It is rather technical for the layman to grasp, but, in a nutshell, whereas the Dry method calls for the coffee fruits, or cherries, as they are called, to be laid on a stone floor and exposed to the sun, the Wet method requires galvanized spouting and a water supply to convey the cherries from the field to a tank where a pulping machine liberates the seeds and reduces the fleshy parts of the cherries to a pulp. After several more stages, what we refer to as parchment coffee is produced, as the beans are enclosed in a silver skin of parchment. The parchment coffee requires further treatment before the item you would recognize as a coffee bean is arrived at.'

'Gosh,' said Jack, with a disarming smile. 'I didn't realize there was all this science involved – you know, galvanized spouting and pulping parchment and so on. I'd always assumed coffee was just coffee.'

Frederick Hunt's air of self-satisfaction increased at this laughable admission of naivety. 'A common mistake, Major. Most understandable.'

'What did your nephew do for entertainment, sir? Did he have any hobbies or interests?' Apart from wetting coffee, he added to himself.

'Entertainment?' Mr Hunt frowned as if the idea was an alien concept. 'He went to dances, of course, as all you young men do, and he was a member of a number of clubs. The Cicerone on Dover Street was his favourite, I believe. He was a good shot, hunted occasionally and was, I gather, fond of tennis and golf. He enjoyed motor racing, but only as a spectator. My niece's husband is Gregory Jaggard of Jaggard Cars, and he would always make a point of attending Brooklands when Gregory was racing.'

Mr Hunt put down the pencil. 'I am afraid I feel somewhat at a loss, Major. I was – am – fond of my nephew but for an assessment of his character, you would be far better to ask his contemporaries. I can only tell you that he was scrupulously honest and moderate in his habits.'

A rattle of crockery in the corridor announced the arrival of the tea trolley. Cup in hand, Jack changed tactics. 'I'm obviously interested in what happened on the ninth of January, Mr Hunt. You and Mr Helston had a meeting with Senhor Valdez on that day, didn't you?'

'Indeed we did, sir.' His eyes gleamed behind his glasses. 'I understand Captain Smith informed you how disgracefully we were let down by Senhor Valdez. It was all most unsatisfactory. I gave the clearest instructions to Valdez and I expected them to be implemented. Instead, the wretched man left our employment without even the courtesy of a note. We were gravely inconvenienced, most gravely inconvenienced. Our business, Major Haldean, obviously depends upon South America, but it is a constant trial to depend upon South Americans! They do not have our sense of loyalty or stability.'

'What was Senhor Valdez like? Did you get on with him, I mean?'

Mr Hunt tutted disapprovingly. 'I find your line of questioning very awkward, Major. I always found Senhor Valdez perfectly amiable. Until he let us down, I had no reason to complain of him.'

Jack tried a new cast. 'What did he look like? Was he dark or fair? Did he have a beard or moustache or wear glasses?'

'For a Brazilian he was very fair.' He paused, cast a covert glance at Jack's olive skin and dark eyes, and gave a disconcerted cough.

Jack knew what Frederick Hunt was thinking as clearly as if he said it out loud. 'Fairer skinned than I am, perhaps?' he suggested.

Frederick Hunt looked embarrassed and relieved at the same

time. 'Yes, now you come to mention it, yes. Exactly right. Precisely so. Senhor Valdez had no beard but a small moustache. He wore gold-rimmed glasses. His hair was dark, but he could easily have passed for an Englishman. His speech gave him away though. He spoke good English but very heavily accented.'

'And was the meeting of the ninth of January the only occasion Senhor Valdez saw either you or Mr Helston? I gather he arrived in England on the twenty-eighth of December.'

'We met the day after he arrived, on the twenty-ninth. He spent the New Year in Paris. His meeting here on the ninth of January was the last before he sailed for Brazil on the tenth.'

'And did Mr Helston attend that earlier meeting? The one on the twenty-ninth, I mean.'

'No. It was not necessary for my nephew to be present on that occasion. The subject was Valdez's report on the current state of the plantation with particular reference to a stand of Liberian coffee trees, which had been planted as an experiment. The Liberian tree is, as you may know, rather hardier than the Arabian tree, but lacks its flavour. It was my father who had insisted on growing Liberian coffee on account of its greater productivity but, although the trees have flourished, we shall only be using the coffee in our cheaper blends.'

'Why wasn't Mr Helston at the meeting? I'd have thought he'd have been interested to hear how the plantation was doing.'

'Oh, he was, but young men must have a social life, my dear sir. He spent Christmas and the New Year hunting in Leicestershire and did not return until the fifth.'

'What was the tone of the meeting on the ninth? The one between the three of you, I mean. Was it amicable?'

Mr Hunt paused. Picking up his tea, he finished his cup then, placing it back on the saucer, ran his finger round the rim. 'No, it was not,' he said eventually. 'If my nephew had a fault, Major – which I am not prepared to admit – it was that he could be rather short-tempered with . . . with . . .' He cast another sideways glance at Jack and coloured slightly.

'Foreigners?' prompted Jack, who was used to these evasions.

'Foreigners,' agreed Mr Hunt, gratefully. 'There had been a suggestion when Mark first joined the firm that he should go to Brazil permanently and, indeed, he was willing to do so. However, it wouldn't have done at all. The Brazilians as a people are very free and easy and, in my opinion, rather too wedded to a rough-and-ready democracy which did not fit with Mark's strict ideas of efficiency. Mark disagreed with some of Senhor Valdez's decisions, and Senhor Valdez resented his tone.'

'I see. Was there any decision in particular Mr Helston disapproved of?'

'Not really.' He sighed. 'Mark wanted the Brazilian end to be tightened up and put forward various suggestions as to how this could be accomplished. Senhor Valdez took exception to the implication that his methods needed correction. I'm afraid that tempers got slightly strained.' He drummed his fingers on the desk. 'It could be Mark's rather high-handed approach which led to Valdez's abrupt departure. When it became evident that he had left the firm, I was annoyed but not particularly surprised.' He glanced at the clock. 'Excuse me, Major, but was there anything else you wanted to ask? If so, I would be delighted to see you when I have rather more time at my disposal.'

Jack got to his feet. 'Not at all, sir. I'll push off now. I'm grateful to you for seeing me at such short notice. There's just one more thing. Which hotel did Senhor Valdez stay in?'

'He stayed at the Montague Court, I believe.'

'And in Paris?'

'I'm afraid I can't tell you, Major.'

'Never mind. It's probably unimportant. Thanks again. I'll see myself out.'

This, however, did not prove necessary. Jack reached the stair-well when he heard his name called. It was Meredith Smith.

'Hi! Don't go yet. I'll walk down with you. How did you get on with Mr Hunt?' he asked in an undertone as they clattered down the stairs. 'Bit of an old fuss-budget, isn't he?' Jack pulled a wry face. 'Like that, was it? Tell me more outside.'

As they walked towards the factory gates, Smith burrowed for more information. 'Could he tell you anything about Valdez?'

'Not much. Are you certain the firm hasn't heard from him?'

'Quite sure.' Smith cocked an eyebrow at Jack. 'Putting two and two together?'

'Perhaps. I might be horribly wrong, of course. Look, Merry, could you ask around for me? Was Helston fairly imperious in his manner, particularly with foreigners – Brazilians, I mean – or was he reasonably easy-going? Don't let Mr Hunt know you're asking questions, otherwise he'll know I'm checking what he said, and I don't want to put his back up. There's another thing. Apparently Helston thought Valdez was a bit of a slacker and had a set-to with him at this meeting on the ninth. I'd like another account of that meeting. Mr Hunt says there were voices raised, so someone might have heard.'

'They might have, old man. There's nothing like an office for gossip, especially when there's been a quarrel.' He ran a hand through his hair. 'Look here, Jack, I know this sounds a bit melodramatic but, granted Valdez has disappeared, I don't suppose Mark Helston could be responsible, could he?'

'You mean did Mark Helston bump off Valdez and then scoot?'

Meredith Smith winced. 'That's putting it very bluntly.'

'Very bluntly, yes. It could have happened the other way round, of course. Valdez could have bumped off Helston. Or the two disappearances could be nothing but coincidence.'

'There has to be more to it than coincidence,' muttered Smith. He looked at Jack anxiously. 'I don't like this. H.R.H. is a great old boy. I've got tremendous respect for him. If you do dig anything up, be certain of your facts, won't you? His heart's not as strong as it might be and the old bird really cared about Helston.'

Jack stopped by the gates, hands in pockets. 'It might come to nothing, Merry. Thinking of old Mr Hunt, I hope so. But if someone asks you to dig, then, like a good dog, you've got to show them what you've unearthed.'

'Yes,' said Smith unhappily. 'I suppose you have.'

Gregory Jaggard paused, cocktail shaker in hand. 'Would you like another, Pat?'

She smiled cynically. 'It's all right. You can drop the pretence. Inspector Rackham and Major Haldean have left.'

His lips tightened. 'Pat – please! We can be civil to each other at least. We can't go on like this.'

She raised her eyebrows, her head cocked to one side. 'Why not, Gregory? After all, the arrangement seems to work.' She fixed a cigarette in its holder, lit it and blew out a long cloud of smoke. 'I'd like a cocktail, thank you.'

Jaggard poured two cocktails, gave one to his wife and leaned back against the mantelpiece with sudden boiling irritation.

Home! Home, sweet bloody home. Pat picked up her glass with elegant hands. Everything about Pat was elegant; the way she dressed, the way she moved, the way she held her dark glossy head on that perfect neck. Not many women could wear their hair cut close but it framed Pat's high-cheekboned face with her cool blue eyes to perfection. But there were dark smudges around those eyes and around her mouth were faint lines of strain. 'You were damn late last night,' he said brusquely. 'I don't care for Eve Lahone's crowd.'

Pat's eyes opened wider, then she looked away. Jaggard knew what she was thinking. *That's rich, coming from you.* And, God help him, she had a point. Rather more than a point to be fair. *I shouldn't have done it.* He knew that. He'd known it at the time, but Pat had been away, the firm was in its usual state of crisis and all he'd really wanted was some sympathetic conversation over dinner.

He'd broken off with Elise before he was married. He had had the honest intention of being faithful but . . . Elise knew the rules and he had been wretchedly alone. It didn't mean anything. No messy emotional scenes, no heartbreak, no ghastly recriminations. Just one night of their old relationship of lover and mistress, which had, fool that he was, continued.

Then, of course, some kind friend felt it 'Her duty' to write to Pat and Pat locked herself into this hurt shell of mannered indifference which nothing could crack. It was so horribly *civilized.*

He didn't want to be civilized, not with Pat. Pat was, and always had been, the only woman he cared for. He knew just how much he'd wounded her but if only she would tell him so! He'd welcome a row, a scene, a chance to fight and be forgiven. All she gave him was cold decency. If she would only smile at him with that heart-stopping lift of the mouth . . . If only she'd want to throw something at him!

Yet, even before he fouled his nest, that time which he now regarded as a golden age, he had the bitter honesty to acknowledge that things weren't perfect. He knew Pat had been married before. If anyone had told him it would have ever mattered he would have laughed out loud. For, after all, what had Pat's married life amounted to?

She had been desperately young and had spent, when Laurence Tyrell was killed, a total of sixteen days with her husband.

Thousands of war-widows married again. But it did matter. It mattered damnably.

Second best. He'd never been anything else. Tyrell's picture was on her dressing table and Tyrell's shadow stalked through their lives, all the more potent for being unmentioned. He had been measured by an invisible standard and found wanting. He could have fought Tyrell in the flesh but this wraith defeated him. And the irony of it was that Laurence Tyrell had precious little to recommend him. He'd heard stories which painted that gentleman in a very different light to the one in which Pat regarded him. Stories which he couldn't, in common decency, pass on.

'I said, do you think they'll find Mark?' It took him a moment to realize that she had spoken. He wrenched his thoughts back to their recent visitors.

'Inspector Rackham seems an improvement on that other policeman. I like Haldean. I've met him before.'

'Have you? I didn't care for him much.'

'He's not so bad, Pat. Did you know he's a friend of Meredith Smith's?'

'Is he? My mysterious cousin?' She played nervously with her cigarette. 'I think if I were Meredith Smith I'd rather resent things being as they are. After all, he seems to have as much right to my Grandmother's money as we do.'

'I don't think Smith sees it that way.'

'Very noble of him.'

'Well, you never minded that Mark scooped the pool.'

'Didn't I?' A very faint smile touched her lips. 'I did, actually. But Mark would have played fair. He'd have shared Grandmama's money. He knew she was absolutely silly about him. She never made any secret of the fact she preferred men to women. Why, my dear, she only arranged things as they were because I was married to you.'

'It's your money, Pat,' he said stolidly.

She gave him a sideways glance. 'Not in the eyes of the law, it isn't. Joint beneficiaries. What was the legal phrase Mr Stafford used? *Cestui que use.* For your use and mine.' She finished her drink, then hesitated. 'I . . . I heard from one of the Lahone crowd that you could use some money, Gregory.' She looked at his face with sudden, sharp attention. 'My God, it's true, isn't it?'

'No.' It was a lie, but it salved his self-respect. 'Even allowing for income tax, how can it be?'

'And there's always the firm,' she said softly.

'There's always the firm,' he repeated. 'Actually, I stand to make a goodish bit in the next couple of weeks.' He swallowed. 'There's a race coming up. I've got a bet with Johnnie Miller on the strength of it.'

He looked up and surprised an expression which made him catch his breath. Then, just as quickly, it was gone. Did she know – how could she know? – the desperate nature of his gamble with Miller? She was looking at him with odd intensity. He smiled humourlessly. 'It adds a bit of spice, don't you think?' She dropped her gaze and he gave an involuntary sigh of relief.

'Perhaps.' Her voice was cold and uninterested. 'It's occurred to me a couple of times that you might find Mark's disappearance and the way things have worked out a welcome break.'

'Pat! I was damn fond of old Mark, you know that. I don't know what the devil's happened to him but the sooner we find out, the better.'

She took another cigarette from the box. 'I can't see Major Haldean's going to be much use.' She shuddered. 'I hated the way he wanted to turn us inside out. You didn't volunteer much, did you? I noticed you skirted round the fact you were away after the New Year.'

'I couldn't see it was relevant. Besides, you were away, too.'

'I was at the Massinghams. You said you were in Birmingham. Business, I believe.'

'So I was,' he said flatly.

'Yes . . . You don't think Mark's in Brazil, do you?'

'Brazil?' He was genuinely surprised. 'Whatever gives you that idea?'

'All those questions Major Haldean asked. "Did Mark enjoy his trip to Brazil? Did he get on with Brazilians? Did he like Ariel Valdez?" That sort of thing. Uncle Frederick said that Mark and Valdez had quarrelled about the plantation and I thought he might have gone to see for himself and . . . and met with an accident over there.'

'We'd have got to know about it. Look, I'm sorry to say it, but the longer he stays away, the more likely it seems he isn't coming back.'

'You mean he's dead, don't you?' She drew a deep breath. 'I wish we could prove it!' she broke out passionately. 'If Mark is dead I want to *know*. Anything would be better than to be stuck in this limbo. What if we never know? What then? What did Mr Stafford tell us? It's seven years before the law assumes some-one's dead. In seven years' time and not a day before, I can mourn for Mark properly.'

'Seven years is a bit arbitrary,' he said awkwardly. 'It doesn't mean anything. It's just a legal thing to do with the trust and the money.'

Again, the oddest expression flitted across her face. 'And in the meantime neither you nor I can touch the capital.'

'Unless we can prove the poor blighter has bought it, no.'

A sudden hope clutched him. If they could prove it, that would make everything so easy . . . Things couldn't be that simple. God, what a mess. 'I'm going out,' he said abruptly.

Pat stood up. 'So am I.'

He couldn't ask where; he'd lost that right. But he *didn't* like her running with the Lahone crowd. They drank too much, gambled too much and he was sure Tim Lahone used dope. Eve was hard and . . . and cheap. Funny word. The amount of money she flung around was anything but cheap. Money. Pat had seemed damn interested in money . . .

Bill put his half of stout down on the pub table. 'We know Ariel Valdez arrived in Southampton on the morning of the twenty-eighth of December. He booked into the Montague Court Hotel off Tavistock Square at four o'clock that afternoon. He had his first meeting with Frederick Hunt at the Southwark works at two o' clock on the twenty-ninth. He sailed for France on the thirtieth. I've been onto the French police and they located his Parisian hotel easily enough. He stayed in the Hotel Maurice on the Avenue Victoria. Before he left the Montague Court, he reserved his room for the eighth, remarking to the clerk at reception that he'd rather spend New Year in Paris.'

'And who can blame him?' said Jack. He drew out his pipe and, filling it from his leather pouch, struck a match.

They and two clerks standing at the bar, earnestly discussing the fortunes of Crystal Palace, were the only customers of the Heroes Of Waterloo at this early hour of the day. In half an hour's time the stone-flagged pub would be bulging with the lunchtime trade, but, for the moment, they had the place to themselves.

'So far all's according to Cocker,' said Jack, flicking the match into the ashtray. 'I see you've checked where Valdez went with the hotel and the shipping company.'

'That wasn't difficult. Did you manage to verify Helston's movements before he disappeared?'

'To an extent. As the Jaggards told us last night, Mark Helston had taken up his standing invitation to join the Failfords in Leicestershire to do the British fox a bit of no good. I spoke to Mrs Failford on the phone this morning. There's no doubt he was there,' said Jack, picking up his glass.

'Failford and Helston were old Navy chums and knew each other well. Helston arrived on the twenty-third and should have stayed until Sunday the eleventh. However, he got caught in the rain and developed such a snorter of a cold that any hunting was out of the question. After a few days of misery he decided to go back to London, which he did on Monday the fifth. I got hold of Helston's valet, Robert Carlton, who's taken a position with a Mr Charteris of Bruton Street. He said Helston returned home feeling wretched. However, after a couple of days of bed and hot whisky he began to feel more the thing. He played golf on Wednesday and by Thursday was well enough to look in at Southwark. Meredith Smith tells me that gossip says Helston's arrival took everyone by surprise as they weren't expecting him back until the following Monday. He spent the afternoon working on a new roast for United Stores and arranged to have lunch the next day with Martin Crowther, their chief buyer.'

Jack took a thoughtful sip of beer. 'The only thing which puzzles me slightly is that Frederick Hunt gave me to understand that the meeting between himself, Valdez and Helston was a cut-and-dried arrangement. In fact, Helston only happened on it by chance. Frederick Hunt was out of the office on Thursday and didn't know that Helston had returned. It was Helston's clerk, Miss Mandeville, who now looks after Smith, who told him of the meeting on the Friday morning. Apparently Helston was astonished to find that Valdez was in the country.'

Bill frowned. 'Did Hunt deliberately lead you up the garden path?'

Jack clicked his tongue in irritation. 'That's it, dammit. He said that Helston had returned on the fifth. I assumed that "returned" meant "returned to work" but he could simply have meant "returned to London". I'd hate to say that Mr Hunt *meant* to lead me astray, as it could just have been a misunderstanding.'

He took a brief sip of beer and carefully put the glass back in the exact centre of one of the many beer rings on the table. 'He said nothing about Helston returning unexpectedly but, on the other hand, I didn't ask him. Here's something else for you to chew over. Hunt stated that the meeting between the three of them was a bit rocky. Now Meredith Smith's clerk, Miss Mandeville, says that after the meeting Helston was "not himself". Incidentally, there'd be worse people to get in touch with than Miss Mandeville for the low-down on Helston. I must dig her up. Anyway, Helston was very abstracted and couldn't settle. Miss Mandeville thought it might be his cold playing up again, and asked him if he wanted to cancel his lunch appointment with Martin Crowther. Helston seemed in a world of his own, which was quite different from his usual manner. Helston thought about it, but decided to go, saying words to the effect of, "I don't see why the work of the entire firm should be disrupted because of one man".'

'What did he mean by that, I wonder?'

'I only wish I knew.' Jack puffed at his pipe thoughtfully. 'Pronouns are the devil, aren't they? "One man" could mean Hunt, Valdez, Mark Helston himself or even, although I think it's unlikely, Martin Crowther from United Stores. At this stage it's impossible to guess. What I do think odd, though, is this. The Jaggards both told us that Mark had no prejudice against South Americans. According to Pat Jaggard, Helston enjoyed his trip to Brazil and had shown no animosity towards Valdez. But Frederick Hunt said that Helston felt the weight of the white man's burden to such an extent that the cause of the quarrel was Helston's dislike of, as he delicately put it, foreigners. I helped him out a bit with that. He was so obviously trying not to say *Damned dagoes*.' He glanced at his friend. 'You're looking pensive, Bill. Why? Is it deep thought or the horsehair upholstery?'

'Well . . .' Bill shook his head slowly, then grinned. 'I don't want to be personal, but I do wonder if you were the right person to ask Patricia Jaggard that question. I mean, your face is your face and although it's perfectly decent as far as faces go . . .'

'It's not the most Anglo-Saxon mug you've ever seen?' Jack laughed. 'D'you think that's all it is? I didn't feel she was going out of her way to be gracious.'

Bill's grin widened. 'Your much-vaunted charm failed to bring home the bacon, didn't it? You usually have girls eating out of your hand in the first five minutes.'

'Bill!' Jack was shocked. 'What a revolting idea. Messy, too. I don't charm and I certainly don't vaunt. I'm merely polite.'

'Come off it. I've seen you switch it on.'

'Drop it, will you?' pleaded Jack. 'You make me sound like an advert for Gleamo toothpaste. However, leaving these gross personalities to one side, Helston, we know, was alive and well at half past seven on the ninth of January. What's the last time anyone saw Valdez?'

'The manager of the Montague Court Hotel says that the last they saw of Valdez was at seven o'clock or thereabouts on Friday the ninth when he handed his room key into the desk clerk. He was carrying a small case and mentioned that he was meeting a friend and might end up staying out overnight. The desk clerk assured him that was perfectly in order from the hotel's point of view, and off he went.'

'Hang on. He was due to sail the next day, wasn't he? Didn't anyone smell a rat?'

'Not then, no. By the time Sunday morning came round and Valdez still hadn't returned, the manager began to get uneasy and entered the room. All of Valdez's things were still there. Now at this point the manager should have informed us, but he hesitated until the Tuesday morning.'

'Didn't anyone think to ask the Hunt Coffee people?'

'There wasn't anything in the room to connect him with Hunt Coffee. As far as the manager was concerned, Valdez was a private visitor. After all, hotels don't usually grill their guests about the purpose of their stay.'

'No, I can see that. What about his passport?'

'It was in his room. There was no money there, but all his clothes and personal belongings were untouched. The manager assumed that Senhor Valdez had met with an accident and so did we. We contacted the hospitals, but no one answering to his description had been admitted and there, I'm sorry to say, the matter rested.'

'Didn't Inspector Murray think it was odd?'

'I don't suppose Inspector Murray knew anything about it. They were different enquiries, you see. Murray had been told Valdez had sailed for Rio de Janeiro on the Saturday and, as far as he was concerned, Valdez was now out of the country. A note was put on the file to check Valdez's details against any unnamed accident victims and that, I'm afraid, was that.'

'Talk about the left hand not knowing what the right is doing . . .' Jack refilled his pipe. 'Now we *do* know, let's see where it gets us. Valdez and Helston are both missing and the *a priori* assumption is that the two events are connected. They met that morning and, whatever the cause of the disagreement, the meeting left Helston shaken. If there's a connection, they must have met again. It sounds as if they should have gone to Oddenino's, but for some reason they didn't. So where did that second meeting take place? Not at Valdez's hotel or the desk clerk would have mentioned it. Yes?'

'Yes. Valdez was by himself when he left the hotel, that's for sure.'

Jack frowned. 'What was Valdez wearing? Evening clothes?'

'No. I asked that. His evening things were in his wardrobe.'

'Helston was wearing evening dress.' Jack frowned. 'That probably explains Oddenino's, by the way. I don't think they let you in unless you're properly togged up. You'd think if they'd arranged to have dinner together, Valdez would be in evening clothes as well.'

'Maybe he didn't know Oddenino's rules. He's a South American, after all.'

'Yes, but he's not Tarzan of the Apes, is he? He'd just had a holiday in Paris, for heaven's sake. The fact that no one enquired for him at Oddenino's makes me think it was Valdez he was planning to dine with but the pair of them met up and decided to go elsewhere. Mrs Jaggard said Helston had always seemed perfectly friendly towards Valdez. Valdez left his hotel saying he might be spending the night "with a friend". If Mark Helston was the friend, you'd think Valdez would be wearing evening dress.'

'Valdez could have hoped to have made a friend in the course of the evening, if you see what I mean,' suggested Bill delicately. 'At a night club, perhaps?'

Jack grinned. 'So he could, but if he was planning a night on the town, he'd still be wearing evening dress. Who the devil could the friend be, Bill? Mrs Jaggard said she thought Valdez had been to this country before, but he wasn't a frequent visitor. The question of dress is a real poser.' He shook his head in irritation. 'The more I think about it, the odder it seems. If Helston and Valdez met, where did they meet? Where did they go? Not at Helston's flat or any of his clubs, either. Neutral ground. Somewhere both men have access to.'

'A pub?' suggested Bill, looking around the rapidly filling bar of The Heroes.

'Perhaps. I can't help thinking that, as Helston was in evening dress, that makes a pub a little unlikely at that early hour of the evening. Not impossible, but it wouldn't be my first choice. A hotel bar seems a better bet.'

'They could have simply bumped into each other on the street,' suggested Bill.

'So they could, but unless one of them resorted to violence right away, they'd still have to go somewhere. I wish we could have got onto this sooner. The chance of anyone remembering two men having a drink nearly four months ago is pretty slight. Did Helston run a car?'

'Yes,' said Bill. 'It's still in the garage. Helston last used it before Christmas.'

'So we can wash that out.' Jack drummed his fingers on the table. 'We've assumed they've met, presumably in some public place, and one of them either impulsively or with malice afore-thought, decides to make away with the other. Not in a hotel bar. They're nasty, crowded places to do a murder in and people have a tiresome habit of noticing that sort of thing. So they leave the hotel—'

'Or pub.'

'Or pub – and go where? And how? If Helston had his car, that could have been anywhere, but they're limited to feet, the tube, buses or taxis.'

'I don't know about a taxi,' said Bill. 'There was a real hue-and-cry about Helston. I can't help thinking that any taxi driver who'd had Helston as a fare that night would have come forward.'

'The tube or a bus? Not completely out of court, but not my first choice. It's awkward lugging a corpse around on the tube and I honestly don't think bundling a dead body onto the luggage rack of a Number Eleven bus is on the cards. It'd take up so much space for one thing and the conductor would probably want to charge for excess baggage.'

'What if the victim wasn't dead?' suggested Bill, then stopped as he saw Jack's smile. 'What are you grinning at me like that for?'

'I thought that as proposals go, it'd be a lulu. Come with me to some lonely dockside wharf, some unfrequented alleyway or, possibly, Epping Forest or Wimbledon Common. Because, don't you see, if our murderer is going to make his victim walk to his own grave, where he can hide the body so it defies detection, then you're asking the victim to be awfully trusting about the whole process. Unnaturally so, you might say.'

'But . . .' Bill stared long and hard at his half-empty glass. '*Either* the murderer finds a way of carrying the dead man to where he's going to leave him, *or* the victim gets to the spot under his own steam where he gets knocked on the head. He could have been invited to come and see a friend. There could easily have been some ruse like that.'

'A friend,' repeated Jack thoughtfully. 'I'd like to know if Valdez really did have a friend, know. And I'd love to know if Valdez and Helston really did quarrel at the meeting. We've only got Frederick Hunt's word for it that they did.'

Bill laughed. 'Why on earth should he lie about it? Frederick Hunt can't have bumped either of them off. He was at a Mansion House dinner that evening with dozens of witnesses. Besides, it's not very likely, is it?'

Jack conjured up a mental picture of the paunchy, self-satisfied, fluffy-haired figure and shook his head. 'No, it isn't.' He picked up his glass and finished his beer with a sigh. 'We need evidence, Bill. So far, all we've got to go on is two missing men. It's not enough.'

Jack didn't know why he had come to the Montague Court hotel. He could tell nothing about Valdez from gazing at the outside of the hotel and Bill had investigated the inside thoroughly.

Bill was very confident that any taxi driver would have come forward. Maybe Valdez had hired a car; maybe they had simply walked. But where to? Where, in this whole teeming city, could a body vanish? There were plenty of places where a man could be murdered but very few where he could remain undiscovered.

Without any clear purpose in mind he set out from the Montague Court Hotel and wandered aimlessly through the maze of streets, coming eventually to Russell Square and Montague Place.

He had no idea there were so many hotels in this part of London. He walked to the corner and turned into Gower Street. Bloomsbury was behind him, Tottenham Court Road, with its crowds and traffic, lay separated by a cluster of interlocking streets. On the right was University College, where the academic life of London went its ordered way. On the left was row after row of stone-fronted, railed-off houses. Some obviously belonged to whole families. Others had been split up into flats. He was in boarding-house London, where no man knew his neighbour.

Isolated cards advertising vacancies caught his eye. He walked on. It was rare to see an entire house for let.

One house stood apart from its fellows. Still dingy white under a shroud of soot, it looked particularly dilapidated. The area railings needed cleaning and a lick of paint wouldn't come amiss. There were weeds between the cracks of the steps leading down to the kitchens and cobwebs and dust grimed the windows. Empty, obviously, and for some considerable time; but it wasn't for sale or to let. It seemed simply forgotten. Why? Why, in the midst of a housing shortage, with houses and flats being desperately sought after, with premium payments on top of the rent being demanded and paid, would anyone let a whole valuable house stand untenanted and unused?

He walked along the street, turned the corner, and found the backs. High walls with gates. Lines of washing beyond. A smell of cooked cabbage – why was it always cabbage? – and, like bookends, two high and haughty cats sitting on opposing ends of stone-topped walls.

He counted down the number of gates to the empty house, but it wasn't necessary. It stood out in unpainted neglect. He put his hand on the latch finding, as he expected, that it was bolted. The backs were deserted. An overpowering desire swept over him to

see inside. Catching hold of the top of the gate, he put his foot
on the handle, pulled himself over and dropped to the yard below.
Cracked, green-slimed flags and emptiness met his eyes. With a
quick glance round, he cautiously approached the house.

A ground-floor window was open, with darkness beyond. A
bluebottle settled on the window before indolently crawling over
the sill. His senses tingled. There was a faint and foul smell.
Drains? It wasn't drains.

There's nothing here, he told himself. Not here. Not with the
roar of the Tottenham Court Road traffic at his back. Not in
the very heart of London. It couldn't be here.

With shrinking reluctance, he walked to the window and looked
into the room. There was nothing in the room but the oddest,
moving, black shadow in the middle of the floor. And then he
realized there was no light to cast a shadow; and the pool of
darkness was composed of innumerable, languid flies.

THREE

Frederick Roude, M.R.C.S., L.R.C.P., stood in the open
doorway. Wiping his hands on a cloth that smelt of disinfectant, he nodded to the sergeant before standing aside to
admit Jack and Bill. The capricious May sunshine illuminated a
hall, which showed elegant lines and fine proportions under
a thick layer of grime. A fat bluebottle crawled into the patch
of light.

The doctor followed Jack's fascinated gaze. 'Bloody flies,' he
said tersely. He jerked his thumb towards the room at the end of
the hall. 'Well, he's in there, but it's not a pleasant sight. He's
been dead for fifteen to sixteen weeks at a guess but I'll know
more when we get him to the mortuary. The van's waiting to
take him away as soon as you've finished. The cause of death
appears to be stabbing, but I'll have to confirm that later. What's
that? Any means of identification?' He frowned. 'Not on the
body itself. The features have all given way, as you would expect
after this length of time, which means his face isn't identifiable
and there aren't any fingerprints. He was stripped naked, for

some reason, but there's some of his things on the mantelpiece. I haven't touched those, of course. If you've got anyone in mind, I suppose we can compare their dental records, if any. That's the only way you can say for certain who he was now. I'll leave you to it, gentlemen.'

With a certain unwillingness, Jack walked past the two policemen on duty in the hall and pushed open the door of the room. An angry buzzing met his ears. There was a stomach-churning smell composed partly of dust, damp and disinfectant but chiefly, and sickeningly, of decay. It's only a dead man, he told himself firmly. You've seen plenty of those in the war. France. Think of France. But this wasn't France and it wasn't a battlefield. It was a terraced house on Gower Street, and from outside came all the humdrum noises of everyday life. The room had a high ceiling, bare boards and a fake Adam fireplace. Soot streaked the sill of the open sash window. All these were irrelevant details to avoid gazing at the thing on the floor. *You've seen this before* his mind insisted and in sudden anger at his own hesitation, he forced himself to take a steady look. Beside him, Bill made a noise as if he were choking.

An odd shape sticking out of the ribs caught his eye and, walking across to the body, he crouched down beside it. 'I say, Bill, look at this. It's a knife. Silver at a guess, but it's too badly tarnished to be sure.' He peered at it closely. 'We'd better not try and move it. It looks too well glued in to me.' He glanced round. 'Bill? Are you all right?'

'I will be in a minute,' said Bill, tightly. 'Yes, I can see the knife. Let's get it – him – taken away, shall we?'

'Wait a minute.' Jack looked closely at the dead man's hand. 'He's wearing a ring. Third finger, right hand. It's a bit obscured by . . . well, it's a bit obscured, but it looks like gold to me with . . . yes, I'd say that was a diamond.' He rocked back on his heels. 'Now why should someone take the bloke's clothes, yet leave a valuable ring?' He glanced up at the mantelpiece where a little heap of possessions lay. 'Or, for that matter, all his bits and pieces?'

'God knows,' said Bill. 'I can't think straight with that thing there.' He called to the men outside.

After the body had been removed, Jack walked slowly round the room, coming to a halt by the mantelpiece. Stacked in a neat pile were a silver card case, a leather wallet and a gold cigarette case. Sitting on top of them lay a pair of gold-rimmed glasses and a fob watch, its chain curled neatly round in a circle. Everything was thickly coated with dust.

'Don't touch those,' called Bill. 'I want to get them checked for fingerprints first.'

'Give me some credit, old thing.' He walked to the window, avoiding the tracks on the floor.

'This is the usual futile lock. A babe in arms could get in here.' He stooped down and peered along the dirty floorboards. 'Come and have a squint at these footprints. What d'you think?'

Bill joined him. 'They're a bit smudged. I suppose that's only to be expected with the window open like that. Hmm. One man, size nine shoe at a guess, with smooth soles.'

'Not bare feet,' volunteered Jack.

'No.' Bill inched forward slightly. 'There's more tracks by the fireplace. Different shoes. There's a small depression in the heel as if he had a patch there.'

'Yes.' Jack straightened up. 'Look along the top of the mantel-piece. The dust has been disturbed and settled again but there's a shape underneath.'

'It's a sort of curved rectangle,' said Bill. 'I know! It's a hip flask.'

'Bingo,' said Jack. 'Well done. I bet you're right.' Stooping down, he pointed his finger at the marks in front of the hearth. 'Smooth-soles and patches stood by the fireplace. What sort of lock is on the front door?'

'It's a Yale, sir,' contributed one of the policemen. 'We had to break it to get in.'

'Thanks,' said Jack briefly. 'That must have made it easier for him . . . How about this for an idea? Smooth-soles breaks in through the window but he opens the door to patches. The impli-cation is that patches is the victim because he entered by the more conventional route, but that's not certain. They either have a drink together or, what's at least as likely, smooth-soles does the deed and has a drink afterwards.'

'More likely, I'd say,' put in Bill. 'So smooth-soles stabs his victim . . .' He walked slowly around the room. 'There's no trace of bare feet anywhere, so the clothes must have been removed after death. For some reason he can't have wanted him to be identified. But in that case, why leave all his belongings? I wonder if there was any damage to the chap's face? It's impossible to tell at this stage, but the post-mortem will show that. After the murder, smooth-soles can simply walk out of the front door, leaving his victim behind. He must have had a case or a bag of some description.'

'A small overnight case?' asked Jack with a lift of his eyebrow.

'By God, yes!' said Bill excitedly. His face fell. 'It looks as if we've found Mark Helston, poor devil. We'll have to check it, of course, but I can't say I'm looking forward to breaking the news.'

'No,' said Jack, remembering an old, veined hand resting on a photograph frame. 'Neither am I.'

Meredith Smith paced restlessly round Jack's rooms. Where the dickens was he? The table was set for breakfast, complete with a neatly folded newspaper beside the empty plate. The percolator on the spirit lamp had ceased to make plopping noises and now steamed contentedly, awaiting the return of its owner. A heap of notes beside the typewriter on the desk by the window had attracted his attention, but they turned out to be ideas for a detective story. Stories, for God's sake! He looked at the tall bookcase in the alcove with disgust. Weren't there enough books in the world without churning out more? He pulled down Bartlett's *Dictionary of Familiar Quotations* and flicked through this repository of knowledge without reading a single word. Damn the man. Where was he?

The door opened and Jack, dressing-gowned and damp, came into the room. He stopped short with a smile of welcome as he saw his visitor. 'Hello, old man. You're an early bird. I was in the bath.' He rang the bell, then pulled up a chair to the table. 'Sit down, Merry. Have you had breakfast or will you join me? There's kippers on their way and we can probably run to a couple of eggs as well.'

'It's not eggs I want, Jack, but an explanation.'

'An explanation of what?' asked Jack, picking up the coffee pot. ''Scuse me for mentioning it, old thing, but you seem rather agitated. Milk in yours? Oy! Careful with that book. Don't chuck it down like that. I couldn't write without my Bartlett.'

'Write! I want you to do more than write.'

Jack put down his coffee cup and gazed severely at his visitor. 'Merry, old bean, if you won't actually come to the point and tell me what it is you do want, then this conversation is going to prove an uphill struggle. I haven't a clue what you're talking about and I'm blowed if I'm going to have raised voices before breakfast. In fact . . .' He glanced at the clock and then back at Smith. 'What are you doing here at this hour of the morning? I thought you'd be toiling away, earning the daily crust.'

Smith seized the newspaper from the table, ignoring Jack's protest. 'I'll tell you what I'm doing here.' He opened the paper and searched it briefly before jabbing a finger at a column on page three. 'Read that. Just read that.'

Jack, eyebrows raised, took the *Daily Messenger*. '*Gruesome Discovery on Gower Street. The decayed body of a man was found yesterday in a deserted house on* . . . Oh, Lord. *Violent means . . . Well-known author and investigator* . . . Oh, crikey . . . *Inspector Rackham, one of Scotland Yard's most able* . . . He'll like that. *The body has not been identified but is thought to be that of the missing businessman Mark Helston* . . . Hell's bells! How the devil did they get hold of this?'

'That's what I want to ask you,' said Smith, grimly. 'H.R.H., who still gets up at the crack of dawn, found that waiting for him when he came down to breakfast. He got me on the phone before I left for work, and left me in no doubt about his thoughts on the matter. He wants you to go to the house and explain things to him as, not unnaturally, he feels he should have been informed before the press got hold of it.'

'But there's nothing to tell him,' said Jack. 'Not yet, anyway.'

'That's not what . . .' He stopped as the door opened and Mrs Pettycure came into the room, carrying a tray.

'Here we are, Major,' she said cheerfully. 'Kippers with a dab of mustard sauce, just how you like them. And your porridge, of course.'

Jack took the tray from her hands. 'Thanks, Mrs Pettycure. Do you want anything to eat, Merry?'

'No, I don't,' said Smith, forcibly.

'Well, it's up to you. Now then,' Jack said, when the landlady had left the room. 'I can see that you're upset and I don't blame you. But honestly, old thing, we don't know if it's Helston or not.' He pulled a chair up to the table and, removing the cover from his bowl, poured milk onto his porridge. 'Do stop pacing up and down. It's putting me off my feed. The only definite thing I can tell you is that we found a body yesterday in a deserted house.'

'And what took you there?' asked Smith, suspiciously. 'Luck?'

'Partly,' agreed Jack between mouthfuls of porridge. 'Bill and I worked out that Helston and Valdez had met up in the evening. The probability was that Helston went to see Valdez, rather than the other way around. Valdez had been staying at the Montague Court, so I went for a walk – a jolly long walk – in a rough circle round the hotel, hoping to pick up some notion of where a murderer could deposit the doings so it would remain undiscovered for all this time. Obviously, after I'd tumbled to it, the police were in and out and the mortuary van was outside the door, so it didn't take long for the bright lads of the press to roll up. All they were told though, were the bare facts of what was found, how long it had been there and that it was murder. Stanhope from the *Messenger* got hold of me, but I stayed stumm as regards who it might be. The only thing I can think of is that he married up the date of Helston's disappearance with the age of the corpse and made a guess.'

'Murder,' muttered Smith. 'Are you sure it's murder?' he demanded, rounding on Jack.

'Certain, old scream. The corpse was still wearing a knife. About the only thing it was wearing apart from a ring,' he added. 'That's why we can't say who it was,' he added, pushing his empty bowl to one side and turning his attention to the kippers. 'He was naked.' He tapped the newspaper with his knife. 'It says so in there. So that means no tailor's tags and no laundry marks. There was a little heap of personal stuff on the mantelpiece, which looked as if the man had emptied his pockets, but who those pockets belonged to, I don't know.'

'What about his face?'

'Come on, Merry. You were in the war. The doctor said the body had been there for the best part of four months or so. It didn't *have* a face. It hardly had a body, if you see what I mean. Between you, me and the gatepost, we've assumed, as a working proposition, that it is Helston and the murderer's Valdez, but unless Mark Helston went to the dentist and therefore left a record of his teeth, we're stuck. Teeth don't decay,' he said, then seeing that Smith was trying to make sense of this statement added, 'well, they do, of course, but not after you've popped your clogs.'

Smith shook his head. 'I wish I knew what to tell H.R.H. You'll have to see him. He's blistering.'

'Hrr-o-eh?' asked Jack, considerably hampered by kippers.

'Yes, really. I've never seen him angry before. I'm not anxious to repeat the experience. I've heard before how he ruled the company. Benevolent, you understand, but definitely the boss.'

'The iron fist,' Jack offered, able to speak once more, glancing at the copy of Bartlett which had fallen open on the table. 'It says as much here. "The iron fist in the velvet glove".'

'Exactly. He really cares. I'm willing to bet that's one of the reasons why he was so fond of his great-nephew. Frederick Hunt, between the pair of us, is a bit of a washout. He's competent enough but he's got no enthusiasm. He couldn't care what the factory turned out as long as he gets a living from it. It wouldn't matter to him. Now Helston did share H.R.H.'s love of coffee. He wanted to know all about it, from the soil the plants are grown in, to the temperature it's roasted at. H.R.H. was a real pioneer, you know. I mean, coffee essence has been around for ages, but he experimented with getting exactly the right strength, then mixed it with condensed milk and syrup so all you have to do is add hot water.'

'Dear God,' said Jack, who loathed bottled coffee.

'I know, I know. I don't care for it either, but a lot of people do. You must have seen Royale Coffee with the blue and yellow label.'

'Oh, I've seen it all right,' agreed Jack dubiously. 'I've had to drink it on occasion. My landlady's under the illusion it's fit for human consumption. I didn't know it was made by Hunts. I take it "Royale" is a pun on H.R.H.?'

'That's right. He's tremendously proud of it. And before you turn your nose up, you should know that it sells by the million. That brand alone is worth a fortune and there's so much chicory in it, it's actually very cheap to produce. It's good business, Jack. But I honestly don't think it was just the money H.R.H. was after. It was all the excitement of seeing something he'd made really take off and become a household word. Helston, by all accounts, felt like that too. He was very keen on new sorts of trees and different flavoured roasts. As far as Frederick Hunt's concerned, coffee's coffee. All he's really bothered about is getting a decent income.'

'And old Mr Hunt wanted a bit more fire and passion?'

'That's right. He thought he'd found it in Helston. You have to see him.'

'I will, I will,' said Jack, holding up his hands. 'Pax, *Kamerad*, and all of that, but I need to know more. Rackham will have the post-mortem reports today, he'll have looked at the stuff that was in the room, and I know he was going to speak to Helston's dentist, if he had one. Then we've got some hard thinking to do. How did the body come to be in the house? Why was it naked? There were two sets of shoe prints in the room and the hall and no track of bare feet. Were only two men, the murderer and the victim involved, or was there a third man who helped to carry the body into the house? And, what, hanging over all those questions, was the motive? At least one, and I hope more, of those questions can be answered today and when they are we'll have a better idea of the answer to the others.'

'So you will see H.R.H.?'

'Yes, dash it, of course I'll see him, but before I do, I must get in touch with Bill. Depending on what else he's got planned, I imagine we'll both call on Mr Hunt. To have enough time to get the various reports that we need, I should think it'll be around teatime. Say four o'clock and you won't be so far off.' He glanced at the clock. 'But if I'm going to get hold of Bill, I can't do it in my dressing gown.' Smith didn't move. 'Which means, old thing, that I want to get shaved and dressed in reasonable privacy. I'd like you to pop off and tell Mr Hunt that I'm very sorry about the stories in the press, but it wasn't me, honest, guv.'

Smith still hesitated. 'Between the two of us, Jack, do you think it was Helston?'

Jack pulled a face. 'Between the two of us, I really don't know, but it very well might be.'

'And so, Major Haldean, you are unable to tell me any more than the bare facts that the body of a man has been discovered.' Old Mr Hunt accompanied this remark with a reproving glare, but Jack met his eyes squarely.

'At this stage, sir, that is all I *can* say. I hope Inspector Rackham will be able to add to our knowledge. When I spoke to him earlier he said he would be here. I don't think he expected the entire family to have turned out though.'

For Jack, like a latter-day Daniel, had walked into a den of Hunts. He had expected old Mr Hunt of course, and it was no great surprise that Frederick Hunt should be there as well. Hovering protectively by his father's chair, he had favoured Jack with the curtest of greetings. He hadn't bargained for Gregory Jaggard though, who stood stiffly by the window, and still less for Patricia Jaggard, who occupied the other end of the large sofa from Meredith Smith. An odd family trick of expression stamped them as relatives. Disapproval hung like a rain cloud in the air.

Frederick Hunt puffed his chest out. 'I need hardly say, Major, that the item in this morning's press occasioned us all very great alarm and, furthermore, a sense of outrage that you should have betrayed our confidence in this public manner. I think I speak for the entire family when I state that our thoughts flew to my father, who has invested his trust . . .'

Mr Hunt reached up and placed his hand on his son's arm. 'Major Haldean has explained himself, Frederick.'

He stopped as the doorbell sounded, followed by the heavy tread of the butler's footsteps down the hall. Still holding onto Frederick's arm, he rose slowly to his feet as Bill entered the room. He took a deep breath and looked at him with crackling anticipation. 'Well, Inspector?'

'It's good news, sir,' said Bill. 'It's not your great-nephew.'

There was a rustle of reaction in the room. Jack, who knew what Bill had to say but who had been asked to keep quiet, covertly watched everyone's response. Mr Hunt closed his eyes in momentary relief. Patricia Jaggard relaxed. Gregory Jaggard, on the other hand, seemed disappointed. Meredith Smith looked puzzled and Frederick Hunt gave a smug snort of disapproval.

'*Not* Mark? We have been put through all this for nothing?'

'Quiet, Frederick,' said Mr Hunt sharply. There was a sharp intelligence in his next question. 'Then who is it, Inspector? How can you be sure it's not Mark? Please, do take a seat.'

Bill sank into an armchair. 'Thank you, sir. We traced your nephew's dentist from his address book, which is in store with the rest of his effects from his flat. The dentist confirmed that whoever the man is, it's not Mr Helston. As to who it actually *is* – well, I'm afraid it looks as if it might be Senhor Ariel Valdez.'

'Valdez?' rapped out old Mr Hunt. He sat down and put his hand to his mouth. 'Valdez? That's awkward. That's very awkward indeed.'

Bill felt in his inside pocket and taking out his notecase, opened it and produced a white visiting card. 'This was found in the dead man's card case, together with a number of cards bearing the name of Ariel Valdez.' He held it out to Frederick Hunt. 'This card is one of yours, sir. Can you confirm that you gave it to Senhor Valdez?'

Hunt took the card and looked at it, turning it over in his hand. 'Yes, Inspector, this is one of mine. Look, here on the back I've scribbled a note of the time and date of our meeting in January. I remember giving it to Senhor Valdez at our first meeting in December.'

Old Mr Hunt moved impatiently. 'The newspaper said the man had been dead for a matter of four months. Is that an accurate statement?'

'Yes, sir.'

Mr Hunt's lips compressed. 'Then your next move is obvious. But you're wrong, Inspector, totally wrong. If only you had known Mark you would understand how wrong you are.'

Frederick Hunt looked at his father in bewilderment. 'What on earth are you talking about?'

'Oh, don't be a greater fool than God made you, Frederick. I'm talking about murder. Until Valdez was discovered the police had no explanation for Mark's disappearance. Now they believe they have. I am right, aren't I?'

Bill nodded reluctantly. 'I wouldn't put it quite as baldly as that.'

'For heaven's sake, man, do stop trying to spare my feelings. To state the matter plainly, you believe that the missing man and the murdered man are part of the same puzzle. I have dealt in facts all my life, Inspector. I cannot blame you for your very natural assumption. But I have one fact you do not, and that is a knowledge of my nephew's character. Granted sufficient provocation, I can imagine Mark hitting out in blind fury and even, although I do not think he would go so far, wresting the knife from the other man's grasp and using it. But what he would *not* do is conceal his actions. He had enough faith in English law to believe that a distinction would be made between manslaughter and murder.'

Frederick Hunt had gone very white around the lips. 'Murder? Surely not. That was merely sensational newspaper talk. It has to be an accident.'

'Nonsense,' snapped Mr Hunt. 'The man was stabbed.'

'Mark *couldn't* have murdered Valdez or anyone else,' broke in Pat. 'It's a ridiculous idea.'

Jaggard nodded in support. 'Absolutely. Valdez went back to South America.'

Jack swapped glances with Bill, then shook his head. 'Not as far as we can tell.'

'You are wrong, Inspector,' said Mr Hunt with deadly calm. 'Mark *cannot* be a murderer. I engaged you to find my great-nephew, Major Haldean. The production of a body, even the wrong one, is proof of some sort of zeal. At least it's more than that fatuous fool, Murray, ever did. To that I add a further commission. Clear Mark's name of this monstrous charge.'

Jack hesitated. 'I don't know if I can, sir.'

Mr Hunt gave him a shrivelling look. 'You too, eh? Then discover the truth. You will find it amounts to the same thing.'

'Look here, Haldean,' said Jaggard. 'You're barking up the wrong tree if you think Mark bumped off Valdez.'

'Thank you, Gregory,' put in Mr Hunt quietly.

Jaggard shrugged. 'It's not the sort of thing Mark would've done. Like H.R.H., I can just about credit an argument that went wrong, but not this hole-in-a-corner business in an empty house. I mean, they might have disagreed about running the plantation, but that's no reason for seeing the bloke off. If Mark felt as strongly as that he could have had the chap sacked.'

Jack's eyes slid to Frederick Hunt. 'It's been suggested that Mark's aversion to Senhor Valdez was based on more personal grounds. An uncomplicated dislike for dagoes?'

'Rubbish!' averred Mr Hunt vigorously. 'Frederick, you met both of them on that last day. You can vouch that Mark had no feeling of that sort.'

'Well, er . . . I rather thought he did.'

Jaggard shook his head. 'Not old Mark. That's not like him at all.' He looked curiously at Frederick Hunt. 'Whatever gave you that impression?'

Hunt shifted uncomfortably. 'It was the tone Mark employed during the meeting.'

'How d'you mean?'

'I am uncertain at this distance of time as to the precise terms used, but they were definitely concerned with Senhor Valdez's origins. More than that I am not prepared to say.'

'I think you'd better,' said Mr Hunt grimly. Frederick gave him an agonized look. 'Later, if you prefer, but I want to know, Frederick. However, *if* Mark had a quarrel with Valdez I find it frankly incredible that was the cause. As you know, I always thought you placed far too great a reliance on Valdez's judgements, but that is another issue.' He rose very stiffly to his feet. 'And now, Major Haldean, Inspector Rackham, I will not presume upon your time any longer. If the body is indeed that of Senhor Valdez, surely it is easier to believe that some tramp lured him into the house for purposes of robbery, violence ensued and the tramp fled, leaving his victim. Mark cannot have had anything to do with it.'

'Perhaps, sir. This could prove to be nothing more than a mare's nest.'

'I am glad to hear you say so, Major. Whoever killed Senhor Valdez – and I would dearly like to know – it was certainly not Mark.'

FOUR

P at Jaggard sat back as Gregory's practised hands steered the great car smoothly through the traffic. She enjoyed Greg's driving; able without ostentation. Not like that lout, Tim Lahone. He crashed the gears, over-revved the engine and flung the car from one side of the road to the other in a swaggering display of what he fondly imagined was skill. He *liked* cutting up other motorists and watching pedestrians scurry at his approach. And then he had stopped the car . . .

She winced at the thought of Tim's alcoholic breath, gin-soaked endearments and pawing hands. Greg had been right about him. When Greg used to hold her, she remembered feeling nothing but pleasure. He was good at that, too . . . So why, *why* had he betrayed her? If it hadn't been for Greg she would never have been in Tim Lahone's car in the first place.

Greg half turned his head to her. 'Anything wrong?'

'Tim Lahone tried to make love to me.' The engine stuttered briefly. *That* gear-change wasn't so smooth, she noted with satisfaction.

His lips set in a thin line. 'I see. What d'you want me to do about it? Endure it politely or knock his block off?'

At one time he would have acted, not asked. His knuckles where he gripped the steering wheel had gone white. Dangerous hands, she thought with a shock. 'Do you mind?'

'Mind!' He almost shouted. 'Of course I mind. You're my wife, for God's sake.'

'It's a pity you didn't remember that before.'

For a few moments he said nothing, keeping his gaze rigidly ahead. Then he shook himself like a man coming up from underwater. 'Pat . . .' His eyes stayed fixed on the road. 'If . . . If you want to call it off, then tell me. Let's have a clean break. I don't know how much longer I can go on living like this. If you want me to say I'm sorry, I'll say I'm sorry. God knows, I'm sorry. I don't want to split up but I'd rather have anything than keep dragging out this charade.'

'Can you afford a divorce?'

He did look round then. 'Whatever d'you mean?'

'You talked about the truth. I'd like the truth, Greg, about a few things. For instance, do you need Mark's money or don't you?'

'I don't,' he said tightly.

And she knew, with an inner conviction that nothing could shake, that he had told her another lie. She sighed and rested her arm along the sill, feeling the cool air rush over her hot skin. She suddenly felt utterly weary. What the hell was the point anyway? If he wanted a divorce she supposed she'd play the outraged wife when some slimy photographer turned up with evidence from a hotel somewhere. Perhaps he could get *that woman* – his mistress – to play the part. Keep everything cosy, as it were. Then, at least, the outrage would be real. It was with a slight shock she realized he was speaking to her.

'I said, what other things would you like the truth about?'

She roused herself with an effort. 'It doesn't really matter any more, does it? Not now it's all over.'

'I think it does.'

'Why. I suppose that's the question. Why?'

To do him justice he thought about the answer, and when it came it surprised her. 'Laurence Tyrell.'

'Laurence? My husband, you mean? Whatever's Larry got to do with it?'

He smacked the steering wheel. 'Ever since we've been married it's been like living with two people. You and him. You've always judged me against him but he's dead. I can't fight a ghost. You've built up this glorious picture in your mind and it's false, Pat, utterly false. Why did he marry you in the first place?'

'Because *he* loved me,' she snapped out, stung.

'Oh yes? What about his godfather's will? Did he tell you about that? Tyrell got his godfather's money when, and only when, he got married. He needed that money, Pat.'

'You've got that all wrong. His godfather wanted to make sure Larry had enough money to get married on. Don't shake your head in that *I know best* manner. It's the truth.'

'So what happened to it? Tyrell's money, I mean? He ran through it pretty damn quickly, didn't he?'

'He was unlucky.'

'Luck! He threw away a small fortune and landed you with a sackful of gambling debts. I paid the last of them, if you recall.'

'How very kind of you to remind me,' she said icily.

He winced. 'Oh, *hell!* I take that back. I really do, Pat. It's just that when I think of him and how you feel about him it makes me see red. He's always there and I hate it. Then I . . . I made a fool of myself. I'm sorry. Dear God, I wish you could guess how sorry I am, but something had to crack. We couldn't have gone on as we were.'

'Nor, apparently, as we are.' She was still smarting about the attack on Larry.

He executed two corners, before bringing the car to a halt in front of the garage on Tanyard Mews. Switching off the engine he turned round in his seat. 'So which is it to be?'

A grey weariness enfolded her. It was difficult to think . . . and all the time, Greg's voice sounded as if from the other end of a tunnel, pushing her, needling her to make a decision.

She didn't care if he was sorry. She wouldn't believe him if he said he was. She didn't really care about living any longer. One day and then another day and every day like this. Let him do what he liked. She didn't care about anything at all. It had all been so different when Larry had been alive.

Jack watched the Jaggards drive by with a feeling of admiration. That was some car Jaggard had built. The meaty, yet well-bred engine sounded as if it could match anything on the road. He was looking forward to talking engines with Jaggard. There was fifty-brake horsepower at a guess under that sleek maroon bonnet. Match the engine with a lightweight body and the speed would be . . .

'I don't think much of the idea it was a tramp,' said Bill, interrupting these wayward reflections as they continued up the street together. It was a cold, blustery day where March seemed to have displaced May. Bill stopped, gave his gloves to Jack to hold and did up the top button of his overcoat. 'You don't really think it's got anything going for it, do you?' he asked, taking back his gloves.

Jack shook his head. 'No. It's not impossible, of course, and it would explain the clothes being pinched. A tramp wouldn't want to leave those but if the bloke's got a strong enough stomach to take the clothes and shoes, then he'd hardly leave all the other bits and pieces. Incidentally, you owe me a thumping great debt of gratitude. Following your instructions to the letter, I kept mum before you arrived, although I was longing to put poor old Mr Hunt out of his misery. Why are you so certain it's Valdez? All you really told me on the phone were the results of the post-mortem.'

'The man's age is about right for Valdez, and, as far as we can tell, the body fits the description in his passport, but the identification hinges on the things which were in the room. They're all his. We know he wore gold-rimmed spectacles, the card case has his cards in it, as well as the one from Frederick Hunt, the watch has his name engraved inside, and both the wallet – which was empty, by the way – and the cigarette case had his monogram on them. The ring he was wearing was his, too. It had *A.V.* engraved on it.'

'None of which are inextricably part of him, if you see what I mean. Someone could have simply left them in the room.'

'Yes, but why? If the murderer was trying to confuse us, then he was going a jolly funny way about it. It's a damn funny business altogether. You'll hardly credit the story behind the house. Apparently it's the subject of a long-running legal wrangle between two branches of the same family. It's been empty for the last year and a half. Can you imagine leaving a house like that standing empty in this day and age? Some people really do have more money than sense. They couldn't even agree to put a caretaker in, so it's been left to moulder.'

'Could the murderer know that?'

'I don't see how. The body could have been found the next day. The post-mortem proved that the face had been untouched and the hands, which had been complete with fingerprints, were still intact. If we'd have found a complete stranger in that room, we'd have known it wasn't Valdez, no matter how many of his bits and pieces were scattered around. Now if someone had tried to make out it was Helston who was dead, I could see some sense in it. Helston's death would benefit Gregory and Patricia Jaggard very directly and, for all I know, Uncle Frederick might not be sorry to see the back of him, but no one gains from Valdez's death.'

'No one we've come across, that's for sure. Yet why take his clothes? Especially if you're going to leave all his things.' Jack sighed impatiently. 'I'm going to chase up Miss Mandeville, Helston's clerk. She should be able to tell me more about Helston other than that he was old Mr Hunt's white-headed boy. What about the knife, Bill? Was it silver? It looked like it.'

'The hilt was made of strands of silver wire set into a solid silver bar. The blade was inlaid steel and the whole thing must be worth a few bob. There's no prints on it, worse luck, but we might have expected that. It's a nice little thing in its way. I'd say it was a paperknife from a gentleman's study.'

'A gentleman, eh? That goes with the hip flask whose traces were on the mantelpiece. The knife and the hip flask are the only things we've come across which seem to belong to the murderer rather than the corpse. Speaking of gentlemen, what d'you think of Frederick Hunt?'

Bill shrugged. 'He didn't enjoy being put on the spot about Helston's feelings towards Valdez, did he? Which could either mean that his account of the meeting wasn't true or that he didn't want to shatter his father's illusions.'

'Would his illusions be shattered? There are worse things you can say about a man other than he doesn't like dagoes. God knows, it's a point of pride with some people. Jaggard didn't believe it, though. Talking about old Mr Hunt, he was damn quick on the uptake about the implications of the body not being Mark Helston's.'

'I'll say. Old or not, he's nobody's fool. He's certainly got more about him than his son.'

'Frederick's certainly not the human dynamo, is he?' said Jack with a grin. 'I'll tell you something that struck me, though. When you announced the dead man was Valdez, Frederick Hunt radiated smugness. It was almost as if he was expecting it.'

Bill nodded. 'Yes. I picked that up, too. However, if the quarrel between Helston and Valdez really was bitter, he might have had his suspicions of Helston all along. Obviously he wouldn't want to say so in front of the family, but he was the only person who seems to have known both parties at all well. Mark Helston's our obvious suspect, no matter what his relatives believe. Like you though, I want to know why the clothes were taken.'

'I suppose there could be some clue on the clothes, some stain or other that would give the game away, but *what* game for heaven's sake?'

They turned into Grosvenor Place, wincing against the wind which whistled across Buckingham Palace Gardens. 'Any alibi Helston might have was shot when he disappeared.' Jack shrugged himself further into his coat and kicked out at a paving stone. 'I don't get it. As you said, the only corpse that would do anyone any good is that of Mark Helston, but we know it's not Helston because of the dentist's evidence. If we'd found the body straight away, as we could've done, there wouldn't be the slightest doubt about who it was.' He frowned. 'I suppose you've cabled the Brazilian police?'

'I have,' said Bill, quickening his pace against the wind, 'but when we'll get a reply is anyone's guess, if we ever do. By the way, I've asked a couple of the right people about Jaggard's car firm. It's hovering on the brink of Queer Street, all right. Apparently disaster's only been staved off this long because of

Helston's money, otherwise it would have gone under a couple of months ago.'

'That means it's only Helston's death which would benefit Jaggard. He *might* be trying to accuse Helston of murder and thereby get him hanged but we've got to lay hands on Helston first. Having the chap vanish into thin air doesn't help anyone.'

Ruby, the parlour maid, came down the hall to greet the Jaggards on their return. 'You've got visitors, ma'am. Mr Stafford from the lawyer's office and another gentleman. I showed them into the drawing room. They've waited ever such a long time but Mr Stafford said as how it was important and he didn't want to leave without seeing you.'

'I wonder what Stafford wants?' said Jaggard. He glanced at the grandfather clock. 'It's past his office hours.'

'It'll be something to do with the trust, I expect,' said Pat absently. She couldn't get up enough energy to be curious. 'You see to him, Greg. I want to go and change.'

She walked up the stairs to her room and shut the door behind her. Greg would deal with it. It would be strange to have a world without Greg in it. Empty . . . Peaceful? She supposed so. She wished Mark was still here. She could have talked to Mark. She never realized how much she did talk to Mark until he was gone.

A vision of Mark, quite wonderfully indignant on her behalf, rose up. A very faint smile curved her lips. There was at least as good a chance that Mark would have squirmed with embarrassment. She could almost hear his voice. 'You'll have to handle it yourself, Pat. You can't expect me to get involved. Besides, I like old Greg.' And he had liked Greg, too. More than he'd liked Larry. It was horrible what Greg had said about him. A spark of anger flamed through the dull greyness. How *dare* he . . .

A knock sounded on her door and Greg walked in. 'You'd better come downstairs,' he said abruptly.

'Why?'

He seemed to be finding it difficult to speak. 'Just come downstairs, Pat. Now.'

Without waiting for a reply he strode off. Shrugging, she followed him. He was waiting for her outside the drawing room. Silently, he opened the door and stood back for her to enter. With a puzzled shake of her head she went into the room. Mr Stafford looked up as she walked in and gave a little cough.

'Ah, Mrs Jaggard. Thank you for coming. This is a very delicate business and it seemed best to see you as soon as possible.' He indicated the man beside him. 'This gentleman . . .'

A tall, fair-haired man was standing by the fireplace. She looked at him with a vague feeling of recognition, then there was a buzzing in her ears and her mouth went totally dry. She felt dizzy, as if she were going to faint. 'Larry?' She gasped out the word. 'Larry? You're dead.'

He smiled and it was as if the picture on her dressing table had uncannily moved and come to life. Then his hands caught her and they were real hands. Living hands of flesh and blood, not images in a frame. Strong hands. She looked down and with a catch in her throat she saw the little finger with the twist where he had broken it long ago. She'd forgotten that. It was hidden on the photograph and she'd forgotten it. She'd seen him as a flat picture in black and white for so long, she'd forgotten what the real Larry was really like. She looked up and found his grey eyes fixed on her. She'd forgotten his slate-grey eyes.

His arm slid round her shoulders. 'I've given you an awful shock, Pat.' His voice was deeper than she remembered, more virile, more *real*. 'I wish I could've warned you in some way. Please. Come and sit down.'

FIVE

Miss Sheila Mandeville decorated the bottom of the top copy of the weekly accounts with a line of neatly interspersed noughts and dashes, pressed the release lever on her typewriter, and taking the top copy, carbon and flimsy out of the machine, started to read it through. The bell on her desk rang, causing her forehead to wrinkle in a faint line of annoyance. Gathering up the papers, she went to answer it.

'I'm terribly sorry, Captain Smith, I haven't had time to check . . . Oh!' She stopped short. Sitting beside Meredith Smith's desk was the tall, rather foreign-looking Major Haldean she had shown into Captain Smith's office half an hour ago. As she entered the room he rose to his feet and inclined his head with an easy courtesy.

'Miss Mandeville?' He had a pleasant, low voice in which she could hear his smile. 'We met earlier, but we weren't properly introduced. Forgive me for asking, but I wondered if you'd heard what I'm doing here?'

Sheila Mandeville smiled bashfully. 'I did hear something about it, Major.'

Meredith Smith grinned. 'You're too well known, Jack. It caused an absolute sensation in our little world when you came the other day.'

Jack looked wryly at Miss Mandeville. 'I can't say I enjoy everyone knowing who I am, but it does save a lot of wearisome explanations.' He hesitated. 'The thing is I could do with talking to someone who knew Mark Helston and, as you looked after him, I wondered if you'd be kind enough to spare me some of your time. I know it's jolly short notice, but would you allow me to buy you tea? My car's outside and we could run up to the Ritz or somewhere. I know it's a beastly cheek imposing myself, but you really would be doing me a favour. Captain Smith will vouch for my table manners and the fact that I wash behind my ears and behave myself in public places and so on.' He looked at her with mild anxiety, waiting for her answer.

Bless the man, she thought indulgently, mentally replacing her tea-shop poached egg on toast with a vision of Palm Courts. He isn't worried I'll refuse, is he? He looks as if he is. Even if I don't really know him, he's obviously all right, especially as he's a friend of Captain Smith's.

She liked Captain Smith, and his friendship with the famous Jack Haldean, which had been dissected over tea and biscuits three mornings running – '*He really knows him well, Sheila. He was in the war with him and everything. Have you read any of his stories? They're awfully clever*' – added a welcome tinge of glamour. She was pleasantly conscious that she would share in this reflected glory. 'I'd be delighted,' she said, noting with satisfaction how pleased he appeared.

'Then that's all settled. Good. When do you finish for the day? Five o'clock?'

'Oh, go now,' said Meredith Smith in a put-upon voice. 'Have the extra quarter of an hour with the compliments of Hunt Coffee and welcome. Will you be at the club tonight, Jack?'

'I should be.'

'Good-oh.' Smith smiled at her. 'You're in luck, Miss Mandeville. When he wants something from me, I usually end up buying the drinks myself. I've never managed to get a meal out of him yet.'

'So how,' said Smith over the whisky which, despite the comments he had made earlier, was on Jack's account, 'did you get on with my Miss Mandeville?' There was an unconscious emphasis on the word *my*.

'*Your* Miss Mandeville . . .' Jack paused and shot a swift look at Smith.

Smith met his gaze, colouring slightly. 'Well, what about it?'

Jack sighed. 'Merry, you prize idiot, the last thing I want to do is put your nose out of joint. You should've invited yourself along. If it comes to that, why don't you invite her out yourself? Why didn't you tell me you felt like that about her?'

'There's nothing to tell,' said Smith, defensively. 'And you know how it is. Private life and business don't mix very well. For one thing, she's so horribly efficient. It stops me in my tracks every time. She's a highly competent confidential clerk and I have to tell her what to do. It's not as easy as you might think when you work with a girl.'

'Yes, I can see that. If you're used to asking someone to take a letter, bunging in your hand and heart at the end of it may prove awkward. Even a small sherry might be difficult.'

'You've got no idea,' agreed Smith, earnestly.

Jack sipped his whisky. 'Failing all other solutions, you can always write to the queries page of *On The Town* for advice to the lovelorn. Setting aside your natural bias in her favour, do you think she's trustworthy, old thing? I mean, how objective would she be about Mark Helston?'

'Totally, I would think.'

'Umm. She liked him, obviously, and thought he was honest and hard working, if not, perhaps, the brightest of sparks.'

'She should know. She was with Ainsworth and Richards before she came to us. Ainsworth was bright enough for anyone. When the crash came she was out of a job for over a month.'

Jack put down his glass. 'That explains why brightness wasn't something she particularly appreciates. I'm beginning to get a picture of Helston. A conscientious, solid sort, with conventional hobbies who was quite happy to continue in the path his great-uncle, old Mr Hunt, laid down for him. Not much originality there, perhaps, but a desire to do the best he could. By the way, he was really keen on going to Brazil, but Frederick Hunt stopped him by pointing out how valuable he was at home. Apparently he got on with Valdez perfectly well.'

Smith frowned. 'I don't see how Miss Mandeville knows that.'

'She was going off what Helston said about him. Er . . . If I tell you what she said, am I speaking to Meredith Smith, the eager beaver of Hunt Coffee, or Meredith Smith, the human Sealed Tomb?'

'Oh, the Sealed Tomb all the time,' replied Smith with a grin.

'Good . . . because, to put it bluntly, she thinks Valdez was a crook but doesn't want anyone to know she said it. He oozed too much sex appeal for her liking. She said it was as if he'd heard what a South American charmer was like and was trying to live up to it. Rather like a cross between Rudolph Valentino and a dance-band leader.'

'How the devil does she know? She never met the man.'

'But she did. She saw him on the twenty-ninth, before his first meeting with Frederick Hunt. She spent a good few minutes with him whilst he was waiting to be shown in to Mr Hunt. As Helston was away, she was filling in by doing various bits and pieces, and that morning she was chief hand-holder to any visitors.'

'So what? The fact she didn't like him doesn't make him a crook. Besides, he can't have been up to anything. Someone would have spotted him.'

Jack gave him a significant look. 'Maybe they did. It's a glimmer of a motive for the quarrel which took place between Valdez and Helston on the ninth, at any rate.'

'But . . .' Smith stopped, trying to put his thoughts in order. 'If Valdez was up to something rum, it'd have stopped after he died, wouldn't it?' Jack nodded. 'That's not happened, Jack. As far as the financial side's concerned, there's been no change. Did Miss Mandeville have any idea of what form the crookedness might take?'

'Yes. She worked for a stockbroker before she came to Hunt Coffee . . .'

'Ainsworth and Richards.'

'Ainsworth and, as you say, Richards. She got into the habit of checking the City page in the papers. Well, according to her, the spot-market prices for coffee have recently varied from between one hundred and eleven shillings to one hundred and ninety-four shillings a hundredweight, depending on the quality. Now, the cost of the coffee from Hunt's own plantation is one hundred and fifty-four shillings and upwards which she says is crazy, when you consider they actually own the thing.'

Meredith Smith took a cigarette from his case, absently offering one to Jack. He struck a match and smoked for a while in silence. Then he rubbed his hand through his hair and looked up with a rueful grin. 'She's got me there. Apart from to see how the market's doing in general, I haven't checked the City page for ages, and certainly not the small print of the spot markets. One hundred and eleven shillings, eh? That must be East African or Indian. South and Central American coffee always carries a premium. The one hundred and ninety-four shillings will be peaberry.' He brooded over his cigarette.

'But what d'you think of the idea?' prompted Jack. 'Could there be some sort of jiggery-pokery going on? You said yourself not so long ago you thought there was something odd.'

'Yes . . . Although that was based more on meaningful conversations with H.R.H. than anything I'd seen for myself. He'd told me to keep my eyes and ears open.'

He clicked his tongue in irritation. 'You see, although it seems a very simple comparison, it's not as straightforward as all that. We don't just pay the plantation for coffee, we make a regular payment which not only covers the cost of the coffee, but such things as wages and salaries, maintenance of the equipment and buildings, processing, shipping costs and replanting. The very high-quality coffee, such as the peaberry, is also included in the flat payment. There's other things as well, but those are the main expenses. We also buy unprocessed coffee in Brazil, as we don't produce anything like enough to meet our demand. Any comparison is bound to be misleading because you're not comparing like with like. However . . .' He stubbed out his cigarette with a gesture of finality. 'I'll look into it. It seems damned strange when you put it like that, I agree.' He hesitated. 'Did she think it was likely that Helston was guilty? Of seeing Valdez off west, I mean?'

'Absolutely not. She was emphatic about it. She believed he could've had a quarrel with the man, but would have stopped far short of murdering him. Everyone seems very definite about that. But if Helston didn't account for Valdez, who did? The murderer has to be someone to do with Hunt Coffee.'

'But who does that leave? There's only Frederick Hunt and H.R.H. – I'm not counting the junior staff – and I can't see either of them stabbing a naked man in an empty house. Incidentally, if Valdez was up to something dodgy, Frederick Hunt would be bound to discover it eventually.'

'Could he be in on it?'

Meredith Smith laughed. 'You don't pull your punches, do you? I suppose he *could*, but I'm blessed if I know how he'd work it. The accounts are all A.O.K., you know.'

'What about Frederick Hunt's private life? What do you know about that?'

'Not much.' Smith shrugged. 'He has a taste for gambling, but that's not a crime. He often goes to the races, he holidays in Monte Carlo and I had a very peculiar phone call the other day which was wrongly put through to me instead of him. If the bloke on the other end wasn't a bookie, I'm a Dutchman.'

'What was the tone of the call? Friendly or threatening?'

'Oh, friendly, definitely. Why?'

'Because if he was in need of money, it'd be interesting to know.'

'But Valdez's death didn't benefit him and neither does this business with Helston. In fact I can't see Valdez's death benefits anyone, which makes it a real puzzler.' Smith rose to his feet. 'D'you fancy a game of billiards? Inspiration might strike while we're playing. I'm blowed if Helston sounds like the bloke responsible, yet it's more or less got to be him because everyone else is accounted for.'

'As far as I can see no one gained, except Pat and Gregory Jaggard,' said Jack, putting down his glass. 'And even they didn't know they were going to. Not that that helps with Valdez, of course. Oh, to hell with it. I'll play you a hundred up and the loser stands the tab.'

He got up and led the way to the billiard room. 'We're in luck, the table's free,' he said, then stopped. Gregory Jaggard was sitting slumped by the table in the corner. 'I'm sorry,' he began, then stopped as he saw Jaggard's flushed face.

'Smith and Haldean,' said Jaggard. He laughed. 'Sounds like a gun I had. A Smith and Wesson, don't you know? Must find it. It'll come in useful.' He attempted to sit upright, glaring at them. 'Won't it?'

'It might,' temporized Jack, trying to gauge just how drunk Gregory Jaggard was.

Jaggard slumped back. 'I'll need a gun to shoot myself.'

Jack and Meredith exchanged worried glances. 'Why do you want to shoot yourself?' asked Jack cautiously.

Jaggard waved his hands expansively. 'Or him. Can't shoot her. Not my . . . my . . . But she isn't any longer, is she? He's back, you know. Why didn't the swine stay dead?'

'Who?' demanded Smith. 'Mark Helston?'

'Mark?' He squinted at them truculently. 'Talk sense. Mark's gone. He won't come back. He killed Valdez, didn't he? Didn't think he would. Not Mark. Shouldn't have done that. Oh, God.' He buried his head in his hands. 'Leave me alone, will you?'

They quietly left.

'We've got to get him out of there before he causes a scene,' said Jack. He strode into the lobby to find the porter.

'Mr Jaggard, Major?' said ex-Sergeant Sutton. 'He's staying here tonight. If both you gentlemen could help, I'm sure we could help Mr Jaggard up to his room. We don't want him making a fuss in front of the other members. Mr Jaggard wouldn't like that at all. He'd be mortified once he realized what he'd done.'

Confronted with their joint force, Jaggard allowed himself to be persuaded up to his room, where he lay, fully clothed and incapable, on the bed.

'I don't know how long he's been drinking,' said Sergeant Sutton, 'but they shouldn't have served him, poor sod, begging your pardon, sir.'

Jaggard opened one eye. 'Where's that bloody gun?'

'Never mind about that now, old man,' said Jack soothingly. 'You can't do it tonight. It's far too late.'

Jaggard's face crumpled. 'Too late. Oh, God, I feel sick.'

Jaggard was sick. It was some time, some rudimentary housework and much talk before they could leave, but, as Sergeant Sutton comfortingly said as they walked down the stairs, 'He'll be all right now, gentlemen. I'll keep an eye on him. I should report this to the Secretary, though.'

Jack felt in his wallet and drew out a pound note. 'This is for your help, Sergeant. We couldn't have managed without you. Unless you feel you absolutely must, I can't see there's any need to bother the Secretary about it. I don't want to inconvenience Mr Jaggard more than is absolutely necessary.'

'Right you are, sir,' said the sergeant, pocketing the money. 'Least said, soonest mended.' He grinned to himself. 'But I wouldn't like to have his head tomorrow.'

Bill Rackham, entering his office considerably before nine o'clock the next morning, was surprised to find Jack waiting for him. 'Hello, old man. What's up? I'm up to my eyeballs today. I've got to be at the Old Bailey to give evidence in the Leigh Abbey case, so I can't spare you much time.'

'This won't take long, I hope. I knew you were tied up today which is why I'm here at this unearthly hour. Who, in the Valdez-Helston business, is connected with Jaggard and called Larry? He's obviously got right up Jaggard's nose. I think I know the answer, but I want to make sure.'

Bill frowned. Walking to the desk he opened the drawer and picked out the file. 'It doesn't ring any bells. Here we are. Gregory Jaggard . . . Nothing there. Patricia Jaggard . . . There's a Laurence, if that's any help. He could be called Larry, I suppose. He was Patricia Jaggard's first husband. He was killed at Third Ypres.'

Jack nodded. 'That's what I thought. I'll have to go into this, Bill, but it looks as if the army might have made a mistake. Jaggard was at the club last night, very much the worse for wear. If I understood him correctly, Laurence Tyrell arrived in London yesterday.'

Bill gaped at Jack. 'What? Are you *sure*?'

'Nearly sure.'

'I don't believe it.' Bill put the file back on the desk like a man in a daze. 'I've never come across a blinking case like it. A man we didn't know was missing is murdered, a missing man we assumed to be dead is suspected of murder, and now another man, who we all thought was safely dead years ago, strolls in, restored to life. Where the hell's he been all this time?'

'That's one of the questions I want to ask.'

Bill looked at the clock and swore. 'You'll have to ask it by yourself. I've absolutely got to be in Court. But here's a thought, Jack. How on earth will it affect that trust fund of the Jaggards?'

'That, old son, is another one of the other questions. But from what I can remember, I wouldn't be at all surprised if Gregory Jaggard got the wooden spoon. Can you pass me the file? I want to check the solicitor's address.'

'I need scarcely tell you, Major Haldean, we are not accustomed to impart confidential details relating to our clients.' John Gervase Stafford peered disapprovingly at Jack over the top of his half-moon spectacles. 'However, in light of Sir Douglas Lynton's telephone call, I feel that an exception may be made in this case. Although why we pay rates when the police force deems it necessary to call upon amateurs, I really do not know.'

'The officer in charge has to be at the Old Bailey this morning in connection with another case. As I've been retained by Mr Harold Hunt to investigate an associated matter, Sir Douglas thought it best for me to see you, rather than brief another officer previously unconnected with the affair,' said Jack, blessing the foresight which had made him prompt Sir Douglas to ring Kyle, Stafford and Bruce.

'I see,' said Mr Stafford, with the suspicion of a sniff. 'As you have the confidence of both Mr Hunt and Scotland Yard, it would be churlish of me to object any further.' He permitted himself a thin smile. 'Please smoke if you so wish. I do not myself indulge in the habit. I consider tobacco to be the cause of most of the nervous agitation so sadly prevalent amongst your contemporaries.'

Jack's hand froze on the way to his pocket and he contented himself with bringing both elbows up to the desk and resting his chin on his interlocked hands. Mr Stafford leaned back in his chair and steepled his index fingers together under a prim mouth.

'Well, Major?' he asked, after a short pause. 'You do have some questions for me, I presume?'

Having thus established the prickly Mr Stafford in the role of imparter, rather than withholder, of information, Jack relaxed with a smile. 'Oh lots, sir. The first and most important is about this chap who turned up yesterday. He is Laurence Tyrell, is he?'

'Undoubtedly, sir. His wife, the former Miss Patricia Helston, currently known as Mrs Jaggard, identified him at once.'

'I see . . . Bit of a shock for everyone, what?'

'A most severe shock. Indeed, had I any inkling of the upset it would cause Mrs Jaggard I would have refrained from letting him confront her without warning.' He hesitated. 'To be honest, Major, I thought there must be some mistake, either deliberate or accidental. As far as I was aware, there was no doubt that Laurence Tyrell had been killed at the Third Ypres, and I harboured a suspicion – unworthy as it transpired – that the man claiming to be Mr Tyrell was an impostor. There is a considerable sum of money at stake and, in such cases, I regret to say that false claimants are not unknown. Rather than be a party, however innocent, to any deception, I thought it was best to take immediate action to establish his *bona fides*.'

'Why did he come to you, sir? Why not go straight to his wife?'

'He was not furnished with her address. I gather he arrived in London yesterday morning. He consulted the telephone directory for a Mrs Tyrell but, naturally enough, found no one listed under that name. He had no idea that his wife had remarried. As the marriage had taken place in good faith, there can be no question of an action for bigamy.' He glared at Jack as if suspecting him of wanting to drag his client bodily into court.

'No, no, of course there won't be,' Jack assured him hastily. 'But where did the chap spring from? He seems to have popped up like the demon king.'

'For that information you must apply directly to Mr Tyrell himself.'

'Okay . . .' Jack ran a hand through his hair. 'Won't this upset the apple cart rather? I mean about the trust fund and what-have-you?'

'The point you raise has not escaped my attention, Major. Indeed, I was so exercised upon the question that I have decided to take Counsel's opinion upon the subject. The rules regulating the operation of trusts are principally determined by the large body of case law upon the subject. In this situation, which I venture to suggest is unique, case law will, I fear, be of little help.'

'Gosh,' said Jack, with a disarming grin, wondering how it was that Mr Stafford could so successfully turn an admission of ignorance into what sounded like a display of knowledge. 'It sounds as if this Counsel's opinion might be fairly key to the whole thing. D'you mind if I come along?'

'Well really, I . . .' Mr Stafford broke off and gazed uncomfortably at the leather blotting pad on the desk in front of him.

'Who've you asked?' put in Jack, easily. 'I was wondering if I'd ever run across him. My godfather's a K.C., you know. He's called Archie Wilde, if that means anything to you.'

Mr Stafford brightened visibly. 'Indeed it does, Major. We have never briefed Mr Wilde as ours is an exclusively civil practice, but I am, of course, familiar with the name. I have an appointment with Thomas Littleton, K.C. at his rooms in Lincoln's Inn at three o'clock this afternoon. In the circumstances it would, perhaps, be in order for you to accompany me.'

'That's very good of you, sir,' said Jack, rising to his feet. 'Shall we say the Chancery Lane entrance outside Stone Buildings at quarter to three?'

And I only hope, he added to himself as he took his leave and walked out onto Southampton Row, that the learned Mr Littleton is rather more forthcoming than the reticent Mr Stafford.

Meredith Smith laid down his pen and looked thoughtfully at the open ledger in front of him.

The accounts, *as* accounts, were fine, culminating in a row of figures scored under with a double line and resulting in a worthwhile profit. And really, he thought, looking at the signature of Francis Mason, Chartered Accountant, who had audited and signed last year's accounts, he wouldn't have expected anything else. Mason and Schofield was a well-respected firm; if there was anything dodgy it was unlikely to show up in the official records. They were scrutinized far too closely.

So why, in the face of all the evidence, to say nothing of his own careful accounting, did he think something was wrong? H.R.H.'s hints? Maybe, but the hints had been so guarded that he might have read too much into them. He'd been nettled, too, by Miss Mandeville's spotting of the discrepancy between the plantation price and the spot-market price. He should have been aware of that. Having their own plantation ensured a regular supply of high-quality coffee and that, surely, was worth paying a premium for, but . . .

He pulled down a set of accounts at random. 1919. That was

too early. The market was still settling down after the war. He
went forward a couple of years. Prices had steadied at 115 shillings. The next year showed a total rise to 131 shillings and the
year after that it had shot to 146 before rising to 154 where it
had been for the last two years. They were buying a lot more
chicory than in previous years but that price had fallen slightly.
Instead of buying chicory in Yorkshire, they were shipping it
from Belgium, which, oddly enough, was cheaper. The total
production of the factory had remained about the same for the
last three years.

Hang on. If coffee was being bulked out by chicory, and the
production was the same, that should mean less coffee – expensive, taxable coffee – was being imported which should mean a
reduction in costs. So where was the saving? He glanced over
his figures again, drumming his pencil on the table. Surely the
profits should have risen more? There *was* a profit, but he would
have expected it to have grown. With the last three years' accounts
in front of him, he ran his eyes up and down the columns of
figures while the idea for a fraud took root and grew in his mind.

He suddenly became aware of the complete silence of the
office; lunchtime. He glanced at his watch. The siren had sounded
ages ago. He had roughly half an hour to test out his idea. Through
the open window overlooking the factory yard came the shouts
of an impromptu game of football. The factory would be deserted
too.

He walked rapidly down the stairs, out into the yard and across
to the factory. The bottling department was eerily quiet. The great
green-painted machines stood ready to clank into rattling life,
jetting clouds of steam into innumerable waiting bottles before
they each received a precise eight fluid ounces of ready-made
Royale Coffee. When he had been here before it had resembled,
with the heat, the noise and the hissing steam, a picture of a
mechanical hell.

He had to shout at the man next to him to make himself heard;
now his footsteps rang out on the tiled floor. He opened the far
door into the outside air and skirted round the various buildings
until he got to the warehouse, walking through the towering piles
of sacks, with their clean, sharp smell of jute, until he reached
the far doors looking out onto the slowly flowing Thames.

The watchman sat dozing in a chair pulled up to the open

doors of the dock entrance. He looked round with sleepy eyes as Smith approached and put down the newspaper that covered his knees. 'Would you be wanting anything, sir? The offices is round the other side.'

'I know,' said Smith with a friendly smile. 'I work there. I thought I'd come and have a look at the warehouse instead of sitting at a desk all day.' This eccentric behaviour was met with a nod which implied 'suit yourself', better than any words could have done. 'Smoke?' he asked, offering his case.

'Thanks, guv. Don't mind if I do,' said the watchman. 'There's many,' he said, obviously feeling called upon to make some remark, 'who'd do better to come rhand 'ere a bit more often. Take old Mr Hunt now. He knew everyone who worked for him by name. Saw a lot of him, we did.'

Smith let this remark drop into silence. 'There's an awful lot of coffee in there,' he said, with a glance into the warehouse. Now that was an idiotic thing to say. Of course there was a lot of coffee in there. 'What happens when it comes in?' he asked quickly. 'I mean, how d'you know where to put it all?'

'It all depends. There's some bags we put up the side for storage and there's some going to be used right away. Mr Wilkins, the foreman, he takes care of that. He tells the lads where to put everything right enough.'

'Do you store coffee for a long time?'

'Sometimes. There's sacks in there we've had for the last two, three years and more.' He gave a slow smile. 'Don't ask me why.'

'I suppose you know how much you've got?'

'Mr Wilkins does. He keeps tabs on it all. We don't want no one sticking one of these bags under their arm and walking orf with it, do we?' he said with a smile, jerking his thumb to indicate the warehouse.

This was the opening Smith had been waiting for. 'They'd take some lifting, wouldn't they? They must weigh a ton.'

'There's a hundredweight to each sack and when you've shifted a few of those you know about it. I've done enough of that in my time. I can't manage no more because of me back, but if I had a penny for every sack I've shifted, I'd be a rich man.'

'I bet you would. Are some sacks lighter than others?'

'Oh yes,' agreed the watchman. 'Mind you, they don't feel

lighter at the end of the afternoon, but you take the old coffee, for instance. I could move two of those for every one of the others.'

'Why's that?'

The watchman shrugged. 'Blessed if I know. But those sacks is a lot less heavy when they go out than when they come in. Mr Wilkins knows all about it. He often says, "Come on, lads, it's an easy job this afternoon." Funny, innit?'

It was funny, thought Smith on the way back to the office. So funny he thought he'd like a word with Mr Wilkins. He felt a sense of tingling excitement. It seemed as if his idea just might be right after all.

'Sherry, eh?' Thomas Littleton, K.C., taking Jack's assent for granted, jerked the liquid into a glass, completely heedless of the splashes on the silver tray or the faded but beautiful Turkish carpet and handed it to his guest. 'What d'you think?'

Jack's eyes widened in appreciation. 'It's a very fine oloroso, sir. In fact –' he took another sip – 'I'd say it was what my Spanish grandfather would call a *palo*.'

'Would he, by George? That means it's good, eh? Appreciate your opinion, sir.' He spoke in a succession of short barks and Jack found himself irresistibly reminded of a stout, tetchy but agreeably inclined Jack Russell. 'I can't tell one from another myself but I got a case from a client. Oakshot versus Imperial Alloys, Stafford. Remember that?'

'Indeed I do,' said Mr Stafford with feeling. 'And I may say it was fortunate for Oakshot that you took the brief. He would have been a much poorer man without your assistance, although I cannot feel that justice was truly served.'

'Justice?' Littleton flung himself in an armchair and raised two bristling eyebrows at Mr Stafford. 'You mustn't confuse yourself with notions of justice, man. Justice is what the judge says it is or where would we poor barristers be? If the law was a simple matter of justice then every man could be his own advocate, the courts would be clogged with every Tom, Dick or Harry who has a fancied grievance and complete anarchy would reign.'

Mr Stafford mildly disassociated himself from any desire to inflict elemental chaos on the law courts, but Littleton had turned his attention back to Jack. 'You ever read for the bar? I ask because you always get it right in your books. They're some of the few detective stories I can read without wanting to argue with the author.'

Accepting this, as indeed it was, as a compliment, Jack shook his head. 'I've no legal training myself, but I check anything I'm not sure about with my godfather, Archie Wilde.'

'Ah. I thought there was some expert knowledge there. So you're Wilde's godson, are you? Sound man.' He pugnaciously wriggled forward in his chair. 'So what's your interest in trusts? Going to put them in a book?'

'I sincerely hope not,' exclaimed Mr Stafford, shocked.

Littleton grinned suddenly. 'Make a damn dull book, eh? Smoke if you want to, Major. The box is on the table beside you. I understand sherry's one of the few wines you can smoke with, not that it ever bothers me. So, what's it all about? I know the rough outline of Stafford's query, but what's your interest in the matter?'

'I've been asked by Mr Harold Hunt to look into the disappearance of his nephew, Mark Helston. As the trust concerns Mark Helston's money, it might be relevant to the case.'

'So old Hunt's got you involved in that, has he? Yes, that makes sense. It was you, wasn't it, who turned up that body on Gower Street the other day? I was glad to read in this morning's paper it wasn't Helston after all. I came across him a few times.'

Littleton relaxed back, his hands folded across his chest, and when he spoke it was in a softer voice. 'Damn fine boy, Helston. He was with my son on the *Jupiter*. He came to see me on his first leave after Andrew had . . . Well, that's all over now. No point living in the past.'

He picked up his sherry and for a moment concentrated very hard on the light refracting through the glass. 'Yes, a damn fine boy. Old Hunt did his best to ruin him, of course, together with that precious grandmother of his, but he came through unscathed. Anything that boy wanted he could have, which is the quickest way to the devil I know of, but he weathered all their efforts to spoil him. There's a sister, isn't there? Wouldn't be surprised if she had more than a touch of jealousy about the way they glorified young Helston. It'd only be natural.'

Mr Stafford gave a little legal cough in the back of his throat.

'It is about the sister I wish to consult you. As far as I am aware, her relations with her brother were always cordial, although, as you say, there was a marked difference in the treatment of brother and sister by my client, their grandmother, Mrs Enid Burbage. I might have ventured to remonstrate with her about the extremely unequal division of her property, but, at the time her will was drawn up, I had no idea of the sums involved. She gave no indication that she was a wealthy woman and, indeed, I questioned more than once the expense she incurred by her lavish partiality for Mark. She insisted on making him a most generous allowance which I believed she could ill afford.'

'What was Mark's reaction?' asked Jack. 'How did he feel about getting the dibs?'

'He had considerable reservations, Major, if I understand your question correctly.' Mr Stafford gave a thin smile. 'However, he managed to overcome them, as I believe most young men would. To be just, he probably believed Mr Harold Hunt was his real benefactor. He was rather inclined to accept matters at face value and not probe too deeply into what lay behind them. As he was aware that the situation pleased his grandmother and most certainly suited him, he was content to let sleeping dogs lie.'

'What about this trust?' snapped out Littleton, rather in the manner of an abruptly wakened dog himself.

'I have the original documents with me,' said Mr Stafford, 'but the essence of the case is this: under the terms of Enid Burbage's first will, Patricia, née Helston, received two thousand pounds free of duty, but, after various small bequests to servants and charities, the whole of the residue went to Mark. Now, I may say that Mrs Burbage was a very strong-minded old lady, but her physical condition was no match for her mental state. She was very upset by Helston's disappearance, the more so because of a tactless remark made by the police officer in charge of the case. Two weeks after his disappearance, she suffered a minor heart attack. As far as she was concerned, the writing was on the wall and she felt it her duty to make a new will in case Mark's absence should be prolonged. Acting upon her instructions, I drew up a will whereby she put her entire property, minus the bequests to servants and charities, which were to be paid upon her death, into a trust.'

He paused. 'I may say that at the time I drew up the will I had

no idea of the amounts involved. Her property, which was chiefly
in shares, amounted to two hundred thousand pounds, which
results, as it is currently invested, in an annual income of eight
thousand pounds. Patricia and her husband, Gregory Jaggard,
could draw upon the income from the trust, but the capital sum
was to remain untouched. If Mark reappeared within seven years,
then the provisions of the original will as they related to himself
and Patricia, would stand. However, if within seven years following
Mrs Burbage's death, Mark was proved to be deceased or there
was still no trace of him, thus allowing the legal presumption of
death to be made, the trust would be dissolved and Patricia Jaggard
would become her grandmother's residuary legatee.'

'No mention of the husband in that final disposition?'

'None.' Mr Stafford sat even straighter, if that were possible,
in his chair. 'Mrs Burbage, remember, thought Mark would return
in the near future and none of these provisions would, in fact,
be enacted. If the trust did come into operation she wanted
Gregory Jaggard to have an equal hand in the administration.'

'I see. So what's your problem?'

'The problem, Mr Littleton, is this: the trust documents refer
to Gregory Jaggard in his capacity as Patricia's husband.' Mr
Stafford paused with an unconscious flair for drama. 'Last night
that marriage was proved to be invalid.'

'Good God! Why?'

'By the return of her first husband, Laurence Tyrell. Laurence
Tyrell married Patricia Helston in April 1916, whilst serving as
a lieutenant in the Irish Guards. He was later reported missing,
presumed killed, at the battle of the Third Ypres—'

'Passchendaele.'

'Or, as it is more popularly known, Passchendaele. Patricia
remarried two years ago in the firm belief that she was a widow.
I need hardly tell you that the question which most concerns me
is the implication for the trust.'

Mr Littleton's eyebrows shot up to alarming heights. 'The
question which concerns me is the human one. Good Lord, Major
Haldean, this is like one of your books. Have you met the feller?'

Jack shook his head. 'Not yet, no. I bumped into Gregory
Jaggard last night though. He's taken it rather badly.'

'I bet he has. What's this chap Tyrell like, Stafford? Disfigured
at all?'

'By no means.'

'That's something.' He got up and strode around the room, hands behind his back. 'What's the girl's reaction?'

'She seemed very happy to be reunited with her husband.'

'Did she, by jingo? A divorce seems the obvious step but if she's happy to see the man, that could put the cat amongst the pigeons. Let me see the papers,' he added abruptly. 'Help yourself to more sherry.'

He flung himself into a chair with the documents Mr Stafford produced from his case, muttering comments to himself. He eventually tossed them down on the table beside him before producing a deep-bowled briar which he proceeded to stuff with astonishing quantities of jet-black tobacco.

'Simple,' he growled, once his pipe had been ignited. 'No question at all.' He glowered at Mr Stafford through a haze of blue smoke. 'I'm surprised you needed to consult me, Stafford.'

'Does Gregory Jaggard lose out then?' asked Jack, seeing that some reply, which Mr Stafford obviously wasn't going to commit himself to, was needed.

'Lose out? Of course the man loses out. He's had his wife snatched from him by a chap who's played dead since nineteen seventeen. If he's got any emotions at all he'll feel he's very much the loser, wouldn't you say?'

'I would, certainly. But what about the money?'

'Oh, that's all right. He gets to keep his income under the trust. Not that that's much consolation, I should imagine.'

'Does he?' asked Mr Stafford, startled into speech.

'Of course he does. Look man, it's here in black and white.' He picked up the papers and ruffled amongst them, before stabbing the page with the stem of his pipe. '*Gregory Jaggard, husband of the aforesaid Patricia Jaggard.* He's a beneficiary because he's Gregory Jaggard, not because he's Patricia Jaggard's husband. *Error nom nomine.*'

'*The error is not in the name,*' said Jack slowly.

'Correct,' said Littleton, casting him an approving glance.

'So financially speaking, Laurence Tyrell won't be any better off for his reappearance?'

'Strictly speaking, no. However, his wife does receive an income under the rules of the trust. I suppose he might persuade her to part with some of that.'

Mr Stafford took off his glasses and wiped them carefully. 'You sound unduly suspicious of Laurence Tyrell's motives, Mr Littleton.'

Littleton gave a crack of laughter. 'Unduly suspicious! I'll say I am. Ask him what he's been doing for the last few years and why he's only decided to come home now there's some money in the offing. Half of four thousand is a significant sum. He might've thought he was going to get Jaggard's share too. What is it?' he added, swinging round on Jack, who was nursing his sherry thoughtfully.

'I was just wondering,' said Jack, slowly. 'At the moment the trust and all the whatjamajigs don't seem to be affected by Tyrell's return. But what if Mark Helston's dead?'

'If that can be proved – and wait seven years and it doesn't have to be proved – then Patricia, whatever she chooses to call herself, will be a very rich woman.'

'And the husband?'

'Will be the next of kin.' His eyes narrowed and he sat back, sending up a huge cloud of smoke. 'I see what you're getting at, Major. Ugly thought, isn't it?' He turned to Stafford once more. 'I don't suppose you'll get anywhere with her, Stafford, because in my experience women will not take the most obvious precautions to protect their interests against their family, but it wouldn't hurt to suggest she makes a will leaving her property away from her husband.'

'But . . .' Mr Stafford repolished his spectacles furiously before replacing them. 'That sounds as if you are suggesting my client may be in danger. Surely there can be no foundation for such a monstrous idea. I cannot possibly be responsible for putting such notions into her head. Why, Mr Littleton, you talk as if you expected her to be murdered.'

'Do I?' said Littleton, with a lift of his eyebrows. 'Well, it occurred to Major Haldean and it occurred to me. But she's your client, Stafford, and you must do as you think best.' He took his pipe from his mouth and gazed at the ashes in the bowl, before glancing up at Stafford once more. 'Let's just hope that it doesn't occur to anyone else, shall we?'

SIX

Ruby was quite definite; Mrs Jaggard wasn't in, nor was the master and she couldn't tell when either of them would be back, not if you offered her a hundred pounds.

Jack stopped short of such fantastic inducements but, aided by an excess of charm that made him feel slightly hot under the collar to think of (Bill was right, damn him! He *could* switch it on) elicited that the house was at Sixes and Sevens.

A Man had mysteriously appeared and the mistress had taken on ever so before going off with him. The master had looked *reelly* ill – as white as a sheet – before leaving the previous night. Mrs Jaggard was stopping with her uncle, as she knew for a fact, as she'd sent round for Ellen, her maid, to bring some clothes that morning and if Major Haldean could tell her, Ruby, what was behind it all, she, Ruby, would be very glad to know as neither she, or Cook, or any of the other servants knew what it was all about or even if they'd still have a place at the end of the month; no, not even Mr Kennett, who was Mr Jaggard's valet and had been with him all through the war.

14, Neville Square did indeed prove to contain the missing lady.

'Mrs Jaggard, sir?' enquired Fields ponderously. 'I will enquire if she is At Home.'

Jack, left in the hall like a parcel, waited with as much patience as he could muster. Mrs Jaggard, it transpired, was At Home but currently engaged with Mr Hunt and Captain Smith. If Sir would care to step into the morning room, Mrs Jaggard would join him shortly.

Sir, ridding himself of his hat, coat and stick, did care. There was, as Fields informed him, as he led the way to the morning room with elephantine tread, a lady in the morning room, also waiting to see Mrs Jaggard.

The lady turned out to be an old friend.

'Anne!' exclaimed Jack with genuine pleasure.

It was Anne Lassiter, a brown-eyed, brown-haired, capable,

kindly, thoroughly good sort, who was married to one of Jack's old friends, George. He shouldn't, Jack thought, be surprised to see her here. After all, it was George's grandfather, old Mr Lassiter, who had urged Mr Hunt to seek his help and he knew that Pat Jaggard and Anne Lassiter were good friends. He couldn't think of anyone better for Pat to turn to.

'Have you heard about Larry Tyrell, Jack?' asked Anne, clasping his hand warmly. 'Pat rang me first thing this morning. You know Meredith Smith's here? He's with old Mr Hunt. I think he's got some news about Mr Tyrell.'

Jack's forehead creased in a frown. 'Whatever sort of news can Merry Smith have about Tyrell?'

'I don't know the ins and outs of it,' said Anne, 'but Pat said Mr Hunt asked him to call. It's something to do with Brazil. Apparently Larry Tyrell actually worked for Hunt Coffee in Brazil.'

'*What?*' Jack stared at her. 'Pat's husband worked for Hunts?'

'I know,' said Anne nodding vigorously. 'Isn't it amazing?'

'Didn't anyone notice he was there? Come to that, didn't he think to mention who he was?'

'No, that's just it. He didn't know who he was.' Anne leaned forward earnestly. 'It's something to do with the war. He was badly blown up and suffered from shell shock. He lost his memory and it's taken him ages to find out who he really is.'

'Blimey,' said Jack, settling down in a chintz-covered chair. 'That'll be a story worth hearing.' He took out his cigarette case. 'Do you mind if I smoke?'

'Not at all,' said Anne, taking a cigarette from the case Jack offered her.

'How does Mrs . . .' Jack broke off and grinned sheepishly. 'D'you know, I was about to say "Mrs Jaggard" but I don't suppose it's right to call her that, is it? How does she feel about it all?'

'Confused, I think,' said Anne. 'She certainly sounded confused on the phone, but there's more to it than that. There's going to be some very unkind people who'll think Pat planned this in some way, but I can tell you she honestly believed Larry Tyrell was dead until he walked in last night.'

'I'll take your word for it, Anne. Why on earth should anyone think she planned it?'

Anne shook her head distractedly. 'Pat wasn't happy with Greg. You know the beastly construction people put on things, but it wasn't her fault.' She looked at him quizzically. 'You like Gregory Jaggard, don't you?'

Jack shrugged. 'I've always got on with him.'

'Most people do.' Anne clicked her tongue. 'The trouble is that Pat always looked on Greg as second best. It worried me. I tried to talk to her about it, but you can't live other people's lives for them, can you?' She looked at him helplessly. 'I knew they weren't happy. He was always too polite to her, if you know what I mean.'

'I know exactly what you mean,' said Jack. 'That's a very good way of putting it.'

'It was almost inevitable it would go wrong and, of course, it did.'

'What happened? Did Jaggard – let me think how to put this – did Jaggard stray off the straight and narrow?'

Anne let out a long breath of relief. 'You are quick on the uptake, Jack. That's exactly it. Pat was terribly hurt. She retreated into a horrible cold, hard shell. She runs round with that beastly Lahone crowd for no other reason, I'm sure, than to spite Greg. He hates it, but he really only has himself to blame. Have you ever heard of Elise Molnar?'

Jack frowned. 'The name's vaguely familiar for some reason. Hang on. Is she a singer?'

'That's right. It's a few months ago now, but George and I went to the Dead Lucky in Piccadilly with Pat and some friends. Elise Molnar was singing. I knew something was wrong. Pat told me the whole story.'

She leaned forward confidentially. 'Gregory Jaggard saw an awful lot of Elise Molnar before he married Pat. She's Scandinavian, with very striking fair good looks. She makes rather a hobby of rich, good-looking men, if you see what I mean.'

Jack raised his eyebrows. 'Jaggard fits that bill.'

'Absolutely he does. Well, Pat found out that he'd started seeing her again. Men can be such fools, Jack. Pat knew perfectly well there was something going on. He'd have unexplained nights away – sometimes as much as a week – and expect her to believe some cock-and-bull story about where he'd been. When she found out it was Elise Molnar, the fat really was in the fire.'

'Poor beggar,' commented Jack. 'Has the affair continued, do you know?'

'I don't,' said Anne with a shrug. 'Pat says she couldn't give a damn. Whether that's true or not, I don't know. The rotten thing is, I'm sure Greg cares about Pat, cares a lot.'

'I think you're absolutely right,' said Jack. Jaggard's behaviour the previous evening was still vivid in his mind. 'The idiot had a pretty rum way of showing it, though.'

'I know. I can't excuse him, but I must admit I feel sorry for him. I like Greg and Pat's one of my best friends. I hoped that eventually the pair of them would make it up, but now Larry Tyrell's returned, there's no hope of that.'

'Have you ever met Tyrell?'

She shook her head. 'No. Pat thought the world of him. So much so, I don't see how anyone *could* be as wonderful as she thought he was. I'll tell you something else, Jack.' She crushed out her cigarette in the ashtray. 'It may be very mean spirited of me, but I can't help feel suspicious of his motives. Why's he come back now? Now Pat's got some money, I mean?'

'That,' said Jack, dryly, 'is precisely the question that occurred to me.'

In the drawing room, the question of Laurence Tyrell's motives was also up for debate. Mr Hunt closed the file Meredith Smith had brought with him. It was a little while before he spoke. 'So, according to our records, it would seem that Mr Tyrell's account of himself – Mr Tyrell's *remarkable* account of himself – is true.'

Pat pushed an impatient hand through her glossy hair. 'Of course Larry's telling the truth. He has to be telling the truth.' She bit her lip. 'It's beastly to check up on him like this.'

Harold Hunt and Meredith Smith exchanged glances.

'It's as well to be sure, my dear,' said Mr Hunt. 'You cannot blame me for wanting to be as certain as possible under the circumstances.' His sharp blue gaze fixed on her. 'What are you going to do?'

'I don't know,' she said miserably. She was, as Meredith Smith warily saw, close to tears. 'It's all so *difficult*.'

Mr Hunt drew a deep breath. 'Don't rush into things. Your welfare is very dear to me, Pat. You are welcome to stay here until you come to a decision. Out of sheer justice to both Laurence Tyrell and Gregory Jaggard you will have to decide, but your happiness is the most important consideration.'

Pat blinked away sudden tears and kissed him impulsively. 'H.R.H, you're an absolute dear. You don't know how grateful I am.' She braced herself. 'I'd better go and see what Major Haldean wants. Anne's waiting, too. Do you want to see Major Haldean, Meredith?'

'As a matter of fact, I'd appreciate a word with Mr Hunt on a matter of business. Is this a convenient moment, sir?' asked Merry, glancing at Mr Hunt. Mr Hunt nodded in agreement. 'After that, I really had better get back to Southwark. I'd be obliged if you could give Haldean my regards and make my excuses.'

'Of course,' said Pat.

Once she had left, Mr Hunt turned to Meredith Smith with interest. 'Now, m'boy. What is it?'

'You know you thought there was something amiss in the firm, sir? I think I've discovered what it is. I haven't said a word to anyone, but it's a question of the weight of the coffee sacks.'

Meredith Smith had no reason to complain of Harold Hunt's lack of attention, but, as he outlined his theory, he didn't get the reaction he'd expected. To Merry's surprise, the more he spoke, the nearer Mr Hunt seemed in the grip of what, in a younger man, would be called a fit of the giggles. Not only was it very disconcerting, it made him lose his thread. As he faltered to a halt, he couldn't for the life of him think what the joke was.

'That,' said Mr Hunt, drawing a flag-sized linen handkerchief out of his pocket and wiping his eyes, 'is one of the funniest things I've ever heard. I was seriously concerned when I saw your solemn face. I thought you had discovered something shocking, then to hear what you said . . .' He dabbed his eyes and turned an amused face to Smith. 'I'm sorry, young man. It's too bad of me. You really have no idea of what this is about, do you?'

'I'm sorry, sir, no. I haven't,' said Smith, rather stiffly.

Mr Hunt waved him to a chair. 'Sit down and stop looking as if you're sucking lemons. As far as trying to find if something is amiss, I applaud your undoubted diligence. You interpreted my hints very ably and you acted with great rectitude in coming to me first. There. Have I said enough to smooth your ruffled feathers? I mean every word.'

Smith moved awkwardly. 'Well, of course, sir . . .'

'Oh, call me H.R.H. to my face, man,' said Mr Hunt genially. 'To tell you the truth, I like it.' He put the handkerchief away and leaned forward in his chair. 'You see, Meredith, I've always had a fairly keen instinct for how things should be. Don't ask me how I know; I can't tell you. Mark had it too. He didn't know what was wrong but he was uneasy. However, this business about the weights is not it.'

He got up and, going to the glass-fronted bookcase, selected a dumpy, calf-bound book blocked in gold lettering. 'Perhaps I should have shown you this earlier.'

Smith got up and took the book from his hands. *Notes Upon Coffee Growing And Processing In The Southern States of Brazil With Observations on the Prevention of Fungal Growths and Ceylon Coffee-Leaf Disease.* The author was one H.R. Hunt. 'What will this tell me, sir?'

'It will tell you how the finest coffees are obtained. A central part of that process is time. Pick a good coffee and you have the makings of a fine roast. Let it mature for two or even three years and you have a great one. It has to do with the amount of oil in the seeds. However, this is not achieved without some loss. Over the maturing period the stored coffee loses weight with great rapidity. It can be as much as a stone in the hundredweight. That elementary fact is what you so sedulously discovered and, quite frankly, why Wilkins, the foreman, didn't tell you as much defeats me. You say you asked him about it?'

'He said he didn't know why the sacks were always lighter after a long time in storage. He just accepted it, I suppose.'

'Dear me. No spirit of inquiry.'

He looked up as the door opened and Frederick Hunt came into the room. 'Ah, Frederick, there you are. Meredith called to see me with some information about this extraordinary situation Patricia finds herself embroiled in.'

'A situation which I disapprove of intensely,' said Frederick Hunt with a sniff. '*Most* distasteful and not one you should be forced to confront at your time of life. I have every sympathy for my niece, but I really cannot see why, with two husbands available, she cannot choose one and leave you in peace.'

'Perhaps I don't want to be left in peace,' said his father, briskly. 'And as for Patricia, I enjoy her company. She, at any rate, does not feel the need to shield me from what is going on. Talking of which, I understand that our use of chicory in proportion to coffee has substantially increased. Why is that?'

Frederick Hunt paused with his hand on the sherry decanter. 'It's . . . it's all this buying on the Brazilian commodity exchange that's done it. A lot of the coffee simply can't meet our standards and we've been forced to bulk it out. Besides that, the French roasts, which call for a lot of chicory, have proved to be very popular. I really don't think you should bother with such small details, father.' He cast a poisonous glance at Smith. 'I didn't think it important enough to bring it to your attention.'

'Why not? I'm interested in anything which affects the firm. You must remember the misgivings Mark expressed.'

'There's nothing to have misgivings about. Please don't upset yourself. You know it isn't good for you. Mark got some odd ideas in his head at times, all of which have proved to be wrong.'

'Have they?' said Mr Hunt, sharply. 'I'm not aware you've taken any action to investigate Mark's ideas.'

'There's no action to take. The profits aren't as buoyant as I would like, but as I've said when we've discussed this previously, we are doing as well as can be expected under the circumstances. With the present conditions of world trade, exacerbated by the move back to the gold standard, there are forces at work which you never had to contend with. The attempt to restore the pre-war exchange value of sterling and the dollar is, in my opinion, utterly futile and has cost us dear. I have quite enough to do without chasing after some vague, melodramatic notion of Mark's.'

A warning glint came into Mr Hunt's eyes. 'Mark was not given to melodramatic notions, Frederick. I have wondered if the failure of the profits to rise might be caused by something closer to home than the fluctuations in world trade. Something that you would be well advised to look into.'

Frederick Hunt looked from his father to Meredith Smith and back again. 'I beg your pardon, father. I think I must have misunderstood you. It sounds as if you believe there might be some form of illicit activity in progress.'

'That is exactly what worries me. How often do you visit the factory floor and the warehouse?'

'Why on earth should I visit either? I have too much to do without wasting valuable time replicating my staff's responsibilities.'

'Maybe,' said old Mr Hunt, unconvinced. 'How well do you know the men who work for you?'

'Well enough to assure you there is nothing to worry about. If there was anything wrong, it would have shown up in the accounts long before now.' He turned to Meredith Smith. 'I take it there's nothing wrong with the books?'

'Nothing at all.'

'In that case, there is no cause for concern. You must get this idea out of your head, father. You're talking about nothing less than fraud. It's impossible.'

Mr Hunt sat back in his chair and regarded him thoughtfully. 'I'm glad you think so, Frederick.'

He didn't, Meredith Smith noticed, say he shared that opinion.

SEVEN

Although Pat was keeping a tight rein on her emotions, her eyes had dark shadows and she was as taut as piano wire. 'Thank God you're here, Anne,' she said, coming into the morning room. 'Larry said he'd call this morning.'

Jack very much wanted to meet the mysterious Mr Tyrell, but he had no intention of muscling in on a reunion. He stood up. 'Perhaps I'd better leave.'

'Please, Major Haldean, don't go.' She pushed a lock of hair distractedly away from her face. 'I owe you an apology. I didn't like you nosing around. I thought you did this sort of thing just to get publicity for your books. I hated the idea of you using Mark as part of some sort of stunt, but Anne said you wouldn't do that sort of thing.'

'Of course I wouldn't,' said Jack. 'I wouldn't dream of it.'

Her shoulders went down and he realized she was close to exhaustion. She slumped back in her chair. 'You know what's happened?'

'Yes. I ran into Jaggard last night at the club.'

'Oh!' Her eyes widened. 'How is he?'

'Upset, but you'd expect that, wouldn't you?'

'I suppose so. Did Greg ask you to call?'

'No. I tootled along off my own bat. Jaggard was a bit foggy on the details but he said enough to let me know something pretty cataclysmic had happened. I wanted to see if you were all right.'

'Thanks.' Pat took a cigarette from the box on the table and lit it with shaky hands. 'It was a terrible shock. I believed Larry was dead. I never doubted he was dead.' She smoked in silence for a while. 'It seemed so *unfair* that he died. We'd had so little time together.' She looked at him defiantly, eyes suspiciously bright. 'Grandmama didn't want me to marry Larry in the first place.' There was a hard edge to her voice. 'Maybe she was right. He left lots of debts – gambling debts. I had to settle them all.'

'Didn't your Grandmama help you?' said Anne.

'She would if I'd begged, but you've no idea how grateful I would have to be. She would've never let it drop. It was different when I met Greg. She approved of Greg. He went out of his way to flatter her. She'd been a great beauty in her time and liked it when men paid her attention.'

'Flattering your grandmother sounds like nothing but tact on his part, but I'm surprised it didn't put you off him altogether,' said Jack.

She looked at him in sharp surprise. 'So you do understand? I wouldn't have thought anyone would. Greg was – well, nice. I did like him. He even looks a bit like Larry. It never struck me until last night, but he does. I think I was tired. Tired of always having to fight everything and so desperately tired of being broke. It's not much fun, you know.'

'I know,' said Jack with a certain amount of ruefulness.

'Greg sorted everything out. He was ever so decent about it and there were no strings attached. I honestly think I married him more out of gratitude than anything else.'

Anne and Jack looked at each other. 'I wouldn't have thought that was an awfully good reason, if you'll excuse me mentioning it,' said Jack, shifting in his chair.

'It's a rotten reason,' she agreed vehemently. 'And damned unfair to Greg, too. I always knew he was just a substitute.'

'That sounds very harsh,' said Anne. 'I can't believe that's all it was, Pat.'

Pat drew hard on her cigarette. 'You always did think the best of people. Well, it went wrong, badly wrong. What I really wanted was Larry.' She tried to smile. 'I got what I wanted.'

The doorbell jangled in the hall.

Pat crushed out her cigarette. 'That'll be Larry.' She looked at them anxiously. 'You will stay, won't you? It's stupid but I feel nervous about being alone with him.'

The door opened and Fields entered the room. 'Mr Tyrell, madam.'

A fair, grey-eyed man followed Fields into the room. Jack was immediately struck by the truth of Pat's remark. He did bear a superficial likeness to Gregory Jaggard but it was a likeness of colouring only. He wasn't as tall as Jaggard and there was a glint of wary humour in his expression that was quite missing from Jaggard's face. There was a squareness about his shoulders which hinted at hard muscle earned by hard work.

'Pat, I . . .' He stopped short when he saw Jack and Anne, his eyebrows lifting inquisitively.

'This is Major Haldean and my friend, Mrs Anne Lassiter,' said Pat hurriedly. 'Major Haldean's really here on business, Larry. H.R.H. asked him to find out what happened to Mark. He was asking me a few questions.'

Tyrell sat down on the sofa beside Pat. He reached out and gave her hand an affectionate squeeze. 'You'll appreciate my wife and I would like some time together, but I suppose there's plenty of time for that. Funnily enough, Haldean, I was going to look you up. I understand you're the feller who discovered Valdez. I don't know how much you've heard of my doings, but I worked with Valdez in Branca Preto, on the Hunt plantation in Brazil.'

'Did you? I'd heard you worked for Hunts in Brazil, but I didn't know you knew Valdez.'

'I knew him quite well. He was officially in charge, but, once he saw I was competent enough, he let me do things my own way. When he didn't show up, I assumed he'd got a job in Rio or somewhere. He had quite a taste for the high life. He used to complain about being stuck out in the coffee country, miles from anywhere. I never dreamed anything had happened to him.'

'Can you think of anyone who might have had it in for him? Who might have borne him a grudge?'

Tyrell shook his head. 'I can't say I do. However, he had quite an eye for the ladies and was a keen gambler. He might have fallen foul with someone over a dispute about cards, say.'

'That would clear Mark altogether,' said Pat eagerly.

'Mark?' asked Tyrell with a frown. 'What's Mark got to do with it?'

'It's nonsense, of course,' said Pat, 'but the police suspect Mark of killing Valdez. They think that's why Mark disappeared.'

'What? That's crazy. Mark wouldn't do a thing like that. Why on earth should he?'

'It was just a theory,' explained Jack. 'The two men disappeared at more or less the same time and the coincidence of the dates seemed significant.'

'That's all it ever was,' said Pat firmly. 'A coincidence, nothing more.'

'Mr Tyrell, did Valdez get on with Mark Helston, do you know?' asked Jack.

'I haven't a clue,' said Tyrell with a shrug. 'He never mentioned him.'

Anne looked at him with a puzzled frown. 'I don't understand. How did you come to be in Brazil?'

'Why don't you tell Anne and Major Haldean the whole story, Larry?' said Pat.

Laurence Tyrell gave a world-weary sigh, then laughed. 'If you say so. I seem to have gone through this about a hundred times already.' He looked at Pat affectionately. 'All right. Once more won't hurt.'

He took a cigarette from the box, lit it, and blew out a long mouthful of smoke. 'I think it started with Polygon Wood. You know Polygon Wood, Major?'

'Rather too well for my liking.'

Tyrell grinned. 'As you say. In August'17 I was in the Guards doing my bit to take Westhoek. God knows why anyone would want it. It was just ridges of soft mud filled with holes of softer mud, with nine-twos bursting beside us and machine-gun bullets slashing down like rain. On the sixteenth we moved forward, and I lost twelve of my platoon straight away. I don't know if they were dead or wounded. I remember going forward to see if I could get in touch with Captain Hart and that's the last I actually remember until I woke up in a casuality-clearing station.

Apparently I'd been found with a bunch of dead Anzacs in a
shell hole between Polygon Wood and Westhoek. We'd obviously
stopped a shell.' He hesitated. 'You'll excuse me for mentioning
it, ladies, but the odd thing was that I was in my birthday suit,
so to speak. The explosion must've torn my uniform off. I didn't
have a stitch on.'

Jack nodded. 'I've heard of that sort of thing before.'

'Given the circumstances, everyone assumed I was an Anzac,
of course. I couldn't contradict them because I couldn't remember
a thing about who I was or where I was supposed to be. I was
clutching an ID tag for one John Marsden, a Private in the
Sixteenth Battalion, Royal Western Australian Regiment, and
that's the name I've been using until a few weeks ago. To cut a
long story short, I wasn't much good to the war any longer, so
I got shipped off, first to a hospital in England and then to what
everyone told me was home.'

'Australia?'

'That's right.'

'Didn't anyone guess you were English, Mr Tyrell?' asked
Anne. 'You don't sound like an Australian.'

'I'm glad to hear it,' he said with a grin. 'My accent wouldn't
count for anything, Mrs Lassiter. There's thousands of Englishmen
in Australia. John Marsden didn't seem to have any family but
he'd enlisted at Perth, so that's where I went. I roamed around
the outback for a while, picking up jobs in mining towns and
sheep stations and so forth, and eventually John Marsden began
to have a life of his own. The past was a complete blank, you
see. My life had started in that casuality-clearing station. Then,
one day, I was in Mullgarrie, Western Australia. It's part of the
Coolgardie Goldfields and I'd been sweating it out in one of
the deep shaft mines. Mullgarrie isn't much of a town but it
had the usual cheap hotel that sold food and drink. I was sitting
up at the counter and asked for a cup of coffee, and the barman
reached down a bottle of coffee with a blue and yellow label.'

'Royale Coffee,' put in Pat, with a smile.

'That's right. Royale Coffee. Well, for some reason the sight
of that bottle meant something. I asked the barman to give it to
me and, as I held that bottle, my memory started to stir. You know
all that stuff on the label? About how it's made from finest coffee
from our plantation in Brazil and so on? I sat there with the bottle

in my hand, letting my ham and eggs go cold, until the chap behind the bar must've thought I was nuts. But I knew that my past had something to do with this Royale Coffee. I wondered about going to London, where it was made, but I'd been in England and nothing had registered. Could I have lived in Brazil? It didn't spark any memories, but I decided to give it a go.'

'I can't imagine just setting out for Brazil,' said Pat. 'I think it was very brave of you.'

'You must remember how rootless I was. I knew I had a past somewhere and I wanted – wanted more than anything – to find out who I was.'

He laughed. 'It sounds crazy, but on the strength of that label on a bottle of coffee in Mullgarrie, I trekked down to the Trans-Australian Railway at Karonie and stayed on it all the way to Sydney. In Sydney I got a place on a boat – the *Furneaux* – as a deck hand, calling first at Wellington then at Rio. That's a journey of over ten thousand miles because of a cup of coffee. When we reached Rio I hung over the ship's rail, waiting for my memory to stir.'

His face fell. 'Nothing happened. Nothing at all. The view as you sail into Rio harbour is one of the best sights on the earth, but it'll always spell disappointment for me. You see, it was all so utterly strange and I wanted to come home.'

Pat reached out and squeezed his hand gently.

'Well,' said Tyrell, 'there I was in Rio. I left the ship and, feeling as if I was on a fool's errand, started to find out a bit more about Royale Coffee. I hadn't realized what a barrier the language would be. I assumed, God knows why, I'd find plenty of people who could speak English, but apart from a few words, everyone talked Portuguese. However, there's nothing like being in a country for getting to grips with the lingo. Within a few days I worked out that coffee grew in São Paulo, so I got on the train and headed down there. São Paulo City is a big, bustling place with trams and traffic everywhere and, as I got off the train with my bottle of Royale Coffee still in my pack, I felt pretty hopeless, believe you me.'

Tyrell put his hands wide. 'I won't bore you with all the ins and outs of what I did, but you know how the label on the bottle has a picture of your Uncle Harold on it, Pat, as he looked in about 1890? It gives his name underneath and eventually I came across a reception clerk in a hotel who knew the name of Hunt. There was a sort of conference with everyone adding their bit, and it eventually came out that this Senhor Hunt used to live in São Paulo a long time ago but must, so everyone thought, be dead by now. I'd wondered if he was a relative of some sort, although the name didn't ring any bells. I seemed to have come to another dead end. However, one of the men knew that the Hunt Plantation was still in existence, although the chief was a Brazilian called Ariel Valdez.'

Jack leaned forward expectantly.

Tyrell grinned at his expression. 'The rest was surprisingly easy. Valdez turned out to be well known in the town and I also learnt that, although the plantation was up at a place called Branca Preto, in the coffee country, Valdez was a frequent visitor to São Paulo, and the man himself was expected at the hotel in the next few days. I hung around and introduced myself to Valdez when he arrived. He was intrigued by my story. He didn't know of any connection between John Marsden and the company, which wasn't surprising, but the upshot was that he invited me up to Branca Preto to see the plantation for myself. It ended by Valdez inviting me to stay on as assistant manager. I think he fancied having a European around the place. He tended to be a bit dismissive of his fellow Brazilians. In July of last year I officially went on the payroll of Hunt Coffee.'

Pat shook her head wonderingly. 'It's incredible to think I believed you to be dead while Uncle Frederick was paying your salary.' She turned to Jack. 'That's why Meredith Smith called this morning. He brought the wages book and so on, that showed Larry worked for us in Brazil.'

'Was your uncle checking up on me?' asked Tyrell with a frown.

'You can't blame him,' said Jack quickly, seeing Pat was stuck for an answer.

'I suppose so,' said Tyrell, in a disgruntled way. He thought it over, then shrugged. 'I'm not used to having my word doubted, that's all. Anyway, after a time I began to think I'd imagined the whole idea of a link between my past and Hunt Coffee. Valdez never mentioned the name "Helston" or something might have twigged, but all Valdez talked about was the Hunt family, and Senhor Frederick in particular.'

'Did you think of trying to trace the Hunt family in England?' asked Jack.

'No. It seems like the obvious thing to do, but I'd been invalided back to Blighty without any memories stirring and I thought I'd covered that end of things. You must remember I was convinced I was John Marsden, an Australian. Of Pommy origin as the Aussies say, but definitely an Australian. In the end, I made my mind up to move on. I'd decided to leave when Valdez returned from London. He left me in charge quite happily. It was just a case of keeping the place ticking over and sending off the occasional report to the head office in London. He sailed on the thirteenth. Unlucky for some, eh?'

Jack nodded. 'What were his plans while he was in London? Did he talk about meeting up with any old friends?'

'I don't think he had any old friends in London. He'd been here before, but that was about three years ago.'

'That's right,' said Pat. 'Mark knew him, of course, and so did Uncle Frederick and H.R.H., but they're business acquaintances, not friends.'

'Valdez never mentioned anyone in London apart from your family, Pat,' said Tyrell. 'What he was really looking forward to was spreading himself a bit in Paris. Rightly or wrongly, he thought Paris had more to offer him than London. I suspect he was probably right about that but I didn't enquire too closely.' He grinned. 'That was his affair.'

'So he didn't have any worries about his trip? Business worries or any other sort?'

'None whatsoever. As I say, he was looking forward to it.'

'There's been a suggestion he quarrelled with Mark Helston. Can you imagine what that quarrel might have been about?'

'How could I? I was thousands of miles away. There certainly wasn't anything wrong with the plantation, that's for sure.'

'No . . . You'd know if there was, I suppose?'

'Certainly. Don't forget I'd been there since July and had sole charge of the place whenever Valdez was absent. It was a decent post, as I say, but I'd had enough. I had a hankering to see what the rest of the country was like. The coffee country is fertile but not much to look at. It's a series of dusty red plains, stretching endlessly for miles. I had a yen to go further afield, up to tropical Brazil. According to the stories you hear, there's gold and gems for the taking all along the Amazon and I thought I'd try my luck. I'd done a good bit of prospecting in the Outback and thought I stood as good a chance as anyone. With that in mind, I waited for Valdez to return.'

'But he didn't come back.'

'No.' Tyrell crushed out his cigarette in the ashtray. 'He should have got to Rio on the twenty-fifth, but I didn't think anything of it until a couple of weeks later. As I said, I thought he'd stayed on in Rio. After a while I cabled the head office in London to see if he'd been delayed, to be told that, as far as they knew, Valdez had sailed on the tenth.'

'Did you inform the police?'

Tyrell shook his head. 'No. I agree that's what you'd probably do in London but Branca Preto isn't London or anything like it. As he had all his valuables with him, I assumed he'd upped and left. I stuck it out at the plantation until March. I left the foreman, De Oliveria, in charge.'

He smiled. 'I didn't bother too much about that part, to tell the truth. I felt I'd been left holding the baby when Valdez hadn't showed up, so the first London knew of my departure was my last report when I told them I was off. When I got to Rio I tossed a coin and got a boat which eventually wound up at Para, on the mouth of the Tocantins. I'd meant to get onto the Amazon itself, but I met up with three Brazilians on the boat who told me that they intended to get a launch up to Maraba and there get a boat of their own up the Araguya, where, according to them, the river virtually ran with gold.'

He looked at them ruefully. 'That's where things went badly wrong. To listen to these three talk, you'd think they knew the jungle like the back of their hand. After a couple of days on the launch it was obvious they'd never been away from the coast in their lives. We got to Alcobaca and they refused to move another step. I pressed on to Maraba, convinced I could do better by myself. It was a crazy thing to do but having come so far, I didn't want to back down. I did get a boat, but that's the only thing which went right. It holed on some rapids, I cracked my head on the rocks and only just managed to make it to the shore, where I lay, thinking my last hour had come. I can't really tell you what happened next but it was a priest, a Freire Jose, a Dominican missionary, who picked me up from the riverbank. I got him to write down what had happened afterwards, because I couldn't remember any of it.'

He lit another cigarette. 'I don't know if it was the bang on the head that did it, but I woke up in the whitewashed room at the Dominican mission knowing I was Laurence Tyrell of the Irish Guards. I didn't know where I was or how I'd got there. The last thing I could clearly remember was the war. Eventually, over the next few days, it came back to me. It was the oddest sensation, I can tell you. I stayed at the mission until I was well enough to travel, then I got back to Para and there took a ship to Madeira and so on to London. Fortunately my wallet and passport had been buttoned into my shirt pocket when my boat capsized, so they were safe. I travelled home as John Marsden, as my papers were in that name and I didn't want to explain myself to any officials.'

He leaned back on the sofa. 'And that's just about that. It came as a bit of a facer to find you were married, Pat. Mr Stafford, the solicitor, annoyed me. He so obviously didn't believe I was the long-lost Larry Tyrell, even when I showed him Freire Jose's statement, that I wanted to prove it to him. When he suggested I come with him to see you, I jumped at the chance. It was only in the taxi to your house that he told me you'd remarried.'

'Is the statement from Freire Jose still at the solicitors?' asked Jack.

Tyrell raised an eyebrow. 'Yes, it is. Why?'

'Oh, no reason, really. It's just a fairly important document. I'm glad to know it's in safe hands.' He rose to his feet. 'My congratulations on your return, Mr Tyrell. What do you plan to do now?'

'That rather depends on my wife,' answered Tyrell with an affectionate look at Pat. 'I don't know if I can settle in this country any longer, but that's up to her.'

'There's . . . there's other things as well, Larry,' she said.

'Jaggard you mean?' He pursed his lips. 'I grant it's tough on him, but there's nothing I can do about it. Now that I've got you again, I'm damned if I'm going to step aside in his favour.' He put his hand under her chin and turned her face towards him. 'Not unless you want me to.'

'No,' she said. Jack caught the hesitation in her voice. 'I don't want you to go again.'

'Talking of going,' said Jack, 'I think I better be off myself.'

Anne picked up her handbag. 'I think I'll go as well, Pat.' There was an unspoken question in her voice.

Pat stood up. 'I'll see you to the door. You stay there, Larry. I'll be back in a minute.'

She saw them into the hall.

'Pat,' said Anne quietly. 'Will you be all right?'

Pat put her hand to her mouth. 'To be honest, I just don't know.' She was silent for a few moments. 'You must think I'm crazy,' she said passionately. 'All I ever wanted was Larry and now he's here I don't know what to *do*.'

Jack took her hand between his, meeting her worried eyes. 'Take your time. It's too important not to. It's your life. It's not a straight choice between them. You may decide you'd be happier on your own.' He would have said more, but the door-bell rang.

Fields came into the hall and walked towards them with a steady tread. 'We'd better let him answer it,' said Pat quietly, with the glimmer of a smile. 'Otherwise he'll think I'm trying to do him out of a job.'

Fields opened the door. Outside stood Gregory Jaggard. With a feeling of apprehension, Jack realized he was not quite sober.

'Hello, Fields. Is Mrs . . . Is my . . .' He shook his head impatiently. 'Damnit, you know who I mean. Is she . . .' He caught sight of Pat in the hallway and breathed a sigh of relief. 'Pat! Thank God you're here.' He walked into the hall. 'Anne! Nice to see you again. Just off, are you? Hello, Haldean. I believe I owe you an apology for last night.'

'Don't mention it,' said Jack.

'No? Well, thanks, anyway. Pat, we've got to get all this . . .'

'Larry's here,' she broke in.

His face hardened. 'Is he, by Jove?'

'Yes, I am,' said Tyrell from up the hall. He had come out of the room and was leaning against the doorframe. 'Any reason why I shouldn't be with my wife?'

'For goodness sake, let's go back in the room,' said Pat, with an agonized glance at Fields, whose fascinated eyes belied his impassive face. 'We can't possibly talk out here.' She caught Jack's eye in a desperate request and, together with Anne, he followed her back into the morning room.

'Now,' she said when, much to Fields' disappointment, she had shut the door firmly behind them. 'What is it, Greg?'

He passed a hand over his forehead. 'I wanted to see you. I called at the house but you weren't there. I tormented myself last night with the thought you were in a hotel somewhere. If I'd known you were here I'd have . . .'

'This is only a temporary arrangement,' put in Tyrell, smoothly. 'My wife and I, will, of course, be moving shortly.'

Jaggard flinched. 'Pat, please listen to me. You can't do this. All he's after is your money. That has to be the reason why he's come back after so long.'

'And all you're worried about is the chance I'll get it,' drawled Tyrell.

Jaggard turned to face him, looking at him properly for the first time. 'You keep out of this.'

Tyrell smiled warily. 'You'd like that, wouldn't you? Well, you'd better get this into your head. I'm here and I'm stopping here and there isn't a thing you can do about it.' He came closer, balancing on the balls of his feet. 'Now run along and play.' He waved his hand in front of his face. 'And next time you call on a lady, don't drink so much first.'

'No!' shouted Pat as Jaggard's face flushed.

She darted towards the two men, but before she could reach them, Jaggard's fist shot out. Tyrell avoided the blow easily and landed one in return. Pat and Anne, their faces white, looked on in shocked horror as Jaggard stumbled backwards across the room, staggering into the mantelpiece. His foot caught the fire irons as he fell, sending brush, shovel, tongs and poker clattering into the silence.

Tyrell walked across the room and stood over him. 'Get out.'

Jaggard, sprawled on the hearth, shook his head in mute defiance.

Tyrell stooped down, so his face was inches away from Jaggard's. 'I said get out. My wife doesn't want to see you again.'

Jack saw the moment it happened. A murderous glaze came into Jaggard's eyes as he reached for the poker beside him. At that instant he was capable of anything.

Jaggard scrambled to his feet with the steel-shafted poker raised to strike.

'Stop!' screamed Pat and Anne together.

With the cries of the two women loud in his ears, Jack hurled himself between Jaggard and Tyrell. The poker thudded down, catching him on the upper arm.

Furious with pain, Jack wrenched the poker from Jaggard's hand, threw it across the room, then grabbed hold of Jaggard's shoulder. 'Stop it, you *bloody* fool! You'll murder him at this rate.'

Jaggard shook off Jack's restraining hand. Ignoring Jack completely, he stood rigidly still, glaring at Tyrell. 'I'm going to kill you,' he said, very softly.

'You?' Tyrell laughed. 'You terrify me. You're rotten with drink and good living. You'd had it your own way for far too long. I've been told all about you. You never cared for Pat. The only reason you want her now is to waste her money on your lousy cars. Well, Pat's mine and the money's mine, so you can damn well whistle for it.'

'The money isn't yours,' said Jack, curtly. Red hot needles of pain were lancing up his numbed arm and he was reining in his temper with an effort.

Both men turned to stare at him.

'What d'you mean?' asked Tyrell.

'The money,' said Jack shortly. 'The money from the bloody trust. Jaggard keeps his share.'

Tyrell's voice cracked in disbelief. 'Who says so?'

'The law says so. Now if you two have finished trying to kill each other, I think we should all leave.'

Tyrell recovered himself with an effort. 'Pat? Do you want me to go?'

'Please. It'd be better if you did.' She rang the bell to save further discussion, and, rather subdued, the three men, shepherded by the two women, walked into the hall.

Jack was conscious of an absurd feeling of anticlimax as Fields helped them into their coats. His arm was on fire and it was a very necessary help as far as he was concerned.

Once out of the house, Jaggard walked away without another word. With an expressive look at Jack, Anne crossed the square.

Furious with himself for having blurted out the information about the trust, Jack strode down Neville Square. He stopped and turned as he heard running footsteps behind him. It was Laurence Tyrell. 'Haldean! Wait a moment, will you?'

'What is it?' asked Jack abruptly. His arm was very sore.

'I want to say thanks.' Tyrell brushed away the hair which had tumbled into his eyes. 'Pat was upset and I had to see she was all right, but wanted to tell you I really am grateful. If that lunatic had managed his party trick with the poker I'd be a goner by now. I'm surprised he didn't break your arm.'

'Oh . . . Well, that's all right.' Jack met Tyrell's eyes. 'Why on earth did you provoke him like that?'

'He annoyed me with his filthy insinuation I was only after Pat's money. She's my wife, not his. He's going to have to get used to the fact that the good times have ended.'

'So you don't want the money?'

Tyrell drew his breath in. 'Of course I do. Why shouldn't I? I've as much use for money as any man, but I'm damned if he's going to tell me that's all I care about. As far as I'm concerned Jaggard's a past chapter in Pat's life. I'm not going to let him pester her any longer.'

'As long as this trust's in operation he's going to have to pester her to some degree.'

Tyrell looked at him with eyes that were suddenly hard. 'You were very pat with that bit of law. I hope you haven't been checking up on me.'

'Of course I've checked up on you,' said Jack, wearily. 'God damnit, man, you appear from nowhere years after everyone believed you were dead. What d'you expect us to do? Clap?'

'I expect you to keep your nose out of my business,' said Tyrell quickly, then stopped. 'Look, Haldean, I don't want to quarrel, because I owe you one. I wish you could find out what happened to Helston. It'd put Pat out of her misery and sort out this damned legal rigmarole we seem to have got enmeshed in. I loath the idea of Jaggard having any say in Pat's money. The quicker it's sorted out the better, but I'm blowed if I'm having you or anyone else snooping around. It's going to be hard enough for Pat as it is. I'm no fool. It's obvious that she's going to need some time to get used to things. It won't help if you're watching my every move. You do get me, don't you?'

'Oh yes,' said Jack evenly. 'I get you.'

Tyrell nodded and turned away, walking swiftly back to the house.

That, thought Jack, as he watched him go, could be a dangerous man. He was certainly a very determined one. He rubbed his arm ruefully. On the other hand, if that poker had got home he would now be the chief witness in a murder trial. It would be a damn sight better for Jaggard if he laid off any more strong-arm tactics. He wasn't sure who would come off worse.

EIGHT

'At least,' said Bill, 'the coroner managed to stop the jury pinning it on Mark Helston.' It was early on Wednesday evening, the day of the inquest on Ariel Valdez, and Bill Rackham and Meredith Smith had taken up Jack's invitation to come back to his rooms. 'Honestly,' he continued, relaxing gratefully into a shabby leather armchair, 'when you think of the petty-fogging rules and regulations we have to obey giving evidence, it's shocking what members of the public will believe without any proof to back it up.'

'I've never been to an inquest before,' said Meredith Smith. 'It's not a bit like a trial. I mean, the coroner can't actually do anything, can he? I can't really see the point of it all.'

'An inquest is supposed to establish the facts of a case,' said Jack, pulling the cork from a quart bottle of Bass. 'Beer all right for you both? Move those papers off the sofa, Merry, and park yourself there.'

Meredith Smith swept the pile of newspapers to the floor and took the glass from Jack. 'Take this afternoon,' said Meredith, warming to his theme. 'We all know Valdez was murdered by a person or persons unknown. I can't see why we have to go and sit in a stuffy room with all my relatives trying to look sorry when they're told as much.'

Jack grinned. 'At least the verdict *was* murder by person or persons unknown. I thought old Mr Hunt was going to assault the foreman of the jury for the pointed remarks he made about the coincidence of Helston's disappearance and Valdez's death. You could hear the inverted commas in the chap's voice.' He gravely regarded the head on his beer. 'I can't blame him, though. After all, it's what we thought ourselves.'

'It's an idea we considered,' corrected Bill. 'It's a far cry from seeing the possibility to saying that's what happened. Inquests can be useful, though. From my point of view, I got to have a look at this Laurence Tyrell who's caused all the rumpus and, at the very least, we got to hear Frederick Hunt's story again. He stuck to his guns about the quarrel between Helston and Valdez, didn't he? According to him, Helston didn't like Latins and that was that.'

'And Patricia Tyrell-as-was-Jaggard contradicted him. It was all very polite and so on, but she didn't agree. I'm inclined to believe her. And yes, before you tell me again, I know that's just her opinion. Dickens of a lot of reporters around, weren't there?'

'All with their cameras pointed at Pat and Laurence Tyrell,' said Meredith. 'It's not hard to guess whose picture's going to be on the front of the newspapers tomorrow. Ever since the *Messenger* ran the story about Tyrell's reappearance there's been a constant stream of press-hounds at Neville Square asking for interviews. What beats me is how they got hold of the story.'

He rummaged in the newspapers beside the sofa. 'Look at this. *War Hero's Return From The Grave. A Wife Who Despaired. Husband's Dilemma.* Columns of the stuff. How on earth do they know? I'm damn sure she didn't tell them. H.R.H. nearly went pop. He wondered if you'd said anything, Jack, but I told him . . .' He broke off and gazed at his friend accusingly. 'Why are you looking like a stuffed frog? You *didn't*, did you?'

'Of course I didn't,' said Jack impatiently. 'It's just – well – you know Jaggard's living at the club at the moment? I bumped into him there after he'd done his trick with the poker. He started on a long, involved apology and was what you might call unguarded in his speech. Ernie Stanhope of the *Messenger* was sitting at a nearby table. His ears were flapping so hard they were causing a draught. I saw Stanhope and tried to choke him off, but it was like stopping a steam train. As I left, Jaggard was pouring out his heart to Stanhope, helped by whisky, and Stanhope was looking like a child on Christmas morning.'

Meredith Smith whistled. 'It's just as well Pat doesn't know. She'd hand Tyrell the poker herself next time. It beats me how that Jaggard feller ever drives a car, let alone makes them. He seems to spend all of his time half cut.'

Jack shook his head. 'You're being unfair. He's not really a lush. He's been stone cold sober for the last few days and he's been working flat out down at the track. He's got a race coming up at the weekend.'

Bill swung his feet comfortably over the arm of the chair. 'All this is a bit beside the point, isn't it? The point being Valdez's death and Helston's disappearance.'

'Not entirely,' countered Jack. 'Don't forget what concerns Jaggard concerns Laurence Tyrell, and Laurence Tyrell knew Valdez in Brazil.'

Bill smiled cynically. 'If he was ever in Brazil, that is. I can't be the only one who's wondered exactly what that gentleman has been up to for the last few years.'

'As a matter of fact, as far as the firm's concerned, his story's true,' said Meredith. 'H.R.H. is nobody's fool and asked me to check our records. John Marsden was employed at the plantation in Branca Preto from last July onwards.'

'John Marsden being . . .?' asked Bill.

'The name Tyrell was using,' said Meredith. 'There's the entries in the wages book, Valdez's note to London that he was taking the man on and Tyrell's own reports from Branca Preto when he was running the show. We've even got the cable he sent enquiring what had happened to Valdez. Then, come March, he ups and offs, leaving the deputy in charge.'

'The rest of his story seems to be true as well,' said Jack. 'Mr Stafford, the solicitor, showed me the statement from the Dominican missionary. It's in Portuguese, which I worked out with a little effort. It bore out everything Tyrell said. Furthermore, there really is a Freire Jose of the Dominican Mission at São Estevão, which isn't far from Maraba on the Araguya. I know, because the Dominicans at Chalk Farm looked him up for me. I also paid a visit to Bingo Romer-Stuart, my pal at the War Office. Private John Marsden of the Sixteenth Battalion, Royal Western Australian Regiment, was invalided back to Australia after Passchendaele. The only thing which did make me hesitate was that, before he apparently left us for a better world, Lieutenant Tyrell was a whisker away from being hauled up for conduct unbecoming. However, as far as that goes, we already knew he left a slew of gambling debts. Pat Tyrell said as much.'

Bill was unconvinced. 'Don't you think it's convenient that he's reappeared now there's some money in prospect?'

'Of course I do,' said Jack. 'Admittedly he's biased, but Jaggard certainly thinks so. By the sound of it, it occurred to H.R.H. as well. Tyrell doesn't actually gain directly, though. Jaggard gets to keep his share of the trust fund and the rest of the money has Helston's name on it. All I would say, is that it came as a nasty shock to Tyrell when he realized the money was tied up in a trust.'

'Have you had any more thoughts about the murder, Jack?' asked Meredith Smith, reaching for the beer. 'Because I can tell you,' he said, concentrating on filling his glass, 'that H.R.H. isn't happy. As he sees it, all you've done is to give the police a motive for Helston to disappear. Between you and me, he's regretting that he ever asked you to look into it.' Meredith cast an acute glance at Bill. 'It has made it worse, hasn't it? For Mark Helston, I mean.'

'It's a compelling theory,' admitted Bill. 'We have an argument, a body, a disappearance. It's hard to say they're not connected. I wish we could get some sort of lead on the knife Valdez was stabbed with. The jeweller I showed it to said it was probably made to order abroad. I've ordered every jeweller in London to be contacted about it, in case it was sold in London, but so far there's nothing. If we do get a result, it could help enormously.'

'The trouble is, this is Mark Helston we're speaking about,' said Jack. 'Everyone who knew him says that he was kindly, honest and straightforward. I must say I'd like to know if there's anything in this idea that it's not all as mother makes at Hunt Coffee.'

'Is there anything going on, Smith?' asked Bill.

Meredith pulled a face. 'H.R.H. thinks so, that's for sure. Frederick Hunt doesn't, and was pretty ratty when he found I'd talked to his father about it. There was a discrepancy with the amount of chicory to coffee, which he explained away – not terribly convincingly I thought – but I'd hate to take him up on any technical point to do with production. I stuck my foot in it good and proper over the disparity of weights of the various sacks of coffee in the warehouse and, for all I know, he's telling the exact truth about the chicory. H.R.H. told me that Mark Helston suspected something dodgy was going on, though. I'm hanged if I can guess what it is, if there is anything. It certainly hasn't shown up in the accounts, that's for sure.'

'I wonder . . .' said Bill. 'Let's say there is a swindle of some sort. Valdez gets on to it and challenges Frederick Hunt. He might even try a bit of blackmail. That would be at the meeting on the twenty-ninth of December. Valdez then goes off to Paris, leaving Hunt to mull it over. Hunt carefully doesn't tell Helston about the meeting arranged for the ninth, either because he wants to buy off Valdez or give him some explanation which wouldn't wash with Helston. But Helston arrives unexpectedly and makes a third at that meeting.'

'Why should it be fraud?' asked Meredith. 'It could be simple incompetence. Frederick Hunt wouldn't want his father to know he'd been asleep on the job. If Valdez had spotted something wrong, Frederick Hunt might very well want to keep it quiet. He'd want to keep Helston out of it, as telling Helston would be tantamount to telling H.R.H.'

'That's true enough, Merry,' agreed Jack. 'We know Helston was worried and abstracted after the meeting. That sounds to me like a man who's making up his mind what to do next, rather than a man who's been confronted with something definitely criminal. From what I've learnt of Helston, I think he'd reach for the nearest policeman as soon as he knew something was really wrong. At the very least, he'd go and ask H.R.H. for advice. What he *did* do, if we follow our earlier line of reasoning, is arrange to meet Valdez again that evening.'

'D'you think Valdez asked Helston for money in return for keeping quiet?'

Jack shook his head. 'If he had done, Helston would've gone off like a rocket. If Valdez tried, Helston might very easily have tried to slug him. He wouldn't, if what everyone says about him is true, take the man off to a deserted house on Gower Street, strip him naked and stick a knife in him.'

'Are we sure Helston was such a knight in shining armour?' asked Bill.

Jack looked at Merry. 'I think so. If he wasn't, he fooled a hell of a lot of people.'

'I agree,' said Meredith decisively. 'I've heard it too often to think anything else. His clerk, Miss Mandeville – she works for me now – thinks he was very likable and honest.'

Jack stubbed out his cigarette. 'She should know.'

'I hardly like to suggest it,' said Meredith, 'but could Frederick

Hunt be the murderer? I can't imagine him doing anything of the sort, but I suppose it's possible.'

'Unfortunately, from my point of view, it *isn't* possible,' said Bill. 'Frederick Hunt's alibi from seven o'clock onwards on the ninth is about as cast iron as it's possible to get, and we know Valdez was alive and well at seven o'clock, because that's when he left the Montague Court Hotel.'

'Is there any chance the Valdez who left the hotel was an impostor faking an alibi?' asked Jack, hopefully.

'None whatsoever,' said Bill with a laugh. 'The desk clerk recognized him. That just isn't on the cards. At seven o'clock, Frederick Hunt was at a Mansion House dinner, with heapings of the great and the good. That's borne out by dozens of witnesses. The dinner started with a reception at seven and broke up about half eleven. Frederick Hunt arrived back at Neville Square just after midnight with a guest, a Mr Alistair Buchanan, of Buchanan Glassworks. Mr Buchanan had a nightcap and stayed until about half one.'

Jack finished his beer. 'Fair enough. Frederick Hunt couldn't go anywhere until Mr Buchanan had left and, granted Valdez and Helston were together from half seven or so, it'd be damned odd if they waited until about two in the morning for Frederick Hunt to turn up. To be honest, I can't see him murdering anyone. Not violently, at any rate.'

'What about Pat?' said Meredith Smith. He flushed as both men turned to look at him. 'I don't like the idea but she does benefit from her brother's disappearance.'

'She'd benefit a damn sight more from her brother's death,' said Jack. 'Leaving it up in the air like this isn't much use to anyone. Besides that, not only was Pat Jaggard, as she was then, away on the ninth of January, the footprints we found in the house were made by a man. She's in the clear.'

Meredith breathed a deep sigh of relief. 'I'm glad to hear it. I hate the thought of any woman mixed up in a gruesome business like this. Does it have to be someone connected with Hunts? Why can't Valdez have been killed by a stranger?'

'It won't work, old thing,' said Jack. 'Valdez and Helston have both got to be accounted for and the idea of a stranger seeing them both off just won't wash. As far as I can see, there're only two real possibilities. Either Helston killed Valdez and ran for it, or both were killed by a third man. Either way, it's a thin prospect for Helston.'

He filled up his glass and seemed to be considering the head on his beer. 'I do wonder where Jaggard fits in to all this. Anne Lassiter told me that, come Christmas or thereabouts, Jaggard took up with his old mistress, Elise Molnar.'

Meredith Smith gave a long whistle of surprise. 'Are you sure, Jack? After helping to shovel him into bed the other night at the club, I'd have said he was crazy about Pat. He certainly wasn't happy about Tyrell's return, was he?'

'That's putting it mildly. I can't help feeling sorry for him. From what I can make out, his company's one jump ahead of the Receiver, his personal life is a mess and now Tyrell's come on the scene to round it all off. However, leaving my feelings to one side, the fact is that if Helston didn't murder Valdez, someone else did.'

Bill looked up sharply. 'And you think that someone might be Jaggard?'

Jack winced. 'It's a possibility. I don't like it, but it's a possibility. We've been concentrating on what you might call a business motive for bumping off Valdez, but it could just as easily be a private motive. Jaggard could've been very anxious his wife didn't find out about his affair.'

Bill raised his eyebrows expressively. 'I'd be anxious, if I was him. Pat Whatever doesn't strike me as a very forgiving type. How does that involve Valdez though? He couldn't know anything about Jaggard's shenanigans.'

'That's just the trouble, Bill. He could. Valdez was in Paris over the New Year. Jaggard said he was in Birmingham after the New Year. He wasn't.'

'Wasn't he, by George?'

'No. He was with Elise Molnar in Paris.'

'Now we're getting somewhere,' said Bill in satisfaction. 'How on earth did you find out?'

'I took Elise Molnar out to dinner. She's currently singing at The Frozen Limit.' He grinned. 'My word, that woman's got the digestion of an ostrich. It cost me two bottles of champagne, a fair old bit of caviar and lashings of lobster mayonnaise.'

'And maddened by mayonnaise she simply told you everything?' said Bill in perplexity. 'What did you do? Hypnotize the woman?'

'I spun her a yarn. Quite a good one, actually. It certainly brought home the bacon.'

'What did you tell her?'

Jack rubbed the side of his nose in reluctant amusement. 'Well, if you must know, I said I was madly in love with a beautiful young Russian girl called Sofia. Sofia, despite her ethereal looks and air of mysterious grace, hadn't done what any other Russian with an ounce of sense had done and opened a hat shop, but was eking out a life of grinding poverty as a humble servant. I rather went to town over that part. I'd discovered, although I was sworn to secrecy, that Sofia was really, if all had their rights, so to speak, the Grand Duchess Vladimorovia. All her family had been slaughtered by the Bolsheviks, you see. Her only asset was an emerald necklace, the legendary emerald necklace of the Vladimorovs, which her dying mother had pressed into her hands.'

'Good God,' muttered Bill. Meredith Smith merely gaped at him.

'She fled Russia disguised as a peasant, her feet bound in rags, suffering appalling privations, before eventually reaching Good Old Blighty and freedom. Here things hotted up for the girlfriend. She realized, in the nick of time, that she was being pursued by a gang of evil Bolsheviks who wanted the necklace. In order to escape the villains, she took a post as the aforesaid humble servant at a grand house in Birmingham.'

'Blimey.'

'As you say, blimey. Anyway, disaster struck when, at a grand ball at the grand house, the necklace was stolen. The Bolsheviks are convinced that the thief is none other than Miss Molnar's old friend, Gregory Jaggard. He said he was at the ball, you see. Now, I know he wasn't there. I'm convinced, I said, looking her straight in the eyes, he had lied about being at the ball and had lied for the best reason in the world, to protect a lady who was very dear to him. Gregory Jaggard, although he doesn't know it, is in deadly peril from the Bolshevik gang.'

Jack grinned broadly. 'At this point Miss Molnar, identifying herself correctly as the lady in question, was nearly overcome with emotion. Could she, I asked, tell me where Jaggard was after the New Year? If I knew – really knew – I could draw the Bolsheviks off and set them after the man who I believe really stole the necklace, who is none other than the leader of the Bolshevik gang, a black-hearted traitor who deserves all that's coming to him because he has designs on my lovely Sofia.'

'You mean to say she believed all that rigmarole?'

'It's a damn good story,' said Jack. 'So good, in fact, that it'll probably appear in a forthcoming issue of *On The Town*. Yes, of course she believed me. She hung on my every word. And that, Bill, my old pal, is how I know that Miss Molnar and Gregory Jaggard spent a week in an apartment he'd taken on the rue de la Paix, near the Tuilerie Gardens. Miss Molnar has expensive tastes.'

Meredith Smith filled up his glass, laughing. 'Did the gullible Miss Molnar say when she and Jaggard were in Paris?'

'Jaggard was there from the first to the seventh of January.'

'Valdez was killed on the ninth,' said Bill slowly. 'Was Jaggard in London?'

Jack nodded. 'Yes, I'm afraid he was. Elise Molnar stayed on in Paris for another fortnight, but Jaggard left on the seventh. He spent the evening of the seventh on the boat but the evening of the eighth and the next few evenings he spent at the Young Services Club. I've checked that. All this time, of course, he was supposed to be in Birmingham. He was meant to have arrived back on the eleventh.'

'That puts him firmly in the frame,' said Bill. 'I'm glad you got the information, Jack, but the trouble is I can't see there's any chance that Elise Molnar will testify, not after you've convinced her it's all a communist plot.'

'You could always ask the concierge of the apartments on the rue de la Paix to identify him,' suggested Jack.

'That's true. Valdez stayed in the Hotel Maurice on the Avenue Victoria. How close is that to the rue de Whatsits, where Jaggard was?'

'I imagine it'd take about half an hour to walk there, but it doesn't really matter. The rue de la Paix is one of the most expensive, glamorous streets in Paris. Any visitor is more or less bound to end up there. We can't, of course, prove that they met or that Valdez either saw or recognized Jaggard, but they were certainly in the same area at the same time.'

'Jaggard's well known,' said Bill thoughtfully. 'Very well known in motoring circles, and, of course, there's the connection with Hunt Coffee. It's not too much to suppose that Valdez would recognize him.' He finished his beer pensively. 'What's in your mind? Blackmail?'

'That's about the size of it.'

'It's an idea, Jack. We know Helston was worried about something the day he disappeared. We've taken it that he was worried about the firm, but it might just as well be his sister he was bothered about.'

'It sounds as if he was justified,' put in Meredith. 'My clerk, Miss Mandeville, told me that Helston was very protective of Pat. If Valdez told Helston he'd seen Jaggard in Paris, Helston wouldn't like it one bit.'

Bill rested his chin on his hands. 'Valdez said he was going to meet a friend. The friend could easily be Jaggard. He wouldn't take kindly to being blackmailed. I think he could be dangerous. Say he did see off Valdez. If Helston found out about it, Jaggard would have to kill him too to keep him quiet.'

He sucked his cheeks in reflectively. 'I think I'd better check exactly what Jaggard says he was doing that evening.' He took in Jack's unhappy expression. 'What's the matter? Don't tell me you can't see Jaggard committing murder.'

'That's the trouble,' said Jack, unhappily. 'I can. I've seen him drive and he's got an ice-cold nerve. He's more than bright enough to dope out a scheme that would work. However, saying that he could do it is a million miles away from saying that he did do it. And, of course, we've got the question of what happened to Helston's body.'

'He could have loaded it in his car and dumped it anywhere,' said Bill. He lit a cigarette and blew the smoke out thoughtfully. 'I think you might be onto something, Jack.'

Meredith Smith tramped morosely down Chandos Place before turning up Bedford Street towards Leicester Square and home. The name Primrose Street caught his attention. In some odd way it was familiar. The name brought a little tinge of pleasure in its wake. He stopped to fill his pipe at the corner, idly wondering why.

Primrose Street itself was unlikely to generate any sort of pleasure. It was dominated by a huge and hideous bulk of blackened brick and grimy glass, built, so a plaque told him, by the charity of one Josiah Dunthorpe in 1883 as dwelling for Artisans, Labourers and their Dependants. It was so encrusted with soot it seemed to have been carved from some dull jet.

And then, incredibly, Dunthorpe Mansions became a thing of beauty; for there was a tap on his arm and beside him stood Sheila Mandeville.

'Hello! What brings you here?'

'Miss Mandeville!' He raised his hat. 'I was just on my way home. I don't live very far away.'

'Really?' She nodded towards Dunthorpe Mansions. 'I live here.'

Of course! That's why Primrose Street was familiar. 'Isn't it full of artisans and things?'

'Oh, they wouldn't be seen dead in a place like this. It's flats, you know, all full of people like me.'

'Impossible,' he returned, gallantly, and he saw her colour deliciously as she caught the implication. That did it. He paused again, then rushed on. 'Have you eaten yet? There's a decent A.B.C. tea shop in Leicester Square. How about mangling a bun with me?'

Sheila Mandeville took his proffered arm with a smile. She *liked* Captain Smith.

NINE

J ack Haldean was the cause, albeit the unwitting cause, of Meredith Smith and Sheila Mandeville dining at the Ritz.

Seated in the A.B.C. teashop with scrambled eggs, a pot of Ceylon tea, a plate of mixed cakes and Sheila Mandeville, Meredith Smith was completely happy. The only jarring note occurred when Sheila, dabbing her lips with her napkin, had remarked that it was a real treat to be taken out to tea and when Major Haldean had taken her to tea at the Ritz . . .

The rest of the sentence was lost on Meredith Smith. He regarded his coconut pyramid with sudden dissatisfaction. An A.B.C. tea shop was *all right* and there was nothing wrong with tea, but there were, dash it, other places and other meals.

Dinner at the Ritz?

Sheila Mandeville tentatively objected that they both had to work in the morning. Work was dismissed in a lordly fashion. Sheila Mandeville was in the mood to dismiss work and consented to be called for at quarter to nine.

And now, dinner over, the hour was nudging towards the fashionable, and the Ritz was filling up with those fortunates for whom work was something that other people did.

'Good Lord,' said Meredith Smith, looking at the new crop of arrivals. 'There's Pat Tyrell. She's got Laurence Tyrell in tow.'

'Really? Where?' Sheila Mandeville looked out discreetly from behind the vase of flowers that stood on the centre of the table. There weren't many dancers on the floor and she had a good view of a dark-haired woman and a fair-haired man sitting at the other side of the room. 'Oh, yes.'

She stopped, blushing. 'I suppose I ought to pretend to know nothing about it, but it was in all the papers and it's difficult not to take an interest, especially as she's Mr Hunt's great-niece.'

'And even more difficult not to talk about it?' asked Smith with a grin.

Sheila looked at him apologetically. 'You know how it is in the office. The subject did crop up. I'm sorry. I shouldn't have gossiped about her. She's your cousin, isn't she?'

'Yes, but I didn't know she existed until H.R.H. introduced us.'

'She's lovely,' said Sheila, and added, with a certain amount of envy, 'I wish I could dress like that. It must be wonderful to come to places like this and to feel you really belonged.'

'You look as if you belonged,' said Smith admiringly. 'Absolutely to the manner born. I don't know what you've done to your hair, but it's absolutely knockout and that dress is a smasher.'

Sheila Mandeville smiled. She was pleased with her hair, but well aware, even if Meredith Smith wasn't, of the difference between her dress ('*price forty-two shillings and sixpence – original price eight guineas – of knitted artificial silk made in a new fancy stitch from best quality yarn in a very becoming style*') from Derry and Tom's January sale, and the Real Thing, so casually and energetically displayed on the dance floor by the other women in the room.

It was different for men; they could cheerfully say 'I haven't got a bean', and everyone laughed. But all they needed was one set of evening clothes whereas she *couldn't* give this dress another airing for at least another fortnight without feeling positively dowdy. What on earth could she wear next time? She glanced at his admiring eyes and felt a stab of pleasure. She was sure there was going to be a next time.

That dinner was damn good, thought Meredith Smith. She looks beautiful. Perhaps next time we could just go dancing? A few more meals like that would punch a real hole in the weekly envelope, even on the money I'm pulling in from old H.R.H. If only I hadn't had so many debts! That couple of months off work really did for me. Maybe dancing would be okay. We'll need a taxi, of course. I'd rather walk but girls always seem to have such awkward shoes. It'd be fun to walk through London. Just the two of us. Stop by a coffee stall somewhere and watch the sun come up over the Thames. I wish we didn't have to work tomorrow. I'd like to dance until three, but I suppose I'd better have her home long before then.

He looked at her profile as she gazed across the dance floor and caught his breath. I'd like to give her a better home than that poky flat in that hideous building. Maybe . . .

'I felt sorry for her husband,' said Sheila, concentrating on the Tyrells. 'Mr Jaggard, I mean. It must be awfully hard on him. I like him and he's so glamorous, isn't he? He used to call at the office sometimes for Mr Helston. What's this man like?'

'Laurence Tyrell?' said Meredith Smith, suppressing a surge of jealousy. 'I've never met him to speak to, but he was at the inquest this afternoon.'

Sheila peered from behind the flowers once more. 'He's vaguely familiar, for some reason. He looks a bit like Mr Jaggard, doesn't he? Not properly, I mean, but at first glance. I wonder if . . .'

Meredith Smith coughed. He wanted to talk about himself, herself, his feelings, her feelings and perhaps touch on his plans for the future. He would be more than happy to explore Sheila's views on these matters, but he had no intention of talking about his cousin and her matrimonial problems. 'Shall we dance?' he asked, with his most inviting smile and was rewarded, minutes later, with the sensation of her in his arms.

*   *   *

'Oh, look,' said Patricia Tyrell. 'There's my cousin, Meredith Smith.'

Laurence Tyrell glanced up. 'The chap who works for Hunts, you mean? I'd never heard of him until the other day.'

'I didn't know he existed until a few months ago until H.R.H. suddenly produced him. It's all bound up with some desperately mysterious Victorian scandal.'

Tyrell's eyes narrowed as he followed the couple round the room. 'Who's he with?'

'I can't remember her name, but I think she works for the firm. What is it, Larry? You look as if you recognized him.'

He laughed. 'He seemed familiar, that's all.' His eyes continued to follow them. 'I must be mistaken.' He touched her arm as she raised her hand to wave across the room. 'No, don't call them over, Pat. I don't want crowds of people round. I'd like there to be just you and me – for a time anyway. In fact . . .' He hesitated and took her hand. 'Don't go back to your uncle's tonight. Stay with me. I've booked a room.'

Her hand moved in his. 'I can't, Larry. I haven't got anything with me.'

'Does it matter?' he said passionately.

'Of course it matters.'

He let go of her hand and stared down at the table for a long moment. 'All right,' he said eventually. 'I'll be patient. God knows, I've waited long enough.'

He broke off as a waiter came to the table. 'Yes?'

'Mr Tyrell, sir? There's a telephone call for you.'

He frowned in annoyance. 'I don't know who that can be.' He rose to his feet. 'Excuse me, will you, Pat?'

He left the room. Pat watched the dancers for a few moments, idly noticing that Meredith Smith was no longer amongst them. If only she knew what to do! Maybe a talk with Anne Lassiter would help. She shook her head in irritation as the hackneyed succession of thoughts started once more. She fumbled in her bag for her cigarette case.

As she took out her lighter a familiar voice said, 'Let me do that for you.' She turned, startled.

It was Gregory Jaggard.

He pulled out a chair and sat down, gazing at her admiringly. 'You look absolutely stunning.'

'Greg, I'm with Larry,' she said urgently. 'You're not going to make a scene, are you?'

Jaggard shook his head. 'No, I'm not. I'm sorry about what happened at Neville Square. Nothing like that will happen again, I promise. I know Tyrell's here. I got rid of him for a few minutes.' He grinned. 'I had an ally. I met that nice girl in the lobby who used to work for Mark and she promised to hold him up. I simply had to speak to you.'

He looked at her, rueful yet shy. 'I made you a rotten husband. I know you were unhappy but there were all sorts of things going on that you didn't know about. If there's any chance at all, it'd be different, Pat.' He looked suddenly haggard. 'It's driving me nearly insane, seeing you together. You're my *wife.*'

'We're not married,' she said coldly. 'We never really were.'

'I know, damnit,' he said with a flash of his old temper. 'I'm sorry. I didn't mean to go into that.' He dropped his hand onto hers. 'I want you to do something for me. It's the race on Saturday, my race with Johnnie Miller. Will you come and watch me?'

'I – I don't know if I can.'

'Please, Pat. You don't have to come to the sheds or the owners' enclosure. Just knowing you're in the crowd would be enough.' He smiled hopefully. 'Please. You've always watched me race. It wouldn't be the same without you. Wear your red hat. I can always spot it. You see . . .' He stopped and swallowed. 'This race could change everything, Pat. If I win on Saturday, things will be different. Will you come? If you could come to the sheds afterwards, that'd be wonderful.'

'It might be difficult, Greg.'

He grinned suddenly. 'Do your best.' He stood up, raised her hand to his lips and, before she had a chance to protest, kissed it. 'I love you.'

She watched him leave in bewilderment. Thank God Larry hadn't seen him. Why was he so insistent that she should come to the race? She always had watched him, but there was more to it than that. She glanced up as Tyrell walked across the room. That had been a close-run thing. She felt a sudden loathing of deception. Why on earth shouldn't Greg come and talk to her? After all, she had been married to him.

Larry sat down beside her with an annoyed expression.

'Whoever was on the phone had rung off before I got there.' He motioned to the waiter. 'More champagne, please. Mind you, I got held up on the way. That silly girl your cousin's with barged into me in the lobby and scattered the things from her handbag everywhere. I could have sworn she did it on purpose. I had to stop and help her pick them up.'

She brought her chin up in determination. 'Greg spoke to me while you were away.'

His eyebrows rose. 'Did he, by jingo?' He gave a humourless laugh. 'At least I know who the telephone call was from. What did he want?'

'He wants me to watch his race on Saturday.'

Tyrell's eyebrows crawled upwards. 'Are you going?'

'I'm not sure. Would you mind?' She was relieved when he shrugged.

'Go if you want to, my dear. I'm your husband, not your keeper. You'll excuse me from attending, won't you? I don't think I'd get an awful lot out of it.'

She felt irrationally grateful to him. 'I thought you'd object.'

He shrugged again. 'Not in the least.' He gave a sudden, attractive smile. 'I can't put you in a box and I don't want to. I know how hard this is for you, Pat. When I woke up in that Mission Station it was as if the years since Passchendaele had been wiped out. It took me ages to realize how much time had passed. At first I thought we could simply take up where we left off. Perhaps that was stupid of me.'

Her hand tightened round his, but she said nothing.

'You go, my dear. D'you know the one thing I envy Jaggard? The fact he has an occupation. I need a job. I want something to do. I've talked to your Uncle Frederick about working for Hunt Coffee.'

'Have you?' she asked, startled.

He broke off as the waiter arrived with the champagne. When he had gone, Tyrell raised his glass. 'Here's to us. And to work, and all sorts of other worthy notions I never thought I'd espouse. But, most especially, to you.'

'I can't drink my own toast,' said Pat, laughing.

'Oh yes, you can. And then, Mrs Tyrell, you're going to dance the night away and then, long, long after your bedtime, I'm going to take you home.'

He was as good as his word and, thankfully and unusually, there was no further mention of the room he'd booked.

For the first time since his return, the tacit pressure on her to declare openly she was his wife and his wife only had been lifted. She responded by enjoying his company more than ever before. There was a tense excitement about him that she'd never known before. If he asked me now, she thought . . . but he didn't and it was with real regret she said goodbye to him on the doorstep of 14, Neville Square, long after the first dawn greyed the sky.

There were roses on her dressing table next morning. The maid, bringing in her morning tea, nodded towards them.

'Mr Tyrell left those for you, ma'am. He had breakfast with Mr Frederick, but he said not to disturb you.'

'Thank goodness for that, anyway.' She read the card with a smile and a slight blush.

Breakfast with Uncle Frederick? Larry must be serious about having a job. Maybe he had changed.

She was startled by the ferocity of hope the thought brought with it. She'd been scared. Scared at the thought of being landed with his debts once more while she struggled and pinched and faced real, actual want . . .

That was all over. She was a rich woman. She would never again face that awful blank despair of days with not quite enough to eat, rent to pay and appearances to keep up. Greg had saved her from all that biting worry. She would always be grateful to Greg for that.

But if Larry was sincere about work, that put a whole new complexion on things. He was going to call for her that evening. She was looking forward to it.

'Who was buying the biscuits this week?' demanded Rosie O'Connor of her fellow labourers over morning tea in the typists' room of Hunt Coffee, Limited, Southwark. 'All the custard creams have gone *again*.' She looked up as Sheila Mandeville came in. 'I'm sorry, Sheila, but there's only Rich Tea left now. There always is on a Friday if you're not here first thing.'

'Never mind about biscuits,' said Sheila, helping herself to the teapot. She was brimming with news. 'I had a letter this morning from *The Daily Messenger.* I've won the Spot The Stars competition!'

There was a chorus of awed congratulation. 'What have you won?' demanded Cynthia Cullen raptly.

'Twenty pounds and free tickets for two for a month to the Shaftesbury Pavilion,' said Sheila with shining eyes. 'It's not bad, is it? I had to match ten film stars with their films. There's a reporter coming to see me this evening. They like to publish details of the winner.'

'That's to show it's a genuine competition,' said Margaret Ross from Dispatch knowingly.

'I wonder what the reporter will be like,' said Eileen Wilks, whose favourite reading was the weekly romance in *Peg's Paper.* 'He might be ever so good-looking. You never know your luck,' she added enviously.

'He might be all right,' said Sheila absently. With Wednesday at the Ritz still golden in her memory, she wasn't interested in reporters. She hadn't told the girls about dinner at the Ritz. That sort of gossip would go round like wildfire. It was a pity in a way. The girls would simply *adore* hearing about her encounter with Mr Jaggard, to say nothing of Mr Tyrell. It was the oddest thing about Mr Tyrell. She was sure she'd seen him somewhere before. Meredith (*Meredith! She had better think of him as Captain Smith in the office!*) said she was imagining things, but she wasn't.

'What will you spend the money on?' asked Rosie O'Connor, interrupting her thoughts.

'A new dress,' said Sheila Mandeville dreamily. 'And a bag and shoes and gloves. Something really special.'

Standing beside the Brooklands track, Joe Hawley watched the great maroon and silver car come round the banking, throttle back and coast gently to a standstill. Jaggard revved the engine once more, then let it idle into silence.

Hawley ran to the car as Jaggard climbed wearily out. 'I've got the lap times, Jag. They're damn good. One-oh-three point six on that final stretch.'

Jaggard pushed up his goggles, unbuckled his helmet and tossed them into the car. He passed a hand over his face, leaving streaks of burnt castor oil. 'One-oh-three? It's not nearly enough, Joe. That chain-driven monster of Miller's can go like the clappers.'

He buried his head in his hands. Hawley had never seen him look so exhausted.

'We've got to *win*,' Jaggard muttered fiercely. 'We've *got* to get more speed.'

'You're all in, old man,' said Hawley, practically. 'Why don't we go and get something to eat?' He broke off as a boy approached. 'Yes?'

'I've got a message for Mr Jaggard, sir. There was a telephone call for you.'

Jaggard took the note, read it, then looked up, grinning broadly. 'It's from Pat. She wants to meet me this evening at Miss Mandeville's flat. I'd rather go there than Neville Square, that's for sure.'

He fumbled inside his overalls and, bringing out a shilling, tossed it to the boy. 'Here you are, sonny.'

'Thanks, guv,' said the boy, catching the coin with alacrity.

'Now, about this car,' said Jaggard, turning to Hawley. He looked suddenly refreshed and the deep lines on his forehead had disappeared. 'The rear wheels are locking as I brake and she's shifting under the weight, which means I brake down too soon and lose speed on the curves. If we saw about two inches off the rear brake shoes, that just might do it. Help me get her into the sheds, Joe. We'll get to work, then I can take her out again this afternoon.'

In the kitchen of 42, Dunthorpe Mansions, Mrs Chard put down the potato peeler, sighed ominously and went into the attack. She disapproved heartily of her next-door neighbour, Miss Mandeville – Mrs Chard disapproved of most of her neighbours – and she most certainly disapproved of the noise in the hall.

She sallied forth to see a solid, well-dressed, fair-haired man, who was certainly old enough to *know better* raise the knocker on Miss Mandeville's door yet again. 'Young man! Must you make all that racket? If Miss Mandeville was at home she would have surely answered the door by now.'

Gregory Jaggard turned. A woman with repressive spectacles, a repressive hairstyle and an alarmingly repressive expression was looking at him from the open door of the neighbouring flat.

Jaggard forced himself to smile. 'I'm sorry if I disturbed you. I haven't been able to get an answer.'

'I'm not surprised,' said Mrs Chard with a sniff. 'She's been out till all hours the past couple of nights. She knows I'm a *martyr* to insomnia and yet I heard her giggling in the hallway. *And* she had a man with her. If it occurs again I shall have to speak to the management.'

Jaggard ignored her. To the accompaniment of a sharp intake of breath from Mrs Chard, he knocked vigorously on the door once more and rattled the handle. Much to his surprise, the door swung open.

He looked into the empty hallway of the flat. 'Pat? Pat? Are you there?'

'Miss Mandeville's Christian name is Sheila, I believe,' said his unwelcome companion.

Jaggard turned his head impatiently. 'I'm not looking for Miss Mandeville, I'm looking for my wife.' He stepped cautiously into the flat. 'It's all right,' he said as the woman made to follow him. 'You needn't come in as well.'

Mrs Chard drew herself up. 'Indeed I must. I consider it my responsibility – my duty even – to see that Miss Mandeville's flat is not ransacked. You say you are looking for your wife. How do I know that story is not a complete fabrication?'

'Look,' said Jaggard testily. 'If I wanted to break in, I'd hardly come hammering on the door, would I?'

The woman sniffed. 'That's as may be.' She was darting glances around her, obviously enjoying this chance to explore. 'The sitting room is directly ahead.'

The room, which also did duty as a dining room, was empty, but a handbag lay on the sofa.

'She's been in, then,' said Jaggard, pointing to the bag.

'Oh yes,' agreed Mrs Chard. 'She's always in at this hour. She usually switches on the wireless. I have frequently had occasion to speak to her about the noise, but my views, I am sorry to say, apparently count for nothing.'

Jaggard glanced back into the hall. A coat was hanging up on the pegs beside the door and a hat was on the shelf by the mirror. 'This is damned strange,' he said. He paid no attention to Mrs Chard's intake of breath and scandalized protest of '*Language!*'

He quickly looked into the tiny kitchen before pausing self-consciously at the bedroom door. 'Er . . . d'you think you could?'

'Certainly.'

Mrs Chard pushed open the door. The bed stood empty against

the wall. A chest of drawers, a ponderous wardrobe and a chair were the only other furnishings. There was no one in the room.

'This is ridiculous,' muttered Jaggard. 'Where the devil is she?'

He strode back into the hall, pausing before the only door they hadn't opened. 'What's in here?'

Mrs Chard hesitated. 'The . . . er . . . facilities,' she said, primly.

He rapped on the door before pushing it open. The bathroom was as empty as the rest of the flat.

'I've had enough of this,' declared Jaggard. He threw back his head and shouted. 'Pat! Miss Mandeville! Pat!'

The only sound was the quiet ticking of the sitting-room clock.

'I trust,' said Mrs Chard, gazing at him in fascinated horror, 'you will not do that again.'

'Don't worry,' said Jaggard, restraining his temper with difficulty. 'I won't.' He looked at his watch impatiently. 'It's nearly half past six. She should have been here twenty minutes ago.' He went back into the sitting room and, scribbling a note, left it propped up against the clock.

Meredith Smith raised the knocker of 43, Dunthorpe Mansions, once more, but, before he could bring it down, the door of the neighbouring flat flew open and an alarming woman, her face suffused with fury, issued forth.

'Will you . . .' she began, then stopped. 'I beg your pardon,' she said in a tone which made it clear she thought Meredith Smith should be begging hers. 'I assumed you were the *other* young man.' She looked at him with distaste. Clearly the change was no improvement.

Meredith Smith raised his hat. 'I'm sorry if I disturbed you. I was looking for Miss Mandeville.'

'Well, that's something,' said the woman with a sniff. 'Miss Mandeville is clearly not at home. As I told the other young man . . .'

'*What* other young man?' demanded Meredith.

'The one who was here earlier. I didn't care for his manner *at all*, although I'm sure I went out of my way to be helpful. I even went so far as to look round Miss Mandeville's flat with him, otherwise I am convinced he would still be hammering at the door. I am a *martyr* to neuralgic headaches and find this constant disturbance *most trying*.'

Meredith Smith tried his hand at pacification. 'Look, I'm awfully sorry to have bothered you, Miss . . .?'

'I am a married woman, young man,' she said, drawing herself up to her full height. 'My name is *Mrs* Chard.'

Meredith briefly marvelled at the reckless heroism of the absent Mr Chard before trying another dollop of oil on troubled waters. He didn't want to set Sheila at odds with her neighbours. 'I'm sorry you've been disturbed, Mrs Chard, but I've nothing to do with anyone else who was here. Er . . . How did you get into the flat?'

'The door is unlocked,' she replied icily.

Meredith tried the handle. 'No, it's not.'

Mrs Chard strode to the door and tried the handle. The door remained closed. 'Well, all I can say it was open earlier. And really, although there is a very nice class of people in these flats, I think that leaving a door unlocked in that manner is nothing less than putting temptation in the way of those who may be *weaker* than oneself.'

Meredith stood undecided in front of the door. He looked at his watch. Half past seven. The show started at eight o'clock and Sheila had promised she'd be ready. She might have made a mistake, of course, and assumed he was going to meet her at the theatre. He'd better be off, or else he might miss her there . . .

'But she wasn't there, Jack,' he said next day on the telephone. 'I hung around the theatre until the interval, then left her ticket at the box office in case she showed up later. I called round to her flat again, but she still wasn't in and this morning she hasn't shown up for work. I did wonder if she'd been called away unexpectedly, but it seems odd she hasn't let me know. I'd have expected her to send word that she wasn't coming into the office at the very least.'

'It does sound odd,' said Jack. Smith could hear his hesitation. 'Look, I'm a bit stuck at the moment. The Lassiters are calling for me. They'll be here at any minute. We're going to Brooklands with Pat Tyrell to see Jaggard's race this afternoon. Hold on a minute, Merry.'

Smith could hear the sound of muffled voices over the telephone.

'I'll have to go. Can you meet me in the club at six o'clock? Try not to worry. There's probably a perfectly reasonable explanation.'

And so there might be, thought Meredith Smith, staring sightlessly at the ledger in front of him. It's just that he was damned if he could think of it. He put down his pen and strolled to the window, where he leaned on the sill, looking out over the factory buildings. Where the blazes was she? Damn, damn, damn! To be stuck here on a Saturday morning . . . At least he had the afternoon free.

He looked impatiently at the clock. He'd like to go to Dunthorpe Mansions now, but he was seeing Wilcox from Buchanan Glassworks first thing on Monday morning and the costings needed work. Reluctantly he went back to his desk and, pulling the ledger and a sheaf of letters towards him, tried to bury himself in estimates. Work was better than having nightmares about Sheila.

When the twelve o'clock hooter sounded, all his ruthlessly subdued fears suddenly sprang into overwhelming life. He put the cap on his fountain pen with shaking hands and left the office at a run.

At 43, Dunthorpe Mansions, the door remained obstinately closed. Meredith Smith pounded on the door. Mrs Chard, thank God, must be out. Just for once, she'd have every reason to complain about the noise he was making. Sheila could be out, too, but . . .

Meredith Smith swallowed hard and went to get the porter.

Grumbling, the porter reluctantly left his cubbyhole in the basement and consented to unlock Sheila's door with his pass key.

Merry pushed past him into the hall. 'Sheila!'

There was no response. He knew there wouldn't be. She simply *couldn't* have ignored the hammering at the door, but a feeling of intrusion made him shout her name once more.

He opened the door to the sitting room. He'd told himself that he was a fool to worry so, that he was allowing his imagination to run away with him, that he was a complete idiot . . . and everything he dreaded was suddenly true. Only the real thing was far, far worse.

Sheila's broken body lay slumped on the floor against the couch, her face distorted and her eyes staring.

The porter, still grumbling, came into the room behind him. 'And I'll have to tell the management . . . *God Strewth!'* He made a noise as if he was going to be sick. 'The police! We'll have to get the police! She's been *murdered*!'

TEN

Gregory Jaggard watched the blue Bugatti of Sandy Keyne streak past on the inside. Never mind. The Bug was lighter, but his car, with its greater weight and low-revving engine, needed time to build up speed. The wind tore at his face and he felt the muscles in his neck and shoulders take the strain as he swung the six-cylinder car up the banking under Member's Bridge. He pulled the air intake control out to full, then floored the accelerator as the Railway Straight opened out in front of him.

He was gaining on the Bugatti now, the roar of the crowd on the bridge coming faintly to him over the deep thrum of his engine. His revs were building as the long stroke picked up the power. Keyne was slowing, trying to see a way past the huge Frazer-Nash in front of him. Jaggard touched the wheel and saw a window of clear track ahead, blocked by Johnny Miller in the Miller Special.

The smell of cut grass twanged his senses. The grass had been cut by a car crashing off the track. There it was! Reggie Palmer in an overturned Voisin, broadside on, its wheels still spinning in the air. He caught a brief flurry of movement by the wrecked car. Palmer should be all right.

He eased off the accelerator slightly before pressing down hard. The engine, the beautiful, handcrafted, lovingly tuned engine, responded like a nervy horse and shot forward, passing both the Bugatti and the Frazer-Nash. A flick of the wheel saved him from disaster and he was past Miller with only Ronnie Noble's Mercedes and Barnato's Bentley to master. He took the high ground on the Byfleet Banking and settled down to wear out the Merc.

'They're coming!' shouted Pat Tyrell, crammed against the

iron railings in the enclosure. With a ground-shaking rumble, as if an earthquake had been canned and set on wheels, the race leaders streaked past the white grandstand, leaving a trail of smoke and the heady smell of burnt castor oil in their wake. 'Did you see him?' she called, clutching at Jack's arm in an agony of excitement. 'Did you see him? He's past Miller. That's what he cared about. He's past Miller.'

The grin that Jaggard wore as he flashed past the grandstand hardened into a frown. He *knew* Pat was there, willing him on. He'd caught a glimpse of the distinctive red hat she always wore on race days as he'd gone to the car and he thought he'd seen her wave.

He caught up with the slow-moving cars at the back of the field and the next few minutes were pure concentration. Hillhouse's Fiat was there, seeming to stand still. He must be having trouble with his supercharger. Jaggard distrusted superchargers. They were quick but unreliable . . . Ah! The Fiat coughed its way to the side of the track and Jaggard weaved in and out of the remaining traffic, playing follow-the-leader with the Mercedes. He touched the brakes, feeling the lightened brake shoes slacken the speed just long enough to avoid disaster with Noble's Mercedes before a throaty roar a note or two below his own well-bred sound warned him that Miller was on his coat tails. Then the leaders were away once more and Jaggard settled down to slug it out for second place.

'They're coming round Byfleet Banking once more, ladies and gentlemen,' crackled the public address system. 'They should be in sight very shortly. In the lead is Captain Woolf Barnato in the Bentley followed by Mr Ronald Noble in his four-cylinder Mercedes . . .'

The cars thundered past. 'Where's Greg?' cried Pat. The third car past the grandstand was the Miller Special.

The address system crackled once more. 'We're getting reports of an accident on the Byfleet Banking, ladies and gentlemen. The marshals are going to the scene now.'

Pat turned a white, agonized face to Jack.

'It's Mr Gregory Jaggard in the Jaggard Six. The car's on fire, ladies and gentlemen.'

Pat raised a hand to her mouth.

'The driver was flung clear and . . . Yes! He's on his feet. He seems quite unharmed.'

Pat made a choking noise.

'Miller is running a superb race in third place, gaining on the Mercedes . . .'

'I must get to the sheds,' said Pat. All the colour had drained out of her face. 'I must see him. Oh, poor Greg. He's lost his race.'

With George and Anne Lassiter beside him, Jack took her arm and led her out of the crowd. 'The race doesn't matter, surely?' he said.

'It *does* matter,' insisted Pat. 'Greg was keyed up about this race. He had a bet of some sort on with Johnnie Miller. I'm sure he had a lot riding on it. More than money, I mean.'

It took them a long time to get through the enclosure to the sheds. By the time they arrived, there was quite a crush outside the double doors. Pat determinedly made her way though, Jack and the Lassiters following on behind.

Gregory Jaggard was sitting on an upturned oil drum, with a man in a tweed jacket, who was obviously a doctor, dabbing at his forehead with piece of damp lint. Jaggard seemed completely oblivious of the doctor's care.

'It's all over, Joe,' they heard him say to the man beside him. He looked utterly beaten. Then he looked up and saw Pat.

He made a fluttering motion with his hand. Pat drew in her breath as she looked at the deep, dirty gash that the doctor had only partially cleaned. 'It's only a graze,' Jaggard said, and repeated it three or four times. 'Don't fuss. It's only a graze.'

'It's rather more than a graze,' said the doctor, soaking the cloth and wringing it out in the bowl of water beside him.

'I'll say,' said Joe Hawley. 'That was a hell of a smash you had, begging your pardon, Mrs Jaggard. The poor beggar's tyres blew. The car's burnt out. You were damn lucky, old man.'

Jaggard shuddered. 'It doesn't matter.' He tried to fend off the doctor's hand. 'Just leave me alone. It's all over.'

'Whatever's the matter with you, Greg?' demanded Pat. 'You're still in one piece. You're alive, for heaven's sake.'

He looked at her with blank eyes. 'Alive? I wish to God I wasn't.' With a sudden burst of temper he forced the doctor's hands away. 'For Christ's sake, *stop it*! I don't need help! You don't understand, Pat. You don't know what I've done.'

There was a movement at the back of the crowd and turning, Jack saw, to his absolute astonishment, two uniformed policemen force their way into the shed followed by, of all people, Inspector William Rackham.

Bill nodded to him. 'I knew you'd be around, Jack. I'll talk to you later. This is official business.' He approached Jaggard and, with a sympathetic look at Pat Tyrell, tapped him on the shoulder. 'Gregory Jaggard? It is my duty to arrest you for the murder of Miss Sheila Mandeville. You do not have to say anything, but anything you do say may be used in evidence . . .'

He stepped back in alarm as Gregory Jaggard, his face paper-white, clumsily staggered to his feet, made as if to walk forward, then collapsed in a dead faint.

With a swift movement, the doctor knelt beside Jaggard, supporting the unconscious man's head. 'Clear a space everyone,' he said peremptorily. He pointed to Hawley. 'You! Help me sit him up.'

Together he and Hawley sat Jaggard up against the oil drum. As the doctor loosened Jaggard's collar, he spared a glance over his shoulder for Rackham. '*What* did you say you were doing? Arresting him for *murder*? Nonsense, man. I've known Mr Jaggard for years. There must be some mistake.'

'There's no mistake, I'm afraid, sir. I'm Inspector Rackham of Scotland Yard. I've got a warrant for the arrest of Gregory Jaggard.'

The doctor snorted disparagingly. 'Absolute poppycock. Well, I'm sorry to disappoint you, Inspector, but Mr Jaggard isn't going anywhere except hospital. That cut needs properly cleaning and stitching. Ideally I'd like to keep him under observation for a couple of days. In my opinion he's suffering from severe concussion and I can only hope he's not fractured his skull.'

Rackham pursed his lips. 'When will he be fit to answer questions?'

The doctor shrugged. 'Certainly not today and I'd be unhappy about him saying much tomorrow. I know you're eager to make an arrest, but this man is my patient.'

Rackham held up a conciliatory hand. 'Don't worry, Doctor. I've no desire to see my name in the papers as an example of the third degree. Take him to hospital by all means, but this is a serious charge he's facing. We'll need to have a police officer present.'

'If you must, I suppose you must, although it's a lot of damned nonsense.' He turned to Hawley. 'Did you send for an ambulance, man? Well, for God's sake, go and do it! Never mind what Mr Jaggard wanted. The poor devil's in no state to make any decisions.'

He glanced at Pat who, frozen with shock, was gazing down at Jaggard. He looked at the worried faces of the group. 'This woman needs some help. Who's with her? Anyone?'

'I am,' said Anne Lassiter, coming forward.

The doctor looked relieved. 'Take her away. Make sure she's all right. She's in no fit condition to be left alone.'

'Greg,' said Pat, forming the words with difficulty. 'I want to stay with Greg.'

Anne Lassiter looked at the doctor, who quickly shook his head. 'Greg's in good hands,' she said, slipping her arm round her. 'George,' she said, turning to her husband. 'Help me get Pat out of here. Come on, Pat. We'll take you home.' With great patience, Anne Lassiter escorted the protesting Pat out of the shed.

Bill Rackham turned to Jack with relief. 'I'm glad she's out of it.'

'What the devil happened, Bill?' asked Jack in a low voice. 'Is it true? Sheila Mandeville's been *murdered*?'

'Only too true, I'm afraid,' said Bill. He motioned with a jerk of his head for Jack to follow him and stepped outside the doors of the shed. It was good to be in the open air again. Outside, the thrum of engines and the noise of spectators from the track came to them clearly. It seemed strange that the whole world hadn't come to a halt, transfixed by tragedy.

Rackham lit a cigarette and drew on it deeply. 'We found Miss Mandeville's body in her flat. She'd been strangled.'

Jack felt sick. 'Dear God. I liked her, you know. Liked her a lot.' His stomach twisted. 'What the devil can I say to Merry? I was meant to be seeing him at the club at six o'clock.'

'That's one task you're spared, at any rate,' said Bill grimly. 'It was Captain Smith who found her. He was in a hell of a state. I didn't realize there was anything between them.'

'There wasn't until a couple of days ago.' Jack lit the cigarette Bill offered him. 'Where is she? Miss Mandeville, I mean.'

'At the mortuary. Do you want to have a look at the flat? The

Chief won't object, I know.' He glanced back over his shoulder into the shed. 'I'll get my laddo in there safely disposed of and we can have a look round together.'

'This is where she was killed,' said Bill, in the sitting room of Sheila Mandeville's flat. 'She was lying slumped by the sofa.'

Jack looked round Sheila Mandeville's sitting room. It was neat and well cared for, with only the finest film of dust on the table under the window. The curtains moved gently in the breeze from the window and a vase of daffodils splashed a rippling reflection of yellow on the polished wood. The fabric on the chintz-covered arms of the sofa had worn smooth and, for some reason, this innocent evidence of use made him swallow hard.

He didn't sit down. It felt wrong to even consider the idea. If Sheila were still alive he'd have had to ask her permission. She'd probably have apologized for the shabby condition of the furniture and he'd have thought of some light-hearted remark to put her at her ease, as he had done that day at the Ritz.

He leaned on the mantelpiece, resting his forehead on his hand. 'Tell me again what happened,' he said, finding his voice.

'Dr Roude, the Divisional Surgeon – he was the doctor called into Gower Street – says she was killed between five and nine yesterday evening, give or take a reasonable margin. The cause of death is strangulation and, from the bruising on the neck, it appears that a scarf of some sort was used.'

Jack frowned. 'Between five and nine is four hours. That's a fairly long time.'

'It is, but we can narrow it down a bit. Jaggard called here yesterday evening at ten past six or thereabouts. The neighbour, a Mrs Florence Chard, heard him knocking at the door. Mrs Chard – who between you and me is a bit of an old fidget – came out and asked him what he was up to. Now, the funny thing is, is that he said he was looking for his wife. He said she'd arranged to meet him here. Anyway, after banging at the door again, Jaggard tried the handle and found the door wasn't locked. Jaggard came into the flat, still apparently searching for Mrs Tyrell. Mrs Chard came in with him, thinking it was her bounden duty, as she more or less said, to see he didn't sack the joint. According to Mrs Chard, the place was deserted. It was obvious, however, that Sheila Mandeville had been home, because her handbag was on the sofa and her coat and hat were hanging up in the hall.'

'Could she have slipped out for a few minutes? To a neighbour, say?'

'She could have done, very easily. I've got a couple of lads going round knocking on doors now. Needless to say, there was no sign of Mrs Tyrell. After a while, Jaggard gave up and left a note propped up against the clock. That was half past six or so.' Bill opened his briefcase and handed a folded half sheet of paper to Jack. 'We found the note. That's it.'

Jack read out the note. '*Dear Pat – I called as you asked but missed you. I'll be at the R.A.C. all evening and the track tomorrow. I hope all's well. Please get in touch. Love, Greg.* What happened next, Bill?'

'What happened next is that Captain Smith called. That was just before half past seven, according to both Captain Smith and Mrs Chard. She heard him knocking and sallied forth to do battle again, thinking it was Gregory Jaggard who had returned to disturb her evening. Anyway, the door was locked and Miss Mandeville obviously wasn't in.'

'Could Jaggard and Mrs Chard have locked the door as they left the flat? Without knowing it, I mean?'

Bill shook his head. 'No. The lock's the Chubb type, which you have to turn with a key.'

'Which means, of course, that either Miss Mandeville locked herself in when she returned or that the murderer took the key and locked the door after him.'

'Exactly. Now, Captain Smith had asked Miss Mandeville out to the theatre. He thought there was just a chance she'd mistaken the arrangements and gone to meet him there. When she hadn't shown up by the interval, he came back, but she still wasn't in.'

'I know,' said Jack. 'He rang me this morning. She wasn't at work and he was worried about her.'

'That's right. He called round as soon as he finished work this lunchtime and this time, when he still couldn't get an answer, he went and found the caretaker for the flats. The caretaker let them in with his pass key and they found Miss Mandeville. That would have been about one. Captain Smith contacted us at once, and I came over with Dr Roude.'

Jack winced. 'It's damn rough on Merry. D'you know where he is now? I'll have to see him.'

'He went off to tell the Hunts – old Mr Hunt in particular – what happened. I don't think the shock had really hit him when I saw him. He's probably better doing something rather than sitting brooding about it.'

'Yes, I bet you're right about that. How was the murder actually committed?'

Bill clicked his tongue. 'What I imagine happened is that Jaggard came to see Miss Mandeville. He knocked on the door, not realizing how the sound would travel, and, when Mrs Chard appeared on the scene, made up a cock-and-bull story about meeting his wife here. As soon as he decently could, he got rid of Mrs Chard, then re-entered the flat and waited until Miss Mandeville came back.'

Jack gave him a puzzled look. 'But why, Bill? Do you suspect Jaggard just because he was seen here? On those grounds Meredith Smith's equally suspect.'

'No, it's not that.' Bill opened his briefcase again and took out an envelope. 'I found this in Miss Mandeville's handbag. It's an unfinished letter. Come and have a look.' He took out a typed sheet of paper and laid it flat on the table.

'*Dear Mr Jaggard,*' read Jack. '*I'm shocked you should think I could be bought off with a few pounds. I had no intention of saying anything until I saw you at the Ritz, but now I really think I should tell the police about that day at the booking office in January* . . . January, eh? That sounds as if she saw him booking tickets for Paris.'

'That's what I thought,' said Bill. 'In the envelope were four five-pound notes. It clicks into place, doesn't it? Meredith Smith says Jaggard was at the Ritz on Wednesday night, as were Mr and Mrs Tyrell. Jaggard wanted to speak to Mrs Tyrell alone. He got the waiter to tell Tyrell he was wanted on the telephone and asked Sheila Mandeville, who he'd met in the lobby, to hold Tyrell up for a few moments by bumping into him and dropping her bag.'

He shrugged expressively. 'It sounds as if Jaggard might have said something about this encounter at the booking office. I can't imagine Sheila Mandeville attached any importance to it, but it looks as if Jaggard tried to bribe her, which, of course, would make her realize there's something to conceal.'

'It all hangs together,' agreed Jack. 'There's more than enough evidence there for a circumstantial case.'

'That's why I got the warrant. We should be able to trace the banknotes fairly easily and the typewriter shouldn't present any problems. Obviously I'm going to ask Mrs Tyrell if she did arrange to meet him here, but I'll be very surprised if the answer's yes. I didn't want to question her at Brooklands. I thought she was so bowled over that doctor would've had my guts for garters.'

He broke off as a knock sounded at the door and a uniformed constable came into the room. 'Well?'

'We've been round the flats, sir. There's a couple of people we haven't managed to get hold of, but no one we've spoken to saw Miss Mandeville last night.'

'Thank you, Collins. Make a note of who you haven't spoken to and call back later. I think we're about finished here. Jack? Is there anything else you want to see?'

'Well, there's something I wouldn't mind doing, actually. I know Mrs Chard heard Jaggard knocking. What else could she hear, I wonder? Was she able to say what time Sheila Mandeville got home?'

'No, she wasn't,' said Bill. 'She didn't hear her come in yesterday.'

'In that case . . .' Jack stood for a moment, frowning. 'Look, would you mind going next door? I'm afraid it means coming up against Mrs Chard again, but I'd be interested to know what sounds do come through these walls. If you hear me shout, yell back, would you?'

'Mrs Chard?' asked Bill, warily. 'All right, if I must. How long shall I give you?'

'I'll knock on the door when I've finished,' promised Jack.

Once alone in the flat, Jack took the chance to look round undisturbed. He found it very easy to imagine Sheila at home. A silver-framed photograph of a middle-aged couple stood, amongst others, on the highly polished small table in the alcove. Her parents, at a guess.

Everything was clean, but with a cheerful, lived-in air. The mantelpiece contained, as well as the clock, little china ornaments from various south-coast resorts and a jar of coloured spills. The paper rack by the side of the fireplace contained a week's copies of *The Daily Messenger*, *Film Star Weekly* and the latest copy of *On The Town*. He winced when he saw *On The Town*. His name was on the cover. She'd probably bought it on the strength of meeting him. He put the papers back in the rack, idly noting that Sheila had clipped out the entry for the competition in Monday's *Messenger.*

With a feeling of trespass he went into the bedroom. It was a small room, floored in oilcloth with two bright rugs. He kneeled at the door and squinted along the floor, but it looked as if the oilcloth had been recently mopped.

He opened the wardrobe thoughtfully, shaking his head as he saw the dresses and skirts hung up, all covered with cotton bags. Six pairs of shoes and two suitcases stood on the bottom of the wardrobe. He lifted a suitcase slightly, seeing its outline marked by a thin line of dust. He replaced it carefully and shut the door.

The top of the chest of drawers was covered with a plate of thick glass and on it lay her hairbrushes, a hand mirror, a powder compact and a lipstick. The powder compact was open with a scattering of powder dropped from the powder-puff which lay beside it. Jack frowned at these for a moment without touching them, then, with a glance at his watch to mark the time, threw back his head and shouted. No call answered his.

The neatly made bed was an iron frame, the sheets and blankets covered with a blue candlewick bedspread. Jack knelt down beside it and lifted the bedspread to look under the bed. The floor underneath the main part of the bed was clean, but dust rimmed the edges against the walls. He let the cover drop and went into the kitchen, lifting the kettle from the hob. A cup, saucer, egg cup, plate and teapot stood on the draining board and the dishcloth was hung up to dry.

All the time he kept listening for sounds from the flat next door but no noise came through the walls.

The tiny bathroom was as clean and well cared for as the rest of the flat. A toothbrush in the rack, a cake of soap in the dish with no smears of soap, a towel hung up on the rail and a tooth-glass turned upside down to dry. The underside of the soap was damp.

A tall cupboard outside the bathroom held, on the one side, an ironing board, a mop bucket, an ordinary bucket, a long brush and a mop. A short brush and a pan stood against the wall while a bag proved to contain nothing more exciting than clean, washed rags. The other side was divided into shelves of neatly folded towels and linen.

The topmost sheet looked more crumpled than the rest and, taking it out, he carried it through to the sitting room, laid it out on the sofa and unfolded it along the ironed lines. A very faint dark mark was etched in one of the creases. Wetting a finger, he touched the mark, smelled it, then brought it to his lips.

Soot. The laundry mark was inked in red at the bottom and beside it was a small snag where a thread had pulled.

He shook his head and stepped back into the hall. Here, for the first time, he caught the faint murmur of voices from next door.

There was a key hanging down on the inside of the door from a long piece of string beside the letterbox. He opened the door and, standing outside, put his hand through the slit. He found the string easily and pulled, bringing the key through. He shut the door, then opened it with the key. He fed the key through the letterbox so it hung once more on the inside.

He paused before knocking on the door of the Chards' flat and thought of the woman whose home had been full of prosaic happiness. It seemed unbearably sad.

It was Monday morning, a day and a half since the discovery of Sheila Mandeville's body. Sir Douglas Lynton, Assistant Commissioner of Scotland Yard, glanced at the clock on his desk, then at Jack, leaning against the windowsill of his office.

A knock sounded on the door and Rackham entered. He nodded a hello to Jack before speaking to Sir Douglas.

'I'm sorry I'm late, sir. I had to wait at the hospital and the business at the bank took a little longer than I expected.'

'No matter, Inspector. Come in and sit down. Has Jaggard made a statement?'

'Yes, sir. The doctor in charge, Dr Woodcote, was unhappy about it, but Jaggard insisted. I've made a note on the file of Jaggard's condition. He's suffered severe concussion and his head wound needed seven stitches. There's nothing much in the statement. To put it in a nutshell, Jaggard denies the charge completely.'

Sir Douglas raised an ironic eyebrow. 'Does he, indeed? Did you trace the banknotes found in Miss Mandeville's handbag?'

'Yes, sir. They're part of a series paid to Gregory Jaggard by the Wool Street branch of the London and West Country Bank, where Jaggard has an account, in payment for a cheque he cashed for fifty pounds on April the twelfth. The letter itself was typed on Miss Mandeville's typewriter at Hunt Coffee. Acting on information earlier received from Major Haldean, I requested that the Paris police question the concierge of an apartment on the rue de la Paix, Paris. The concierge identified Jaggard from a photograph shown to him by the Paris police and confirmed that Jaggard stayed there from the first to the seventh of January. I've also established from the secretary of the Young Services Club that Jaggard stayed there on the nights of the eighth, ninth and tenth of January. That was when Jaggard was supposed to be in Birmingham. There's no doubt in my mind that the motive for Miss Mandeville's murder is the fact that she was in a position to prove Jaggard made a false statement regarding his movements around the time of Valdez's murder.'

'I agree entirely,' said Sir Douglas.

'Jaggard needed a reason to be at Miss Mandeville's flat. He says Pat Tyrell telephoned him at Brooklands and left a message, asking him to meet her there. Mrs Tyrell denies making that call.'

'Does she indeed?' said Sir Douglas in satisfaction.

'However, there was a call, sir. The steward who took the message says as much. The interesting thing is, that although the caller gave their name as 'Pat' it was a man who telephoned. The steward didn't think anything of it, of course, as Pat's a man's name as well as a woman's.'

'So who telephoned?' demanded Jack. 'Have you traced the call?'

'I have,' said Bill. He couldn't help but pause for effect. 'It was made from Weybridge Station. I think Jaggard slipped over the footbridge from the track to the station and made the call himself. I think he wanted the steward to be an independent witness who could testify he'd been asked to turn up at Sheila Mandeville's flat.'

'Good work, Rackham,' said Sir Douglas. 'This is building up nicely.'

'Thank you, sir. There is a question as to when the crime was committed. Captain Smith called for Miss Mandeville at half past seven. Our assumption is that at half past seven, Miss Mandeville was dead, otherwise she would have surely answered the door. Now the neighbour, Mrs Chard, saw Jaggard leave at half six.'

'So the crime was committed between half six and half seven.'

'So I thought, sir, but at seven o'clock, Jaggard was in the bar of the R.A.C. with his riding mechanic, Joseph Hawley. The barman confirms that, by the way. Hawley states he was with Jaggard all evening until about eleven o'clock. I'd assumed that Jaggard returned to the flat after looking round it with Mrs Chard and waited for Miss Mandeville, but that leaves him very little time. However, Major Haldean has a few ideas on that score, sir.'

Sir Douglas looked at Jack expectantly.

'Yes . . . Fundamental to all this is the fact that Sheila Mandeville kept a spare front door key hanging down beside her letterbox. It's awfully easy – as it's meant to be, of course – to reach in, grab the string, and get into the flat. We tried a little experiment, Rackham and I, and established that, although you can hear someone knocking on the door from the next flat, you can't hear someone letting themselves in with a key. My idea is that someone—'

'Jaggard,' interposed Bill.

'Who *might* have been Jaggard,' corrected Jack, 'did just that. Now, Sheila Mandeville generally got home about half past five or thereabouts.'

'The Hunt people said she left at five o'clock,' put in Bill. 'That was her usual time.'

'Good. That sounds about right. She went, I think, first into the bathroom to have a wash – the underside of the soap was damp – and then into her bedroom. The rest of the flat was undisturbed but in the bedroom her lipstick was on the dressing table and her powder compact was open. There was a scattering of powder from where she'd dropped the powder puff on the dressing table. I think she was attacked when she was doing her make-up in her bedroom. I shouted fairly loudly and Inspector Rackham tells me he couldn't hear a thing from the next flat.' He sucked at his cigarette, then studied the glowing end. 'Which means, of course, she was murdered not in the sitting room, but in the bedroom, shortly after she returned from work at around half past five.'

'She can't have been,' said Sir Douglas. 'It has to have been

after half past six. That's when Mrs Chard looked round the flat.
Sheila Mandeville wasn't there.'

'I think she was, sir. The top sheet in the linen cupboard wasn't
as neatly folded as the others. It looked crumpled, as linen always
does when you disturb it. I opened it out and found a little mark
of sooty dust along one of the ironed-in creases. What I believe
happened was that the murderer wrapped her body in a sheet
from the linen cupboard and put her under the bed. It has to be
under the bed, because there's nowhere else in the flat to hide a
body. The wardrobe was a possibility, but it was evident that
nothing in there had been touched.'

'But . . .' Sir Douglas stopped, lost for words. 'Why on earth
should anyone go through that performance?' he said at last. 'It
means two trips to the flat. One to kill the girl and to hide the
body, then to bring her into the sitting room. It doesn't make
sense.'

'Nevertheless, sir, I think that's what happened. The sheet had
a small flaw, as if a thread had been pulled out. It looked as if
it'd caught on a ring, a watch or a shoe.'

'And had it?' asked Sir Douglas.

'Yes, sir,' said Bill. 'When Major Haldean told me what he'd
found, I alerted Dr Roude to the possibility of finding a thread.
He found it snagged on Miss Mandeville's shoe. There's photographs in the file. In the face of that evidence, I agree with Major
Haldean that Miss Mandeville was murdered shortly after she
got home from work, at half past five.'

'But *why*?' demanded Sir Douglas plaintively. 'Why should
anyone give themselves two trips to the scene of the crime? He'd
have to come back within four hours, otherwise rigor would set
in and it'd be perfectly obvious the body had been moved.'

Jack nodded. 'I agree, sir. That brings us up to an outside time
of half nine for moving Miss Mandeville into the sitting room.
It doesn't make any sense, unless someone's trying to cover up
the fact that they've got no alibi for half past five.'

'What's Jaggard's alibi for that time?' asked Sir Douglas
sharply.

'He hasn't really got one, sir,' said Bill. 'He left Brooklands
at just gone four. Jaggard states he drove to Tanyard Mews where
he garages his car and walked to Dunthorpe Mansions. They're
only lock-up garages, with no one in attendance. He could easily

have driven straight to Dunthorpe Mansions and been there much earlier than ten past six. It's not much of an alibi, unlike his story for later in the evening. I think Major Haldean's right. He knew that part of his story was weak, so he deliberately drew our attention away from the early evening by trying to make us think the murder had been committed after half past six. I think Jaggard got back into the flat after having been seen by Mrs Chard, rearranged the body, and went off to meet Hawley.'

'Excellent,' said Sir Douglas approvingly. 'I really think that covers everything.' He looked quizzically at Jack. 'Is something wrong, Major? You don't look very happy.'

Jack clicked his tongue. 'I'm not,' he admitted. 'It's possible, I know, but I don't like it.'

'You've always been soft on Jaggard,' said Bill reprovingly. 'It's not admissible evidence, so I haven't put it in the file, but when I turned up to arrest him he was in the middle of telling Mrs Tyrell that she didn't know what he'd done. What was that about? It sounds suspiciously like a guilty conscience to me.'

Jack moved impatiently. 'It could mean anything. He'd just lost his race for a start, poor devil, so it could be that. I grant you that the case against Jaggard seems pretty black and I'd lay long odds you'd get a conviction, especially with the letter, the phoney phone-call and the banknotes to back you up. I must say, I don't like those banknotes.'

'They're damning,' said Bill briskly. 'And think of what else we've got. He lied, and can be proved to have lied, about being in Birmingham on the ninth of January. I think Valdez found out about his affair with Elise Molnar, tried to blackmail him and was murdered for his pains. What happened to Helston is anyone's guess, but I wouldn't be at all surprised if Jaggard accounted for him, too.' Bill looked at his friend and sighed good-humouredly. 'I can see you're not convinced.'

'Oh, yes I am,' admitted Jack. 'I'm convinced there's an absolutely solid case. Believe me, if he murdered Sheila Mandeville, he deserves everything that's coming to him. But . . . what if he didn't? I want to know two things that haven't been explained. One, what happened to Mark Helston, and two, why were Valdez's clothes removed?'

Bill shifted in his chair. 'We'll find an explanation, I'm sure.'

'Yes, but we haven't done so yet. There's an odd, artificial flavour about all of this. I smell the faint odour of rat.'

'I'm investigating a murder, not the drains.'

Jack grinned. 'You get me. What if Jaggard's been set up? It'd be very much to, say, Laurence Tyrell's benefit, if Jaggard was out of the way.'

'And so he murdered Sheila Mandeville simply to drop Jaggard in it? Come *on*.'

'It sounds ridiculous,' admitted Jack. 'So ridiculous that it can't possibly be the reason. I do wonder about Tyrell though. When Miss Mandeville saw him at the Ritz, she mentioned to Captain Smith that he looked vaguely familiar. I must admit she remarked on the similarity between Tyrell and Jaggard, and ascribed her feeling of familiarity to that.'

'That's probably all it amounted to,' said Bill.

'She also told Smith that Tyrell looked startled to see her when she bumped into him in the lobby.'

'Well, if he'd just had the girl run into him, I imagine he did look startled. You would, wouldn't you?'

'I suppose you would,' said Jack without enthusiasm.

Sir Douglas sighed and laced his fingers together. 'The trouble is, Major Haldean, I've known you too long to discount what you say. By all means, consider Tyrell as a possible suspect if it makes you feel any happier. I, for one, have a very healthy distrust of his motives for suddenly reappearing when there seems to be some money up for grabs. What I would say, is that the only murder that would benefit him is that of Patricia Tyrell. And she, as we know, is still very much alive.'

Jack wriggled impatiently. 'Of course Tyrell hasn't murdered his wife. If Pat Tyrell died now, all that would happen is that her income would be reabsorbed back into the trust. Besides that, he's not a complete fool. It'd be a bit obvious, wouldn't it?'

'Obvious or not, he hasn't harmed a hair of her head. But why invent problems? It's the actual murder of Sheila Mandeville we've got to crack, not the imaginary murder of Patricia Tyrell. And, incidentally, while Jaggard's removal might make things pleasanter for Tyrell, he's not a penny better off for it. Say we do convict Jaggard and he gets his just deserts, then his money from the trust goes back into the trust, just as Mrs Tyrell's would. Laurence Tyrell wouldn't benefit. I believe in evidence, and the evidence tells me that Jaggard should stand trial. If the verdict's guilty I won't lose a wink of sleep over it, I can tell you.'

The telephone on Sir Douglas's desk rang. With a frown the Commissioner reached forward and picked it up. Jack watched as Sir Douglas's face altered and became grave. Snapping out a few instructions, he replaced the earpiece, then looked at Bill. 'You'd better get down to the hospital. Gregory Jaggard's escaped.'

ELEVEN

In the corridor of St Luke's Hospital, Police Constable Brockley flicked his eyes to his superior's face, before resuming a close study of the wall one inch to the side and three feet behind Inspector Rackham's head. He said nothing. Experience had taught him that this was the best way.

'And you call that keeping watch, man?' Rackham's voice was thick with disgust. 'Of all the incompetent, blundering, bungling idiots who ever wore a uniform, I'd put you at the top of the class. You were told to watch him, yes? *In the room.* Not hanging about in the corridor, dallying with the nurses.'

'But, sir . . .' Constable Brockley tried to find words to express his feeling of acute injury and failed.

'I think what the officer is trying to say, Inspector,' said Dr Woodcote, intervening for the sake of common humanity, 'is that he is not responsible for Mr Jaggard's escape.'

Rackham adjusted his features into a semblance of civility. 'Would you care to explain that, Doctor?'

Doctor Woodcote ran a hand through his grizzled hair. 'Well, the fact of the matter is that I asked the constable to leave the room while I conducted an examination of my patient. Whilst the examination was in progress I was called to attend a complication that had arisen in another case. I did not anticipate being away for any great length of time. I may say that I could not possibly have foreseen such an action on Mr Jaggard's part. Indeed, he seemed to have slumped into a kind of torpor.'

'He snapped out of it jolly quickly,' muttered Bill.

'Er . . . yes. Remarkably quickly, I agree.'

'And you didn't think to ask Constable Brockley to step back into the room while you were gone?'

'Er . . . no. I am not accustomed, Inspector,' said Dr Woodcote testily, 'to having my hospital treated as a prison, nor, indeed, having to combine the functions of a doctor and a jailer.'

'I had to do what the doctor said, sir,' said Brockley, mournfully. 'And I weren't mucking about with any of the nurses, sir, honest.'

'All right, Brockley, dismissed,' said Rackham wearily. 'Although what,' he added to Jack, when they had stepped inside Jaggard's room and safely out of earshot of the hospital staff, 'that doctor thought he was playing at, I don't know. You'd think we had police posted here because we thought they could do with a nice rest.'

He sourly regarded the curtains flapping over the open window. 'Imagine leaving a man facing a murder charge in an unguarded room with an open window and a flat roof beyond. Honestly! It's obvious Jaggard's been waiting his chance. Torpor, indeed! I'd like to shake that damn doctor out of his torpor. Jaggard's got the best part of an hour's start on us. He'll be across the Channel before we know it.'

Jack shook his head. 'I doubt that. He'll know there'll be a watch on the ports and he'll be pretty conspicuous with a bandage round his head. What clothes was he wearing?'

'Pyjamas, dressing gown and slippers. His own clothes had been removed.'

'Did he have any money?'

'Not as far as I know. He had a few personal bits and pieces – a watch, cigarette case and so on – but that was the height of it.' Bill brightened visibly. 'He'll find it a hard job to get anywhere.'

'His main need'll be for a change of clothes and some shoes,' said Jack, propping his elbows on the windowsill. 'He won't be able to call in any shops, obviously. Keep an eye on anywhere where there's clothes, Bill. Washing-lines in back gardens – I can see some from here. Sheds, garages, anywhere he can hole up without being disturbed.'

'A washing-line?' said Bill, stepping to the window. 'That's a thought.' He turned in annoyance as the door opened. It was Constable Brockley. 'Yes?'

'Mrs Tyrell's here, sir, to see Mr Jaggard. I didn't say nothing, but she knows something's up.'

'Damn! I haven't really got time for her, but she'd better be told.'

'I'll see her,' offered Jack.

Bill shot him a glance of gratitude. 'Thanks. Maybe she'll have some idea of where he could have got to. If she has, telephone the Yard. Brockley! Come with me and see what you can do to make good the damage. Although, my lad,' he added, bitterly, unfairly, but quite understandably, 'it's mainly down to you that we're trying to shut the stable door after the horse has bolted.'

'Kennet!'

The voice was a low whisper but it made the valet jump as if it had been the crack of a gun.

'Kennet!' came the voice again. 'Over here, man.'

There was a rustle in the shrubbery fringing the path. Kennet threw away his cigar, which he had been enjoying in the night air, and moved cautiously towards the bushes. 'Is that you, Mr Jaggard?' he asked quietly.

'Of course it's me. Is it safe to come out?'

Kennet glanced round the garden. The French windows into the drawing room were open, but the rest of the servants were at the other side of the house. 'I think so, sir. The house is being watched front and back, though. There's a couple of bobbies walking around. They've called here to ask if we'd seen you.'

The bushes parted and Jaggard stepped out, grunting as he straightened himself up. 'That's more like it. I know the police are about. I got into the gardens at the bottom of the row and climbed over the walls. That wretched little pug of the Price-Norrises nearly gave the game away but I managed to scarper before anyone came.'

'Sir . . .' wavered Kennet. 'Your clothes!'

His master, who was normally so impeccably dressed, had on a pair of filthy, oil-smeared overalls, boots from which his toes were sticking out and a cap in which the pattern had long since merged into grime. His face was streaked with oil, but under the dirt, Kennet could see he was ghastly white.

Jaggard tried to laugh. 'I broke into a garage and stole them. I managed to slit the boots, thank God, otherwise I'd have been crippled. I've been lying under the tonneau of a car all day until it got dark enough for me to move.' He swayed and clutched at the valet for support. 'I'm in a hell of a mess, Kennet. I need help.'

'Sir, it's not true, is it?' asked Kennet urgently. 'What the papers are saying about that young woman an' all?'

Jaggard gave a very tired smile. 'No, it's not true. I've done a lot of things I'm not very proud of, but funnily enough, that's not one of them.'

'There!' said Kennet in triumph. 'I knew it wasn't. I told the others, I said, Mr Jaggard's never done it. I've been with Mr Jaggard all through the war and I know what he would do and what he wouldn't do. He's been upset recently and no wonder, with Mrs—'

He was stopped sharp by an angry grunt from Jaggard. 'Leave your mistress out of this, Kennet.'

'Yes, sir. I beg your pardon, I'm sure.'

'I need some money, some better clothes and some food, then I'll take myself off again.' He swayed once more as he spoke.

Kennet glanced up and down the garden once more. 'You'll do no such thing. Let me get you up to your room. You'll be perfectly safe there and you can have a proper night's sleep. I won't say a word to anyone, sir. I'll tell Janet to leave cleaning your room in the morning. She won't need much persuasion and not a soul'll know you're here. Steady, sir!' Jaggard's eyes had closed and he had nearly fallen. Kennet slipped an arm under his shoulders. 'In you come and no more argument.'

Jaggard's eyes flickered open. 'I've got to get away.'

'And you will,' said Kennet cheerfully. Jaggard slumped against him. 'Poor little sod,' he said tenderly, and half walked, half carried Jaggard into the house.

Ruby was cleaning the picture frames in the hall when the front door opened and Patricia Tyrell walked in. Ruby quickly got down from the steps and came to greet her. 'I'm that glad to see you, mum. I didn't know you were coming this morning, or else I'd have had the drawing room ready. Janet hasn't finished in there yet.'

'That's quite all right, Ruby,' said Pat, taking off her gloves and unpinning her hat. 'I need to sort out a few things in my room. Is Kennet about? I could do with his help.'

'He's upstairs in the master's room, ma'am.'

'Good.' She walked towards the stairs but was stopped by a cough from Ruby.

'Er . . . ma'am, what I want to say is, that I don't believe a word of them wicked lies they're saying about the master, but Cook's gone and taken herself off saying she could have been murdered in her bed any time this twelvemonth.'

'Good riddance,' said Pat. 'She was a rotten cook anyway.' She smiled. 'I appreciate your loyalty, Ruby. These are very difficult times for all of us, but you can tell the staff that I value the way they've stood by me, and, as a mark of my appreciation, I'd like to raise everyone's wages by ten shillings a month. I'll have a word with you all later, but first of all I really must go and have a look at my room.'

Ruby watched her walk up the stairs in a much happier frame of mind. Load of rubbish, all that stuff in the papers was *and* she'd never cared for the police. Ten bob extra a month? That'd come in handy . . .

Kennet froze and put a finger to his lips. Jaggard heard the foot-steps on the landing and quietly slipped into his dressing room. The door opened – it would have caused too much comment if it had been locked – and Pat walked in. Kennet breathed a sigh of relief. 'Thank goodness it's you, ma'am. This is a nerve-racking business. There's only me knows he's here.'

'How is he?' asked Pat anxiously. 'I got your note, Kennet, and came as soon as I could . . .' She trailed off as Jaggard came into the room.

'Thanks for coming, Pat,' he said softly. 'I knew you wouldn't let me down.'

Kennet tactfully faded into the dressing room, shutting the door behind him.

Jaggard tried a smile. 'Kennet's been a brick. I didn't want to stop here because of the risk of getting him into trouble, but he wouldn't hear of me going. I . . . I was in a pretty bad way last night and he took charge. I can't stay for much longer. Someone's bound to discover where I am and he'll be for it.'

She walked across to him, rested her hand on his arm and

searched his face. He was very pale and still wore a bandage over his forehead. Deep lines of strain were etched round his mouth and there were shadows under his eyes. He looked like a beaten man. 'Why did you run for it, Greg?' she asked softly.

'It seemed better than waiting to be hanged.'

She flinched. 'It won't come to that.'

'Oh, won't it?' He gripped onto the doorframe. 'Excuse me, I'll have to sit down.' He slumped onto the bed and, after the slightest of pauses, Pat sat down beside him. He clasped his hands and looked at his palms. 'They're convinced I murdered Sheila Mandeville,' he said at length. 'God knows why. They've got some evidence to prove it. I don't know what.' He turned to look at her. 'Pat, you don't think . . .'

She shook her head. 'No. There must be some terrible mistake.'

'Thank you.' His face lightened in gratitude. 'Thank you, my dear.' He paused. 'Why did you ask me to meet you at her flat? I got your message but you never turned up.'

'I never sent a message,' she said. 'Inspector Rackham asked me about it, but I certainly never asked you to meet me at Miss Mandeville's. After I saw you at the Ritz, I decided to come and watch the race, but I never attempted to get in touch with you. There must be some mistake.'

His mouth set in a grim line. 'Either that or someone's set me up.'

'But who?' She read the answer in his face and stiffened. 'No, Greg, no. You can't think Larry's responsible.' She sensed his complete disbelief and an ember of anger smouldered into life. 'He wouldn't do that. He's my husband, Greg. He doesn't *need* to get rid of you. He's got me anyway.'

'Has he?' Jaggard asked quietly.

She flushed. 'I wasn't going to tell you, not after the accident and everything that's happened, but I'm going to live with him. It's only right,' she added defensively.

Jaggard's shoulders slumped and he shut his eyes tightly. 'I was expecting this,' he said eventually. He opened his eyes and looked at her very closely. 'You're right, you know. He's your husband. I made a rotten fist of it. I know I was only ever second best.'

'Don't,' she began, infuriated at his self-pity, then her anger drained at the sight of his white face. She reached out for his hand but he jerked away as if he'd been burnt. 'I'm sorry,' she said formally.

She reached out again and this time he let her hand rest on his. 'Greg, I've thought a lot about what went wrong. I trusted you, Greg. I believed you loved me. I think I'm as much to blame as you, but . . .' She shook herself in irritation. 'When I found out about that woman I was so *hurt*!' she broke out bitterly. 'Why did you do it?'

He got up and walked across the room, leaning his forehead on his arm against the door. 'There's many reasons,' he said flatly. His face was turned away from her. 'I knew I only had a limited claim on your affection.'

He motioned her to keep quiet. 'I got tired of never quite coming up to scratch. That was one thing. Then – and this is nobody's fault but my own – I tried too high with the car business. They're good machines, Pat, some of the best on the road, but I wanted them to be the very best. I started to have big ideas. I got in way over my head. I poured money in. Nothing mattered but perfection. I've been taking ghastly losses. I ran through all my money and borrowed more. It's been hell. I *couldn't* make it pay but kept on tormenting myself with the idea it might. You can call me a bloody fool if you like, but the truth of the matter is that I'm flat broke. Ruined.'

'Ruined?' she repeated. 'You mean you've got no money at all, Greg?'

'That's the height of it. I'm totally skittled out. When things were at their very lowest ebb, I ran into Elise again. Don't get me wrong. She was never more than fun, but I liked her. She demanded nothing but hard cash. I managed that . . . There were no emotions with Elise. She never pretended to care and would have laughed if I'd said I loved her. Just for once, I was being honest. I knew what I was buying was false, but, for a time and on conditions, it felt like the real thing.'

'Why couldn't you tell me?' she asked. 'I was your wife, Greg. I knew something was badly wrong. I tried to talk to you, remember? Why didn't you tell me?'

'You?' The twist in his voice knifed into her. 'You? All I'd ever had to offer you was money. It's gone, Pat, gone. All I've got are debts. I couldn't tell you.'

Pat drew her breath in. Money. It was like a shock of ice-cold water. Money. She'd hated Greg's mistress, despised a woman who could sell herself, but now? It was like looking at a reflection in a mirror. Why *should* Greg believe he had nothing to give but money? That money was all she'd ever valued him for? Because he's right. A small, objective, damning voice sounded in her mind. Because he's right.

She walked across the room and tentatively put a hand on his back. She didn't want him to be right.

He shuddered as she touched him, then turned his head to look at her. She tried to find words, but failed. He took her shoulders in his hands, studying her face intently. Then his lips were on hers in a passionate, desperate embrace. 'I love you,' he said. It sounded like a death sentence. 'God help me, I love you.'

She stood, encircled by his arms, truth burning through her like acid. She'd been hag-ridden by a dream of Larry, bitten with worry, made cynical because Greg thought he could buy her, despising herself because she was up for sale.

He kissed her once more – tenderly this time – then pushed her gently away. 'It could have worked, couldn't it?'

'Yes.' There was a world of loss in the monosyllable.

He squared his shoulders and took a deep, ragged breath. 'D'you know, that makes it better? God knows what'll happen to me, but that really will make it easier to bear.' His eyes grew thoughtful. 'Perhaps, in the circumstances, it was just as well the race turned out the way it did.'

'What's that got to do with it, Greg?'

A ghost of a smile twitched his mouth. 'It was my big scheme to put everything right. Miller knew I was in deep trouble and offered to buy the firm. He's a sportsman, old Johnny, and I told him the truth. I couldn't afford to sell because I'd have to square up the debts. I didn't pull any punches and what I had to say made him think a bit. Anyway, he came up with the idea of a bet. He's always thought the world of that old aero-engined monster of his and offered me a race. If I won, then he'd come in as a partner with enough money to put us back on the right lines. It'd still be my show, but he's got some American connections that could be worth a fortune with the right car. If I lost, then he'd have the firm and take all the existing stock in lieu of the debts. If the cars sold, which they would, then it'd work out slightly to his advantage. It's the interest payments that crippled me. He'd start with a clean sheet. It seemed to solve everything. Not only was it a way out but I believed if I won, we could start again. You thought I was a wealthy man. I've been sailing under false colours. I had nothing left to give you and . . . and . . .' He shrugged. 'I thought it mattered.'

'Poor Greg.'

'Well,' he said in an attempt at a businesslike voice. 'That's water under the bridge. My immediate problem is how to clear out for long enough to let the police get to the bottom of this murder charge. If I could convince Haldean I'm innocent, he'd help, I know he would.'

'Major Haldean? D'you think so? H.R.H. thinks he's a washout.'

Jaggard grinned. 'Don't you believe it. He's the goods all right. Anyway, that's a side issue. I'm going to clear off and lie low for a time. Did you bring any money, Pat?'

'Yes.' She swallowed. 'How can I let you go? I mean, after all this?'

'I'm afraid you're going to have to.' He took her hand and kissed it. 'Pat, don't take this the wrong way. I know you're not my wife. You can't expect me to like Tyrell. I accept that I'm not the most impartial judge, but I don't trust him. Please be careful.'

'Careful of what?'

'Yourself.' He hesitated. 'Try looking at it without prejudice, Pat. Don't you think there's a chance he's after your money? I'm sure that's what most men of the world would say.'

'Mr Stafford, the lawyer, hinted as much. But what can I do, Greg?'

'What did Mr Stafford suggest?'

'Well, as far as I could follow him, he seemed to be suggesting I should make a will.'

Jaggard looked up sharply. 'Of course! That's it. If you did that, Pat, then I could rest easy. At the moment all your money goes to Tyrell as your next of kin, doesn't it?'

'I suppose so. I've never made a will.'

'Then make one. Leave your money to anyone you like. The Dogs' Home or some stray tramp. No, stick to charities, they're safer. The point is to get it away from Tyrell. What's more, you must tell him that's what you've done.'

'Oh, this is too silly for words.' Jaggard didn't reply. 'He's my *husband*, Greg.'

'That's the point,' said Jaggard drily. 'If he wants you and only you, he'll accept it. He must see that by coming back now, when you've got an income of eight thousand . . .'

'Half of it's yours.'

'I can hardly claim it, can I? Look. The longer Mark's away, I'm afraid the likelier it is that he's gone for good. I feel rotten putting it as bluntly as that because he was a damn good scout, but there it is. In seven years' time he'll be legally dead and you'll be a very rich woman.'

'So, according to you, I've got seven years of safety.'

'No.' Jaggard sat on the bed and put a hand to his head. 'If you, God forbid, die in the meantime, Mark's money, which was coming to you, goes to your husband unless you will it otherwise. I'm honestly frightened for you. Please make a will. Look on it as a last favour to me if you like, but make a will. After all, if Tyrell is as honest and as trustworthy as you believe, you can always make another one in a few years.'

'Are you sure you're right? About the legal side of it, I mean?'

'Not a hundred per cent,' said Jaggard. 'I know enough to be worried, though, and that's good enough for me.' He took her hands once more and looked earnestly into her eyes. 'Make a will, Pat. You might hurt his feelings, but that's a small price to pay for safety.'

Harold Rushton Hunt kept to the old-fashioned custom of ordering a selection of newspapers. They stared up at Jack from the Hunts' drawing-room table and, on a day in which there had been a dearth of news, there was no doubt which item had caught the attention of the Press. *Jaggard Escapes!* screamed the *Daily Messenger*, and the same story was repeated with variations of text, type and emphasis in all the other papers. It was obvious they'd all been read.

Although the *Messenger* story carried no byline, Jack knew, because he had been told as much that lunchtime, that its author was his old pal, Ernie Stanhope. He had successfully run Stanhope to ground in the Cheshire Cheese. Brooding over a melancholy whisky, Stanhope had accused Jack of deliberately making his load heavier to bear. 'I know you're in on it, Jack, You've got to give me a break. The Yard've clammed up. Who'd be a poor bloody reporter?'

It was with difficulty that Jack persuaded Stanhope that he didn't know where Jaggard was, hard work to convince him that he had no knowledge of any special relationship between Sheila Mandeville and the missing man, and a real uphill struggle to get him to believe that he simply didn't know if there was any connection between Sheila Mandeville's murder, Ariel Valdez's murder and the disappearance of Mark Helston.

'So what do you want?' asked Stanhope morosely. 'You didn't come to Fleet Street to gaze into my beautiful blue eyes.' He listened incredulously. 'The film competition? The *film* competition? What has that to do with . . .? Okay, have it your own way. If you say it's important, it's important. You'd better see Frankie Taylor. He does all the competitions. Well, let me finish my drink . . .'

The winner of last Monday's Spot The Stars had been a Miss Margery Westbury of Walthamstow. Had Miss Mandeville won any of the newspaper's competitions? No, she had not. Was he sure? Of course he was sure. Interview the winner? For a twenty-quid competition? Frankie Taylor was highly amused.

But, thought Jack, as he took his leave to keep his appointment with old Mr Hunt, that hadn't tied in with what Rosie O'Connor, Cynthia Cullen, Margaret Ross and the rest of the clerical staff of Hunt Coffee had told him earlier that day. According to them, Sheila Mandeville had been determined to get home on time last Friday because she'd had a letter from the *Daily Messenger* to say a reporter was coming to interview her about the pleasing fact that she'd won twenty pounds in Monday's Spot The Stars competition. So who had written the letter? Someone who wanted to make sure she'd be at home early on Friday evening . . .

He gazed at the spread of newsprint in front of him. The drawing-room clock continued to tick in its mellow, unhurried way. He checked the time with his watch. Old Mr Hunt was keeping him waiting. That had been a very curt note requesting him to call. Jack had an uncomfortable suspicion that he wasn't top of Mr Hunt's list of favourite people . . .

Laurence Tyrell had been at Hunt Coffee on Friday; all after-noon, Agnes Clement, Frederick Hunt's confidential clerk had told him. He'd been shown round by Mr Hunt. She thought they'd gone to the club after they'd left. She didn't know which club. Frederick Hunt, impatient at being interrupted, had curtly confirmed he'd been with Tyrell all day. Dash it, Major Haldean, that did include the early evening as well. Tyrell had come for a couple of drinks at the club and had been persuaded to have a spot of dinner before leaving at about half past nine to go back to his hotel to change. Which club? The Archias on Carteret Street, St James's, not that it was any of his business.

The porter at the Archias remembered Mr Tyrell well. Nice gentleman, Mr Tyrell, with a very pleasant way with him. Mr Tyrell and Mr Hunt had come in at quarter past five. His watch had stopped and he'd asked for the time. Oh yes, he'd been around all evening. The steward could bear him out. He must have left about half past nine or so. He'd said goodnight on the way out. No, his watch hadn't stopped again. Mr Tyrell had said as much, he'd said, 'Good, I see my watch is still working.' Plenty of people had seen him, including the waiter who had served him.

Jack frowned. Was there a chance there? There was an insistence on the time, which seemed fishy, but any idle remark seemed fishy if examined long enough. Tyrell couldn't, simply couldn't, have moved the body after half nine. By that time it would have started to stiffen and it would have been obvious it had been moved.

Besides, he didn't have time to get from the Archias to Dunthorpe Mansions, then back to his hotel to change before calling for Pat that evening. Tyrell had certainly arrived at Neville Square at ten o'clock, in full evening dress. Pat Tyrell had told him so. Poor Pat. There was no doubt that Jaggard's escape had been a complete shock to her.

Jack looked at his watch again. Where the devil was old Mr Hunt?

As if in answer to his unspoken question, the door opened and Mr Hunt, supported on Fields' arm, came into the drawing room. He walked with obvious difficulty, stopping to draw breath, and his lips had an unhealthy blue tinge. He looked at Jack but did not speak until Fields had settled him in the winged chair by the fireplace. When he spoke it was to the butler. 'You can go now.'

Fields didn't move. 'Are you sure you'll be all right, sir?'

'Of course I'll be all right!' He waved an irritated hand at the bottles on the tray beside him. 'I've got every sort of medicine for every complaint known to man – not that any of it is a farthing's worth of use – and I am perfectly capable of ringing the bell should it be necessary.' Fields still didn't move. A thin smile touched Mr Hunt's lips. 'You're a stubborn man, Fields, and your concern does you credit, but I don't intend to die just yet. Off you go.'

Reluctantly the butler left the room.

'Now, sir!' said Mr Hunt, as if calling a meeting to order. 'I suppose I should thank you, Major, for calling in response to my note. However –' his thin hand grasped the arm of the chair – 'I must own I am extremely disappointed in your progress. The newspapers this morning were a disgrace. My family's name has been dragged through the gutter and for what? Are you any closer to discovering what happened to Mark? No, you are not. I am not a complete fool. I know what people are saying. If you had deliberately set out to blacken my family's name you couldn't have made a better job of it.'

Jack was prepared to take a good deal from an old man, espe-cially one who looked so very frail, but he was not prepared to take that. 'I think you're being unfair, Mr Hunt. I admit I haven't managed to trace your nephew but I warned you at the time it would be difficult. As for blackening your name . . .'

'You have been only too successful. Thanks to you, everyone – *everyone* – believes that Mark is guilty of murdering Ariel Valdez. Laurence Tyrell has returned in a blaze of publicity which was certainly not of my making . . .'

'Or mine.'

'Really? I'd like to know exactly how the papers did get hold of it, then. Patricia assures me she was not responsible and I refuse to credit that any of my family, servants or employees would carry such tittle-tattle to the popular press.'

Jack bit his lip. He felt disinclined to lay any more blame on Gregory Jaggard's shoulders. 'Gossip will almost always get out, sir.'

'Gossip! You tell me my family is the subject of gossip and expect me to be cheered? But that, Major, is almost by the way. A young girl has been murdered and, yet again, there is a damning connection with Hunt Coffee. She was my employee and I cannot help but feel responsible for her. If that was not enough, her murderer has escaped justice. Although Jaggard is not and, apparently, never was, part of the family, the link is there and the papers have pounced on it.' He stopped, gasping for breath. 'My drops,' he croaked.

Jack crossed swiftly to his side, quickly found the small brown bottle Mr Hunt was pointing to, and, shaking some into a glass of water, held it to his lips. Very gradually the colour came back to the old man's face.

'Thank you,' he said eventually. From the hall came the jangling of the front-door bell, but Mr Hunt ignored it. He closed his eyes and waited for a long moment.

'I have rarely,' he said at long last, 'felt so helpless.' He opened his eyes. 'I have had a long and varied life, Major. I was eighteen when I sailed for Brazil. I made an expedition up the Amazon and held a gun against a revolutionary mob. I carved the plantation out of virgin land and always, always, relied on my own wits and abilities. If I still had a fraction of my strength I would hunt down Jaggard and make him confess to Valdez's murder. If Jaggard killed this girl then surely he killed Valdez as well. It can't be Mark. You see that, don't you? Mark's name would be cleared and Patricia would be free for good.'

His hands clenched momentarily. 'I have to rely on others! Age makes such idiots of us all. But old or not, I wish I could get to grips with Jaggard. I've rarely been wrong about a man but I was wrong about him.' A new light crept into his eyes. 'I've said some hard things to you, sir. Perhaps it's only my age that made you listen. I mean them; I mean everything I've said. But the hardest thing for me to realize is that Jaggard deceived me so completely.'

'Have you considered that Jaggard might be innocent?' asked Jack tentatively.

'Don't be a damn fool, man,' began Mr Hunt, then stopped, keenly searching Jack's face. 'You've got something in mind, haven't you? Out with it, sir!'

Jack shook his head. 'I'm afraid I can't, Mr Hunt. For all I actually know, both you and the police may be correct.'

'But you've got other ideas than the official ones, haven't you?' he said, continuing to stare at Jack acutely. 'I wonder if old George Lassiter was right about you, after all. Well, ideas are not enough. There's a girl murdered. Ideas didn't save her, did they? If you knew what was going on, why didn't you take some action?'

'Because I . . .' Jack stopped in exasperation as the door opened and Fields entered the room.

'There's a Mr Robert Waldron to see you, sir.'

For a moment Mr Hunt looked blank, then he gave a broad smile. He looked suddenly younger and fitter. 'Robert? Robert Waldron? John Waldron's son? My word, I had no idea he was in London.' He tried to lever himself out of his chair before glancing impatiently at Fields. 'Give me a hand up.'

'If you would care to wait here, sir, I will show the gentleman in.'

'Wait here? Stuck in this chair? I'm going to meet Robert standing on my own two feet, not lolling about like some old fogey.' Fields, resigned to the inevitable, helped his master to stand. 'That's better. No, not your arm. Pass me my stick.' He slowly walked into the hall, obviously trying to recapture some of his former strength. Jack glanced at Fields, and the butler gave him the very slightest suspicion of a shrug. If the man had said, 'What can I do?' his meaning couldn't have been clearer.

They followed Mr Hunt into the hall. Standing by the front door was a sallow-skinned, wiry man in his vigorous early sixties. He strode forward to take Mr Hunt's outstretched hand with pleasure.

'Mr Hunt! You're looking remarkably fit, sir.'

'Don't flatter me, Robert, I'm nothing of the sort. I'm older than your father was when he died. My word, though, it's good to see you again after all this time.'

He broke off as the door to the morning room opened and Pat, followed by a very disgruntled-looking Laurence Tyrell, stepped into the hall.

'My mind's made up,' she said over her shoulder to Tyrell. 'Those are the only terms I'll accept.' She stopped and looked at the men in the hall. 'I'm awfully sorry, Uncle. I had no idea you had visitors.'

'Major Haldean is just leaving us, my dear, but this is a very old friend of mine who's turned up out of the blue. Robert, this is my great-niece, Mrs Patricia Tyrell, and her husband, Laurence

Tyrell.' He said the names with an air of defiance, but they clearly meant nothing to Waldron.

'Larry's just going as well, aren't you, Larry?' said Pat. There was an odd deliberation in her choice of words.

Mr Hunt went for the sound rather than the sense. 'Is there anything wrong?'

'Wrong?' Pat pushed her hair back from her face and laughed. 'Nothing much. After all, Larry's got what he wants, haven't you, my dear?'

For a man who had, apparently, got what he wanted, Tyrell was clearly finding it quite a struggle to be civil. 'We'll talk about it later, Pat.' Then he relaxed and smiled. 'I'll call for you this evening as we arranged.'

The hall was lit by a long window over the stairs and, as Tyrell spoke, the sun came out from behind a cloud, lighting up Tyrell's face as if he were under a spotlight. Maybe it was that which gave Jack a sudden feeling of unreality. It was like watching an actor. Tyrell's smile was as attractive as ever, but his eyes were calculating and very cold. Jack felt Mr Hunt stiffen beside him. He had seen it too.

For a split second Jack felt as if he had stepped out of time. It was as if he was watching a group of statues, then Tyrell had hold of Pat's hand and the odd, frozen moment passed.

'When shall we say? Ten o'clock? I'll be here earlier if you like. Why don't you ask your friends, the Lassiters, to come?' He turned to Jack. 'Would you like to join us? We'll have supper at the Savoy, but we can always go on somewhere else if you fancy it.'

Jack was stupefied by the implications of that look. With a huge effort he spoke as naturally as he could. 'Thanks very much. I'd be glad to, especially if the Lassiters are going to show up.'

'Good. Half ten in the Savoy?' He squeezed Pat's hand affectionately. 'Do ask your friends, Pat. After all, we've got something to celebrate.'

Mr Hunt and Mr Waldron retreated into the drawing room. Fields opened the door to show Jack and Tyrell out but, as he opened it, Jack drew back, patting his pockets.

'I think I've left my cigarette case. You go on, Tyrell. I'll see you this evening.' He stepped back as Tyrell went down the steps and the door closed behind him. Fields murmured, 'Excuse me, sir,' and left Jack with Pat.

He grinned apologetically at her. 'I'm sorry. I'm guilty of telling whoppers. I've got my cigarette case, but I wanted a few moments alone with you.'

She looked at him apprehensively. 'Why? What is it?'

He nodded in the direction of the front door. 'Laurence Tyrell. I'm sorry if this sounds like vulgar curiosity, but I would like to know what you've got to celebrate.'

She shrugged. 'There's no reason why you shouldn't know. It'll be common knowledge soon enough. I'm going to tell H.R.H. when his visitor's gone. I've decided to live with Larry as his wife.'

Jack nodded slowly. 'I see. Are you sure you're doing the right thing?'

'No, I'm not!' she broke out. 'I'm not certain of *anything*, but I can't go on like this.' She gave him a challenging stare. 'Everyone thinks Larry's after my money. Do you?'

'It'd crossed my mind.'

'Well, it's crossed mine, too. I hate all this. I'd love to be able to trust him absolutely but I just can't. Anyway, I've taken a step which should give me the truth of the matter.'

Jack looked at her inquisitively. 'And that is?'

'I've made a will. At least, I've given instructions to Mr Stafford and he's drafting it for me. I'm leaving all my money to the Red Cross. Larry asked me why, and, of course, I can't spell it out for him.'

'He'll have guessed,' said Jack.

'Yes . . . It's horrible to be so cold blooded about it, but I can't think what else to do.'

Jack looked at her thoughtfully and decided to back a hunch. 'Was this Jaggard's idea?'

Her intake of breath told him he was right. 'What d'you mean?'

'You've seen him, haven't you?'

She gazed at him speechlessly, then slowly bowed her head.

'It's a pretty good idea,' continued Jack conversationally. Apart from a fairly major flaw, he added to himself.

'How did you know?' Her voice was a whisper.

'You, principally. Oh, it's nothing you said, but after he escaped you were desperate. You're still worried, but it's about Tyrell, not Jaggard. Therefore something's happened to make you stop worrying about Jaggard so much. It's the idea about the will that made me twig, though. You might have thought of it, but I don't honestly think you'd have taken such definite action off your own bat. And,' he shrugged, 'I must admit I was guessing. Jaggard needs clothes, food and money and I thought he was as likely to ask you for them as anyone.'

'What are you going to do?' she asked quietly.

'Nothing very much. Did you meet him at your old house?' She nodded.

'He did jolly well to get through the cordon. Rackham had men posted all round the place. You've been watched, too. Is he still there?'

'He's gone. Please don't betray him. He asked me to help. I couldn't live with myself if I let him down. Whatever he's done, he didn't kill Miss Mandeville. He wants you to know that. He believes you can find out the truth.'

Jack caught hold of her hands. 'Easy, now, easy. Can you contact him?'

She didn't speak but her expression was plain to read. 'Don't worry,' said Jack quickly. 'I won't split. For one thing, what you've told me isn't evidence and, for another, I don't see what good it'll do.' He felt her hands convulsively clasp his. 'Don't be too grateful. I might ask you to tell the police yet, but let's hope for the best, shall we?'

'Someone knows something, that's for sure,' said Bill acidly, later that afternoon. 'My money's on that smooth-faced beggar, Kennet. He'd go to the stake for Jaggard by all accounts and yet I'll swear Jaggard's not been near the house.' He tapped the pile of papers on his desk. 'All these are supposed sightings. I don't believe any of them are a ha'peth of use. I thought he'd try and get in touch with Pat Tyrell, but she's as clean as a whistle. Where the devil can he have got to?'

'I don't know,' said Jack, truthfully enough. 'Bill, you know you've been keeping a watch on Pat Tyrell?'

'And a fat lot of good it's done us. Yes?'

'Could you step it up this evening? For her protection, I mean. I've got the nastiest feeling something's going to happen.'

Bill looked at him curiously then, sweeping a file from his chair, sat down heavily. 'What sort of thing?'

'It's Laurence Tyrell.' Jack shook his head impatiently. 'Stop rolling your eyes at me. I tell you, I'm worried. It's this blasted will she's made. If only she'd not told Tyrell before it was actually signed, it'd be a brilliant idea.'

Bill sighed wearily. 'Look, we've been through this before but I'll say it again. If anything happens to Pat Tyrell, Laurence Tyrell loses out. Mrs Tyrell's income goes back into the trust and he hasn't got a bean. What's rattled you?'

'It was a look he gave her,' admitted Jack.

'A look? That's not much to go on.'

'You should have seen it. That, and the fact he'd obviously been arguing with Pat about her will.'

'You can hardly blame the man for that.'

'No. But when I came in on the tail end of it, together with old Mr Hunt and this visitor of his, he switched off his bad temper and suddenly became very sociable. He invited me to join them for supper at the Savoy and wants the Lassiters to be there as well.'

'So? What exactly are you afraid of?'

Jack took a deep breath. It seemed ridiculously melodramatic when he said it out loud and yet . . . 'I don't know how and I can only guess at why, but I think there's going to be an accident. A hundred-per-cent, twenty-four caret, copper-bottomed accident with the Lassiters and me as unimpeachable witnesses. I think Laurence Tyrell is planning to murder his wife tonight.'

TWELVE

The Lahones descended on their table with noisy whoops, bringing in their wake at least six other assorted youths and as many girls armed with toy balloons.

'Pat! Darling!' called Eve Lahone. 'I haven't seen you for a positive *age*!' She sat down and aimed a dazzling smile at Tyrell. 'You've been keeping her all to yourself, haven't you? It's very bad of you. Poor Tim's been absolutely morose without Pat.'

'Life's been just too flat,' called Tim Lahone, pressing his cigarette onto a balloon. 'Let's make it go with a bang.' He roared with laughter at the noise.

George Lassiter stirred unhappily. 'I didn't realize this ghastly crowd would be here,' he muttered to Jack. 'Much more of this and I'm off.'

A girl answering to the name of Binky draped herself round Jack's neck, ruffling his hair. 'Dance with me, darling. You absolutely have to dance. You've got the *wickedest* eyes I've ever seen.'

'Let's all dance,' said Eve Lahone loudly. 'Pat, I'm going to borrow this delicious man of yours. He's simply too good looking for words.'

They all surged off onto the floor. As Jack negotiated the giggling Binky round the floor, he was badly puzzled. Surely Pat would be safe here? He simply couldn't see how Tyrell could try anything in this crowd, and yet why ask him and the Lassiters? It wasn't for love of their company, that was for sure.

He looked round the room and spotted two of Bill's men. They blended in very well. If he hadn't recognized them, he wouldn't have known they were the police. They should have made him feel secure. They didn't. Pat Tyrell was dancing with Tim Lahone, trying, with limited success, to make him keep his hands in the correct position. The music finished and the group drifted back to the table.

'Thanks for nothing,' muttered Lassiter as he sat down beside Jack. 'That wretched girl I was lumbered with has got a shriek like a hyena and I'm convinced she's had more than's good for her. I'm damn sure that feller Lahone has. Look at him! If that was my wife he was fooling around with, I'd rearrange his face for him, but Tyrell doesn't seem to mind.'

'Let's go on somewhere,' said Eve Lahone, pulling out a chair.

'We'll have another drink first,' countered Tyrell, snapping his fingers for the waiter. 'Three bottles of champagne. That'll see us on our way.'

Eve evidently considered this to be a hilarious remark, for she laughed uproariously. 'More champagne, darling. What a lovely idea.'

'I'm going,' said Lassiter abruptly. 'Anne's hating every minute. If Tyrell knew what he was about, he'd get his wife out of it, too. She's not happy either.'

Jack pulled him back down. 'Stay, George. Please. I'll explain why afterwards.'

Lassiter shot him an inquiring look. 'All right. But I warn you, if any of this crowd fools around with Anne, we're off.' He paused while the waiter filled up their glasses. 'Hello! Tyrell's decided to warn off Lahone at last.'

Larry Tyrell, glass in hand, put an affectionate arm round Lahone. 'Come and have some bubbly, old man.' He pulled him round and Lahone's arm, entwined about Pat's waist, knocked her glass, making her spill her drink on the floor.

'Awfully sorry,' said Lahone thickly. 'Has it gone on your dress? I really am awfully sorry.'

'Never mind,' said Tyrell, heartily. 'Pat doesn't mind, do you, Pat?' He tipped a wink to his wife. 'Just come and sit down with me for a few minutes, old bean, and then we'll go on to a club somewhere, yes? Pat isn't cross with you, are you, Pat?' He put another glass into her hand. 'Here, have this. Come on, Lahone.'

'Nicely done,' said Lassiter with grudging approval. 'Better than causing a row.'

With a feeling of sudden apprehension, Jack sprang to his feet. He wanted to stop Pat drinking the glass Tyrell had given her, but Pat, glad to be out of Tim Lahone's clutches, exchanged a laughing remark with Anne Lassiter and drained her glass with enjoyment. Jack sat down again, his eyes fixed on Pat.

'I've just found out who you are,' said a voice from behind. It was Binky. She sat down beside Jack, obscuring his view of Pat. 'Darling, it's just *too* thrill making. I couldn't *believe* it when that nice little girl, Anne, told me you write all those clever stories and catch murderers and things.' She fitted a cigarette into a long holder and put a hand on his knee. 'Light this, darling.'

Jack, glancing past her, caught a glimpse of Pat. She was talking animatedly to Anne Lassiter and looked, if anything, rather more cheerful than before. Jack relaxed. He'd been looking for an accident. This didn't fit the bill.

The hand on his knee increased its pressure. 'I'm waiting,' said Binky.

'Sorry.' Jack struck a match and forced himself to smile at the girl who was looking at him with what she believed was roguish playfulness.

'Skittles!' called Binky to a girl across the table. 'Guess *who* this is. He's just the cleverest man you'll *ever* meet and shatteringly well known. Oh, you are, darling.'

Skittles loudly demanded to be told the nature of Jack's celebrity and for the next ten minutes or so he was at the centre of an admiring group of girls. Out of the corner of his eye he saw Pat Tyrell whirling past, dancing with Tim Lahone once more. She was fine. He'd been brooding about her like an old mother hen, but she was fine. Her laugh rang across the floor. If Tyrell's master plan was to poison his wife, he'd hardly invite half of London to testify that was exactly what he'd done. He breathed out in relief. The girls were pressing him for information and, with an ironic twist to his lips, he settled back to enjoy the pleasures of fame.

He was interrupted by a tap on his shoulder from Lassiter. 'Come on, Jack. We're going, apparently.'

'Where to?' asked Skittles. 'Oh, *not* the Bitter End. It's been raided twice this month. Daddy said he'd cut off my allowance if I was caught there again.'

A shouted discussion followed on the comparative merits of the Seventh Heaven, the Utopia, the Medusa, the Caprice and Hell's Bells.

'How about you, Pat?' called Tyrell.

Pat, her arm firmly wrapped round Tim Lahone, only giggled.

'Let's go to the Fortune,' suggested Lahone. 'It's quite drearily respectable. We'll liven 'em up a bit.' He tightened his grip round Pat. 'D'you fancy that?'

'The Fortune it is,' announced Tyrell.

The night air didn't have any sobering effect on the group. In addition to the balloons, Tim Lahone had a toy trumpet which he blew between shouts of, 'Steady the Buffs!' and 'Gone Away!' The girls found it screamingly funny.

Walking across Lancaster Place to the Embankment, George and Anne Lassiter dropped behind with Jack. 'Would you mind telling me,' said Lassiter, in a voice rigid with disapproval, 'why on earth we shouldn't bunk off? This must be the worst evening I've had for a long time. I can't stand Lahone. He's a vicious little sweep and that sister of his is as hard as nails.'

Jack walked a few more steps before replying. 'I want you to keep an eye on Pat Tyrell,' he said eventually. 'I don't know how, or I'd say, but I honestly think she's in some sort of danger.'

Lassiter snorted. 'She's in danger of a blistering hangover. I always liked Pat, but she's as kettled as the rest of them. She's only standing up because Lahone's holding her. She's making as much noise as the rest put together. What the hell are they doing now?'

They had reached Waterloo Bridge and Lahone, trumpet in hand, scrambled on top of the stone balustrade. 'Hello, fishes,' he called over the side.

'Do come down, Tim,' said Eve Lahone. 'You'll get quite shockingly wet if you go over.'

Lahone danced a couple of steps and nearly missed his footing. 'Whoops! Dare you, Tyrell. Dare you to climb up here and get to the lamp.'

The beautiful wrought-iron lamp standard stood about thirty feet along the bridge. Tyrell laughed as Lahone stepped out along the balustrade. 'You're on!' he shouted. 'Five pounds says you don't make it.' He put his hands on the coping stone and swung himself up on to the top of the balustrade beside Lahone. He held his hand out to Binky who, with a roar of encouragement from the group, kicked off her shoes and climbed up beside Tyrell.

Lahone's face fell. 'Hey! You've got a racing partner. That's not fair.' He reached down to Pat. 'Come on. The two of us'll show them.'

'No, Pat!' called Jack. He tried to push his way through, but he was blocked by the jostling group. 'Get down!' he shouted, but his voice was lost in the cheers of the others.

Pat, very flushed, stood balanced on the balustrade beside Lahone, waiting for Tyrell and Binky. Lahone gave another blast on his trumpet. 'And they're off!'

The crowd surged alongside, yelling. Jack managed to get round to the front, and despairing of getting his message across in any other way, climbed up onto the balustrade himself, blocking Lahone's way.

'Push off, old boy,' said Lahone pleasantly enough. 'There's a bet on, you know.' His breath, sodden with drink, struck rank in Jack's face. 'Plenty of room at the back.'

'Get down,' said Jack as urgently as he could. 'Pat, for God's sake get down.' At the end of the bridge he could see the two plain-clothed policemen.

Lahone turned to look over Pat's shoulder as Tyrell came up behind them. 'There's a blinking hazard here that won't go away.'

The crowd on the bridge started a slow, jeering, handclap.

'Move, Haldean,' called Tyrell impatiently and walked forward. Then, as he got near to Pat, he seemed to stumble and lose his footing. He grabbed at Pat, and the two of them swayed together. For a moment it looked as if they would fall onto the pavement and then, with an agonized cry, they hurtled to the black water below.

The blast of a police whistle mingled with Pat Tyrell's terrified scream. Jack heard the splash, caught a brief glimpse of where they were, tore off his coat and dived.

There was a brief rush of air and light, then the icy water hit him like a solid blow. Coming up from his dive, he shook the water out of his eyes, feeling the giant's pull of the current tugging his legs. With his lungs crunching inside his chest from the cold, he struck out to where he could see a flash of white and an upraised arm. Tyrell was struggling with Pat and as Jack reached them, she went under. Jack plunged down, managed to grab her dress, then a calm voice sounded above them.

'Steady now, steady. Get into the boat. Steady . . . I've got you. Bloody hell! How many are there?'

It was the river police.

Jack bodily brought Pat Tyrell round in front of him, supporting her while the policeman dragged her onto the boat. He'd seen the police boat many times. It was an odd-looking craft, with a roller in the stern to help people get aboard. Bill had pointed it out to him one evening last summer when they'd walked along the Embankment. Suicide Station was the police name for Waterloo Bridge and the suicide boat was moored, day and night, under the shadow of the bridge. A policeman put a blanket round him – he was numbed with cold – and watched as they stoically brought Laurence Tyrell aboard.

'What on earth was behind it all?' asked Bill as they tramped home along the Embankment. Jack, who the river police obviously suspected either of being drunk and disorderly or suicidal, had cut through their protests by insisting they ring Rackham.

He'd refused the offer of a car, preferring to walk to get his circulation going. Despite the hot bath and a change of clothes he'd been given at the police station, he could still feel the Thames water gripping at his chest. Pat and Laurence Tyrell had been taken to hospital.

Bill, roused from his bed, had obviously expected Jack to be pleased that his forebodings had been justified, but Jack felt oddly flat. He only listened to his friend with half an ear. 'I didn't really believe you when you talked about an accident, you know. Are you sure that isn't what it was? High spirits gone astray and all that sort of thing? The sergeant on the boat told me your crowd were making so much of a racket on the bridge that they were standing by to fish someone out of the water.'

'I'm damn sure that's not what it was,' said Jack. 'I'll tell you something else, too. When I reached Pat Tyrell, I was sure that Larry Tyrell was trying to drown her. I hope she's all right. My God, that water was cold!' He made an effort to shed his apathy. 'What happened to Tim Lahone? He was mixed up in it all.'

'He's cooling his heels in the lock-up at the moment. He'll be had up in the morning for being drunk and disorderly. He'll probably get off with a fine.'

Jack smiled grimly. 'Good. I think I'll have a word with Mr Lahone tomorrow. He's either a complete fool or he knows more than's good for him.' He felt in his pocket for his pipe. 'Let me have some tobacco, Bill. My pouch was soaked.'

'Well, don't go adding assault and battery to your record.' He gave his pouch to Jack and they stood together, watching the moon and the soft lamplight play on the water below.

From down the river came the distant chimes of Big Ben. Curled up against the wall lay the usual line of sleepers, too poor to afford a bed.

Jack shivered. He usually loved London at night, when her silent streets gave off a sense of contented waiting, like a drowsy cat in front of a fire, but the city had lost her homely charm. It seemed alien and indifferent to his futile concerns.

'Is it worth it, Bill?' he asked quietly. 'I mean, all this rushing around we do, trying to work things out and make them hang together. Pat Tyrell could have died tonight. All three of us could. I'm meant to think that's important.' He nodded towards the line of tramps. 'It wouldn't matter to these poor devils, and yet their lives are as much in the balance as hers.' He shivered once more and was suddenly bone-achingly tired. He could have dropped down against the wall himself.

Bill clapped a friendly hand on his shoulder. 'It matters. Come on, let's get you home. It's not far. You need a hot toddy and a good night's sleep. You're simply feeling the reaction.'

'I suppose I am,' said Jack, and let himself be led away. There was a dull nag at the back of his mind as if he had overlooked something very important, but he couldn't rouse the energy to try and pin it down. It was connected to this remote, moonlit, unfriendly city, and his sensation of being on the edge of other people's lives. As they crossed the empty road, he looked back at the sleepers and wondered. They must feel the same.

Tim Lahone, his debt to society having been fixed and rendered at the sum of five pounds, got out of the taxi and stood blinking in the spring sunshine of St James's. A hand tapped him on the shoulder and he turned, recognition slowly dawning. 'Hello, Haldean, old man. I see you got out of the jolly old river, then.'

'I did, thank God. Damn cold, these midnight swimming larks. D'you fancy a drink? My club's just down the road.'

'Don't mind if I do,' said Lahone agreeably. 'Funny thing, running into you two days on the trot.' It wasn't funny at all, as Jack had trailed Lahone from Bow Street Magistrates' Court, but he didn't see fit to enlighten his companion.

'D'you know I was jugged last night?' continued Lahone. 'Damn cheek, I call it. There was an absolute swine on the bench. He fired off what he thought were some perfectly priceless remarks at my expense and lifted a fiver off me. Can you credit it? I mean, if you can't have a bit of fun, what's the point? There was no harm in it.'

'None whatsoever, apart from having to be fished out of the Thames,' agreed Jack as they turned into the Young Services. 'What's yours? Gin?' He nodded at Symington behind the bar. 'Two gins, please. Double for you, Lahone? I thought so. We'll take them into the back smoking room, old man. It tends to get rather cheerful in here at lunchtime and you look as if you've got a bit of a head.'

Once in the smoking room, Lahone subsided into a big leather armchair and raised his glass to his mouth. 'That's better,' he said, wiping his moustache. He took a cigarette from Jack's proffered case and rubbed his forehead with the heel of his hand. 'Thanks. Bloody police. That first lot weren't even wearing uniform. How was I to know they were rozzers? And the bed they expect you to sleep on! It's planks, you know, just planks. Have you ever been jugged? Don't do it, old boy. It leaves you fit for nothing.'

Jack smiled. 'That's exactly what I'd have said you were fit for, myself.'

Lahone gave him a puzzled look. 'What d'you mean, old boy?'

'I mean, old boy,' said Jack, still smiling, 'that you've rotted yourself with drink and, if that wasn't enough, you're lousy with dope.' He waved Lahone's protest aside. 'Dry up, man. If I couldn't guess from your looks, I could tell from the marks on your arm. If you don't want people to know, pull your shirt cuff down. What d'you use?'

'What the hell's it to you?'

Jack blew out a smoke ring. 'Nothing, my dear old scream. If you want to go to perdition faster than your maker intended, be my guest. However, what *is* something to me, and what I could really get quite upset about, is the idea that you've been feeding coke or some other foul thing to Pat Tyrell. Now that is naughty. There's a good stiff sentence for dope traffickers and they wouldn't put you in Bow Street, either.'

There was a thread of menace behind Jack's light tone that made Lahone pause and swallow. 'Look, old man, you've got this all wrong. I don't dope . . .' He was brought up sharply by Jack's look. 'All right, I admit it. I do occasionally, but it's only a bit of fun. Livens things up, don't you know? But I haven't given any to Pat. I offered her some – just as a friend, you understand – but she wouldn't have it. I've gone off Pat, anyhow. It was fun trying to get her away from that stuffed shirt, Jaggard, but Tyrell warned me off and . . . Well, there's other fish in the sea.'

'So why did you inflict yourself on us last night? If Tyrell had warned you off, that is.'

'He . . .' Lahone paused and looked round for an escape. Jack, lounging beside the fireplace, was in the direct line of the door. 'We just happened to see you, that's all.'

Jack shook his head. 'Try again.' Lahone swallowed and remained silent. Jack crushed out his cigarette. 'As your memory obviously isn't all it could be, let me help you out. Tyrell asked you, didn't he?'

'So what if he did? There's no law against it, is there?'

'And did Tyrell suggest you climb on the bridge?'

Lahone stood up. 'I've had enough of this. I don't have to answer questions from you or anyone else. I'm off.'

He tried to walk to the door, but his way was blocked by Jack. Infuriated, Lahone aimed a punch but Jack caught the flailing fist easily and sent him sprawling to the floor.

Lahone half rose and hit out again, and this time he found himself face down on the rug with his arm twisted up behind his back in an agonizing grip. 'Let go, damn you! That hurts.'

Jack, on one knee beside Lahone, relaxed the pressure. 'Did Tyrell ask you?'

Lahone writhed and Jack tightened his grip.

'Well?'

'Yes, damnit!' The grip slackened. 'Keep your bloody hands to yourself. Tyrell told me to meet him at the Savoy.'

'When did he ask you?'

'Yesterday afternoon.'

'What else did he tell you to do?'

'Nothing . . . Ouch!' The grip tightened. 'He wanted me to make up to Pat. Be friendly to her . . . For Christ's sake!' The grip eased off. 'Once in the Savoy I had to suggest going on to the Fortune. Bloody dreary place. Then, when we were all outside, he told me to climb up on the bridge and get Pat up there too. I never meant any harm. It was only a bit of fun.'

'What did he give you for your bit of fun?'

'Nothing . . . Ow! Fifty quid. I need it. I get snow from Eve but she's been keeping me short, the cow, because I haven't paid her for the last lot.'

'Did Eve or anyone else give Pat any dope?'

'No. Really, no! They didn't, I tell you. I don't know what happened to Pat. She got bloody drunk. She had to be drunk. Totally canned. She didn't have time to take anything unless it was a pill or something, and Pat wouldn't do that. She wouldn't touch it, honestly. Pat's stuffy about that sort of thing.'

Jack let go and Lahone cautiously sat up. Jack knelt back, his elbow casually draped over his knee. Lahone gave him a frightened glance and nursed his arm. 'If I'd known what was going to happen I'd have never gone along with it but . . . but . . .' His voice broke. 'You don't know what it's like. There's times when

I'm desperate but Eve won't give me anything like enough. I
don't even know Tyrell properly. We've had a drink together a
few times, that's all. I can't stand the man, if you want the truth.
He gives me the creeps.'

Jack stood up and, dusting off the knees of his trousers, kicked
the Persian rug back into place. 'That shows astonishing good
taste on your part. And Lahone . . .'

'What?' asked Lahone, his hand on the doorknob.

'Don't mention this conversation to Tyrell, will you? He might
be cross.'

'Don't worry,' said Lahone, with a shudder. 'That's the last
thing I'll do.'

'Hello, bathing belle,' said Bill with a grin as Jack walked into
his office. 'You'll be glad to know that the river police have been
convinced of your innocence. I didn't say as much last night, but
it was just as well you followed your hunch and were there. In
fact . . .' He coloured slightly and looked down at his blotting
pad. 'It was a brave bit of work, diving in like that.'

'Oh, drop it,' said Jack easily, pulling up a chair. 'Have you
heard how my fellow swimmers are?'

'Mrs Tyrell's been kept in hospital, but Laurence Tyrell's been
released.'

'Hmm. It might be as well if it stayed that way, at least until
Pat Tyrell's signed her will.'

'Jack . . .' Bill broke the point of his pencil on the blotter. 'I
know you said Tyrell was trying to drown his wife, but how can
you be sure? Don't forget, Tyrell fell in too.'

'He'd have to if he was going to finish the job, wouldn't he?
I know that's what happened. I've just seen Tim Lahone and he
spilled the beans good and proper.'

'Tim Lahone? I interviewed him myself first thing this morning
and he didn't say anything.'

'That's because you asked him nicely. I didn't, I'm afraid. The
little swine took a swipe at me and I . . . Well, let's just say I
objected.'

Bill's lips twitched. 'Not something we could do, but that
gentleman deserves everything that's coming to him. Is he still
in one piece?'

'Perfectly whole and entire. You know he dopes? Apparently

he gets the stuff from his sister. It'd be worth your while keeping an eye on her. Eve Lahone keeps Tim on short commons, and he was anxious to bump up his supply. Tyrell saw Lahone yesterday afternoon and offered him fifty quid, which Our Tim proposes to stick in his arm, to go along with his plans last night. Tyrell asked Tim and his crowd to show up at the Savoy and suggest we all went on to the Fortune. Now, the interesting thing about the Fortune, as far as the Lahones and their ilk are concerned, is that it must be one of the dullest clubs going. So why did Tyrell want us to go there? The answer, for which I get no marks because it's too easy, is that all the other clubs mentioned lie to the west, round Piccadilly, whereas the Fortune is off Surrey Street. To get to it we walked along the Embankment past Waterloo Bridge. Now the sight of the bridge apparently inflamed Lahone to become an extra in an acrobatic act, but he tells me that's what Tyrell told him to do and to get Pat up there as well.'

'Couldn't he be making that bit up? He might be feeling guilty and want to shove the blame onto Tyrell.'

Jack grinned and took a cigarette. 'Not ruddy likely. I had to be pretty persuasive to get him to own up to that. It's clever, isn't it? Tyrell can't be blamed. Even the choice of partners was done through Lahone. Tyrell skipped up there taking with him a girl called Binky, who really should know better, so Lahone turned to his companion, Pat Tyrell. It all seemed like the impulse of the moment.'

'Pat Tyrell was pretty far gone, by all accounts. Did Tyrell get her drunk? I heard she was half-seas over. Apparently she climbed up on the bridge off her own bat.'

Jack shook his head. 'I can't work that out. She was perfectly sober when the Lahones joined us, but then Tyrell contrived to spill her drink and offered her his own instead. Now, before she drank it, she was sober. After she drank it, she was tanked. Obviously there was something not as mother makes in that champagne, but what it was defeats me. I can't think of anything that works that fast.'

'So what's behind it?' asked Bill again. 'I know you think it's an attempt to stop Pat Tyrell signing her will, but will or no will, if she dies, Tyrell's out of pocket.'

'He gets nothing at the moment, true. But wait seven years until Helston's death can be legally presumed and he'll be in a strong position to argue that, as Pat Tyrell's next of kin, the money which should have gone to her should come to him.'

Bill clicked his tongue in dissatisfaction. 'He'd probably have to slug it out in the courts. He couldn't bank on it.'

'He could bank on losing the lot if that will was signed.'

'What can I do?' Bill put his hands wide. 'I can't arrest Tyrell. I've got nothing to arrest him for.'

'What I'm concerned about is Pat Tyrell's safety. Why don't we get hold of Mr Stafford, the solicitor, and take him to the hospital?'

'It'd be a waste of time. Mrs Tyrell was very distressed when they pulled her out of the river. She was given a dose of morphine in hospital. She'll be fast asleep for hours yet.'

'Damn!' Jack got up and, hands in pockets, walked moodily to the open window. Below him, past the Embankment, lay the barges on the river. An occasional cry and the faraway chug of an engine drifted up, mixed with the faded music of a great city. On the Embankment a motor horn sounded and he thought of the poor wretches lying so quietly last night, curled up against the wall, while his own drama played out on the bridge. It was extraordinary the difference light made. Now, with the hazy sun catching the water, London was London again, noisy, jostling, smoky, alive. Last night it had been like a city of the living dead . . .

The living dead. His stomach turned over. *That's* where this had started. Find Mark Helston, living or dead.

Forcing his voice to be level, he turned and looked at Bill. 'I say, you remember we were looking for Mark Helston? I've an idea where he might be.'

Jack waited impatiently. How long did it take to get a file? Once again he read the description of Mark Helston, but without taking in the words; he knew them too well to concentrate. Bill, sensing his restlessness, laid a hand on his shoulder. 'Steady, old lad. These things take time, you know.'

Then – thank God! – there was a respectful knock at the door. 'The file you requested, sir.'

Bill took the folder and spreading it on the desk, opened it. 'This is a record of pauper and vagrant deaths for January. If you're right, it should be here. Let's have a look at the tenth . . .'

Jack craned forward eagerly. 'There's three on the tenth. It was a lousy night. Albert Hope . . . he's no good. He's too old. Mary Davenport . . . it's not her, of course. What about this chap? Richard Wainstall, age twenty-seven. Died of exposure, Blackfriars Bridge, Victoria Embankment, during the night of January the ninth. Found by P.C. Brewer, number . . .'

Rackham read the brief entry rapidly. 'The description could easily be Helston's, if that's any comfort to you. There's no dental record noted. There wouldn't be, of course, but that's the only way we'll prove it now. Let's see if there's anyone else who turned up later in the month.'

They read through the descriptions of vagrants together but Jack returned to the entry for Richard Wainstall. He tapped the file with his finger. 'If I'm right, the man buried as Richard Wainstall is Mark Helston. We'll have to dig him up. How soon can we do it?'

'It'll need permission from the coroner,' said Bill doubtfully. 'If I hurry it through then we might be lucky and get it done tomorrow. Are you certain this is Mark Helston?'

Jack hesitated. 'I *was* certain when I first thought of it. It seemed to explain such a devil of a lot. All I can say is that I thought there might be a suitable body and, as there is a suitable body, it seems silly not to take a shufti at it.'

'Exhumation isn't something we do lightly, you know,' said Bill doubtfully. 'If we are going to apply to dig this poor chap up, I'd like something a bit more definite than your inspired guess.'

Jack shook his head. 'I'm sorry. At the moment that's all I've got.'

Bill sighed in irritation. 'Whatever gave you the idea?'

'It was seeing those men on the embankment last night; so many men who had slipped out of normal life. It struck me when I looked out of the window that if you died on the street, then your body would be tidied away and no more questions asked. We asked ourselves right at the start where you would hide a body. I think the answer is that you don't. You leave it in full view.' His mouth twisted. 'It's the old proverb. If you want to hide a thing, put it under the light. I think when light dawned on the tenth of January, Mark Helston was on the embankment.' He reached for a cigarette. 'But there's only one way to find out.'

'Oh hell,' said Bill unhappily. 'I'll apply to the coroner.'

THIRTEEN

The coroner was applied to, the body interred in a pauper's grave in Brookwood cemetery exhumed, and a comparison of Mark Helston's dental records with the corpse showed that the man buried as Richard Wainstall was, indeed, Mark Helston.

'The Chief thinks you've taken to black magic,' said Rackham over the telephone to Jack. 'He was very dubious about applying to the coroner but when we found it was Mark Helston, he was stunned. "Brilliant" was the word he used.'

There was silence on the other end of the line.

'What's the matter?' asked Bill. 'You've just pulled off the coup of a lifetime. You should be pretty pleased with yourself.'

'I don't think pleased is the right word,' said Jack. 'I'm glad we've found the poor beggar, but we still don't know how he died. Besides that, how on earth am I going to break it to Mr Hunt?'

'Come with me,' offered Rackham. 'I'm off to Neville Square to tell him.'

'I can't say I'm looking forward to this,' said Jack, as he and Rackham walked towards Neville Square. 'I'm no doctor, Bill, but I wouldn't say old Mr Hunt's heart was up to much. I'm a bit nervous in case the news sees him off altogether.'

Bill shrugged. 'He asked you to find his great-nephew and that's what you've done. If he doesn't think it's an outstanding piece of work, I'm going to tell him.'

Jack looked at him wryly. 'If you're expecting enthusiasm you'll be disappointed. We've only got half a story. We've found Helston all right, but who put Helston in Richard Wainstall's place? And who the dickens is Richard Wainstall anyway?'

'Now that I can tell you. I looked him up. He's aged twenty-seven, served with the Royal Engineers, promoted to corporal, and was badly gassed at Cambrai. He was demobbed in 1919 and had a variety of casual jobs. He was a doorman for a time, a night watchman and a builder's labourer, but had to give that up because of a chest complaint. He had a sister who lives in Suffolk, but she hadn't seen him for months before he apparently died. As far as I can tell, he has absolutely no connection with Mark Helston, Hunt Coffee or anyone else we've come across.'

'So where's Wainstall now? He's either disappeared on purpose, leaving his identity to Helston, or he's dead himself. Of the two, I'm inclined to think he's dead. If he were alive, it would give him a dickens of a hold over Helston's killer.'

'The Chief thinks he's dead,' said Bill. 'He was only throwing out ideas, but he suggested that the man we found in Gower Street wasn't Valdez but Richard Wainstall.'

Jack wrinkled his nose. 'It can't be. If the murderer had gone to that sort of trouble, he'd hardly leave the Gower Street body untouched. He couldn't have known it was going to be so long before it was discovered. It could have been found within hours. I know Wainstall was on his uppers, poor devil, but someone would have recognized his photo eventually. If the body had been disfigured, then yes, I'd think there was something to be said for the notion but as it is, it won't wash.'

'His other idea,' said Bill heavily, 'is that Valdez is still alive and he murdered both Helston and Wainstall.'

'That's loopy. Again, if that was the case, the Gower Street body would be disfigured in some way.'

'That's what I said. I put it a little more tactfully, of course. I'm sure Valdez is dead. Not only has he utterly vanished from the world, he had a good bit of money tucked away in a bank account in São Paulo. That's still there. From what we know of the man, he liked the good life and he'd need that money to live it.'

'This case is like one of those Russian dolls,' said Jack grumpily. 'However many you open, there's always another one inside.'

Bill looked at Jack and grinned. 'My money's on Jaggard but I know who you want to pin it on.'

'Go on, mind reader. Who do I want to finger?'

'Tyrell, of course. You're itching to find a way it could have been him, but you can't.'

'Go to the top of the class.'

'I knew it!' said Bill in triumph.

'Helston's death does benefit him,' put in Jack slyly.

'But he didn't *know* it was going to, did he? As far as anyone could guess, all Helston's grandmother had to leave was a cupboard full of old china and a couple of cats. Tyrell's account of his motives for coming back to London may be as dodgy as you like, but his account of his actions has got a lot of supporting evidence, and those actions clear him of Helston's murder.'

Jack sighed. 'You're right, old thing.'

They walked for a few paces in silence. 'You know who we've left out as a possible?' said Jack. 'Frederick Hunt. If things are amiss at Hunt Coffee, he very well might have a motive for knocking Mark Helston on the head.'

'But he didn't have the opportunity. He was at that Mansion House dinner, remember?'

'I remember,' said Jack gloomily. 'Anyway, none of this has helped in the least with the immediate problem. What on earth do we say to old Mr Hunt?'

They turned the corner into Neville Square.

It was clear that something was up. The door to number 14 was open and Meredith Smith was on the doorstep, looking feverishly up and down the square. He ran to them with relief. His hair was dishevelled and his face was strained with worry. 'Thank God you're here! I phoned Scotland Yard.'

'Merry, what's happened?'

Meredith Smith swallowed hard. 'Murder!'

'Murder?' Jack felt sick. 'Not Pat?'

'Pat? Of course not.' His voice wavered. 'It's H.R.H.'

'What!' roared Bill. He sprang up the steps. Smith made to go after him but Jack stopped him.

'Merry, wait! Tell me what happened.'

'It's awful,' said Meredith. He was pale and spoke in little, jerky sentences. 'It was bad enough when Sheila was killed. This is dreadful. When's it going to end, Jack? Can't you stop it? When I saw him there . . .'

'Merry! Tell me what happened.' The note of command in Jack's voice had its effect. Meredith took a deep breath.

'H.R.H. was shot. It's a bullet through the side of his head. It must've been instant.'

'D'you know when?'

Meredith shook his head. 'Sometime this afternoon. Tyrell

came to lunch and left about three o'clock. He must have done it, Jack, he absolutely must have.'

'*Tyrell* did it?'

'It simply has to be him. Fields said he'd been to lunch. Poor Fields has taken it very badly. Frederick Hunt's here. You'd better go in. I've come out to look for the police. They're taking ages . . . here they are now.'

A police car, its bell ringing, swung round the top of the square and squealed to a halt. Two uniformed officers got out. 'Are you Captain Smith? We had a telephone call. Is Inspector Rackham here?'

'Yes,' said Meredith. 'Go on in.'

The two men ran quickly up the steps.

Jack caught hold of Meredith's arm. 'Before you follow them, tell me everything you know. Mr Hunt saw Tyrell, you say?'

'Yes, that's right. Shouldn't you be getting after him, Jack?'

'He'll keep for a few minutes. What happened after Tyrell had gone? Did anyone see Mr Hunt?'

'No. They'd been in the drawing room, but when Fields went into the room to clear away the coffee cups after Tyrell had left, H.R.H. wasn't there. Frederick Hunt arrived home about half three or so. He knew Tyrell had been, because he asked Fields if Tyrell was still here. When Fields told him Tyrell had left, he went off to his own study at the back of the house. I arrived about six o'clock or so. That's . . .' he glanced at his watch. 'Dear God, it's only twenty minutes ago.'

'Why are you here?'

'I've been dropping in the last few evenings. H.R.H. enjoyed being brought up to date on what was happening in the firm. I don't think Frederick Hunt tells him much and I was keeping him posted. Anyway, I stood in the hall while Fields went to root out H.R.H. for me. He looked in the drawing room, but he wasn't there, and then Fields went into the library. The poor devil came out as white as a sheet. I honestly thought he was going to faint, Jack. I pushed past him, and there at the table was H.R.H. It was absolutely horrible. Fields went to get Frederick Hunt. He rushed downstairs and then we rang the police. Do come into the house, Jack.'

They walked into the hall. Fields was sitting on a chair by the foot of the stairs, staring sightlessly in front of him. Jack put a hand on his shoulder. 'You need a good stiff drink, man, and so does Captain Smith.'

The butler looked at him, evidently not hearing the words. His eyes were watery. 'No one ever had a better master, sir. I've been with Mr Hunt all my life. All my life. He said to me only yesterday . . .' The butler's voice trembled. 'He said "I don't know what I would have done without you. You've been more than a servant to me . . ." He had such a lot to endure. I always did my best.'

'I know you did,' said Jack gently. 'D'you think you could give Captain Smith a drink? He really needs one, you know.'

Fields stirred as years of training reasserted itself. 'Captain Smith? The master enjoyed his visits. He looked forward to them.' He blinked and his eyes focused. 'Why, Captain Smith, you're here, sir.' He raised himself heavily to his feet.

'Look after him, Merry,' hissed Jack. 'He's bowled over. Don't leave the poor blighter alone. When the doctor arrives, I'll send him along.'

'Right-oh.' Meredith touched the butler on the arm. 'Shall we go to your pantry, Fields? We'll be more comfortable in there. You show me the way.'

Jack walked into the library.

Harold Hunt was sprawled at the desk, a blackened mess of blood disfiguring the white hair over his ear. He looked like a wispy doll. The pistol was under his outstretched hand. Bill and the two police officers were standing by him and Frederick Hunt was by the fireplace.

Bill looked up as he entered. 'Hello, Jack. He's dead all right. We're expecting Doctor Roude.'

Jack nodded. 'Yes. Meredith Smith says Laurence Tyrell did it.'

'What?' Bill swung round on Hunt. 'Tyrell's been here? Why didn't you tell me?'

'Really, Inspector, it never occurred to me,' said Frederick Hunt primly. 'As for Captain Smith's disgraceful suggestion, I would advise you to dismiss it completely.' He licked his lips nervously. 'It's obvious my unhappy father took his own life.'

'That's a great deal more than I know,' growled Bill. 'When did Tyrell leave the house?'

Frederick Hunt polished his glasses. 'Before I arrived home at half three. More than that I cannot tell you. For more precise information you will have to question Fields.'

'The poor devil isn't in a fit state to answer any questions,' put in Jack. 'Smith's looking after him at the moment.'

'Maybe Mr Tyrell will enlighten us. He's at the Fitzroy, or was, at any rate.' Bill turned to the two policemen. 'Conway, Hawkins, call the Yard and ask for another couple of men to join you at the Fitzroy Palace Hotel. It's on Rupert Street off Piccadilly. If Tyrell isn't at the hotel, leave two men there and find him. I want Tyrell at the Yard for questioning by the time I get back. Off you go.'

The two men left and Bill shifted his eyes back to Frederick Hunt. 'Mr Hunt, you have my sympathies, sir. What makes you think your father killed himself?'

Frederick Hunt tutted in irritation. 'Any other suggestion is absurd, Inspector. The gun which my unhappy father used has been in his possession for many years. I cannot, simply cannot, credit that Mr Tyrell would walk in here and shoot my father in broad daylight. What possible reason could he have? It must be self-inflicted. It absolutely has to be.'

'We'll know more about that when the doctor comes. In the meantime, Mr Hunt, perhaps you could give us an account of your own actions.'

'Really, I . . .'

'What time did you arrive home, sir?'

'About half past three, Inspector. I've been at the office all day. My chauffeur drove me here.'

'Did you know where your father kept his gun?'

'Yes. It was kept in its case on the bookshelf, but the bullets were kept in the drawer of his desk. It's ridiculous to suppose that Tyrell could have found both the gun and the bullets, loaded it and shot my father.'

'Did you see your father, sir?'

'I did not.'

'You wanted to see Tyrell, didn't you?' put in Jack.

'I . . . er . . .' Frederick Hunt polished his glasses again. 'Yes. I knew he intended to lunch with my father and I wondered if he was still here. Purely a matter of courtesy, you understand.'

'What was Tyrell's business with Mr Hunt?'

'I really don't know. I imagine it concerned my niece, Patricia.' He stopped as the door opened and Doctor Roude entered the room.

The doctor made a quick examination of old Mr Hunt's body before standing back, shaking his head. 'Well, Inspector, this is a sorry case. The poor old soul doesn't look as if he had much longer to go as it was.'

He looked at his thermometer, glanced at his pocket-watch and did a rapid calculation. 'It's twenty-five to seven now. Death occurred about three and a half hours ago. I'd say you were looking at half two to four o'clock. Death would have been instantaneous. Anyone hear it? No?'

'Could it be suicide, Doctor?' asked Rackham

Roude put the thermometer back in its case and rested his hands on the desk, looking carefully at the body. 'It's the obvious solution, but in my experience it's not the old who take their own lives. It does happen, of course, usually if a man's been told he's facing a long and painful illness, but by and large it's the young who feel they can't face things any longer. By the time you get to his age, you've faced most of the things life has to throw at you. What about the fingerprints on the pistol?'

'It's yet to be tested but it's easy enough to wipe a pistol and press someone's hand round it,' said Bill.

'M'yes. Was there a note?'

Bill shook his head.

'That surprises me.' Dr Roude looked round the tidy library. 'He was obviously a man with a sense of order. It's odd he didn't leave a note.'

'Can you see Fields, the butler?' asked Jack. 'He discovered the body and he's dreadfully cut up over it.'

'I'd like to question him,' said Bill quickly.

'Let me see him first,' said the doctor. 'Where is he? In his pantry? Don't worry, I can find my own way.'

'Now, Mr Hunt,' said Bill, when the doctor had left. 'I think we'll all be more comfortable in another room. The police photographer and the fingerprint men will arrive shortly and then we can make arrangements for your father to be taken away. I still have some questions for you.'

'By all means, Inspector, but I would like to say that, profound as my respect for the medical profession is, I must insist you treat my father's death as suicide.'

'Insist?' repeated Bill with a slight note of warning.

'Insist, sir.'

'Bill!' broke in Jack, sharply.

Bill looked up, annoyed at the interruption. Jack was standing by the bookcase, holding out a paperknife.

Bill's eyes widened. The knife had an inlaid steel blade and a hilt made of strands of twisted silver wire set into a silver bar. It was identical to the weapon they had found in Gower Street.

Bill's voice was a whisper of astonishment. 'What the devil is that doing here?' He took it from Jack and turned to Frederick Hunt. 'Can you tell us anything about this knife?'

Frederick Hunt adjusted his glasses and blinked at the knife. 'That's my father's paperknife, Inspector.'

'Where did it come from?'

'My nephew, Mark, gave it to him, I believe. He had it made during the war when he was out in the East.'

'Did he have any others made of a similar pattern?'

Frederick Hunt thought for a moment. 'I think there were three knives in all. He gave one to his grandmother, one to his sister and the other to my father. Is it of any consequence, Inspector?'

'It might very well be, Mr Hunt. If you don't mind, I'll hold on to it for the time being. I'll issue a receipt, of course. Now sir, if we could go to another room . . .'

In the drawing room Frederick Hunt repeated at some length what they had already heard: he'd returned home at half three, went straight to his own study at the back of the house and remained there until he was alerted by the row at six o'clock.

'Do you think he did it?' asked Bill, once Frederick Hunt had departed.

Jack frowned. 'I think he *might* have done it, but that's a different kettle of fish. Frederick Hunt knew Tyrell had lunched here. He was interested enough to ask if Tyrell was still here, but wasn't, apparently, interested enough to ask his father what had been said. I think that's odd.' He shrugged. 'You don't need me to tell you that Frederick Hunt could've easily gone into the library, shot his father, and then disappeared into his study.'

There was a knock on the door and Cartland, the forensic man, looked round the door. 'We're ready, sir, if you want to join us.'

When Bill returned to the room, Jack was standing by Mr Hunt's old chair, looking at the tray of medicines on the table.

'The pistol had old Mr Hunt's fingerprints on it, sure enough,' said Bill. 'I must say, they looked perfectly natural. Could it be suicide, Jack?'

'That's what Frederick Hunt wants us to think,' said Jack, frowning at the tray. 'He certainly didn't like the idea that Tyrell was responsible.'

'If it comes to that, why aren't you jumping up and down at the thought that Tyrell did it? I'd have thought you'd have leapt at the idea.'

'Because it's the wrong method. Tyrell's an intelligent man. This is far too obvious.' He took a spill from the jar on the mantelpiece and pointed at a brown bottle on the tray. 'Look at this, Bill. It's a bottle of ether. It's nearly empty.'

Bill walked across the room and looked to where Jack was pointing. 'Well? What of it? Ether's common enough.'

'Yes. It's occasionally prescribed for stomach upsets, which is, I imagine, why Mr Hunt had a bottle, but you must have read about people drinking it for fun. A couple of spoonfuls and the effect is as if you were very, very drunk.' He paused. 'Pat Tyrell seemed very, very drunk.'

Bill snapped his fingers. 'Of course! So you're saying that Tyrell laced her champagne with ether? Hang on. Why didn't he just take the bottle?'

'He didn't want the bottle to be missed. He might have got another bottle altogether, of course, but I bet he didn't want to be seen buying it. His fingerprints should be on it. No, blast, they won't be. Say I'm right and Tyrell got the urge to see off Pat after she'd told him about her will. Tyrell called here for Pat in full evening dress. White tie, white waistcoat and, damn it, white gloves. He comes early and gets shown into here to wait, tips some into a bottle he's brought with him, and bingo! And once again, I can't prove a ruddy thing.'

'That'd work if he knew he was going to be alone in here,' said Bill.

'Fields will know the household routine. Tyrell's been here so often he'll know it too.'

'The doctor should have finished with Fields by now. I must say, I'll feel a lot happier when we've got our hands on Laurence Tyrell. Apart from anything else, I want to know what old Mr Hunt said to him. It might give us some idea of his state of mind.'

'Fields might be able to tell us that, too. Let's go and root him out.'

They went down into the kitchen where an elderly maid directed them to the butler's pantry, a comfortable room in the basement of the house. Fields was sitting by the green-baize covered table with the doctor in attendance. Meredith Smith, brandy and soda in hand, had propped himself by the wooden draining board beside the sink.

Dr Roude looked up as they walked in. 'I was just coming to find you. Fields feels a great deal better now, don't you, Fields?'

'Are you up to answering some questions, Mr Fields?' asked Bill.

The butler looked at him warily. 'I've never had anything to do with the police.'

'Of course you haven't,' said Jack. The butler looked at him and blinked in recognition. 'We're just going to ask you a few questions,' he continued, keeping his voice cheerfully matter-of-fact. 'You'll know the answers to most of them and if you don't, just tell us that, too. But the Inspector and I know you'd like to help. I'm sure you want to see this sorry business cleared up as soon as possible, don't you?' The butler sat up marginally straighter and nodded. 'Good man,' said Jack, softly. He glanced at Rackham. Bill nodded for him to carry on.

'Do you remember Wednesday? I was here, if you recall, and so were Mr and Mrs Tyrell.'

'That's the day Mrs Pat had her accident, isn't it, sir?' His voice became stronger. 'It was a mercy she was saved. You helped her, didn't you, sir? That's the day Mr Waldron came to see the master. I remember.'

'Well done.' Jack drew out a chair and sat down. 'Now, on Wednesday evening, Mrs Pat went out with Mr Tyrell. Did Mr Tyrell call for her?'

'Of course, sir.'

'And was Mrs Pat ready when he called?'

The butler gave a ghost of a smile. 'Why no, sir. You know what ladies are. He had to wait at least twenty minutes before she came down. I showed him into the drawing room and he waited there.'

'Was Mr Hunt in the drawing room?'

'No, sir.' Fields looked shocked. 'The master always went

upstairs at half nine, unless we had company, and even then he never stayed up much beyond ten. With him not being as young as he was, it took him a long time to get ready for bed.'

'Was Mr Frederick Hunt in the drawing room?'

Fields shook his head. 'Mr Frederick was at his club that evening. He often dines there. I'm afraid Mr Tyrell had to wait by himself. I hope there's nothing wrong in that, sir.'

'Nothing at all,' said Jack with a smile. 'That's Wednesday evening out of the way. Now what about yesterday? That's Thursday. You must have heard the news about Mrs Pat's accident.'

There was an interrogative grunt from Bill. Jack gently kicked out to warn him to be quiet.

'Indeed we did, sir.' The butler sat up eagerly. 'The hospital telephoned in the morning to say that Mrs Pat had had an accident but she was out of danger. The master was terribly shaken. He wanted to go to the hospital, but they told him Mrs Pat wasn't up to receiving visitors. He sent out for the late editions of the newspapers and read them all. Then, instead of going to his club that afternoon as usual, he went into the library.'

'I know it's not your place to enquire, Fields, but do you know what your master was doing in the library? It might be important,' Jack added, seeing Fields bridle slightly.

'I think he was writing, sir. If he had any correspondence, he always went in the library.' The butler thought for a moment. 'There were some letters in the postbag, sir.' The butler paused. 'If you'll excuse me for saying so, I think it was something to do with his legal affairs.'

'Why's that, Fields?' asked Jack, keeping the excitement out of his voice.

The butler coughed. 'The master had been so long in the library that I took the liberty of going in on the pretence of hearing him ring. He had been so out of sorts that morning I was afraid he might have taken ill and been unable to reach the bell.'

He was encouraged by Jack's smile of approval. 'He told me off for hearing things – I expected that – and sat quite still, as if thinking something out.' Fields swallowed manfully. 'Then he said he knew I hadn't heard the bell, and that I was more than a servant to him. He told me to ring up Mr Stafford, his solicitor, and ask him to step round that afternoon. Mr Stafford came about two o'clock and they spent a long time in the library together.'

The butler frowned. 'There was an odd incident after Mr Stafford arrived, sir. The window cleaners were here yesterday afternoon. Mr Hunt ran the bell and told me to show them both into the library. They stayed for about ten minutes. I don't know why the master should want to see them.'

Jack felt Bill's eyes slap on the back of his neck, but ignored him. 'We'll ask Mr Stafford about that, Fields. Now for this morning. This is going to be very hard for you, I know. Mr Tyrell came to lunch, I believe?'

'Yes, sir. There was a consommé, a cutlet and a sweet omelette. They took their coffee in the drawing room afterwards. The master always went in the drawing room after lunch. He some-times suffered from colic after meals and his medicines were there. He could take them himself without ringing for me.'

'That was very thoughtful of him,' said Jack. 'He was all right today, was he? No upsets at all?'

'Perfectly well, thank you, sir. In fact he seemed more vigorous than usual. He told me to leave him and Mr Tyrell alone, and they would see to themselves.'

'Were he and Mr Tyrell on amicable terms?'

'Oh yes, sir. Over lunch I heard the master compliment Mr Tyrell on his escape from drowning. He wanted to hear all about it.'

'And you didn't go in the drawing room again?'

'Not until I went to clear away the coffee cups, sir. I saw Mr Tyrell in the hall. I was surprised the bell hadn't rung, but Mr Tyrell explained that he didn't want to disturb me, and that the master had dropped off for a nap.' Fields swallowed again. 'I didn't want to disturb him either, sir, so I didn't go into the drawing room for about half an hour, and then, of course, the master wasn't there.'

'How did Mr Tyrell seem when you showed him to the door?'

'Much as usual, sir.'

Jack rose to his feet. 'Thank you very much, Fields. You've been a great help to us by putting things in order. We might have some more questions later, but we'll leave you alone for now.' He turned his head. 'Merry, old son, can I have a word with you?'

'Certainly, Jack.'

With Bill and Merry following, Jack led the way back up to the drawing room and closed the door. 'Whew! I think we're safe to talk in here. That poor beggar, Fields, has been knocked for six all right. Now, Merry, what I want to know is this. Is there anything dodgy going on at Hunt Coffee and did H.R.H. suspect Frederick Hunt was mixed up in it?'

Meredith hesitated. 'Just between us, I don't know but I think so. H.R.H. certainly didn't *know* but had his suspicions of Frederick Hunt.'

'Hang on,' said Bill, forcefully. 'I want to know about this visit from the solicitor. Why on earth didn't you ask Fields about it? I wanted to, but you seemed so damned anxious I shouldn't interrupt your Svengali act.'

'Because if you had interrupted my Svengali act, old fruit, we'd still be there. Fields only talked to me as freely as he did because I'd been a visitor to the house. Besides, what on earth's the point of asking him? A stiff old bird like H.R.H. wouldn't chat about his legal affairs to the butler. Stafford's the obvious person to get hold of. If H.R.H.'s suspicions had got to the point of actual knowledge, I bet he'd cut Frederick out of his will and Frederick might very well react by plugging Dad before it could go any further.'

'You've got an absolute bee in your bonnet about wills and whatnot,' grumbled Bill. 'Still, you're right about one thing, and that's contacting Stafford.' The telephone in the hall rang. 'I'd better answer that,' said Bill. 'It might be the Yard.'

He strode into the hall and picked up the telephone. 'Hello? This is Inspector Rackham speaking. Conway? Have you picked up Tyrell?' There was a staccato buzz of conversation from the other end of the line. 'He's *what*? I don't believe . . . Yes, yes, I see that. Stay there. I'll be as quick as I can. For heaven's sake keep the hotel staff out of that room.'

He put down the phone and turned to them with an odd expression. 'We've lost our chance to question Laurence Tyrell.'

'Has he run for it?' demanded Meredith. 'I told you to get after him, Jack.'

Bill shook his head. 'He's not run for it. He's dead.'

FOURTEEN

I t was the power of the popular press which made Sir Douglas Lynton cancel his Saturday game of golf.

He had been dressing for dinner on Friday evening when Rackham had called with the news and, white tie still in hand, he had listened with a steadily lengthening face. 'Meet me at the Yard at one o'clock tomorrow,' he said. 'Haldean better be there as well. He seems to know as much about it as anyone.'

He thought wistfully of his golf, then dismissed the idea. Jacob Carroll, the crusading proprietor of the Mercury group, who had some hard things to say about Scotland Yard, was a fixture in the clubhouse on Saturday afternoons. The headlines in the papers would be quite bad enough without an account of how the Assistant Commissioner ignored four unsolved murders, a suspected suicide and Jaggard still at large in favour of golf.

When he saw the Saturday newspapers he was glad he'd cancelled his game. *Tragedy Stalks Hunt Coffee!* screamed the *Messenger* and, ominously from the *Mercury*, *Scotland Yard At A Loss!*

Scotland Yard, embodied in the person of William Rackham, looked downright tired. 'The trouble is, sir, that Tyrell's murder has really upset the apple cart. Major Haldean had Tyrell pegged as a would-be killer and, after hearing what Lahone had to say, I agreed wholeheartedly.'

'Not that,' put in Jack, 'we could've got Lahone to admit it in court.'

'No, we probably couldn't,' said Bill. 'However, when we arrived at Neville Square and found old Mr Hunt dead, there was no doubt in my mind it was Tyrell we were after.' He compressed his mouth tightly. 'However, I was wrong.'

'Strychnine poisoning,' said Sir Douglas, reading from the file. 'I see that's been confirmed as the cause of Tyrell's death.'

'Yes, sir. The time of death was between half past three and half past five. We're not sure when it was taken. According to the doctor, strychnine's pretty unpredictable. A meal can slow things up dramatically. Strychnine can kill within twenty minutes or so, or the victim can linger on for a good long while. It depends on their constitution and what they've eaten.'

'Could he have committed suicide?' asked Sir Douglas hopefully. 'He could have panicked, perhaps?'

Bill pursed his lips. 'We thought of that, of course, but it doesn't seem likely. Strychnine must be one of the most gruesome deaths possible. Only a lunatic would commit suicide in that way. That's your opinion too, isn't it Jack?'

'Absolutely. Tyrell wasn't the sort to panic. There's not much chance of suicide, as far as I can see. People do the strangest things, I know – I read about a woman who tried to bury herself alive – but I think it's unlikely.' He linked his fingers together and looked down at his palms. 'So, with Tyrell out of it, we're brought back to the one man who has been in the case from the very beginning and so far has managed to escape serious suspicion.'

'Frederick Hunt,' said Sir Douglas thoughtfully. He pushed his chair back and walked to the window. He leaned back against the sill and, folding his arms, looked at Bill. 'I know you think Frederick Hunt could have murdered his father. Could he have murdered Tyrell as well?'

'It's possible. I questioned Hunt's chauffeur and Hunt arrived home at half past three, after Tyrell had left the house. However, poison's not like shooting or stabbing. Hunt could have simply put a strychnine tablet in the bottle of aspirin by Tyrell's bedside and waited for the inevitable. It's easy enough to get into a hotel bedroom.'

'What about the motive?'

'Inspector Rackham and I have talked about this, sir,' said Jack. 'If Frederick Hunt murdered both his father and Tyrell, then the motive has to be something to do with the running of the firm. Everyone who's been in a position to know – Mark Helston, Meredith Smith and old Mr Hunt himself – thought there was something wrong. Tyrell was interested in joining the firm and certainly talked to Frederick Hunt. Tyrell was a very sharp customer. He could've easily worked out Frederick Hunt was up to no good.'

'Was that why old Mr Hunt invited Tyrell to lunch, I wonder?' said Sir Douglas. 'To find out what he knew?'

'It might very well be the reason,' said Jack. 'If Tyrell did say anything, though, it would have been to his advantage. He was very much out for his own ends. However, he might very well have tried to blackmail Hunt, and used the threat of informing old Mr Hunt to really put the screws on.'

'At which point Frederick Hunt assumes that Tyrell has told his father everything, panics and strikes out,' said Sir Douglas thoughtfully.

'That, I think, is about the size of it,' agreed Bill.

'*Is* there anything wrong with Hunt Coffee?' demanded Sir Douglas.

Bill held his hands wide. 'We simply don't know. Old Mr Hunt certainly thought so, though. His new will tells us as much.'

Sir Douglas sat down on the corner of the desk and rubbed his hand across his forehead. 'You'll have to run through this business about a new will, Rackham. I've got your report, of course, but I've only had time to skim through it.'

'Right you are, sir. I managed to get hold of Mr Stafford, the Hunt family solicitor, at his house last night. Old Mr Hunt asked him to call on Thursday afternoon. Mr Hunt wanted to add a codicil to his will. He owned, at the time of his death, sixty per cent of the shares in Hunt Coffee, with the other forty per cent being held by Frederick. I got chapter and verse on this, how Hunt Coffee Limited is a private limited company by virtue of the Companies Act 1907, as amended by the Consolidating Act of 1908, etcetera, etcetera, with all the various section numbers and what-have-you.'

Bill ran his fingers through his hair. 'As far as I can make out, it's a legal way of having your cake and eating it. It was old Mr Hunt himself who turned Hunt Coffee into a private limited company back in 1909, so he could have all the advantages of limited liability without a board of directors breathing down his neck. He was a pretty shrewd businessman in his day. He had previously made provision for Mark Helston to inherit forty per cent of his holding, which would leave Frederick Hunt as the majority shareholder, with sixty per cent. That, in the main body of the will, remains unchanged, should Mark Helston reappear. However, should Helston still be missing at the time of Mr Hunt's death, then the forty per cent intended for Mark Helston goes to Meredith Smith, who has as much claim upon the title of great-nephew as Helston did. If Mark returned, they would split the shareholding, with twenty per cent each.'

Sir Douglas nodded. 'The only surprise is that he didn't codify his intentions earlier.'

'He never lost hope Mark would return,' put in Jack.

'Yes,' agreed Bill. 'As far as that goes, it seems like a perfectly sensible provision. However, the sting's in the tail. The codicil states that Frederick Hunt gets sixty per cent on Mr Hunt's death if – and this is the nasty bit – Frederick Hunt has not been found guilty of, or is facing prosecution for, any criminal activity, or is subsequently found guilty of any criminal activity for the period preceding Mr Hunt's death. If he *is* facing prosecution but is acquitted, then the original sixty-forty allocation of the shares stands. If he's found guilty, however, Meredith Smith scoops the lot. It makes you wonder what old Mr Hunt thought his son was capable of, doesn't it, sir?'

'It certainly does.' Sir Douglas tapped the desk with his fingers. 'Financial irregularities or murder? Either's covered very neatly by that provision. Was the codicil signed?'

'Yes, sir. The witnesses were Thomas Potter and Joseph Wyre, the window cleaners. Mr Hunt gave them ten shillings each for their trouble. Mr Stafford said that old Mr Hunt was in considerable haste to get the document signed.'

'So if Frederick Hunt did know about it, there was precious little he could do. However, his father certainly suspected he could be guilty of *something*.' He cocked his head to one side and looked at Jack. 'You probably won't like the idea, but have you thought this new will gives Meredith Smith a motive for murder? After all,' he added, 'Smith was on the spot at Neville Square.'

'The thought did occur to me, sir,' said Jack with a grin, 'and, in light of the new will, I thought I'd think it before anyone else did. After all, if we do catch Frederick bending, Smith scoops the pool. With that in mind, I've come hotfoot from Southwark. I wanted to check the facts while they were still fresh in everyone's mind and I'm glad to say Smith's alibi for Friday afternoon is as cast iron as they come. He was seen by loads of people all afternoon – I've jotted down who they are, of course – who say that Meredith Smith was at Hunt Coffee, Southwark, until just after five o'clock.'

'So we're back to Frederick Hunt,' said Sir Douglas. He sighed unhappily. 'It'll be the devil to prove, though.'

He picked up the file and flicked through it at random. 'I see you traced the knife Valdez was killed with, by the way. That proves there's a link between the Hunts and Valdez's murder, not that we doubted it.'

'There's a bit more to it than that, sir,' said Jack. 'Frederick Hunt stated yesterday that Helston had three knives made, one for his grandmother, one for Mr Hunt and one for his sister. But I spoke to Pat Tyrell this morning and she told me Helston had four knives made in all, including one for himself. Now, if it is a lie and not a mistake, then it's a silly, pointless lie, and it makes you wonder why he bothered to tell it.'

Sir Douglas pulled at his moustache. 'Why should it matter how many knives there were? Dash it all, three are enough to be getting along with. Have you traced the others?'

'Pat Tyrell found two for me,' offered Jack. 'Her own and her grandmother's. Old Mr Hunt's makes three.'

'Which means Helston's own knife was the murder weapon,' said Sir Douglas. He continued to pull at his moustache. 'The case against Hunt is purely circumstantial. If we could get to the bottom of what is wrong at Hunt Coffee, that'd help. I'd like to bring Hunt in for questioning, but unless we've got a shrewd idea what old Mr Hunt had in mind, we'll be wasting our time. What one old man thought isn't evidence. Hunt will simply deny everything, kick up the dickens of a row, and we'll end up with egg on our faces.' The spectre of Jacob Carroll and the *Mercury* reasserted itself. 'The last thing I want to do is give the press another stick to beat us with.' He boxed his papers together. 'See me on Monday morning, Rackham, unless there's any developments over the weekend. Thank you for your time, gentlemen.'

Leaving Sir Douglas at his desk, they left the room.

'Can I give you a lift anywhere, Bill?' asked Jack, as they walked out of the door into the yard. 'I've got the Spyker outside. I drove here from Southwark.'

He stopped. Meredith Smith, arms folded, was leaning against the bonnet of the Spyker.

As they approached, he looked up, his face grim. 'So there you are, Jack. I knew I'd find you here. What the devil d'you mean by asking questions in the office about me?'

Jack stopped. 'Ah.'

'You might well say, *Ah*. Do you honestly think there's the slightest chance I'd shoot poor old H.R.H.? Honestly?'

'No, I honestly don't, but in view of this new will, I thought it as well to prove you couldn't. Otherwise you might come up against someone without my beautifully trusting nature.'

'*What* new will?' snapped Meredith.

Jack and Bill exchanged glances. 'You'd better tell him,' said Jack. 'He's going to find out soon enough anyway.'

Meredith listened in bewildered silence. 'I get the lot?' he asked in astonishment when Bill had finished. 'That's crazy.'

'Only if Frederick Hunt's not a good boy,' Jack reminded him.

'But that's still forty per cent. Good God, this is incredible. What did H.R.H. suspect Frederick of? You don't think he killed Sheila, do you?' Unconsciously, his hands twisted together. 'If I thought that . . .'

'There's nothing to suggest Frederick Hunt's guilty of that,' said Bill.

Meredith covered his mouth with his hand. 'Poor Sheila. Why should anyone want to harm her? Who was she?' His face softened. 'Nobody special, I suppose, but I . . .'

Jack stared at him. 'Merry,' he said in an odd voice. 'Would you mind answering your own question?'

Meredith looked at him, uncomprehendingly.

'Go on. Who was Sheila Mandeville?'

'She was my clerk, of course.' He looked doubtfully at Jack. There was a gleam in his friend's black eyes which made him pause. 'You knew that.'

'I did. And I'm wondering how I came to forget it for so long.'

Bill looked at him sharply. 'If you've got an idea, spit it out.'

Jack clapped a hand on his shoulder. 'Not yet. I need more time to think. I'll look you up this afternoon. By the way, you remember Robert Waldron?'

'Who? Hang on, he was the chap who called to see Mr Hunt, wasn't he? What about him?'

'I've got a feeling he knows a whole lot more than we've imagined. Mr Hunt greeted him as an old friend. He didn't know Waldron was in London. I remember looking at the chap and thinking that a man with his yellow, sun-baked skin didn't look as if he belonged in England. Now, where would you expect Mr Hunt's old friends to live?'

'Anywhere on earth except London, I suppose, if he was surprised Waldron was in Town. In Brazil, at a guess.'

'Exactly,' said Jack triumphantly.

'Does that help?'

'It might.' He opened the car door. 'Hop in, everyone. I've got some work to do. For one thing, I need to see Pat Tyrell.'

'I wish I could see what the dickens you're getting so excited about,' grumbled Bill, climbing into the car. 'D'you want me to ask Frederick Hunt about this Robert Waldron bloke?'

Jack paused with his hand on the self-starter. 'No. Not yet, at any rate. It might give the game away. We don't want to flush the birds until we're ready to shoot.' He smiled apologetically. 'I'm not being mysterious on purpose, but I need to get it all taped out. I may find that it's nonsense.'

'Nonsense or not, I'd like to hear it,' said Bill, settling back. 'And you needn't worry that I'll give the game away. I haven't a clue what the game's meant to be.'

It was ten past five that afternoon when Jack arrived at the Archias Club, to find Meredith Smith and George Lassiter already waiting for him. 'Thanks for coming, George,' he said. 'I appreciate it. Hello, Merry. I see you've introduced yourselves.'

'Well, it was pretty easy working out who the other must be,' said Lassiter. 'We've only just arrived. Why did you want us to meet you here, Jack? I showed you round earlier on.'

'This is where Frederick Hunt dined with Tyrell the night poor Sheila Mandeville was killed. I was hoping to pick up a few pointers.'

'I don't see how,' said Lassiter, walking over to the porter's desk. He nodded to the man behind the desk. 'Hello, Stoddart. I'd like to sign a couple of guests in. Shall we have dinner here, Jack?'

'Yes, but later. What I could really do with is a drink.' He looked at the porter. 'Is there a quiet room? We don't want to be disturbed.'

'Well, sir, there's the small smoking room and the library. There's the billiard room as well. That's usually free at this hour.'

'I think we'll plump for the library. That all right with you,

George? Good. Can we have our drinks brought up? Excellent.'
He glanced at his watch. 'I've got to keep an eye on the time.
I'm meeting Bill later on.' He looked at the grandfather clock.
'Is that clock right?'

'Yes, sir. She's just about to chime the quarter now.'

'Good.' Jack adjusted his watch, waited for Lassiter to order
the drinks, then together he and Meredith Smith followed their
host up the marble staircase to the library.

'I don't know what's so desperately important that you have to
meet me here at five thirty-five precisely,' said Bill.

They were standing in Dunthorpe Mansions outside the door
of Sheila Mandeville's flat.

'Perpend, old thing,' said Jack. 'All will be revealed. Did you
get hold of the key? Oh, good egg. Fling wide the pearly gates
without making too much of a song and dance about it, will
you?'

'It's just as well,' said Bill, turning the key in the lock, 'that
this flat hasn't been re-let.'

'Yes. That would put a crick in my plans. We'd have had to
do it in the corridor and I loath performing in public.'

'Do what?' Bill shut the door behind them and turned to face
his friend. 'What are you going to do?'

Jack took off his hat and coat and hung them carefully on the
hall peg before flexing his fingers together. 'I hope you don't
mind, Bill, but I'm going to kill you.'

Alfred Stoddart looked up as Jack approached the desk. 'Yes,
sir?'

'Mr Lassiter wondered if the evening post had arrived. He's
expecting an important letter.'

'No, sir, not yet.' He looked at the clock. 'It's only just gone
quarter past six. The post doesn't usually get here until half past.'

'Never mind,' said Jack with a smile. 'I'll come back later. Is
there much of a crowd in the dining room?'

'Not yet, sir, it's too early. If you'd like to have a word with
the steward, he'll make sure there's a table reserved for you.'

'Good idea. Is it through these doors?'

'Yes, sir. Just go straight in.'

Jack re-emerged from the dining room some ten minutes later.

'That's all settled,' he remarked pleasantly. He glanced at his watch. 'The post is about due. I might as well wait until it comes.'

'I'll bring any letters up, sir. In the library, are you?'

'Thanks, that's very good of you.' He slipped a florin into the porter's hand. 'If, by any chance, Mr Lassiter's letter doesn't arrive, I'd be obliged if you could let us know as soon as possible.'

'Right you are, sir,' said Stoddart, pocketing the money. 'It's a pleasure.'

'There you are, Jack,' said Meredith Smith. 'We were wondering what had become of you.'

Jack grinned. 'Nothing much. I've ordered dinner for seven o'clock, by the way. It's a bit early, but I haven't had much time for food today. Touch the bell, would you, George? I could do with another drink.' He looked up as the porter entered the room. 'Yes?'

'I'm afraid there was nothing in the post for Mr Lassiter, sir.'

'The post?' asked Lassiter, puzzled. 'I wasn't expecting . . .' He stopped abruptly as Jack kicked out under the table. 'Er . . . thanks, Stoddart. Here's a shilling for your trouble.'

Lassiter glared at Jack when Stoddart had left the room. 'I wish you'd be more careful. That was a fairly fruity one on the shin. What's all this about a letter?'

'What's all this about altogether?' demanded Meredith Smith.

'There isn't any letter,' said Jack. 'However, it was a good excuse as any. As to what it's about, Merry, I'm afraid you'll have to wait a little bit longer. Now, this is what I want you to do . . .'

'You,' said Jack, 'should be under the bed.'

'I'm blowed if I'm spending hours under a bed to fit in with some half-brained scheme of yours,' said Bill robustly. 'It's dusty and smells of mice.'

'Well, get under it now, so I can pull you out.'

'What? Oh, for God's sake, Jack, is this really necessary?'

'Shut up, you're a corpse. Stay absolutely still, blast you.'

'You'll be a ruddy corpse in a minute if you don't tell me what's going on. Here, what the hell are you playing at?'

'I'm playing,' said Jack, between clenched teeth as he heaved the startled Bill over one shoulder in a fireman's lift, 'at making you into a beautiful body. Ups-a-daisy. For Pete's sake, Bill, can't you at least pretend to be dead?'

He stood up, one arm grasped round Bill's legs. 'Now into the sitting room with you. Mother of God, you weigh a ton. Don't answer. I can't get into the mood if the remains start chatting to me. Behave yourself and I'll stand you dinner.'

'It can't be worth it,' said Bill, feeling Jack sway alarmingly. 'I don't care if you buy all my meals for the rest of my life. It just can't be worth it.' Jack walked down the hall and into the sitting room, where he lowered Bill onto the sofa. 'Can I be alive again now?'

Jack looked at his watch. 'In a couple of minutes. Why don't you reflect on death for a moment? I'm giving you a very valuable opportunity. John Donne – you know, the "For whom the bell tolls," bloke – used to sleep in a coffin so he could think of death more easily.'

'If he'd met you, he wouldn't have had to bother. I've got no problems connecting the thoughts of you and death at the moment. The idea's making my mouth water.'

Jack grinned. 'Don't be so tetchy. I'll be off, Bill. Give me five minutes or so to get away, then join us at the Archias Club. When you get to the club, this is what I want you to do . . .'

William Rackham approached the porter behind the desk. Alfred Stoddart quickly shoved a copy of *The Pink 'Un* into a drawer and looked up. 'I'm looking for Mr Lassiter,' said Bill. 'He asked me to dine with him.'

'Yes, sir, Mr Lassiter mentioned it. Mr Rackham, is it? Mr Lassiter's in the library. I'll send word for him.'

A few minutes later, George Lassiter, accompanied by Meredith Smith and Jack Haldean, joined Rackham in the lobby.

'I'm glad you could make it, Bill,' said Jack, for the porter's benefit. 'By the way, you know that bet we had on?' He saw Stoddart's quick glance and smiled to himself. The colour of the porter's favourite newspaper had not been lost on him. 'Well, I think Stoddart here is just the man to help us.'

Stoddart, now definitely included by the mention of his name, looked up expectantly. 'Is there something I can do, sir?'

'If you would. I want you to tell Mr Rackham where the three of us have been all evening.'

'What, you and the other gentlemen, sir? You've been here in the club.'

Bill frowned. 'No, they haven't. Major Haldean certainly hasn't.'

'But they have, sir,' protested Stoddart. 'I can especially swear to the Major. He came and asked me about the post, then he ordered dinner.'

'You can't have done,' insisted Bill. 'I saw him myself earlier.'

The porter looked bewildered. 'You must be mistaken, sir. The Major's been here all evening. Tell you what, sir, as it's a bet, why don't you ask the steward who served the drinks in the library? That would be Mulvaney. He'll back me up. He's in the bar now.'

'I'll make a point of it,' promised Bill.

'And he'll say he saw me, because he did,' put in Jack.

Bill leaned closer to Stoddart. 'You know,' he said confidentially, 'Major Haldean is a great one for tricks but he hates losing.' He allowed some coins to chink in his pocket. 'He's put you up to this, hasn't he? Tell me the truth, Stoddart, and I'll make it worth your while.'

'But that is the truth, sir,' protested Stoddart. 'Cross-my-heart honest. The Major's been here all the time.'

'I've won, Bill,' said Jack with a grin.

Bill shrugged. 'It certainly looks like it. I'm going to find this steward, though. When did Major Haldean arrive, Stoddart?'

'He arrived with the other gentlemen, sir. They ordered some drinks to be served in the library. Let me see, that would be about . . . quarter past five. Just before quarter past five it was.'

'How can you be so sure?'

'Because the Major said he had to keep an eye on the time as he was meeting someone later. He asked me special if the clock kept good time and when I said it did, he set his watch by it. She chimed the quarter – that was quarter past five – and they went up to the library. And if you don't believe me,' he added pugnaciously, 'here's Mulvaney now and he'll tell you what these gentlemen have been a-doing of.'

'I still can't credit it,' said Bill, after Mulvaney had been quizzed. 'All right, Jack, you win. Are we going to eat tonight, or was that just a rumour?'

'Be my guest . . . or George's guest, rather. Go on in, I'll be with you in a tick.'

Jack hung back at the desk for a moment. 'Thanks,' he said. 'There was five pounds riding on that and I think you're entitled to one fifth of it.' He handed over a pound note. 'Here you are.' He laughed. 'Poor old Bill. I told him I could be in two places at once but he didn't believe me.'

'Thank you very much, sir,' said Stoddart, taking the note. 'Excuse me, Major, but how *did* you do it?'

'Oh, that's easy,' said Jack. He looked at Stoddart. The man was alive with curiosity. He had to tell the poor chap something. He leaned forward and tapped the side of his nose. '*Twins.*'

'So come on,' demanded Bill over the fish. 'How did you pull off what seems like a version of the Indian rope trick? I know perfectly well you weren't here, and yet you managed to convince the porter and the steward that you were. You didn't bribe them, did you?'

Jack shook his head. 'No, of course I didn't. They might take a bribe if it was only for a bet, but they'd soon come clean if the police were involved. They'd be stupid not to. They'd lose their jobs if it came out and be run in for giving false evidence. No, if you can get people to tell you what they believe to be the truth, it's a lot safer.' He gave a warning glance towards Meredith Smith. 'Without going too much into detail, Bill, you'll grant I had plenty of time to, er . . . commit certain actions earlier on?'

'Oh, I'll grant you that, all right.' He looked at the other two men at the table. 'You're not going to maintain Jack was here all evening, are you?'

'We could,' said Lassiter. 'He wasn't, of course, but as we've got the porter and the steward to back us up, I don't see you could prove we were telling bouncers.'

'It'd be difficult, that's for sure.' He put down his knife and fork and squared his shoulders. 'So how was it done?'

'It was easy,' said Jack with a laugh. 'You've got to know the layout of the place, of course, but George very kindly showed me round earlier on. After drawing the porter's attention to the fact I was here at quarter past five, we ordered some drinks to be brought up to the library. As soon as the steward had gone, I slipped along the corridor and out onto the fire escape. At quarter past six I was back.'

'What if anyone had seen you?' asked Bill.

Jack shrugged. 'I had a good look before I set off and took a chance. There's hardly anyone about at this time in the evening, so I thought I was pretty safe. Meanwhile, George and Merry in the library obliged by finishing my drink. They ordered another one during my absence, but when the steward appeared, first to take the order and then to bring it, there was a cigarette smouldering in the ashtray, as if I'd just put it down, and – Merry, was it you? – came and conversed with the airy nothing behind the tall bookcase on the subject of whether I wanted London lager or Pilsner.'

'It worked like a charm,' said Smith. 'And when the chap actually arrived with the drinks, I merely said, in a carrying sort of voice, "Jack, your drink's here".'

'On my return, I made myself visible downstairs, ordering a table for dinner and talking about the post. As soon as Stoddart saw me *in situ* in the library once more, I shot off again to meet you for a second time. An enquiry about an expected letter was the obvious excuse to get him up there, but a hunt for a lost umbrella or another drink would have served just as well.'

Bill shook his head. 'It's too easy.'

'It worked, didn't it? And whilst to say it can be done isn't to say it *was* done, there's a strong presumption that it might have been done, if everything else fits into place.'

'And does everything else fit into place?'

'One thing certainly has. I've found out where Robert Waldron's got to. He's on the S.S. *Hildebrand* en route for Rio de Janeiro. Can you send him a marconigram, Bill? We want to know the gist of his conversation with Mr Hunt. I'll give you the details later. There's another piece of shipping news I've got for you, but I'd like to match it up with some more evidence. With any luck I should be able to get hold of the chap I want tomorrow. I've left word at the shipping office I need to speak to him and they promised to dig him up for me. However, what I want to do next is strictly unofficial.'

He paused and looked at Bill. 'I'm not too sure if I should sully your ears with this sort of thing, but Merry and I were planning a spot of very gentlemanly burglary.'

Bill raised his eyebrows and took a sip of wine. 'Burglary, eh? What are you planning to pinch?'

'Oh, we're not going to take anything,' said Smith quickly. 'I wouldn't do that. This is more a reconnaissance, isn't it, Jack?'

'Yes. I wondered, Bill, if you could lay your hands on a tame safecracker for us. Not gelignite or anything messy like that, but the real McCoy, who can open a safe without leaving any traces.'

'I might be able to,' said Bill, guardedly. 'Suppose you pair of Raffles stop being so cagey and tell me what it's all about?'

FIFTEEN

'The caretaker's coming!' hissed Meredith Smith from the door. The three men in the room froze against the wall of Frederick Hunt's office.

The steps along the corridor grew louder, then faded away. Smith breathed a sigh of relief. 'I'm glad we're not doing this at the dead of night, Jack. I don't think my nerves would stand it.'

'This is a much better time,' said Jack. 'No one expects to be burgled at eleven o'clock on a Sunday morning.'

'That's true,' agreed Smith. 'I can tell you something, though. If ever I do get to be in charge, I'm going to have the security on this place tightened up. It was sinful to see how easy it was to break in.'

'To be fair,' said Jack, 'we didn't exactly break in. You simply opened the main door with your key.'

'We had to break in here, didn't we? If we were caught fooling around in Mr Hunt's office, the fat really would be in the fire.'

'I wouldn't call it breaking in,' said the Scotland Yard expert. He was a short, stout man with a drooping moustache and lugubrious face who, with his bowler hat, black coat and striped trousers resembled a bank manager who was, albeit regretfully, about to foreclose on the mortgage.

Bill had introduced him as one of the best men with a lock in London. Jack, who had expected a reformed old lag, had been rather overawed by his intense respectability. His name was Hubert Brockbridge and he had, until his retirement, installed safes in the City of London.

'Breaking in means there's been something broken. A blind-folded child with a stick of Plasticine could have opened that door. I hope, sirs, you will be able to produce something more worthy of my talents.'

'We'll see what we can do,' promised Jack. 'Merry, don't waste time fooling around with the desk. Whatever we're after won't be so easy to find. My guess is that Frederick Hunt has a private safe hidden somewhere in this room.'

He looked along the wall, then peered behind an oleograph. It showed an idealized picture of the factory entitled *Hunt Coffee, Limited; The New Model Works At Southwark*, which had appeared, in miniature, on millions of bottles of Royale Coffee. 'Nothing there.'

Mr Brockbridge stood expectantly in the centre of the room, rather like a stout fox-terrier trying to locate a scent. Then he dropped to his knees and rolled back the carpet which covered the middle of the floor, exposing a rectangle of wood with two recessed handles, flush with the oilcloth-covered floorboards.

Mr Brockbridge lifted out the rectangle. Underneath was a safe. 'Here you are, gentlemen.' The moustache lifted in a mournful smile. 'Now this is very nice indeed. The gentleman obviously spent some money having it fitted.' He stroked his moustache. 'It's a Hobbs and Hart ten-lever protector. A lovely lock.'

'Can you open it?' asked Jack.

Mr Brockbridge didn't deign to answer, but, taking off his coat and laying it carefully on a chair, set to work. Metal scraped on metal; a tiny sound, but huge in that quiet room. After seven and a half minutes, Mr Brockbridge gave a sigh of satisfaction and turned the sunken handle of the safe. Without a sound from the well-oiled hinges, he swung back the door. Then, with the contented air of a job well done, he stood to one side.

The contents of the safe didn't, at first glance, seem very exciting. There was a bank book in the name of Clive Harwell for the *Banco do Commercio*, São Paulo, Brazil, and another, also in the name of Clive Harwell, for the Capital and Shires, Lombard Street, London. A thin file of bank statements lay underneath and beside them were a number of letters, all with Brazilian stamps. An account book and a sales ledger lay in a separate compartment.

Meredith Smith picked up the books and took them to the desk, carefully staying out of sight both of the window and the door. After a few minutes, he gave a grunt of surprise and quickly picked up the letters, skimming through them until he found the one he wanted. He read it quickly, then referred back first to the sales ledger, then to the account book.

'What've you found?' asked Jack, unable to keep quiet any longer.

Smith waved him silent, running his finger down the accounts. He shut the book with great deliberation and steepled his fingers in front of him. 'Swine,' he said softly. 'What a thieving swine.'

'It's a very simple but effective fraud,' Meredith Smith said to Bill.

They had carefully replaced everything back in the hidden safe and were now in Bill's office. They had Hubert Brockbridge's assurance that no one could tell the safe had been opened.

'It would need meticulous stocktaking to discover the fraud,' continued Smith, 'and even then it could probably be disguised as being due to the vagaries of the Brazilian commodity exchange.'

'How does it work?' asked Bill.

'Like this. Hunt Coffee, London, pay the manager of the plantation in Branca Preto a fixed sum for coffee. For the last eighteen months it's stood at one hundred and fifty-four shillings a hundredweight. If you tried to buy coffee of that quality on the open market you'd be looking at a price of around one hundred and seventy-one shillings a hundredweight, so the saving seems obvious. However, in a way we're victims of our own success. The plantation doesn't produce anything like enough to meet our needs, so we're forced to use the plantation coffee as the main supply and bulk it up by buying coffee on the Brazilian commodity exchange, supplemented by occasional purchases from the London spot market. That is, naturally, more expensive. Now the London purchases are handled in London, but the additional Brazilian purchases are met by the sending of an additional monthly sum to Brazil which, to get the quality we were after, and disallowing the processing and shipping charges, usually works out about one hundred and fifty-nine shillings the hundredweight.'

Smith lit a cigarette and smoked it thoughtfully for a couple of moments. 'The production figures for the plantation were falsified, so it seemed to be growing far less than it actually was, and we supposedly bought in coffee from other producers at the higher price. In fact, a great deal of the coffee that was meant to have been purchased from other producers was grown on our own plantation. What was bought seems to have been pretty low-grade stuff compared to our premium coffees, and should only have attracted a gross price of one hundred and thirty-one shillings or thereabouts. Frederick Hunt sent the additional payments to the plantation and the plantation manager would be richly in pocket. The manager would keep a chunk of the extra money for himself – it works out at about thirty per cent – and pay the remaining seventy per cent into the bank account of one Clive Harwell in Brazil. Clive Harwell in turn transfers money to his account with the Capital and Shires of Lombard Street. I don't need to tell you that Frederick Hunt and Clive Harwell are one and the same. It says as much in one of the letters.'

Bill whistled. 'How come none of this has ever shown up in the official accounts?'

'There's nothing *to* show up in the accounts. All the coffee imported has been duly taxed and paid for. The fact the plantation's purchase ledger has been falsified to record more purchases than were actually made isn't something that you can work out from the amount of coffee received in London. The number of sacks received tallies with what the plantation says it dispatched. The fact that the provenance of the coffee in those sacks isn't as officially recorded and they contain an inferior grade to what they purport to contain, isn't something an accountant is going to find out. If Frederick Hunt, the Great White Chief, is happy with the quality, who's going to contradict him? Meanwhile he's got a thumping great sum of untaxed money in the bank. But Mark Helston was unhappy and so was H.R.H.'

Bill nodded. 'Valdez would be a knowing partner, of course.'

'Valdez and the current plantation manager, De Oliveria. There's just a chance that Laurence Tyrell, when he looked after the place as John Marsden, might not have been in on it. He was only a caretaker manager, after all. Unless you can find evidence to the contrary, I think we'll have to give him the benefit of the doubt.'

'Yes . . . So old Mr Hunt was right. Frederick Hunt is a crook.'

'Absolutely,' said Smith. 'Poor old H.R.H. obviously suspected him and paid the price. I think Jaggard might be innocent after all, Jack. If Valdez had pressed for more money and Helston rumbled it, Hunt could have seen them off too.'

'This answers a lot of questions, that's for sure,' said Bill. 'You're certain everything in Frederick Hunt's office is just as you found it?'

'Certain.'

'Good. By the time Mr Hunt arrives at work tomorrow he should find an unpleasant surprise waiting for him.' He laced his fingers together and cracked them with a noise that made Jack wince. 'I must say I'm looking forward to this.'

Meredith Smith rose to his feet. 'I won't say I'm looking forward to it, but it'll be a real challenge to get Hunt Coffee up to scratch again.'

Jack looked at Meredith and grinned. 'D'you know, for a moment you looked exactly like H.R.H.'

'Did I? There's worse people in the world to take after. I'm going to get along now, Jack. Are you coming?'

'No. I'm expecting a bloke from the Blue Star shipping line to pay a call.' He looked at his watch. 'He should be here soon. I left word he was to ask for you, Bill. Your name and title has a reassuringly official ring to it.'

A knock sounded at the door and a sergeant entered. 'There's a Mr Michael Lovell to see you, sir.'

Rackham got to his feet as a nervous-looking man was ushered into the room, twisting his cap in his hands. Jack swung himself off the window and advanced with a smile.

'Mr Lovell? It's very good of you to call. This is Inspector Rackham and I'm Major Haldean. We're sorry to cut into your Sunday like this, but we'd appreciate your help. Won't you sit down?'

Lovell shifted from foot to foot. 'I had a message from the office that you wanted me. I hope you don't think as I've done anything wrong.'

'Not at all,' Jack reassured him. 'Mr Lovell, I'd like you to cast your mind back to January. You were a steward on board the *S.S. Albion Star*, weren't you?'

Lovell relaxed and took the chair which Jack had pulled out for him. 'Indeed I was, sir. I was on B deck.'

'Good. Now, Mr Lovell, I know you had certain passengers to look after. Can you tell us if any of these men was among them?'

Lovell took the photographs Jack handed to him. 'It's some months ago now, sir. Mind you, you get to know the passengers quite well, especially on a long voyage . . . That's him!' He tapped the photograph on the desk. 'That's one of my gentlemen. Now, what was his name . . .'

Jack took the photographs back with a broad grin. 'Don't worry about the name, Mr Lovell. We'll supply that. Thank you very much for coming. I'll see you to the door.'

When he stepped back into the room, he found Bill gazing at the photograph with satisfaction. 'Got him,' he breathed.

'I hope so,' said Jack.

At quarter to ten the next morning, Frederick Hunt's chauffeur drove the great Wolseley through the gates of the factory, past the humble rows of bicycles outside the entrance to the works, round the corner of the office building and nosed the car into the six-foot by twelve-foot spot sacred to the director of this temple of industry. Parking the car, he stepped smartly round to the side and opened the door.

Frederick Hunt got out, briefcase and neatly furled umbrella in hand. 'That will be all, Pearson. Please be here at . . .'

He stopped, dumbfounded. Agnes Clement, his confidential clerk, wild eyed and with hair escaping from her bun, rushed up to him and actually grabbed him by the arm.

'Mr Hunt! Mr Hunt! The police! They're in the building waiting for you, Mr Hunt! They've taken the papers from your private safe.'

She waited for reassurance, but with a jolt of horror saw his face crumple and change to become a mask of stark fear. 'Mr Hunt? It's all a mistake, isn't it, Mr Hunt?'

He tried to speak, opening and shutting his mouth foolishly. Then he seized on the inessential. 'How d'you know about my safe?'

'I've seen you use it, sir. Mr Hunt! You must explain to them. Tell them it's all a misunderstanding.'

She was standing between him and the car door. With a sweep of his arm he thrust her to one side and made a leap for the Wolseley. 'Drive, Pearson, damn you, drive!'

Open mouthed, the chauffeur mechanically stepped towards the car, then stopped at the sight of Miss Clement, sprawling in the dirt.

Hunt shook him by the shoulder, his face inches away. 'Never mind her! Drive, I tell you!'

There was the blast of a police whistle and round the corner came the sound of thudding feet. Agnes Clement set up a long, wailing shriek. 'Mr Hunt! Stop!'

With a vicious jerk, he kicked away her grasping hands and, jumping over her body, ran towards the factory gates. There were policemen barring the exit. Hunt, hearing the sound of his pursuers close on his heels, veered off into the only bolthole left to him, the huge open doors of the factory itself.

Heart pounding, feet slipping on the tiled floor, he ran blindly into the bottling department.

Above the clang and clash of thousands of rattling bottles and great whooshes of steam from the sterilizing plant, he heard the repeated shriek of police whistles. A khaki-overalled figure reached out an arm. He lashed out with the umbrella he was still absurdly holding, sending the man crashing into a crate of stacked bottles.

They overturned in a deafening smash, sending loose bottles rolling over the tiles. Tripping and falling, he crawled along the floor, twisting out from under the clutching hands. Then he was on his feet once more, running with sweat filling his eyes, regardless of shouts and whistles, hitting out at everything in his way. He fell against the wall, and dimly saw a door a few yards away. With bursting lungs he staggered, then fell against it. It opened and he lunged through, slamming it shut behind him.

The corridor was oddly quiet. Leaning against the door, breath coming in huge gulps, he heard the shouts from the other side. A tiny flicker of thought took root in the blind panic that swamped him.

This corridor ran the length of the factory and then to the outside, didn't it? His insides twisted as he remembered the policeman at the gate. There would be more men there now . . . Wait! Across the open yard at the back lay the warehouse.

If he could get in there, then he could make his way out of the back doors, onto the wharf where the barges unloaded. Perhaps he could escape along the towpath or even hide on a barge. They wouldn't look for him on a barge. After that, all he had to do was to get back home, collect some money and his passport and get away to Brazil. He had money in Brazil . . . He'd squeeze something out of De Oliveria and he had his account in São Paulo. He'd do it yet.

Very cautiously, he started to walk forward. Then the door behind him was flung back, the noise of the factory swelled, and there was a cry of 'He's here!'

With a sob, he forced his aching muscles to run. The sun streamed through the door at the end. He made it, got out into the yard, dodging round buildings, intent on the black hole that was the warehouse doors in front of him. More whistles blew and he flung up his arm as if to ward off a physical blow.

He hurled himself into the warehouse, a dusty, aromatic place with sacks of coffee piled up on pallets to the roof.

He dived amongst the pallets, trying to find a way between the narrow alleys of brown jute walls. He could hear footsteps and voices. 'He's trapped now, good and proper,' said one.

He shrank back behind a great mound of coffee sacks, creeping round until he was in the dark passage between the sacks and the wall. Trapped, was he? He put a hand to his mouth to shield his laboured breathing. He'd show them. Had they heard him? His gasping must give him away. The footsteps were getting closer. He *was* trapped. He looked round wildly.

The warehouse was dark and he couldn't see the doors to the river. What he could see, between a narrow passage of coffee sacks, was a ladder leading up into the dim recesses of the roof. Perhaps he could hide in the roof. The ladder must lead *somewhere*. Putting down his umbrella, he crept forward, treading as quietly as he could.

The sound of footsteps was muffled by the walls of coffee. He couldn't tell where they were coming from. Sick with fear, he made it to the ladder and started up the rungs. Above him was the box of a cabin with a trapdoor in the floor. If he could make it to the box, then he could hide until this nightmare stopped.

Wheezing with effort, he pulled himself through the trapdoor. Exhausted, he lay sprawled on the wooden boards, dizzy with effort and fright. Gradually his breathing slowed and he realized where he was.

It was the crane! Raising himself to his hands and knees, he crawled towards the crane driver's seat. In front of him was a set of controls that looked like the gear lever of a car and, stretching out from the crane, a long wooden arm.

There was a sort of shuffling silence from the warehouse below. Still on his knees, he risked a glance over the side of the cabin.

A shout rang out. 'There he is!'

He fell back, knocking the controls, and, with a creaking noise, the great wooden arm rose upwards. Amidst his panic, the glimmer of a plan came to him. He seized the controls and yanked them hard. The wooden arm moved left, then right. He pulled the levers feverishly, sending the arm rocking first one way, then another, building up speed until the cabin swayed sickeningly under the strain.

There were sacks of coffee attached to the massive hook and, laughing wildly, he brought the arm, hook and sacks round in a huge destructive arc, crashing into the towering walls of jute surrounding him. The crane cracked and splintered, hurling him out onto the falling mass of sacks.

With a soft whispering that turned to a roar, the sacks slid, bumped and thundered off the pallet. The pile caught another, and another, and across the entire warehouse, tons of coffee cascaded to the floor.

'Look out!' yelled Jack, jumping back, pulling Bill with him. They missed the avalanche by inches, coughing in the thick wall of dust that mushroomed up. The noise of the falling sacks seemed to go on forever, followed by an eerie silence. On his hands and knees and spluttering in the choking cloud, he caught the faint sound of coughing from beyond the fallen mound of sacks.

Jack got to his feet gingerly. The stinging dust was like the worst of London fogs, but, very gradually, it started to settle. He pulled out his handkerchief and wrapped it round his mouth. A vague shape moved beside him. It was Bill. He tried to speak, but the attempt ended in a barking cough.

Jack moved forward, feeling the fallen sacks with his hands. With eyes closed he listened intently, trying to block out the sounds that Bill was making. There seemed to be a scrabbling noise from above him. It was like a giant rat . . . There it was again!

A gust of wind through the open doors blew a tunnel in the murk, showing him Frederick Hunt, climbing over the mountain of sacks, spreadeagled against them like a black spider. A hundredweight of coffee detached itself and bumped down. Hunt turned momentarily and Jack caught sight of the streak of white that was his face.

He cautiously climbed onto the sacks, then the wind dropped and he was in the grey dark. He closed his eyes to keep out the grit, and climbed by touch alone. The scrabbling grew more intense and a sack, kicked by Hunt, lumped past, striking his right shoulder.

Frozen by a jag of pain, he clung on, before grimly starting to climb again. He came out of the dust and saw Hunt clearly a few yards above him. He tried to increase his speed, and fell back as the sacks gave way.

Hunt was kicking out on purpose now, trying to get the sacks to fall. Jack flattened himself, inching forward, feeling as if he was living a nightmare where no matter how hard he ran, the ground rose up and clung to his feet and legs. More sacks slid past him. If one of those hit him squarely . . .

There was a yell of triumph above him. Hunt reached the top, crawling on his knees. Jack vainly tried to grab the flailing ankle, but Hunt launched himself down the other side.

Jack staggered the last few feet to the top and flung himself down the sacks in a wild slide. Shaken, he picked himself up at the bottom, and made a lunge for Hunt, blinded once more by the dust. His fingers closed on Hunt's coat, but he shook himself free with a yelp.

All Jack could see were undefined shapes, but the sound of running footsteps was clear enough. Then came a banging, as if someone were hammering wood, followed by a scuffle, a cry, and a series of choking sobs.

Hands outstretched, he walked forward towards the sobs, saw a blur in the dust and pounced.

'Oy!' the shape said. 'Let go.'

'Merry?' Jack blinked in the gloom. 'Merry, is that you?'

'Absolutely it's me. Let go, will you? I'm kneeling on Hunt. I caught him at the doors. He's staying exactly where he is.'

A voice sounded from outside the doors. 'What the hell's going on in there?'

'Open the doors!' shouted Smith. 'This is Captain Smith!'

There was a creaking noise and light spilled into the dust, revealing the bewildered watchman outside and a black, hunched, sobbing form at their feet.

The watchman coughed as a cloud of dust billowed out into the sunlight. As he saw the destruction in the warehouse, his jaw fell open. 'Blimey! What in Gawd's name's happened? We won't have this mess cleared up in a month of Sundays *and* extra for overtime. Who's the daft sod who did it?'

Jack reached down and pulled Hunt to his feet. The watchman gazed at the battered, grimy figure without a flicker of recognition. 'Who the 'ell is it?'

Jack held the limp man. 'Mr Hunt.'

'Blow me tight!' The watchman stepped back, looked round the warehouse, and slowly shook his head. 'What did he think he was playing at?'

'The police are after him. He was trying to escape through these doors.'

The watchman spat in delight. 'Cor! The boss, you mean? He should've known the river doors are never open on a Monday. No deliveries, see? He should've known that. He never did come round here.'

Bill and three other policemen came round the corner, clambering over sacks. 'You've got him, Jack! Good work.'

'It was down to Merry here, and some very handy closed doors.'

Hunt stirred under Jack's grip. 'What . . . What . . . What is the meaning of this?' he gasped, in a thin caricature of his earlier manner.

Bill smiled with grim pleasure. 'It means, Mr Hunt, that I am arresting you as an accomplice to murder.'

'Murder!' whimpered Hunt. 'You can't arrest me for murder. Not *murder*.' His breathing was ragged. 'You think I murdered my father, don't you? I didn't, I tell you, I didn't.'

'Who's talking about your father?' asked Jack, quietly. 'We never said a word about your father. I want to nail you for what happened to Sheila Mandeville.'

SIXTEEN

It was the early evening when Jack rang the bell of 14, Neville Square. The door was opened by a smiling Pat Tyrell.

'Come in. I've got a surprise for you.' But Jack had already seen the man standing behind Pat.

'Jaggard! My word, it's good to see you once more.'

Jaggard shook Jack's hand with a shy smile. 'Pat phoned and said it was safe to come back. I've been holed up at a friend's place,' he added, leading the way into the morning room. 'I say, he won't get into trouble for that, will he?'

Jack paused with his hand on the doorknob. 'Why don't we draw a discreet veil over that? Rackham's conscience isn't allowed to be as elastic as mine. Where is he, by the way?'

'In Uncle Frederick's study,' said Pat, 'gathering up papers.' She hesitated then spoke in a rush. 'Is it really true Uncle Frederick's guilty of murder? I can't work out what happened.'

'I think I'd better explain everything,' said Jack. He opened the door. 'Merry! I hoped you'd be here.'

'I came with Rackham,' said Smith. 'Legally speaking, I seem to be in charge of the whole shooting match, so I have to be here.'

'You looked just like H.R.H. when you said that,' said Pat.

'As I've said before, there are worse people to take after,' said Smith.

Bill came into the room. 'I thought I heard you arrive. I've just about finished in the study.'

Pat went to the sideboard and poured them all drinks.

'Thanks,' said Bill, taking his whisky. 'I feel I've earned this. Now we've got Frederick Hunt tucked up safe and sound, it's all over bar the shouting. By the way, Jack, there was a marconigram from Robert Waldron waiting for me at the Yard. You'd better read it.'

Jack glanced at the yellow form. 'That's much as we thought, isn't it?'

'Major Haldean – Jack,' said Pat Tyrell. 'Is Uncle Frederick guilty of murder?'

Jack nodded. 'Technically, yes. He certainly knew all about it and kept quiet. The actual murderer was greedy, just like Frederick Hunt, but he was also cool headed, resourceful, and utterly self-centred.'

'Laurence Tyrell,' said Jaggard grimly.

'Laurence Tyrell?' repeated Meredith. 'He can't have killed Valdez or Helston, Jack. He was in Brazil. His reports from the plantation . . .'

'Were sent to Frederick Hunt. They might be dated December or January, but we only have Hunt's word for it that's when they were received.'

'I see . . .' Meredith stopped. 'No, I don't. Did Tyrell come over from Brazil to kill Valdez, then?'

'I think,' said Jack, 'I'd better go right back to the beginning.' He picked up a box of matches and lit his cigarette.

'The beginning, in this case, goes back a long way. In 1917, Laurence Tyrell had run through all his money and was on the brink of being cashiered. In the middle of Passchendaele, with men dropping like flies around him, the thought of dying must have seemed fairly attractive. Especially if he didn't die at all . . . Now, I can't prove this, but I believe he deliberately marked down John Marsden of the Sixteenth Battalion, Royal Western Australian Regiment, as a useful person to be. He was certainly a very convenient person to be, as he had no family to identify him.'

'Larry killed the real John Marsden, you mean?' asked Pat, with a quaver in her voice.

Jack shrugged. 'For what it's worth, I think so, but the Germans might have done it for him. In any event, John Marsden, complete with a total loss of memory and a clean sheet, was shipped off to Australia.'

'What if he met someone who'd known the real Marsden?' asked Meredith.

'What if he had?' said Jack. 'Tyrell had been told by the doctors who'd treated him that his name was Marsden. It wasn't his fault if they'd got it wrong. He told us something of his life in Australia, and I'm inclined to believe most of his story was true. A lie's much more convincing if it's seasoned with truth. I did wonder, though, why, come last April or thereabouts, he left for Brazil. Obviously he wasn't trying to chase his forgotten past and, granted the sort of man he was, I thought there might be a more sinister reason.' He looked at Bill. 'You agreed, didn't you?'

'I did,' said Bill. 'And, although we can't prove anything – as yet, anyway – I honestly think you've cracked it, Jack.'

'I looked in at the British Museum,' said Jack, 'and did some digging in the Australian Press. Tyrell mentioned a town called Mullgarrie in the Coolgardie Goldfields. In March *The Coolgardie Nugget* reported that three miners, who were rumoured to have made a strike, had been shot and killed at their camp at White Flag, which is about fifty miles or so from Mullgarrie. No gold was found at the camp and it's obvious they'd been killed for their finds. Two weeks later the *Nugget* reported that a shotgun belonging to one of the dead miners was sold in Mullgarrie. The police had a description of the man who sold it. He was about six foot tall, fair haired, bearded, and spoke with an English accent. He was never caught.'

Pat reached out for Jaggard's hand and squeezed it tightly. 'Is that Larry?' she asked.

'I think so,' said Bill. 'When I heard Jack's theory, I cabled the Western Australia Police to see if there's more evidence. It fits. Triple murder is as good a reason as any for Tyrell to up and skip to Brazil. There's no British law and it's over ten thousand miles from Western Australia.'

'Why did he turn up at the Hunt plantation?' demanded Meredith.

'The irony of it?' suggested Jack. 'Tyrell had a sense of humour and maybe he really did pick up a bottle of Royale Coffee. It wouldn't take him long to find out that Ariel Valdez was a crook. The fraud, orchestrated by Frederick Hunt and enthusiastically supported by Valdez, had been going on a long time.'

'It's over three years now, Jack,' put in Meredith Smith. 'Frederick Hunt's taken a packet out of the company.'

'Absolutely. Inevitably, Tyrell wanted a piece of the pie. However, if Tyrell came in on the deal, that's so much less for Senhor Valdez. It doesn't take much imagination to see that they'd have words about it.'

He crushed his cigarette out in the ashtray. 'I don't know how, and I don't know when, but I'm absolutely certain that somewhere in Branca Preto is the undiscovered body of Ariel Valdez.'

'Valdez was killed in *Brazil*?' said Jaggard. 'But . . .'

'Valdez was killed in Brazil,' repeated Jack. 'Bill and I are sure of it. You see, it wasn't Valdez who came to London. It was Laurence Tyrell.'

'My God,' whispered Pat. 'I'm starting to understand.'

'Tyrell would want to come to London very much. For a start, Valdez had the trip planned, and it was safer to let Valdez appear to be alive. He would also want to thresh things out with Frederick Hunt. A bottle of hair dye, glasses and a moustache made him look enough like Valdez to pass for the man on Valdez's passport. He might even have had a false passport made, and I think he'd picked up enough Portuguese to pass as a Brazilian. As far as the plantation was concerned, he was safe enough. He had De Oliveria handy to look after things while he was gone. All Tyrell had to do was write his reports and give them to Frederick Hunt to file away in London.'

'This is absolutely horrible,' said Pat with a shudder. 'Uncle Frederick *knew*?'

'I'll say he knew. You'll remember the first meeting between Valdez and Frederick Hunt took place on the twenty-ninth of December, when your brother was away. Hunt wouldn't want Helston there and neither did Tyrell.'

He looked at Pat. 'Did your Uncle Frederick ever meet Tyrell? When you were married, I mean?'

Pat shook her head. 'No, he didn't.'

Jack nodded. 'That's much as we thought. He wouldn't recognize him. Hunt would know immediately, of course, that Tyrell wasn't Valdez, but that needn't, in practical terms, make much difference. Hunt wanted the fraud to continue and Tyrell was a willing partner. I bet Tyrell wanted a sight more money than Valdez though. Tyrell had Hunt by the short hairs all right. All he had to do was to go back to Brazil and, as John Marsden, write an informative letter to H.R.H., and Frederick Hunt would've been dropped right in it. Tyrell left Hunt to think it over and went off to Paris for the New Year, having arranged to meet again on the ninth.'

'Wasn't he taking a devil of a risk, Jack?' asked Meredith. 'I mean, there's a good chance he'd bump into someone who used to know him.'

Jack shook his head. 'It wasn't as risky as you'd think. Dark hair, glasses and a moustache are a fairly good disguise. It wouldn't wash for a minute with someone who'd known him well, but he wasn't going to meet *them*. That's why he went to Paris, among other reasons. Now in Paris, he saw you, Jag. You're a fairly well-known man and Tyrell knew exactly who you were. You were the bloke who'd married his wife.'

Jaggard flushed. 'Can we skip over that bit? Please?'

'Okay . . . but although that information wasn't of any use to him then, it was later on. Tyrell came back to London and, on the ninth of January, arrived at Hunt Coffee for his second meeting with Frederick Hunt.'

Pat swallowed hard. 'That's when Mark came back.'

Jack nodded. 'That's where it all went wrong. The meeting was already underway when your brother walked in. Tyrell probably tried to bluff it out, but it wouldn't work. Helston knew the real Valdez and also knew Laurence Tyrell.'

'How did Tyrell get out of that?' asked Meredith.

'I don't suppose we'll ever know the truth unless Frederick Hunt comes clean,' said Jack, 'but Tyrell must have spun Helston enough of a yarn to keep him quiet. It was probably similar to the story he told us. He'd lost his memory, etcetera, etcetera, and, knowing his wife had married again, he'd turned up as Valdez to see how things were and if there was any chance for him. Pick up any popular magazine and you'll see a heartbreaking variant on the theme of a forgotten husband giving up all for his wife's greater good. I've even written a couple myself, God help me.'

'And he'd believe it?' said Jaggard sceptically.

'The secret's in the telling. And, to be fair to Helston, we believed a version of it. There's enough genuine cases of shell shock and loss of memory to make him hesitate. Helston was a decent man by all accounts, and the decency of gauging his sister's reaction before turning up out of the blue would probably appeal to him. After all, he didn't know Hunt and Tyrell were as crooked as corkscrews. He might be uneasy but he didn't *know*.'

'Wouldn't the fact that Tyrell had borrowed Valdez's identity give him a clue?' asked Jaggard.

'It obviously did make him think a bit, but, as an honest man himself, Helston gave him the benefit of the doubt, at least until that evening when they'd arranged to meet again.'

'How on earth do you know all this?' asked Jaggard, turning his scepticism onto Jack.

'Helston's reactions,' said Jack, reaching for another cigarette. 'If he knew there was something really dodgy afoot, he'd have told H.R.H. and called the police into the bargain. He didn't do that, but he was uneasy.'

'What happened after the meeting?' asked Pat.

'Tyrell had a problem. Helston wouldn't keep quiet indefinitely. Helston had to go, but it's no joke removing a man as cared for as your brother. Tyrell would know if Helston was killed, both he and Hunt, as among the last people to see him, would be under suspicion. That might be all right for Hunt, but it's the last thing Tyrell wanted. His credentials would be blown immediately. However, if Mark Helston didn't die but merely disappeared, he could get away with it. So, with the connivance of Frederick Hunt, he worked out a plan.'

'You mean Uncle Frederick *knew* Larry was going to murder Mark?' asked Pat.

'He certainly knew about it afterwards, but beforehand . . . All I can say is, he probably guessed. Your Uncle Frederick strikes me as a man who can ignore a dickens of a lot if it's in his own interests. One thing which should have alerted him was that Tyrell took your brother's silver paperknife from the office. It made a very nice weapon. I don't know how long Tyrell took to dope out his scheme, but he certainly had everything in place by that afternoon.'

Jack blew out a deep mouthful of smoke. 'I don't like this bit. None of it's nice but this is cold-blooded callousness. Tyrell looked for a man who would roughly fit the passport description of Valdez. He found one Richard Wainstall, poor devil, a man down on his luck. Presumably he persuaded him there was a job in prospect, and he told him to come, that afternoon of the ninth, to the house in Gower Street. The house must have seemed like a good place to leave a body, but he couldn't have possibly have known it was as good as it was. We only found it weeks afterwards because we looked for it.'

'Because you looked for it,' put in Bill. 'We didn't find it.'

'The house stood out like a sore thumb, it was so neglected,' said Jack. 'Presumably that's why Tyrell picked it. He forced a window and got in at the back. Then all he had to do was open the front door to Wainstall. I presume Wainstall had the patched or holed shoes – you remember how the footprints showed up, Bill? There was also the mark of the hip flask in the dust. I bet Tyrell gave Wainstall a drink. The drink would be drugged. When Wainstall was under the influence, Tyrell stripped off his clothes and stabbed him.'

'Why drug him?' asked Jaggard.

'Practicalities,' said Jack with a shrug. 'It's easier to stab someone if they're insensible, and Tyrell wanted Wainstall's clothes without any blood on them. He'd need them for later. Taking the clothes, he went back to his hotel. At seven in the evening he left, having told the desk clerk he was going to meet a friend and might be out all night. He had with him a bag, which must have contained, amongst other things, Wainstall's clothes. By the way, Bill, that explains why he wasn't wearing evening dress. That puzzled us, remember? He couldn't leave the hotel with a suitcase, as he was only meant to be away for an evening, and the bag he had was full of Wainstall's things. He simply didn't have room for a complete change of kit, including shoes, to wear the next day. Once he'd left the Montague Court Hotel, it was essential he didn't return. Valdez was set to disappear as surely as Mark Helston. Considering the real Ariel Valdez's body must be somewhere in Branca Preto, to have him apparently vanish weeks after his death in London was a pretty neat trick.

'Now this next bit is partly speculation, but I bet I'm right. Tyrell had arranged to meet Helston at Oddenino's, but made sure they didn't dine there. He must have known there was a chance Helston would mention the name of the restaurant to someone – he mentioned it to his valet, in fact – and Tyrell wanted Helston to disappear as completely as possible. So, probably using the fact he wasn't wearing evening dress as an excuse, I imagine he met Helston outside and suggested that they dine elsewhere. It would be a very respectable elsewhere to allay any anxiety Helston might feel. From what happened next, I'm certain it was a hotel of the calibre of Claridge's, the Savoy or the Ritz. He seemed to like the Ritz.'

'How come you don't know which hotel it was?' asked Jaggard. 'Can't you look in the hotel registers?'

'We can,' said Jack, 'and we have, but whatever name Tyrell was using, it wasn't his own or Marsden's. In a hotel, dinner can be served in the room, so there's no worry about evening dress and a private dinner, granted they were ostensibly there to talk about you, Pat, would seem perfectly reasonable to your brother.'

Pat Tyrell's lips were a thin line. 'So Larry murdered Mark in a hotel?'

'Not there and then. I think, as with Wainstall earlier, he must have drugged him. Chloral would be my choice. It's readily available as a sleeping draught, has a sweet, fairly pleasant taste which can easily be disguised in coffee or a liqueur, and an overdose results in a speedy, deep sleep from which the victim never awakes.'

He looked at Pat sympathetically. 'If it's any consolation, it's a very peaceful way to go. Tyrell was a very clever man. He didn't leave unnecessary clues, but something like this *must* have happened. With Helston safely asleep, Tyrell dressed Helston in Wainstall's clothes, covering them up with Helston's own coat and hat. Then he'd ring the bell and ask for some help for getting his friend – who, unfortunately had a little too much to drink – into a taxi and home. Any decent hotel would ensure it was done very discreetly. Once in the taxi, Tyrell, very much the concerned friend, could ask to be put down on the Embankment at Blackfriars. Then, knowing that Helston would never wake up, he abandoned him.'

Jaggard put his arm round Pat and held her close.

'It was a horrible night,' she said eventually. 'The cold was bitter and there was sleet. I remember thinking so, afterwards.'

Jack nodded. 'There wouldn't be many witnesses on a night like that. Tyrell was safe enough. He returned to his hotel and, on the afternoon of the tenth, set sail for Rio de Janeiro on the *Albion Star*. He travelled under the name of John Marsden, as he had a passport in that name. A visit to the barbers would take care of his moustache and hair colour. Not only is he on the passenger list, but Michael Lovell, a steward on board the *Albion Star* recognized his photograph from a selection I showed him yesterday. That's why I wanted Tyrell's picture, Pat, when I called the other day. It's that which gave the whole game away in the end, for John Marsden – if we believed what was recorded in the books at Hunt Coffee – should have been peacefully managing the plantation at Branca Preto.'

'Hang on a minute, Jack,' said Meredith with a frown. 'I remember both you and Rackham saying it more or less had to be Valdez in Gower Street because the murderer couldn't know the body was going to be undiscovered for so long. If the body *had* been found shortly afterwards, that would have ruined Tyrell's plans, wouldn't it?'

Jack grinned. 'You'd think so, wouldn't you? But let's ask the expert. Bill, old son, how do the police identify a body?'

'We see what identification's on the corpse. That usually tells us who they are. If we suspect foul play, we drum up someone who knew the person concerned. That's usually a formality, as there's very rarely any doubt.'

'Let's say the body in Gower Street had come to light within a few days. What then?'

'We'd assume it was Valdez, because of his things in the room. Our main lead would be the cards in the card case, which included one of Frederick Hunt's.'

'Who would you've asked to take a dekko at it?'

'None other than Frederick Hunt, I'm afraid. You see, there were only three people in England who could identify Valdez. Helston, who was missing, Mr Hunt senior, and Frederick Hunt himself. It's an unpleasant business, identifying a body and we certainly wouldn't put an old man such as Mr Harold Hunt through it unless it was absolutely necessary. As there had been no attempt to disguise the body, apart from removing the clothes, Frederick Hunt's identification would be the only one we'd require. We'd have taken his word for it, all right.'

'And Tyrell,' said Jack, 'had told Frederick Hunt to identify the body as Valdez. The fact that Frederick could easily have taken Mark's knife was an added fact that Tyrell used to make sure Frederick behaved himself. It would have worked, you know. After all, Frederick didn't know Wainstall. It wasn't as if he was going to be confronted with Helston. The man on the slab would have been a complete stranger. It was very much to Hunt's advantage to do what Tyrell said.'

'He never was called on, was he?' asked Pat.

'No. As things turned out, the body wasn't found until long afterwards and, as time went on, Frederick must have breathed a sigh of relief. John Marsden was safely back in Brazil and the mutually beneficent arrangement between him and Hunt continued to flourish. And then, Pat, a monumentally sized spanner was flung into the works in the shape of your grandmother's will.'

Pat swallowed. 'So it was about money, after all.'

Jaggard gave a bitter laugh. 'I knew it! It must have struck Tyrell as pretty ironic that he'd gone to such lengths to convince us Mark could still be alive and now, with all that money at stake, he'd made it impossible to prove that Mark was dead.'

'Exactly,' said Bill. 'He didn't come straight to London though, did he, Jack?'

'No. He blazed a traceable, provable trail across Brazil to fit in with his character as a rootless wanderer, fetching up on the banks of the Araguya. Here, what I think he intended to happen, was an accident that would account for his sudden reawakening of memory. What actually happened, for the Amazonian jungle is a dodgy place to fool around in, is that the accident nearly saw him off. The statement from Freire Jose, the Dominican missionary, says as much. I believe in Freire Jose. The Dominicans at Chalk Farm vouch for him. Complete with a verified story, Larry Tyrell turned up in London to receive his hero's welcome.'

Jaggard covered Pat's hand with his own. 'Where did I fit in?'

'You didn't, old man. Pat, as he rightly pointed out, was his wife, not yours and besides that . . . Well, he'd been in Paris, don't forget. He knew that your home life wasn't all it could be.'

Pat looked up with very bright eyes. 'Suppose I'd decided to divorce him? What then?'

Jack shrugged. 'He relied on his charm to let you give him a run for his money. In any case, a divorce takes time to arrange. I don't think you'd have lived to see it. Sometime in the future, there would have been an accident. He was betting on a certainty, of course. He knew that Mark was dead. However, then he met Sheila Mandeville.'

He glanced across at Meredith. 'This is going to be a bit rough for you, I'm afraid, Merry. On the ninth of January, Helston should have been on holiday but Sheila Mandeville was at work. With Helston away, she spent the time filling in for other people and acting as a high-class receptionist. She spoke to Valdez for a good few minutes. Tyrell recognized her that night at the Ritz. With the exception of Frederick Hunt, she was the only person in Britain who'd seen him both as Valdez and Tyrell. He was in great danger and acted very quickly.'

Meredith Smith sat very still for a moment. 'She said he looked familiar.' He took a deep, shuddering breath. 'There was something about his hands. She didn't know who he was, though. She didn't know he was Valdez.'

'She could have tumbled to it at any time,' said Jack. 'He had a crooked little finger. Perhaps it was that she remembered. Tyrell just couldn't risk it.'

He looked at Pat Tyrell. 'Did he see Frederick Hunt that night? Perhaps when he brought you home?'

Her brow wrinkled. 'No, but he was here very early the next morning. He had breakfast with Uncle Frederick.' She caught her breath. 'He was excited about something that night. D'you think he planned it then? That's horrible.'

'Yes,' agreed Jack, softly. 'It is. Tyrell knew Miss Mandeville was the girl who'd met him as Valdez, but that was it. Hunt gave him the information he needed. Tyrell must have got into her flat that morning while she was at work. She kept a key behind the door and it was easy to get in. A newspaper with the cut-out coupon for a film competition gave him an idea. He wrote to Sheila Mandeville to say she'd won the competition and, posing as a journalist, requested an interview for half past five on Friday evening. That made sure she'd be on the spot. He thought he'd get rid of Jaggard as well. I'm afraid you helped him, Pat.'

'Me? What did I do?'

'You must have given him some money. Jaggard cashed a cheque for fifty pounds on the twelfth of April. Four of those notes turned up in Sheila Mandeville's handbag. He must have got them from you.'

She looked horrified. 'I gave him some money the evening he arrived. I took thirty pounds out of the desk at home. He needed it to tide him over. He paid me back and after that he always had his own. Why would he have kept it all that time?'

'Perhaps he didn't keep it on purpose, but, when the occasion arose, he realized what damning evidence those banknotes would be against Jaggard. He knew about the race on Saturday, and guessed Jaggard would be working on his car. A phone call to the track confirmed that Jaggard was actually there. He went to Weybridge solely to telephone from the station. When you, Jag, got a message from someone called "Pat" naturally it didn't occur to you to ask if the "Pat" on the phone had been a man or a woman. Later on, when the call was traced, it seemed obvious that you'd nipped across the footbridge to the station and left a message for yourself.

'Then Tyrell went to Southwark. At lunchtime the offices are more or less deserted, and he was able to type a letter on Sheila Mandeville's typewriter without anyone, apart from Frederick Hunt, being any the wiser. Then Hunt and Tyrell went to the Archias Club at quarter past five. With Hunt covering up for him, Tyrell was able to go to Dunthorpe Mansions and kill the poor girl. Jaggard arrived, right on schedule, and drew no end of attention to the fact he was there.'

'It seems very elaborate,' said Jaggard. 'Why not have me walk in and discover the body?'

'Because he couldn't be sure you'd be alone, or what your alibi was for the afternoon. If you could prove that you had been in other people's company up to the time the body was discovered, he'd have been sunk. As it was, the time of death was vague enough for there to be enough doubt about your actions, no matter what you'd been doing. And I think you, Jaggard, should have died the next day.'

'What?'

'Your accident. Your tyres blew, didn't they?'

'Yes, they did.' His eyes widened. 'Damn it, I saw him! I saw someone on the banking just before the tyres went. What did he use? Caltrops?'

'What on earth are caltrops?' asked Pat.

'Wire stars with four points,' said Bill. 'The Aussies used them a lot in the war. Thrown on the road, they're a nasty, simple and effective way to cripple a horse. They work just as well on tyres.'

Jaggard looked grim. 'It's easy enough to get onto the banking from the railway line. The car was such a mess, no one would've noticed a piece of extra metal unless they looked for it.'

'I don't *know* he used caltrops, but it's the easiest solution,' said Jack. 'If you'd bought it, we'd have thought the case was closed before it was really opened. However, you survived. And, then, Jag, you made a suggestion which brought things to a very nasty head.'

'Are you talking about my will?' asked Pat. 'I never did get round to signing it.'

'I am.' Jack lit another cigarette. 'It really rattled him, didn't it? By a stroke of the pen you could disinherit him, and all his efforts would have been for nothing. He had one night in which to act, and act he most certainly did. I *knew* there was something in the air. I saw the look he gave you. It gave me the heebie-jeebies.'

'I can vouch for that,' put in Bill. 'I thought you were over-egging it, but I thought it as well to have a couple of my best men keep an eye on things, just in case.'

'We know what happened. Helped by that little worm, Lahone, he laced your wine, Pat, then tried his very best to drown you. Thank God, it didn't come off.'

'Because of you,' said Pat.

Jack grinned. 'I didn't seem to dry out for days. By George, it was cold! But even Tyrell couldn't plan everything. Not only were you still alive, but H.R.H. had a visitor. Tyrell didn't know it, but that visitor was a dangerous man.'

'Who was it?' asked Meredith.

'His name was Robert Waldron, an old friend of H.R.H.'s from Brazil. I guessed as much at the time and also guessed his visit was responsible for what happened next. He's a coffee planter and his plantation is about a hundred miles or so from Hunt's. As he hadn't approached the family to offer his condolences when H.R.H. died, I thought it was likely he was out of the country and more than likely he was sailing back to Brazil. I checked the shipping lists and there he was. I asked Bill to send a marconigram to the ship. We needed to know the gist of the conversation he had with H.R.H. regarding Laurence Tyrell and John Marsden.'

Jack walked across to the mantelpiece and, taking down the cable form, handed it to Bill. 'You read it, Bill. It was addressed to you.'

Bill took the cable. 'This is Waldron's reply: *Deeply sorry hear news Harold Hunt. Never met Tyrell before. Marsden not at plantation at Christmas. De Oliveria in sole charge.* Now we knew Tyrell wasn't at the plantation at Christmas and could prove it from the evidence of the shipping list and the testimony of the steward, but the significance of Waldron's cable is that it proves old Mr Hunt knew it too.'

Bill put down the cable. 'What I can't work out, Jack, is why

Mr Hunt didn't tell us that Tyrell had lied about being in Branca Preto at Christmas. How much d'you think he knew?'

Jack frowned. 'That's interesting, isn't it? I don't think he got as far as realizing that Tyrell was Valdez, or was guilty of Mark's murder. He would certainly have told us that, if only to clear Mark's name. What he did know, however, was that Larry Tyrell's account of himself was false, and that had quite dreadful implications for Pat. His worst fears were justified by the episode on Waterloo Bridge. The newspapers might have described the incident as high spirits that got out of hand, but H.R.H. knew better. I'm afraid he regarded me as a washout. I'd been woefully ineffective in finding Helston. From his point of view, I'd only made things worse. He'd been a tough, vigorous man and hated relying on others. He had grave reservations about Frederick, and decided to act in the only way open to him.'

Jack took a long drink. 'When he got the news about you, Pat, he wrote to Tyrell, inviting him to lunch the next day. He must have also sketched out some ideas for his new will. Mr Stafford, as we know, called that afternoon and drew up the new codicil.

'The next day Tyrell came to lunch. The coffee was served here, in the drawing room. Mr Hunt, not Fields, served it. Incidentally, Mr Hunt was sharp enough to realize that although it wasn't certain, there was a good chance Frederick Hunt knew that John Marsden was a fraud. You can see his indecisiveness reflected in the new codicil. After Tyrell had left, Mr Hunt went into the library, where, if you remember, he always wrote his letters. The letter he had to write was a suicide note.'

'A *suicide* note,' cried Pat. 'You mean he really did kill himself? But why?'

Meredith Smith looked frankly distressed. 'I don't believe it. That swine Tyrell must have done for him.'

Jack shook his head. 'No. It can't work that way round. Mr Hunt wanted to protect Pat from a man he knew to be a murderous liar. He thought I was hopeless and he didn't trust the police. Every minute Tyrell was alive spelled danger to Pat. So Mr Hunt killed Laurence Tyrell.'

There was a stunned silence. 'You're kidding,' said Meredith eventually. He looked at Jack's face. 'You're not, are you?'

Jack shook his head. 'Consider the facts. There's the new will, hurriedly made effective by a signature. There's the fact that

Mr Hunt asked for the coffee to be served in the drawing room and his determination to serve it himself. There's the fact that Larry Tyrell died after leaving the house and there's also the fact that on his tray of medicines, Mr Hunt had a tonic containing strychnine.'

He got up and walked across the room to the table which still stood with the tray of medicines on it and picked up a brown bottle. 'Here you are. You can see it's nearly empty. It's a tonic syrup which helps the heart, lungs and nerves.'

He put the bottle back on the tray and stood with his arms folded for a few seconds, before shaking his head. 'Strychnine is an appalling way to kill someone. I can only hope that Mr Hunt had no idea of the effects. However, he was desperate. For your sake, Pat, he had to get rid of Tyrell. There must have been a note, though. You can't tell me that a methodical old bird like Mr Hunt would take an action like that without explaining himself. It's simply not in character.'

Jaggard looked bewildered. 'Look here, Haldean, I can quite believe that H.R.H. would kill Tyrell. He was very strong minded and had a ruthless streak to his nature. Pat's told me that since she came to live here they've got a great deal closer. I can see he'd want to protect her. But why kill himself? And what happened to the note?'

'If,' said Pat unsteadily, 'he did kill Larry, he would take his own life afterwards. He'd see it as a matter of justice.'

'As for the note,' said Jack, 'just think what must have been in it. The confession that he'd poisoned Tyrell, right enough, but also the reason why. I believe Frederick Hunt went into the library. When he found his father dead with that note on the desk, he panicked. If the police suspected for one moment that Tyrell hadn't been at the plantation at Christmas, the whole wretched scheme and his part in it would be revealed. He *knew*, you see, and was in a total funk. So Frederick Hunt took the note, went to his study, and pretended to know nothing had happened.'

Bill nodded. 'You're right, Jack. He was scared stiff of being accused of his father's death. I could hardly stop him talking once he realized how much we knew. According to him it's all Tyrell's fault.'

'Tyrell frightened him, of course,' said Jack.

'Frightened?' said Bill with a snort. 'Terrified, more like. Now he's got every chance of getting what's coming to him, he's beside himself.' He glanced at Jack. 'Don't tell me you're feeling sorry for him.'

'Not exactly,' admitted Jack. 'But for a man like Frederick Hunt to come up against Laurence Tyrell must have been like a rabbit meeting a snake. I can feel sorry for the rabbit. I haven't got any sympathy for the snake.'

Jack received a telephone call that evening. It was from Bill.

'You know our case against Hunt?' said Bill in deep disgust. 'It's off.'

'Off?'

'O-ruddy-double-f. He's hanged himself. Oh, well, it'll save the courts some work. The papers will love this.'

They did. The new director of Hunt Coffee, Limited, one Captain Meredith Smith, was quoted on every front page for a week. And then a chorus girl eloped with a Duke, quintuplets were born in Ashton-Under-Lyne, the Dean of Manchester said that Communism was Christianity, a solo attempt to fly the Atlantic failed, Eve Lahone, society hostess, was charged with supplying cocaine and heroin, and Hunt Coffee returned to being an item in the grocers rather than an item in the press.

At the Young Services Club, one month and three days later, the director of Hunt Coffee wiped his mouth with his napkin and sat back in his chair with a smile. 'It seems a long time since we were in here, Jack. D'you remember the evening it all started? I was full of the letter I'd written to you from H.R.H.' He finished his wine. 'I'm glad I didn't know what was going to happen next.'

'It wasn't nice, was it?' said Jack. 'I see Jag and Pat managed to get away on honeymoon without anyone being any the wiser.'

'Yes, thank goodness. The last thing they want is more publicity. You know Jag's coming into the firm? He's selling his business to Miller. I'm looking forward to working with him. I'll give him a couple of weeks to settle down, then I'm off to Branca Preto to make them sit up a bit.'

'Is Jag giving up racing?' asked Jack in surprise.

'Oh no. The racing was the part he loved best of all. He'd

miss the excitement if all he did was work for Hunts.'

Jack smiled broadly. 'That's the last thing anyone from Hunts should complain about.'

'Excitement?' said Meredith with a puzzled frown. 'I wouldn't call it exciting. Interesting, certainly, but not exciting. Mind you, we've got the new roast perfected at last, I've totally reorganized the warehouse and I've got some really radical ideas for the after-dinner . . . That's not what you meant, is it?'

Jack shook his head with a grin and turned to the waiter. 'Coffee, please. Make sure it's Hunt's.'